La'-N.e.w.

Last Anatomical Novel Ever Written.

REGIS ALLISON JR.

outskirts press

L.a'-N.e.w.
Last Anatomical Novel Ever Written.

v2.0

Outskirts Press, Inc.
http://www.outskirtspress.com

ISBN: 978-1-9772-7393-2

PRINTED IN THE UNITED STATES OF AMERICA

Humanity's Last Hope For Survival, Is Love ……

CAST OF CHARACTERS:

1st) **Lieutenant Colonel Wynolla Lafayette** - Micro Biologist, Us Army Germ Warfare Specialist, Ranger and SF Operative. 36 years old, African American Woman.

2nd) **Admiral Jefferson Bullraguard Lee-** US Navy Doctor, Base Commander. Devoted Southern Baptist, 65 years old flag carrying Caucasian, sociopath, sadist and practicing bigot.

3rd) **Doctor Monique Littlefield-** UCLA trained infectious Diseases specialist, Center of Disease control employee, 33 years old of Chinese & Jewish descent. American born female, single.

4th) **Doctor John Hammond/ Convict 997421-** US Air Force trained doctor, designer Gene creator, convicted Murder, father, genius, Taoist , African American, 58 years old. currently on death row.

5th) **Federal Marshal Rene Robin Hammond- Aquilla-** U.S. Marshal assigned to Fugitive Recovery Program, estranged daughter of Convict 997421. 32 year old Afro Filipino female, single.

6th) **Sicaro Enestro "The Ghost" Valdez/ Convict 997619- 28 year old** Feared Mexican Cartel hitman, said to have reached the mile-stone of 100 dead men or women before capture. currently on death row.

7th) **Earl "Chicken Head" Gaines- 35 Year Old,** Convicted Serial Killer, tall, bald, gay and mildly obese. Above average intelligence, Chess Enthusiast and failed contestant on American Idol. Currently on Death Row.

8th) **Sicaro Celeste "Calamity" Valdez/ Convict 997966- 26 year old** Feared Cartel assassin, wife of Enestro Valdez. Beautiful, psychotic, alluring, voice of an angel. Sits in Max security prison for the rest of her life.

9th) **Captain Lance Brown- 25 year old,** U.S. Army, Special Forces, Conventional warfare specialist, Sniper, 28, Six feet tall, African American, brown eyed single and upbeat.

10th) **Colonel David Dunston- 43 year old,** U.S. Air Force logistic and support staff. Second in command on Project. Balding, average height, 41 year old Caucasian. Jazz nut.

11th) **Lieutenant Colonel Kevin Mckinney-** 35 year old U.S Marine Corps, Military Provost Marshal, Confederate flag wearing, crew cut wearing former linebacker from the University of Costal Carolina, 37 years old, twice divorced.

12th) **Sky Harrison-** 26 year old Exotic and gorgeous, 1/3 Cuban, 1/3 Polish, the rest Vietnamese heritage. Stripper by night/ youtube star, part time dental assistant by day. 26 years old, trans planted California girl. Grew up fixing broken cars in San Diego.

13th) **Paradise Hunter-** 23 year old 1/2 Taiwanese, ½ Korean Trans gender, Stripper/youtube star, sultry, seductive, very passable, Black Widow when her heart gets broken, advent reader, real skill, looking fabulous at 24 years old. Horrible singing voice, but that doesn't stop her.

15th) **Deann- 8 year old** One of three immune humans on planet. Of Mixed heritage.

16th) Hana- 8 year old,Two of three immune humans on the planet. Of Mixed heritage.

17th) Indigo Roberson- 55 year old Portly, Prison Social Worker, therapist, 54 year old African American woman with a secret she must not share.

18th) Claire Cherish McGrill- 23 year old drop dead gorgeous African American woman, City college Student- human resources major, stripper/ private dancer and survivor.

19th) James Johansson Jr aka Semaj- Nineteen year old plump fem-boy, in transition Quiet, shy City college student-math major.

2Oth) Nabila Hussein - Fifty one year old widowed High School Chemistry teacher. Legal American resident, belly dancer, one time professional sword swallower and magicians assistant.

MUSIC IS THE KEY TO LIFE:

1st *Don McLean- Bye, Bye American Pie.*

2nd Night Ranger- Sister Christian.

3rd DMX- Party Up In Here!

4th Tina Marie- I need you Lovin.

5th Wu Tang Clan- C.R.E.A.M

6th *Trina- No Panties Coming Off!*

7th Aero Smith- I don't want to miss a thing.

8th Boston- More than a Feeling!

9th Drowning Pools- Let the Bodies Hit The Floor!

10th The Ohio Players- Heaven must be like this.

11th Etta James- At Last!

12th David Bowie and Queen- Under Pressure.

13th Limp Bizkit -Rollin ft. Method Man, Redman and DMX!

14th Whitney Houston- I Will Always Love You!

15th Burt Bacharach-What The World Needs Now.

16th Etta James- I want a Suny kind of love.

17th The Captain and Tennille- Love Will Keep US Together!

TABLE OF CONTENTS

MY 411

Thank you for selecting my material! If you have not already, I ask you to go grab a copy of the first book written about Bethesda Game Studio, Fallout 3, Fallout 4 & Fallout New Vegas! Fallout the Descendants of Vaults 42 43 55. And Hell's Reign, both are horror, sci-fi stories you will like, both books are sold where books are sold!

I'm a retired US Army Veteran, and a one and done filmmaker, who noticed that some many horror projects are written from one perspective only. I found the gene lacked true diversity. For our, America's a magnificent melting pot!

I finished the first draft of this novel in October of 2019 and sat on it until 2024.

For us to move forward as a society, all ISMs must be laid to waste! That's what my writing tends to be about. The death of racism, sexism and ageism. For the American brand our politicians and mega corporations heralded across the globe has faded. Sadly the same 15th-19 century thinking that still rules our land.

Honestly, if you are not actively promoting and pursuing the principles of Truth, Liberty, and Justice for all! Then history states, those who do not remember what came before, will see it once more.

Nonetheless, if you are a Veteran of not and if you enjoy a good horror tale, which might also get you aroused. Then you have found the material to read before bedtime. Now go,

Enjoy.

BACK STORIES:

Every fairy tale and most urban legends must contain the proper back story to lure readers into its awaiting clutches. What's your characters primary motivation? What are the factors that drive their story? This tale is not vastly different. The purists of several of the main characters will be clearly presented for your entertainment. Allowing the reader to comb through their lives with a fine-tooth combo.

Only then will you understand the sacrifice it will take to ensure someone; anyone will survive the **Big Red Death!** Lines will be drawn in the sand as the old concepts of good vs. evil are pitted against the fate of humanity floating in a river of unbridled insanity and the constant army of the recently dead.

The characters you will be introduced to for the most part will fall under one of these categories. The Good, the Bad and the totally indifferent! Have you ever asked yourself what type of person you would be if the rule of law was suddenly thrown out of the blood-stained broken window? How would you behave if all the creature comforts of civilization cease to be at a finger's touch away?

Would you be able to survive in a technological wasteland, a world-wide wasteland where nothing works and whatever did, you had better be able to protect it against bands of Brigands, packs of RAGERS or the hunger of the recently dead?

When the dead rise to wash away the living, I assure everyone most ISMs like sexism, racism, capitalism and ageism will disappear due to the sands of time. Sadly, fascism on the other hand, will never go away quietly! I ask you, will those left to endure the end gladly reinvent themselves? Or wallow in the same mind set of diseased actions that forced our species off the track of evolution and right out to the rails of self-extermination. I ask you to ponder, will this finally be the era when humans work together toward a better tomorrow?

Or will the dreams of humanity die in a flash of weapons fire, a pounding of fist and a gnawing of blood-stained teeth? Gone is a time, where everyone will choose their side based on #hashtags, Professional Sports Team, Political affiliations, High School or College rivalries, which Rap Artist who has beef, Immigrant vs. Native or what section of your Country you reside in. No, no, no. Those days are behind the planet, forever!

In the soon to be present, sides are simply drawn among the living or the dead. Also, will I be able to trust you with my life. All other considerations fall by the waist side in the presence of the **Big Red Death**. Few people will ever have to endure the pain of killing a loved one and fewer people than that will survive the first week of the apocalypse. All because no one who was not in the know, even understood what a RAGER was before it was bashing their head in!

Besides, what came after the RAGERS, no one could fully conceive or even was prepared for. Even those that were entrusted to calculate all the angles did not give their full attention to the aftermath of their truly soul stealing actions.

No one seemed to compute that when you cannot stop the dead from rising to devour the living, then the game is OVER!

However, for the sake of humanity, when so called Monsters find themselves pitted against their real like counter parts. Will they rise to meet the challenge humans have always faced? The question is simple. Shall we fight together or simply against each other?

Nevertheless, this answer remains to be seem.

BE ALL YOU CAN BE.

Long before she was Colonel Lafayette, she was Wynolla Rose Lafayette. A skinny little kid born to loving parents in the small Southern town of Jennings Louisiana. Her father Winston was a thoughtful Doctor and her mother Caroline a wonderful dentist. Both were only but a handful of professional African Americans living in her ethnically mixed subdivision of modernly priced 2-4 bedroom Southern style homes.

Wynolla was born late to aging parents as Wynolla and there wasn't much talk of her older sister. All Wynolla knew was her sister died before she was born, something about her going missing the morning of a bad storm! As Wynolla remembered it her parents never talked about what happened, there was just a small memorial set up in the upstairs hallway.

Her sister was twelve at the time and the sky was overcast and the morning was riddled with thunder. Dressed in her new blue and pink raincoat, the petite thirteen-year-old Laura, left home at 8'05am- as usual- to go wait for her yellow school bus. Sadly, Laura Lafayette was never seen or heard from again! Weeks went by, then months. People that help the worried couple search daily for their lost child, just stop. Few people even knew the words that might comfort the pair. After that it took her parents three years before they could be even intimate with each other once more. The pain of loss, that pain was just too great! Nonetheless, their grief will be replaced by another beautiful baby girl. They named her Wynolla Rose Lafayette, after Winston's grandmother and Rose after Caroline's mother. Much to their concern, their baby girl was born sickly and premature. Born five weeks early to a pair of undeniably excited 41- and 48-year-old parents!

Right off the bat it seems the world had its sights of Wynolla. Born with spinal meningitis and a trace of sickle cell, her doctors had to put the infant in a self-induced comma to control the swelling of her tiny brain. Both parents had nearly worried themselves into an early grave, still they were finally overcome with joy when their baby girl showed signs of improvement in what was a pressure induced three weeks later. However, there was another problem the parents were never aware of, and frankly their fellows' doctors didn't ask for the parents' opinion on the matter! It seems Lafayette's only child was born with both set of reproductive organs! Yes, those things do happen, nature can be a strange chemist.

Like much of the experiences of the early Africans brought to America, it was white doctors determining the fate of a nameless black children! And they took it upon themselves to make a choice that wasn't theirs to make. Using their own religious convictions they assigned the Lafayette's child sexual orientation. Instead of it being Winston III meeting the world. She was Wynolla, and her parents, nor she will never knew the truth.

Growing up Wynolla was indulged by overprotective parents that never let her out of their collective sights.

Her interests were explored instead of ignored and rarely was there a time when Wynolla's happiness wasn't placed before their own. Even though Wynolla was born smaller than most children her age, her parents knew the best thing for her was exercise.

They had Wynolla swimming by two years old and reading by three! Playing chess by five years old and the piano by six. Studying Wing Chun at seven years old and learning to play basketball by eight.

Growing up in Southwestern Louisiana, both of Wynolla's parents grew up in households rich with French, Creole and Spanish dialects. And they passed their love for language, food and life on to their only seed!

From age four until he died and thankfully before the Big Red Death.

Wynolla's father only spoke to her in French. It was Winston's way to ensure his child was in connection with those that had come before her.

While her mother Caroline, the first-generation descendant of Afro Cuban immigrates- not to be out done by her husband; by the time Wynolla turned five, she would only spoke to her child in Spanish.

Wynolla was the only child in their sub-division who came out of the gate speaking three languages! English, French and Spanish. By the time she finished High School with a 4.0 average, Wynolla Lafayette had fielded many offers from colleges across the country. From far away as the University of Hawaii and even the University of Maine!

As well as Georgetown and the University of West Virginia. All were so far away and Wynolla's parents weren't too keen on separation, even if it was for her own sake. She graduated from High School while hosting honors classes, competed on their Regional winning chess team, played on their record settling- in loses- basketball team, played the piano and after thirteen years of rigorous training had been certified to teach Wing Chun by her Sifu Chow Young Park. However, Wynolla knew she needed to get out from under the wings of controlling parents, if she were to ever truly blossom.

With all she had done, sadly Wynolla still had to sneak out of the house, as soon as her weary sixty-year-old parents passed out from long hours at their jobs. Wynolla's parents tried to steer her to pick from Louisiana's traditional Black Colleges like Grambling or the Southern University. Hell, they would even accept USL or LSU if it kept Wynolla close to home!

However, it was one of those late nights where sneaking out the house to hang out at her friend's bonfire with her closest peers. Did events pushed Wynolla to finally decide that it's her own life to start living. Not her parents' life, as here and her friends sang lyrics for songstress Katy Perry Firework.

Later that night when she snuck back inside their home, Wynolla was met by a pair of rude surprises, her parents!

Her mother clutches the phone in her trembling hands, seemingly not sure should she get the police involved. While her father paced the floor with the look of a worry she had never seen on the reserved man.

Once their daughters' key turns in the lock, her parents' emotion turns from fear to anger! Furious, Winston and his wife Caroline unload their panic, pain and frustration of losing their first child onto their second. As usual Wynolla bows her head and sheepishly accepts the guilty trip. This was their norm, they screamed, cursed in various languages until she felt bad about making them worry.

Nonetheless, not this time! It might have been the Red Bull and Sativa or maybe just the Sativa. Or remembering she just had left Megan Hoedel down at Billy Keiwall's house. Where she had put her frighten tongue inside Meghan's hot mouth and frankly Wynolla no longer gave a FUCK!

So, she told her parents she had made up her mind and West Point's the college of choice. And furthermore, since she turned 18 years old one week before graduation there was nothing, they could do to stop her!

That took all the air out of the room and her parents as well. It's not until Wynolla leaves that she noticed how old and frail her parents look! The day they waved goodbye as her train pulled away from the tracks produced a lump of emotion which firmly wedged in tender throat. She didn't fight to hold back the tears washing over her face. For Wynolla felt ashamed, she felt sad and for the first time in her life, the little girl from Jennings Louisiana felt utterly alone! Wynolla tried to get back every holiday she could. However, nearing the end of her last year at West Point, life took its toll on her parents.

While returning from a "routine" Doctors visit, Winston and his wife of 32 years Caroline were killed when a Truck Driver, driving too fast for conditions loses control of his vehicle. It crosses the meridian slamming headfirst into their White Lexus sports coup! Not so FUNFACT, the state of Louisiana led the nation in motor vehicle accidents from 1977 until present. Most outside the state said that stat has to do with drinking and driving. Residents inside the know, claim drivers are always looking for any accident that they can walk away from and sue, sue, sue!

When she got the word of their untimely death Wynolla once again found the strength, fighting with the fear of realization screaming at her that the baby girl was truly alone in this world. All the self-discipline bestowed upon her could not hold back the wave of emotion that had been bottled up in young Lafayette since she arrived at historic West Point.

For Wynolla's first two years, everywhere she went someone was screaming at her! Wynolla had witnessed first-hand as young adults were being broken beyond repair. The physical damage being forced down their collective throats was nothing compared to the emotional distress inflicted seven days a week. Every on freaking Sunday, some asshole finds a reason to scream at you! WTF, right?

The military enjoys placing the personnel they plan to thrust into the throngs of leadership inside pressure filled situations to see who will crack under said pressure. Wynolla held her temper in check for nearly three years. However, there are people and or events that will cause a person to, snap! A soon to be graduating group of older white Cadets, made up of three lackeys and the so called head bitch decided to press the still grieving Lafayette. Not about her character or her ability to grasp military living, but the color of Wynolla's skin!

While exiting the shower, the three older, larger, white Cadet's file into the bathroom- a bit tipsy for sure- and order Wynolla to get her "black ass" out of there! Wynolla had just put in two hours scrubbing toilets, and frankly she wasn't up for anyone's pardon the pun, shit.!

For the first time at West Point, she allowed her temper to speak for her. "What?" Wynolla growls. She recognized two of female Cadets, for they were on the same soccer team, still that didn't matter. Wynolla was going to see how far they were going to push this! She didn't bother getting dressed. Wynolla just stood there, butt-ass naked! Sweat dripping from her pear-shaped breast, rolling down her firm hips and down to her desperately in need of a manicure toes.

She could feel the lust filled eyes of 2 out of 3 of the drunken upper classmen staring at her perky brown nipples. The sole Cadet not interested in eye fucking Wynolla's vagina was the so-called Angry Alpha White Woman, Wynolla grew up hearing his father complaining about, the KAREN! You know the ones who think their whiteness bestows ultimate compliance and utter fucking servitude! Yeah, rude and generally dumb as rocks type of bitches.

The Female Cadet's screaming hate filled words at Wynolla and she's turning red in the ferreted shaped face. The KAREN who was actually named Karen Witmore. She had no idea why she hated seeing Wynolla in West Point. Or in the U.S. Army or in America itself! Karen just DOES. However, it wasn't until the Cadet touched Wynolla, did life get, well fucking real! Army regulations state that at no time will one Cadet make contact with another Cadet in a forceful or aggressive manner.

Wynolla knew that the rules stated if a Cadet could not extract themselves from the situation to alert their superiors. Then said Cadet, has the right to defend themselves in the face of said danger and defend herself she did! Once the bigger Cadet's finger jammed into Wynolla's energetic nipple. She must have sensed something was wrong from the smile Wynolla flashed. It cut through the bullshit and was too cold to be consider fucking friendly!

Cadet Lafayette's strikes were as quick as Praying Mantis and was actually one of the five animals' forms Sifu Park taught young Wynolla so very long ago. Master Park would have been proud to see his pupil control a bigger opponent by locking up her joints and ligaments from the bulky ankle to the boney elbow!

When Wynolla forces the bigger Cadet to her knees, young Lafayette made sure the bully's face was positioned right under her heavenly VJ. The hush from other Cadets, informed Wynolla they had no intention of fighting this battle! Nevertheless, from the desire in their eyes, neither might have a problem ending up on the floor looking up into her love spring as well.

By the time Wynolla was in her fourth year at West Point, she had to choose her MOS or military occupation service. When Wynolla got the autopsy back on her parents, she noticed a mention of two fatal illnesses she never knew her parents had. Caroline had breast cancer and his father Winston had lung cancer!

It was that information that pressed Wynolla into the Preventive Medical Services. *After* graduation she was sent to Fort Sam Houston on the outskirts of San Antonio Texas for the next two years.

After that 1st Lieutenant Lafayette did her residency at John Hopkins. Nonetheless before leaving West Point, Wynolla did manage to lose her virginity to a sweet handsome boy from the great state of Kanas! By the time Wynolla was 23 years old she had been promoted to the rank of Captain. And there was a long line of FUBAR situations before Wynolla once again finds her true calling. It was 2007 and the dreaded disease EBOLA had flared up like wildfire in three African Nations! The U.N. as well as the U.S. Military took interest and united in combating the frightening plague that was EBOLA.

Captain Lafayette had never been compelled to think of what's like for someone dying in their own juices. As their insides turn to liquid and they bled from every orifice, before she set foot in West Africa. Nevertheless, there it was happening right in arm's length of her protective hazmat gear!

To make matters even worst, local Warlords and Islamic Militant regularly hi jack shipments of food, medicine and clean water! Wynolla wanted more out of the US Army. For having to sit by as masked assholes wave AK-47s in her face and steal the necessary items needed for daily living made her goddam blood boil! Wynolla felt she had to get into the fight. She was a goddam warrior and warriors don't hide on the bench when trouble is near!

Several years ago, some of her fellow female Cadets scoffed at Wynolla volunteering to go, Airborne, Air Assault, and do Airborne Rigger training, after she finished their West Point training. Why, they asked, since Wynolla knew she was going to be a doctor? That's what they couldn't understand, Wynolla was tired of fulfilling others' expectations of what she should do with her life! Deep down inside, she has always felt different.

Even though she was in the Preventive medical Services, if a chance to go TDY- temporary duty- for Jungle training in Panama, she did it. Artic training at the South Pole, Wynolla put her name on the list as well!

She even went Pathfinder down at Ft. Bliss- which included knife fighting- taught by a genuine member of the White-Water Apache Reservation. Furthermore Wynolla found the man to be extraordinary as a sexual partner and spiritual guide!

Hell, by the time she made Major Lafayette, Wynolla had managed to earn a degree in Psychology in her eight years before her time to reenlist came up. When she hit twenty-eight years old, it came to time to shit or get off the pot! So Wynolla decided on taking a huge dump! Silently she wondered if her parents would be proud of the woman she has become? Yet now, it was time for Wynolla Lafayette to find her true calling.

The NCO doing her paperwork rubbed his bald head as he needed to know if the officer sitting in front of him was serious or not.

"Ah,.ma'am are you saying you want to reenlist as an Operator? You want to go Special Forces, Major?"

Wynolla knew what he meant; you are a fucking woman! Why do you want to do something like this? She flashes a brief smile before replying. "I am already done most of the necessary pre training Staff Sergeant. Now, it's time to earn the tab."

The recruitment NCO does his best to not insult the officer in his chair when he said.

"You do understand, SF training is a young Soldier's game, Major?"

Once again Wynolla forces her tone to remain even and calm as she reads the NCO's name tag, before saying.

"Staff- Sergeant Shekels, is the bonus still fifty thousand?"

The recruiter shakes his giant baled melon shaped head yes. Only then did Wynolla allow a genuine smile to don her luscious lips as she said.

"Great! That's the startup price for me to continue to BE all I can be."

THE GREAT-GREAT, GREAT, GREAT GRANDSON OF A TRAITOR.

RADM or Rear Admiral Jefferson Bullraguard Lee was born of a proud and not so proud military tradition! He had family members that have fought in every war since the founding of America. Including the civil war where he had relatives die on both sides of that still bitterly felt contest! Surprisingly while growing up, those Northern Lee's were rarely seemed around his family's dinner table. Known to his close friends as J-BULL, Jefferson is a devoted Southern Baptist and University of Alabama fan. Roll tide!

Not to exclude being a xenophobe, misogynist, bigot, practicing sadist, a card-carrying NRA member and %100 certified pure breed asshole. Frankly, Jefferson Bullraguard Lee was groomed to be the miserable son of a bitch that is today! His father wanted a military man, his mother wanted a doctor and his parents got both and not much more out of their only seed.

However, that's not what Jefferson wanted for himself. He fancied himself an ole time fire and brimstone style Preacher! Jefferson wanted to peer into the faces of those pitiful souls in need of spiritual release and sexual guidance and lead them to his will. In turn Jefferson never married, for the U.S. Navy equipped him with a bible and a blanket, but not a willing wife.

He had thought about making concessions and finding some stay-at-home type to wash his clothes, cook his food, occasionally swallow his cock and or course keep his house fucking clean as the board of health! However, that life never interested Jefferson, for he never wanted anyone to see the man behind the carefully crafted mask.

Frankly, Jefferson Bullraguard Lee is a predator and a pure fucking sadist! If he had tortured poor little animals as a child Lee would be a serial-, wait, wait, never mind yeah, he did.

While he was a junior Officer, Jefferson's first duty station was in South Korea. The home of very expensive to real cheap forms of human life. Poor souls kept by greedy proprietors that will let a paying customer do anything they like, including murder! That's where he first indulged in BDSM, becoming a MASTER and owing a pen of slaves.

After he left Korea, Jefferson Bullraguard Lee found himself a junkie hooked on providing others immerse pain! Yet his profession frowned on people who could not control their basic animal desires. So, he became a man with two faces, one who knew when and most of how to play the game! A military man who could go to all the important the Luncheons, or golfing with his superiors and volunteering his services at Veteran's hospice centers without anyone seeing who he truly was. Among Naval Brass, Jefferson Bullraguard Lee was considered a rising star!

He had worked on U.S. Naval bases in Korea, Italy, Japan and Guam and pretty much at every stop Jefferson found a discrete madam or pimp to carter to his dark and twisted needs. While dealing with superiors he must swallow his pride and Jefferson could not wait to visit the cell in which the slave he brought and paid for was waiting for whatever devious acts J-BULL happens to unleash!

It took him nearly 19 years to climb the ranks, by all accounts, Jefferson Bullraguard Lee has the world by the horns.

In 2017 he made RADM or Rear Admiral, that's when Jefferson was assigned to the Great Lakes Training Center in Waukegan Illinois as base commander. J-BULL, was familiar with the Chicago BDSM scene and he could barely wait to see if his old phone numbers were still in action.

SLIGHTLY BLOND, BRILLIANT AND FEARLESS!

Monique Littlefield is a California girl though and though! Born and raised in the Valley, she attended North Hollywood High and went on to attend UCLA. An athletic child, Monique grew up playing volleyball, soccer, swimming and practicing Sun family Taijiquan with her Mother, Linda.

Monique's Mother, Sun Linda Wu was a Hong Kong born National who immigrated to the United States in the summer of 1976. Monique doesn't have memory of meeting her Grandfather the renowned Sifu Sun Peter Gao , all she has to stare at is the only photo, her mother had of her departed family members.

All Monique knew is that Grandfather was a very strict man, and he forced his daughter to study their families Martial Arts, Sun Style Taijiquan, rather religiously! When her mother left home at 19 years old on an American- Hong Kong foreign student program, Linda took to freedom like a robin happily pressed out of the nest to make its way in the world: landing in Berkley California. She worked hard in a local Chinese restaurant by night and attended college by day.

Years later as she practiced the same Martial Arts her father forced upon her; it provided Linda a sense of solace. Growing up under British rule, Linda spoke perfect English as well as Cantonese. Still, years of awkwardness compelled Linda to feel like she didn't fit in. Nonetheless, all that changes on a rainy day when she shares Cab with a blond hair, blue eyed, passionate American man looking to change the world. Samuel Littlefield- a second-year theology major and English Lit minor from Santa Monica- had an infectious nature that bellows welcome to AMERICA!

Standing well over 6'2 tall Samuel had to sort of bend down to talk to the 5'3 Linda about a rally to protest logging that was endangering a species of tree frogs. Once the rain started the conversation continued over dinner. Nature has a way of being a helping hand when it comes to how to get humans to exchange DNA. Surprisingly Linda and Samuel hit it off like warm peanut butter and cool jelly!

Still in 1981 when they both graduated from the University of California at Berkeley- Linda earning a B.A. in Education, while Samuel settled on English Lit. Fear replaced joy with them facing the thought of Linda having to return to Hong Kong. With a hopeful heart Samuel asked for her hand in marriage and his heart sung the song of utter joy when Linda said, YES!

A week later they married, a week after they relocated to his home in sunny Southern California. One of Samuel's fraternity buddies-landed a job as a line producer working on a popular morning game show. He told Sam they were looking for writers and that sports fans are how families get started!

Flash forward five years to June 20th, 1986, and the birth of their only child. A healthy, beautiful baby girl they named Monique. In the last dozen years Linda and Samuel built a wonderful life for themselves. Samuel had moved from writing games shows to writing for, then directing, daytime SOAP Operas!

Leaving Linda, the time to open a small School where she taught her family's Sun Style Taijiquan to any and all that entered through her doors. Instead of the grueling eight-hour practice session that her father peppered her with starting at age five. Linda didn't formally teach Monique until she was eight years old and then it was done with a bit of humanity over a rigid approached.

Linda just asked her daughter to try to follow what she did. This allowed the mother to make gentle corrections along their way. Firmly staying away from her father's practice of negative reinforcement!

PAIN doesn't always entice a person to respond in a prescribed fashion. No, some people will just hide and never excel at what others want.

Monique excelled in practice as well as her choice of musical instruments, the Clarinet. The pretty green-eyed child took after her father when it came to height, by the time she was ready for college. Monique was approaching 5'7 tall and thankfully a diet of American staples like McDonalds, Burger King, Fried Chicken and Pizza. Had the young woman filling out in all the necessary fun in the fun places!

While Linda was thin and wiry at that age, her daughter would be considered a fat American by older Hong Kong Residents. Even so, to the people of her generation, Monique was PHAT, HOT and deliciously alluring! Standing 5'7, 34-25- 36, Monique was more than great looks and booming body! She is rather brilliant when it comes to gene repair theory.

After completing under grad at UCLA, she travels North to get her Medical Degree from her parents' alumina-UC Berkely. Linda and Samuel Littlefield were so proud of their baby girl who they had raised to be vibrant, open-minded, kind and fierce when needed! In 2012 after completing her Residency, Monique's parents are shocked when their baby girl accepted a job with the CDC in Atlanta. Few parents are thrilled when their only child, first child or last child leave the nest. Little secret for the middle child, honestly your parents can't wait for you to leave!

Monique's and her parents had never been more than five hours away from each other, ever. Linda didn't want her daughter to see her cry, yet she was very sad! Not that her daughter was so much like her. Or that Monique would leave her family and travel so far away to start her adult life.

No, Linda was sad, for she knew Monique was beyond her sphere of influence, and from here on out it's a battle of hormones vs. common sense! And early in your life, hormones generally win out!

Secretly, there is a reason that Monique accepted the CDC position over working in the V.A. Hospital in West Los Angles.

It was her undergrad romance- she was in an on again and off again heated love affair with her college flame who had been drafted in the 3rd round by the Atlanta Falcons! Marcus Devon was good at catching footballs and making promises- much like keeping his thick platanna shaped penis in his pants- sadly, he wasn't great at keeping that one.

Monique really thought they could be happy together. However, she grew up around millionaires, big mansions and coked out slutty girls partying on their parent's money! Devon hadn't grown up rich. Now he had "fuck you" money and when he got paid, common sense went out their planned window! Too many Strippers, too many side pieces and too many late nights broke the couple up before they could start. Plus, it didn't help that he was two years younger than Monique.

Which in the long run is the best thing to happen to Monique! Oh, she still has her, one can say addiction to in shape black men. Nevertheless, when one door closes, another one thankfully opens. Even so, Monique had always felt something for exotic looking women. You know hybrids, mutts and interracial love children like herself. And the world pretty much doesn't care who a person loves anymore. As long as that love doesn't interfere with your job! Too bad it takes the end of the world for Monique Littlefield to briefly find her soul mate.

FATHER, SCIENTIST, SCAPEGOAT AND CONVICT.

John Hammond or simply Big John to most of his fellow denizens on Death Row has been in his one-man cell for far too long. Something is wrong! John knew this would be the day he was to get a visit for his estranged daughter Robin.

Each morning John does his best not to dwell on the events that led him to be in a one-man cell next to what most may consider some of the worst people on the planet! Standing well over 6'3 inches tall and bald. The mocha colored, barrel chested man, might have looked menacing. However, John Hammond had to forge himself into that kind of "person" the movement the powers at be threw the book at him!

It's been 14 and ½ years since he was sent to Death Row, now he sits awaiting his expiration date. All his appeals have been exhausted and there was no hope that the asshole Governor of the Great State of Indiana would listen on how he was framed for murder. So, here he waits!

How does a highly respected gene therapist, be tried and convicted of killing his wife, when he was out of town at the time of her disappearance? How do you sentence someone to die, when there isn't even a sign of a crime?

Big John spent the first few years of his prison life reading books on law, any ruling that would get him back to his then thirteen-year-old daughter, Robin. That's when the attacks started, - last once in the shower, once in the cafeteria and the first time in the yard. It was inmates looking to make a name of themselves! That's how the Prison officials summed it up.

It wasn't until a Representative of a Big Pharma conglomerate visited- John had previously worked for at the time of his wife's disappearance- that events began to make sense. For well longer than he would publicly admit John Hammond had been one of those rogue Scientist who actually believed he was playing God!

He was brilliant enough to either create astonishing cures or devise deadly diseases without a hint of remorse. He went from working for the U.S. Air Force, to BIG Pharma, to finally doing his own freelance work. The kind that was supposed to be no questions asked. You deliver their product, and you get your funds deposited anywhere in the world you desire!

John accepted his last contract, one that agreed to his normal request- First class ticket, all work needed to finished in seven days, a king size bed, a case of diet coke and $7,500,000- and that's the way it's worked for John for nearly a decade.

He accepted no more than eight contracts a year, for John enjoyed being a mostly stay at home Dad. His wife Brenda was the more outgoing type and she enjoyed teaching PRE-K down at Duneland Discovery Middle School.

John hated to be away from home, by all accounts he loved his wife, even his mother-in-law. Seeing that John flew Brenda's mother from Manilla to live in with them!

John was an Air Force Veteran and graduate of Purdue University and he's rarely a man given to anger or rash actions. A skilled chess player and a devoted reader, it was hard for anyone that knew him to believe that John Hammond was a murderer! Nevertheless, the State of Indiana spun a tale that convinced twelve of his peers- well not really there were only two people of color on his jury, both women on a jury dealing with a missing wife- that John was crafty enough to stage his entire trip! Sneak back in town, kidnap, then murder his wife, dispose of her body, sneak out of town and arrive back on his prescribed return date acting like he has no clue on what happened to his beloved.

Even though his defense attorney pointed out the last anyone heard from Brenda Hammond was two hours before his plane arrived at Midway Airport. When the jury rendered a verdict of Guilty, even John's high price Lawyer was blindsided! There was no motive, there was not a body and there was no evidence of a crime. Just a missing wife, Yet John Hammond was sentenced to die! His young teenage daughter was left with his mother in-law in the modest seven bedroom- with in the ground pool- home that sat on nine acres of land outside the quiet hamlet of Chesterton Indiana.

Three years into the appeal process, John by this time's doing his own legal work. Requesting information using the Freedom of Information act about a "defunded" Government Program he once worked on while working for the CDC.

That's when the Pharma Rep paid him a visit, they sat across from each other not saying a word. John eyed the expensive suit seat-ing in front of him and waited for him to say something. He simply opened his briefcase, pulled out a single sheet of paper and passed it to John. Even handcuffed John could be a handful if he wanted to be! As he read the information in front of him, threatening the ones he held dear, with bankruptcy and worse. Big John Hammond did his best not to lunge across the table and strangle the shit heel seated across from him!

Now John understood how he got, HERE. The last contract he worked on, held some really nasty stuff, pathogens he had seen in the Air Force while briefly working alongside the CDC. Viral hem-orrhages like EBOLA and viral Meningitis! There was Rabies and even a sample from the genus Ophiocordyceps, AKA the zombie Ant virus. The contract called for the mixture of those pathogens as well as a cure for that same toxic brew. And that was the only time he broke the cardinal rule. Don't ask questions, be reliable, just do your job and go home!

Just before completing his work, John asked his onsite handler. What was his work going to be used for? He got no answer. When John finished completing the gene swap, he asked again. What will the work be used for? Once again, he got no answer, still this time he did get a very angry glare. On the way to the airport, John tried one last time to get an answer to his question. What will the work be used for? Sadly, he received an answer, in the form of his wife's untimely disappearance.

Now as he sits sweating in days old musk, Big John the advent Chess player understood what happened to his Brenda. He broke the cardinal rule, and his opponent sacked his Queen!

THAT'S NO LADY, SHE'S A FEDERAL MARSHAL!

It has been two years since her Manna died and the big Midwestern house has sat empty ever since. Sitting gloomy on a little used tree lined road that leads up to their secluded front door. Robin Aquila had been planning this day for a very long time! And she understood if she went to that house on this morning, there would be no turning back.

Robin looked at herself in the mirror and knew she suffered from lack of sleep, PTSD and probably a yeast infection! She has been a Federal Marshal now for six years, at age twenty-seven she should be considering thoughts of raising a family. Instead, Marshal Robin Aquila is a shit kicking, hard drinking, random guy or gal fucking type of modern woman!

Marshal Aquila's demons won't let Robin come to grip with what's driving her towards self-destruction. Just last week while serving a search warrant for a hardcore wanted felon. Robin failed or maybe just neglected to call for proper backup! In turn two men were shot that day, one died, the other one lived. Sadly, neither was the felon she was in search of! To her credit there was enough drugs and guns to make the shooting if not feel at least look totally above board.

Nevertheless, her superiors must wonder had Marshal Aquila gone into the residence with intent to shoot first and ask questions later? Since day one Robin has been a Marshal that was a spark plug, ready and willing for action! Standing 5'4 and weighing in at 128 pounds on a good day. The Marshal was blessed with a 32-24-35 frame and highlighted by her father's rich mocha color. Still, it's not hard to recognize her mother's Filipino heritage. Yet Robin was far from being laid back or Bubba like!

Robin hated that every time she looks into the mirror, she saw his face and not the mother she struggles so desperately to remember. She was falling off the rails, Robin hated to admit it but every anniversary of her mother's "disappearance", she loses her shit! Whether it's drinking too much, engaging in drunken sex with a willing stranger or strangers, or going looking for Felons to smack around just to get her anger out! Robin has a hole inside her that's filled with anger, rage and lots of confusion.

Which's only getting worse! It hadn't always been this bad, she joined the Indiana State Police Academy straight out of High School. No matter what Robin personally thought of her father, he had taken care of his family.

Big John had set up his mother-in-law Maria Aquila and his daughter Robin with a comfortable life! The property they lived on was paid for. A trust and been set up while John had been awaiting trial, so taxes, monthly bills and medical insurance could be paid for as well. It seems he did everything right, except safeguard his wife!

Her father apparently had a nice size nest egg stashed away, since their never got a dime of insurance mom from their mother disappearance.

Yet for the last 14 and ½ years years, Robin has never had to worry about paying the bills. Understand the lady Marshal didn't trip and fall to go into law enforcement. Robin head and feet first rushed to go into Law Enforcement! She still remembers being thirteen sitting in a hot court room, just to be near her dad, every day of his trial. Her grandmother tried to keep Robin away once, only to find she had snuck out, called an Uber and traveled fifteen miles to the court room getting there with five minutes to spare!

However, when Big John was convicted, their relationship changed. No matter what picture the State tried to paint of her father, there was no way she believed in the lies they were telling about her dad! It wasn't until she found her mother's diary and began reading how Brenda felt John was not always going out of town on business.

She wrote about wondering about what kind of business only lasts seven days at a time. In Brenda's mind John had a girlfriend or maybe even another family that he had to visit. It made no sense, yet to a confused mind it might make total sense. Her father had over eighty million dollars set aside, and his wife had no real clue what her husband did for a living! All she knew it that he invented new types of gene therapy. She liked it better when he was with the CDC, stable hours and government access to black tie-fancy parties, as her writings expressed.

Still, Robin remembers her father wasn't a partying type of guy. Her memory of her father swirls around the books he read, the sport team he followed, the stars they would chart on a clear night, the chess they played. As well as the soulful music John Hammond enjoyed listening to as he loved to call it baby making music!

Robin strips off her sweaty blue boxers and lavender tank top before turning on the shower. She needs a cup of coffee to steady her somewhat toned tummy. The sensation of warm running water down the base of neck, flowing directly down the curve of her back, to the crescent moon of her brown backside felt refreshing. As Robin rubbed the green sponge adorned with vanilla scent soap across her sensitive brown nipples. She thought long and hard about all the events that needed to go right today for her to pull what she had planned off! She couldn't see waiting any longer and there was no other way to get the answers to the burning question that kept her up at night.

Robin's frustration always triggers her fuck, flight or fight response! Even before her mother disappeared, her father enrolled his precious child in six days a week Hapkido lessons. Big John made sure his seed could swim, read, write and defend herself if she must. To her father, those were the keys to having a grounded adulthood.

From age 5 to 26 Robin studied this rare Korean martial art. It's not until she attended the State Police Academy did Robin truly take a step as a Martial Artist and as a woman! As Robin's right hand approaches her shaven vagina, her thoughts are filled with that of her first love. A striking rugged Hispanic Cadet of Puerto Rican descent named Jav and suddenly Robin's index finger traces a small circle around her clitoris.

Robin leans forward, loving the way the warm water hits the back of her neck, rolling down her back, then off the wonderful hills that are her ass cheeks and down the drain!

Her breathing was swallow and Robin knew she didn't have much time to get ready. Nevertheless, everyone does their best thinking when their head is clear of distractions, right? And the quickest way to let go of unwanted stress is to righteous orgasm! Even a stubborn Federal Marshal understands the value of self care.

YOU GO TELL THEM THE VALDEZ'S ARE COMING!

Back in 2000 it was a typical hot and dusty August day in Juarez Mexico for the lanky 15-year-old Ernesto Valdez. Yet that was the day of destiny! For that's when he first met then plump, Celeste Beracruz. Ernrsto's hustle was selling bottles of water to migrant workers longing to illegally cross into the BIG STORE otherwise known as America! The train of Central Americans looking for a better life always stops a piss away from the United States, aka Babylon, aka The Great Satan or the BIG STORE. And it was this hustle that fed, clothed and provided Ernesto a merger existence!

There's an award-winning Broadway play that gave rise to a song that states *"Everything's good in America, everything's GREAT in America..."* Truthful the only thing GREAT about America to immigrates is the ability to make money for their labor. What most bigots refuse to understand is that it's better to work for 4-10 dollars an hour. Then work for eight stinking dollars a day!

Nevertheless, when Ernesto noticed the cute and pudgy girl arguing with what look like a couple of El Salvadoran men. Ernesto knew he had never seen those Coyotes before, and maybe they were not attached to any of the local Cartels. Which was a giant No, no in these parts! Ernesto knew that bounties had been placed on anyone not working directly with the Juarez Cartel.

Juarez was a dangerous city to do business in, and the street tax could vary from street to street! Still, the price may change, yet the cost remains the same. Your fucking safety! Ernesto only sells water and energy bars, nevertheless he had to kick up 20% of what he makes each day he's out working the line!

Even so, whatever the conversation the Coyotes are having with the stout brown skinned girl wasn't going their way. One of the men reaches out to grab Celeste by her sweaty wrist, only to receive a hard kick in his grimy kneecap! The Coyote crashes to the dirt filled pavement as his partner laughs before backhanding the defiant teenager to the dust filled ground.

Ernesto grabs his utility knife from under his shirt and takes off running to the scene. However, before he could make up the thirty or so yards the chubby girl with the pretty face takes matters into her own hands! As the Coyote leans forward to pick Celeste up by her hair, he must not have seen the knife she pulled from her skirt. Making its way directly towards his big fat belly.

Her cut was clean and sure like she has been here a time or two before! As the Coyote reared back to slap the teenager again, he felt the wet sensation of warm water rushing down his pants. Straight through his underwear and soaking into his socks. With hand raised he looks down to see his warm blood nourishing the dry cracked pavement.

That's when the angel faced teenager stabbed him two more times in his prostate shrunken genitals!

The wounded Coyote fell back to the pavement wiggling in pain as the first Coyote to incur Celeste wrath tries to back away from the bloody teenager, begging for his life.

Ernesto could plainly see the look on the girl's face as she leaps on the Coyote and begun to attempt to stab him in his face. It was one of joy! Be in pain or not the older man still had the strength of an adult Male. So, he wrestled with the dangerous teenager until the Coyote was able to flip her on to her back. For a moment Ernesto is confused about what he should do! As the Coyote bashed the teen's hand holding the bloody knife into the ground, until her knuckles bleed and she allows her weapon to go free. He picks it up and screams, PUNTA! While snatching up the bloody knife to slit her deadly throat. That's when the Coyote looks down to find his own 38. sub nose Revolver that he kept in his back pocket, Jammed into his rib cage!

The pretty young girl's face's twisted in utter bitter rage, and she only needs to fire one shot. The force of impact lifted the Coyote of the teenager and propelled his fat ass from toff the dusty he sidewalk and under the wheel of the stopped train.

The crowd was stunned, and no one moved. The sound of police sirens filled the air as Ernesto and Celeste locked eyes. She noticed him holding a knife and slowly her aim adjusted to him. He shakes his head no, and slowly put his weapon away, while holding out his hand. He whispers,

"Come, come with me. Police will be here soon. Come, follow me, please I want to help."

If you ask her why, -Celeste would argue she didn't know. Nonetheless, years later in the dark, as her head rests on Ernesto chest, Celeste will mutter. You had sad understanding eyes! They fled down cramped alleys, before quickly blending into the afternoon crowd. Just like that the young couple embark into a love affair that will endure the end of the civilization.

Ernesto leads a cautious Celeste to his humble one room dwelling on the side of a check cashing place. Once inside Ernesto introduces himself and finds out the 411 on Celeste BeraCruz. The 17-year-old half Costa Rican, and half Panamanian hell spawn was heading to the United States to try out for American Idol. It was difficult yet Ernesto must explain to the willful Celeste that might have to wait. JPD maybe even the Federal Police might be looking for her. Furthermore, even the cartel!

So, this was the start of their something, beautiful to them and very deadly to others! How did they become two of the among the notorious- even among the Sinaloa Cartels standards- Sicaros or assassins? That's another tale worthy of telling however, not right now. What is needed to know is that the couple legally married in 2004 and Celeste never made it to American Idol!

Furthermore, Cartels are always quick to recognized real talent in their mist. They had set up a sort of boot camp for hitman in the isolated desert in their dearest Mexico. Hidden from prying eyes, there future Sicaros learn the dance of Death! Mexican style.

It was a place where the Sinaloa cartel trains their Assassins to be able to kill using guns, knives, machetes, bombs, their fist, feet and their brains. Death was their glorious purpose! Fun Fact disgraced former CIA operatives could not wait to get paid in instructing cartels on intelligence gathering and assassinations.

Anyway, it took a little over a year from when they first met, nonetheless, Ernesto bulked up from 5'6; 113, to 138 pounds of pure calculating mayhem! While Celeste slimmed down considerably, she went from 5'3 174 pounds, to 137 pounds of 36B-26-37, of untainted Calamity!

It was clear to see on their first job why, Ernesto earned the nick name "the Ghost Face Killer" because he was quiet and very efficient at his work. However, it's clear Celeste on the other hand has at least 2.7 screws loose. Some distant traumas she had endured shaped her, molded her or she's just a blood driven psycho slut!

Furthermore, she enjoys killing those that cross her so much, it works her up into a bloodlust that only Ernesto can help her rein in. And by the sounds they make during lovemaking, she's fucking extraordinary! Celeste "Calamity" Valdez is a total wild cat in the streets and in the sheets.

It wasn't until 2015 that events took a turn for the worst when the notorious Sinaloa Assassins after a falling out with their employers on the American side of the border. Lots of people died in Indianapolis Indiana when the couple got into a running gun battle with other Cartel members and the Indianapolis Police Department, the Indiana State Troopers and several armed white do-gooder citizens!

It was right out of a goddammed 90s' action movie! Gut wrenching

Automatic weapons fire, lots of people being trampled or being run over by cars in sheer panic! All while Celeste hurled M-4 fragmentation grenades at Police vehicles. In the end, the Valdez Couple have been gravely wounded. As where twenty even various law enforcement personal had been wounded, in which nine died! As well as twenty-one Indiana residents were injured and four of those also succumb to their injuries Unlucky for Celeste and Ernesto, they survived and Crazy President Trump used them in every negative ad his supporters needed to be them! His agenda of a closed border pushed was quickly passed through by a frighten GOP led Congress.

For their action in which over forty people were injured and 13 died, the Valdez's received the death plenty! Death Row is where they both sit and wait for their judgement day to come. They hadn't seen each other in nearly seven years. Still, something is in the works, some force that shall not be halted. An event which will throw the lovers back in each other's arms.

The million-dollar question was simple has Prison change, them or have they always been who they are now?

CHICKEN HEAD.

Earl didn't like the nick name, Chicken Head! Never take it for granted when you met Earl and call him Chicken Head. If you did, he would probably murder you and drive around three states wearing your head as hat! However, there's a decent chance Earl Grimes might murder you anyway, because you can't stop a hard-working white man that's good at what he does. Born Earl Gaines formerly of Gainesville Florida, now a resident of Indiana's Death Row Population, is more complex than his jailers and observers give him credit for. One must understand Earl only looks mentally handicapped.

Earl "Chicken Head" Gaines stood a hiccup short of 6'8 inches tall and is a biscuit short of 330 pounds on a good day! Earl is a predator elite, he's goddam serial killer! Not just any Serial Killer, he's one that enjoys killing pedophiles- frankly that part didn't start until Prison- if only the dead could complain, right? If Earl had any type of father figure he would be playing in the NFL as a O-Line man, not of Death Row.

Frankly, even before prison Earl was just a regular run of the mill cold bloodied murdering sonofabitch! Being an orphan, Earl has some serious abandonment issues. Being as big as a house and slight artistic it's hard for him to appeal to women, unless he's paying. And then it's still a crap load of assorted NO's!

So, he set his sights of femboys, young gay men and male to female Transgenders aka Transwomen.

As the court records state Earl didn't kill them out of disgust, he stalked, strangled and dismembered their bodies, when they failed to return his calls or texts after what was no more than one night stand! He said he wanted to collect them as slaves in the afterlife. In a sense Earl did, collecting pieces of over twenty-seven victims!

It was some of the same pieces that Police found in a hotel room in Evansville Indiana after responding to naked teen seen running from the area. Dahmer may have eaten his victims, while Earl just wanted to be loved by them! This huge trucker from Florida had a dead Hispanic male hooker in his bed. Along with several pieces of assorted corpses out in the cab of his Peterbuilt Semi truck. Well case closed.

That was in back in 2002, while in 2004 behind bars, Earl takes pride in doing in a Catholic Priest that ended up to close for his comfort! Earl pleaded self-defense saying that the Priest tried to molest him. Yep, that's right, a sixty-eight-year-old former Priest was going to forcibly fuck a thirty nine year old Monster, whose probably four feet shorter than the fabled Bigfoot! Right.

The state of Indiana didn't buy it, they tacked on forty more years to his original 150 years he received in his first trial! Sidenote if it had been Texas or his home state of Florida, Earl would have landed on death row long before he killed his 3rd pedophile! Yeah, third. However, it seems the state of Indiana has a problem with putting people who look mentally challenged to death.

Anyway, by the time Earl got caught strangling a naked University Physician convicted of twenty-one counts of rape and child sodomy Chicken Head tried telling the Guards, it was just rough sex gone wrong! Finally, the Indiana courts where tired of hearing about Earl Chicken head Gaines. This time the Judge sentenced him to death! Asked if he had anything to say for himself, Earl smiled and spoke.

"Well, I be goddammed, is this how you thank me for removing garbage from our home? Anyway, I guess I finally made the big time!" That was in 2009, fourteen years have passed and Earl's next on the list to go screaming into the abyss.

He has been sitting in a cell next to John Hammond and Ernesto Valdez for too many years to count. These men have been through rough and not so rough times on the Row. Nonetheless, whatever happened two days ago has been against protocol!

No lunch has been served, and no breakfast or dinner! A fat man knows when each meal should have been delivered. No guards around anywhere, it's like everyone in charge has just said FUCK IT! The toilets had begun to back up and the screams of inmates were beginning to drive Earl, insane. Which wasn't hard, because he clearly doesn't have far to fucking travel! Earl liked Big John who was fucking smart for a common murderer, and he kept their spirits up by saying someone would have to come check on them sooner or later.

Back when he was making his mind on up on whether to kill John Hammond, this would-be prey, extended to Earl a kindness never bestowed upon him by anyone! He told Earl Gaines that he was his friend and that's all it took. Big John did more than say it, he proved it in Chicken Head's eyes. Behind bars chocolate pudding is a dessert worth killing for and Earl had! Still John always gives his to Earl, because said they give him gas.

And Chicken Head was a bit of a hoarder, so all that pudding came in handy for the last few days. Now all they had to do was survive until help came. Or die in a pool of his own disgusting farts.

AN ASIAN AMERICAN STRIPPER & A TAIWANESE TRANS WALK INTO A BAR!

Sky Harrison was one of those rare jewels that only an interracial pregnancy can produce. Her dad was half Cuban and half German and grew up playing baseball, but never was good enough to get call up for the BIG LEAGUE for more than two months in ten years of D League play! While her mother's one hundred percent Vietnamese professional dancer and real estate agent.

Sky moved to Chicago from sunny San Diego when she got a job dancing for the Chicago Bulls basketball team in 2017. Standing all of 5'3, weighing 118 pounds if you put rocks in her pocket. The 32-23- 34 framed green-eyed sprite captured the hearts of most of the horned-up fans that come to see T & A as much as they do dunks and three pointers!

When she first arrived in Chicago it was the fall, she was all of 21 years old and never had been east of Denver. Now she's 25 1/2 years old, only four pounds heavier and sadly been out of a real job that offers health insurance for nearly a year!

That following year the Chicago Bulls went with a heavy blond; blue eyed and big boobs flavor and she was out of a job. It didn't help that Sky didn't want to explore breast implants. So, she fell into a preferred profession, part time stripper in upscale Gentle's men club. Not the Artist, painter and content creator she strived to be. Sadly, it's kind of hard for a Painter to sell enough canvas to pay the rent. Not alone star in a one woman show!

Sky was on the verge of having to return to San Diego and live with her older/mean big sister. Or take a chance by moving to another city and see if she can catch on cheerleading for another sports franchise. However, fate had other designs for the clever young hottie from Southern California.

Lady Lucky looked down on Sky and smiled, then crapped a pot of renewable gold bars by the name of Paradise Hunter! It was on a cloudy afternoon Sky had gone to visit her local Cannabis club in Lincoln Park when she shared an Uber with an extremely passable male to female- a mixture of Korean, Thai and Caucasian- trans-woman going by the name of Paradise Hunter.

Growing up in Southern California, Sky had been around passable trans persons for all her life. Nonetheless, Paradise Hunter was 40% plastic boobs and booty implants and 60% breeding. Once inside the Cannabis club, Paradise opens up to Sky over two joints of really mellow Sativa!

Her father was half Korean and half Australian visiting, while her mother was Thai sex worker. Paradise grew up in Thailand. an orphan child who at 12 1/2 was sold into a sex trafficking ring and shipped to America. Only to have their container busted by Homeland Security in a sting operation. Lawyers applied for her emergency asylum and crazy has it may sound; the State Department granted it!

After four years and a half year of Foster care in various homes in the great state of Texas. Paradise was finally released into the wild of America, allowed to roam free.

She went out to make her way, standing 5'7 and weighing in 145 pounds on a 34B-26-37 inch frame yielding 7 inches of pure ancient Asian secret! The now twenty-one-year-old Paradise has found a way to monetize her immense sexual appeal without having to actually do porn.

While Sky had been stripping in Downtown Chicago and Northwest Indiana gentlemen's clubs. Paradise was playing video games in lingerie or interviewing skateboard punks no one has ever heard of on new emerging platforms of social media most people had not heard of

It ready didn't matter what she did, Paradise had already been exposed to the key to success in America. Be you a freak or a even super star; whatever you are, you better own that shit! Either way Sky and Paradise hit it off as friends and as coworkers when Paradise brought her in on her ninety thousand subscriber show, one of the first pay for view podcast. That's right, over ninety thousand people paid Paradise Hunter five dollars a month to see her play video games in her underwear! Good work if you can get it, right?

For whatever reason Paradise fancied herself a singer, she has tried out for the Voice, American Got Talent and American Idol. From the sound of it, clearly Paradise has a body built by the toy maker Fisher Price. Nevertheless, she has a voice made by the same people that made whatever in your local fire truck something that entices dogs to howl and lose their fucking minds!

It didn't matter she looked great in tight jeans and come fuck me pumps. Paradise the poor dear, couldn't carry a tune in a bucket if you hung it around her hairless Adam's apple! YES, yes, certain judges tried to screw her behind closed doors. Furthermore, some of those same judges screwed Paradise publicly when a disgruntled Producer recorded every hot mic sound bite of those same Celebrities trashing her!

Most people would have crawled up in a ball and cried themselves to death. However, that's not Paradise Hunter, and that's what Sky marveled in, how confident Paradise is in her own skin! She downloads their sound bites, laced some fairly decent Hardcore Rap lyrics on a trap beat she produced herself and dropped it on youtube!

As a singer Paradise was a bust, however as a hot Rapper, she could make the cut Plus it didn't hurt that Paradise was seated on a swing wearing a bathing suit, and white stripper boots while sucking on a red lollipop as her track loops behind her. She never said a word, just kept swinging on the swing while sucking on that juicy red lollipop! And what was that worth, one hundred million views! Plus, a sponsor in the candy maker of blow pops.

She followed that up with a diss track aimed at her haters! Paradise's content attracted more views than their last ten Winners combined! Same approach, except the swing was replaced by a motorcycle and the hard candy sucker was given proper company in the form of a vanilla ice cream cone melting all over her hands, on her face and on to her heaving chest.

This time four hundred million views! Still, when the world runs itself off the tracks, there's one thing about the internet no one ever dares talk about. Was the success even real?

Book One

Chapter I:

DO YOU REMEMBER THE TIME?

It's been twenty-three years or nearly one generation since the formal death of our world! The virus to end all virus was unwittingly unleashed on February 14st, 2022. There is no way to confirm if it were North Korean hackers paid by Russian intelligence. Or Russian hackers paid by the Iranians. Or Mexican Cartels longing to make Mexico great again! Either way someone went out of their way to crash the North American grid.

All that's known is that a foreign intelligence agency set up a very expensive diversion in an attempt to steal the COVID-MOMREL-6 virus. As in Measles, Meningitis, Ebola, Ophiocordyceps, Leucohloridium parasite and Rabies. Little did the culprits know, their actions opened the door to the end of the world as we know it! At 02:45am the North American power grid went down from Long Island New York to the state of Arizona. Furthermore, what's known is that someone hit the high clearance Proctor & Gamble's lab in Tulsa Oklahoma, killing five and getting away with the first generation COVID-MOMREL-6 virus. Yeah, some real evil scientist shit for sure was being cooked up in those labs!

Whoever knew about the Proctor & Gamble's lab in Tulsa must have known Generations 2-5 were securely stowed away at Area 52- under the White-Water Apache Reservation in the state of Arizona. Sadly, that foreign government must not have known about the sleeper agents deployed in over thirty-eight countries around the globe. Each armed with the remaining versions of COVID-MOMREL-6 mega virus!

Two, four person teams were under strict orders to release their pathogens if America ever fell under attack by foreign or domestic operatives. Meaning if the normal chain of command has been rendered combat ineffective by anarchist, social change or foreign operatives, then it's game on bitches!

Government think-tanks had already envisioned a nationwide collapse of the grid as a sovereign power's first strike option. As it was with various deep state violent American insurgents, whose sole task was to steal and release COVID-MOMREL-6 against all comers. Even if that meant in American's own backyard. You may ask what is the difference between the first several generations of the virus and the last one?

In the first few generations of COVID-MOMREL-6, the gestation of the virus generally took a few weeks. The infected develop flu like systems where they would generally bleed from every orifice while hacking up yellow-grayish puss like substance! In concert with their brains boil to a temperature of 104-118 degrees, as their body shuts down, the infected internal organ's liquidity into a literally a hot bloody mess!

The infected either die a painful death or their eyes turn blood red, as they develop an incurable insane like RAGE. In most cases the infected strength increases three-fold- or three times that of a normal human being. Also, the infected pain threshold rises one hundred-fold. Added bonus, they will kill everything in sight. Everything!

However, there was a strange side effect to the first three generations of COVID-MOMREL-6 virus. If you were infected what was later termed as the RED DEATH, well, some people died and actually stayed dead! Other infected became blood thirsty RAGERs, was all par for the course. However, a strange side effect occurred, a large portion of those that died from the virus didn't stay dead for long! The combination of both so called Zombie parasites,

Leucohloridium and Ophiocordyceps, led to some rather unexpected bumps in the night. Yes, there is a monster under your bed, and at your door!

Once RAGERs died, their bodies would reanimate with the sole mission bent on spreading the virus. The powers at be didn't want Generation one through three of their regime changing tools! No, they wanted a Generation of the killer bug, that went straight to the RED DEATH. Still, they didn't get the pandemic they wanted, instead the powers at be, got the pandemic that ended all. Birthdays, Christmas, Vacations and so on!

Let us Flash-forward many years since civilization came to a halt. Deana had not been to the ruins of the old world in what seems like forever. As she glared across the gloomy landscape of what had once been called Chicago, this shell of a long-lost civilization made the young woman somewhat sad. The last time they were here, she and her twin sister Hanna were nine years old and that was fifteen years ago. It was clear to see that nature has reclaimed pretty much all of the city, once known for its big shoulders.

The vaccine made from her, and Hanna's blood might help shielded them from the RED DEATH. Even so, if a herd of Zombies caught sight or smell of the live humans, all bets were off! Furthermore, RAGERS can still be found and once again they are evolving! Winter has come and gone, the shuffling and moaning of several million Dead Heads will fill the Midwestern sky much like the sound of flies buzzing around shit!

There weren't as many RAGERS as it once were, yet still they exist. Some numbers point to them outnumbering humans around 400,000-1. That doesn't mean anything for the rotten flesh walking about, over five billion corpses didn't just lay down and die-again; just because humanity found out how to protect themselves long after the game was over! Several billion ZOMBIES roam the planet gnawing and searching for a chance to share the gift that keeps on giving, infection. All while the RAGERS, rule over what's left!

The team of seven explorers knew if they draw too much attention to themselves a Z will come shambling along to investigate. If they were to begin their loud death moan, hundreds of thousands of their kin will follow! Before the woman that was Wynolla Lafayette-known as Windu for her love for something she called Star Wars-died doing what her creed and convictions invoked upon her. Their lifelong protector always talked about the keys to rebuilding a society, stashed away in her old office.

Sadly, this area has been devoid of human life for nearly a generation. Deana, much like her twin Hanna are nearly twenty-three years old, in great physical shape and could hear the patented Zombie moan coming from somewhere down the hall. Nonetheless, her team knew to use their suppressor to ensure silent disposal of any Dead Head that gets too close.

The last thing Bravo Team needs is to attract a Zombie herd, who at the time are minding their own business on the other side of the building.

She tried not to hum the words to the song playing soft in her ear buds, **Do McLean Bye Bye American Pie,"** *Long, long time ago I can still remember how that music use to make me smile and I knew if I had my chance that I could make those people dance and maybe they would be happy for awhile.."*

That's when Hanna notices a blur moving to her right. She should have smelt it! Furthermore, allowing herself to be preoccupied should have gotten her dead. If it had not been for her twin sister protecting her back, she certainly would be!

Deana kept her low shooters stand, as she crept right up behind the shambling Dead Head, who's creeping up behind her sister. She calmly fired one 22 caliber round into the rotten bastard's head! Hanna turned around as her sister caught the zombies' body, not allowing it to drop down on the debris ridden floor. Deana gives her twin an angry look, signaling get your head in the game! She wanted to be out of there before dark.

She walked up to her sister and took one of the ear buds and placed it in her own. She picked up the tune with the grace of an angel, while changing the words a bit..

"Bye, Bye Miss American pie. Flew our helio to the levee and we didn't come here to die. Them good ole boys want to about to eat us and that would make me cry. Dead Heads all round us moanin how they want us to die. So pull your head out ass already!"

Deana tosses the ear bud back to her twin and continues to search the vegetation for any signs of the area that holds the keys to re-building the world.

Chapter II:

YOU ONLY HAVE 72 HOURS HEAD START.

Let's return to where it all started, twenty-four years ago to the date, Lieutenant Colonel Lafayette- or Windu to her friends in homage to the Jedi; Samuel L Jackson played in the **Star Wars Attack of the Clones and Revenge of the Sith**!

She had been attending a crisis management meeting in downtown Chicago, Illinois. Along with several other military personnel from all five branches, as well as persons from the mayor's office, the Fire Department, CDC and Homeland Security. Growing Civil unrest has been rapid across the nation due to police shootings.

This forced a national debate on police reform, which has been raging from coast to coast in the form of civil and not so civil disturbances. Chicago in more ways than one, will be the epicenter of all things good and horrible. That's when cell phones around the room began lighting up like the fourth of July.

It had been one week since a nationwide blackout plunged dozens of states in a twenty-hour horror orgy of unwanted violence, and fucking mayhem! Martial Law was just beginning to ease in most urban areas as life does its best to return to semi normal. However, a new pandemic was slowly plodding across the globe. It has flu like symptoms, accompanied with serve brain swelling and body wide yellow puss bearing blisters. Whoops, almost forgot, the infected bleed from the eyes, nose, rectum and mouth. This illness also seems to induce a cationic state that generally leads to seemingly a real painful death!

Lt. Colonel Wynolla Lafayette was seated between an Air Force full bird she has met twice before. A capable and broad-minded white man named, Kevin McKinney from Buffalo New York. He was around forty-five years old, divorced, a bit portly and balding. Colonel McKinney oversaw CIM- Crisis logistic Management- for his air base in Southern Illinois and he was an honest soul.

On the other side of Lafayette was a Marine Lieutenant Colonel by the name of David Dunston. He was the provost Marshal attached to Great Lakes Naval Center about thirty-three miles away. At first assessment, Dunston seems to be an okay guy. You know the type, the seemingly by the book, goofy kind of fuck that does well in the United States Military! Nonetheless those are the same types that go along to get along and will sheepishly watch as the world burns around them. As well as turn their head to silly little things like, rape or mass murder!

That's when Windu saw her seated on the other side of the room. A passionate and fiery CDC scientist, with the girl next door kind of looks. Just about one notch down from any Sports Illustrated Super Model to ever grace their cover. Nonetheless it's not like Wynolla was complaining! It was the second night in their hotel conference area when they caught each other's eye. And even in her quick glance, Wynolla could see that her warm smile was still there. As is the customary flip of her long and slightly blond tinted hair!

Wynolla and Monique struck up several very deep, profound and meaningful conversations over two bottles of wine their first night. They have some much is common from their love of Chinese Martial Arts, to the study of infectious disease! While Lafayette was a New Orleans Saints fan and Monique an L.A. Chargers fan, they both figured they could live with that.

Wynolla wanted to spend the night flipping the slightly curly hair out of Monique's' green eyes. However, she knew they had a big day waiting for them and she simply kissed Monique Littlefield on her lips and left her standing in the frame of her hotel door.

That was two days ago, and they had not had a single moment to pick that conversation up where they had left off. By the number of phones ringing- anyone with a high security clearance pretty much can make out who the other important assets in the room are- it doesn't look Wynolla and Monique will have time for a quick lunch break either!

She can see the frown that crossed Monique Littlefield's lovely face from her seat across the room. As Wynolla reads her own text, she can see it was from the DC and that was never a good thing! Lieutenant Colonel Lafayette got up and tried to find a quiet corner of the room so she could call the Pentagon number that just flashed on her screen.

It has been two years since Lt. Colonel Layette was assigned to her shop at S4-COM- Special Forces Command- based out of Ft. Bragg. Furthermore, she knew the number of the one-star General that ran their shop. Nevertheless, this number was out of Washington DC, and as soon as she dialed it, Windu's sixth sense was right. The call was trouble, with a capital fucking T!

The nasal voice on the other end said. "Major General Rochelle 's office please hold." As Wynolla tries to remember what office the two-star General she's waiting for was assigned to. She could see by the look on the faces of those in the crowd that something horrible was underfoot! When the General picks up the phone, his voice held a bit or worry and a lot of frustration as he grunts.

"Morning Colonel Layette, this is Major General Rochelle."

Wynolla responds in kind. "Good morning, General. Whatever the concern is understand I am not able to reach a secured line."

The two-star General replied. "Roger that. You will grab the next thing smoking and head to Great Lakes Training Center for your briefing. You need to move ASAP Colonel!"

Colonel Layette could see people gathering their things and quickly heading towards prescribed exits. The silence coming from the other end of the phone's beginning to fill Wynolla with a sense of dread.

General Rochelle broke their stalemate of silence by saying. "Did you receive me Solider?"

Windu replied with a simple, "Locked on sir."

It's the Marine Colonel McKinney who offers Wynolla and the Air Force Colonel Dunston a ride to his base, Great Lakes Training Center. However, it's Layette who floated the idea of offering the CDC rep, Monique Littlefield, a ride.

It took the foursome about 55 minutes in horrible bumper to bumper traffic before they reached the Largest Naval base west of the east and north of the west coast!

A young Navy SP waves their Provost Marshal's white RAM pickup with black tinted windows through the main gate without much hassle. From its interior the inhabitants could see the base was indeed busy. Trucks were being loaded and recruits are being pulled out of basic training for some sort of general heavy labor.

FYI, generally, in times of floods, freaky snowstorms or other local natural disaster the United States Navy will assist local law enforcement, fire departments and or civil authorities. Being the entire nation was just now attempting to step back from Martial Law. The activity going on at the Training center might seem somewhat normal.

Yet there was something else, some underlining tension, carving major worry lines across most of the faces involved! Provost Marshal Colonel McKinney drove his passengers straight to the building that housed the office of the base commander, Rear Admiral Jefferson Bullraguard Lee. Inside a video conference room, a huge screen's being erected for many people Colonel Layette has just been with in downtown Chicago. The muttering among the attendees resembles a nest full of angry bees!

The room is quickly packed, and the air is now stale. Five Naval enlisted personnel placed hot coffee and hard donuts down on a metal table and quickly exited the room. Wynolla recognized all letters of the Federal Family, FBI, DIA, ATF, CDC and Homeland Security. She keenly noticed no one was here from the mayor's office or Governor's, which sent red flags up her spine. When Rear Admiral Lee entered the room, someone shouted in typical military bravado. "Attention, Officer on deck!"

Jefferson Bullraguard Lee's stride seemed effortless as he made his way to the front of the cramped humid conference room. At the time to Windu the thing that stuck out about Rear Admiral Lee's that he's a tall man that moves with an air of being in charge. You know the type of middle-aged guy that felt the need to wear patrolman style sunglasses indoors and drive a Porsche!

He signals at ease, so all the Military personnel may relax. The Rear Admiral's never removes his sunglasses as he runs his right hand through his thinning chestnut brown hair. He clears his throat before saying.

"Thank you for joining us at such short notice. We are awaiting a teleconference from the Pentagon, and we will be online shortly."

That was it, he said nothing more, as whispers and private conversations rippled through the room. Meanwhile Colonel Dunston has joined his commanding office. As Colonel McKinney, Colonel Layette and Doctor Littlefield stand at the back of a crowded room. Monique was standing very close to Wynolla, and she was trying incredibly hard not to touch her! Even so, Wynolla could feel the heat from the back of her hand, seemingly leaping out to latches on with hers. It sent goosebumps right down into her spit shinned jump boots!

The sensation of their touch nearly made Monique momentarily forget they were in a room filled with exhausted federal government Officials. All she really wanted to do was lean on Wynolla, allowing her warmth to co-mingle with hers!

Yet, that wasn't to be, for once the Sailor connected the final cable to the video screen. A table of mostly Male, Admirals and or Generals are waiting to be heard. Lee as the base Commander's first to speak.

"Good afternoon, sirs."

Windu recognized the General she had spoken to on her phone at the back of the room. He's a two Star General, but it's clear with the amount of brass crammed in the video feed, shit has finally hit the fan! A burly four-star Air Force General sternly peered into the camera and began filling in the blanks.

"Good afternoon, ladies and gentlemen. I am General Brandon Worth; I need you to save ALL questions until after the briefing! Everyone in this room has been assigned to this need-to-know project is some way, shape, fashion or form. Our nation is facing a crisis that we are not prepared for! In the next few minutes, you receive a series of email blasts with all your need-to-know information. We are past the point that we may even entertain maintaining secure lines of communication."

Just like the burly Air Force General said, IPads, Galaxy Notes, IPhone's, Samsung Galaxy's etc., began chiming and buzzing signaling- You Got Mail. General Worth permits a few moments to past allowing the room to go through the newly received intel. As soon as he feels most people are on board, General Worth continues.

"The attack on our Nation's grid and this growing pandemic are acts of foreign terrorism and domestic bio-terrorism. A group of homegrown domestic terrorist executed their efforts on the behalf of an organized cabal of foreign hostile powers!"

The last part nearly sucks all the air from the room. Eyes glance hard at phone and computer screen attempting to see what they are up against. Wynolla cannot believe her eyes at the email blast of Intelligence released by the Pentagon! General Worth goes on to say.

"The attack or the grid, was a diversion. Their real object was a Proctor & Gamble lab outside the city of Tulsa Oklahoma.

It was a black site used for unapproved, unauthorized experimentation of gene and virus technology. Seems like our pals at the CIA had a shop they didn't want eyes on!"

Once again, the room's silent as a morgue. Everyone in the room's either a Federal or DOD employee. Most have Security clearances, others maybe not. Nonetheless, it didn't seem to matter. When men who operate in shadows lay all the cards on the table, shit just got real! Wynolla looks up from her phone and tunes back into what General Worth's saying.

"The terrorist got away with the first generation of the COVID-MOMREL-6 virus. This weapon attacks the immune system by using a cocktail of diseases such as Measles, Meningitis, the Leucohloridium parasite, the Ophiocordyceps parasite, Ebola and Rabies! It's only a matter of time before our population will begin experiencing flu like symptoms, including fatal brain swelling, yellow and grayish disease spreading blisters, combined with continuous bleeding from most Orifices and more than likely a certainly horrible fucking death!"

The General pauses for a beat, before continuing. "However, an unsought by-product of COVID-MOMREL-6 virus is a bit unsettling, nevertheless undoubtedly goddam real! Hmm, after death, some Corpses may not, stay dead for long... The combinations of the Leucohloridium parasite and Ophiocordyceps parasite otherwise known as Zombie parasites have a somewhat troubling side effect."

The murmur that shot through the rooms palpable! Monique read though the email blast and she could not believe her eyes. Someone in the government and authorized the creation of a Super Bug and now it's loose! She looks up and Wynolla and she glances at her trying to force a smile. Colonel McKinney whispers more to himself.

"Oh, my gracious God...."

General Worth continues, "The bodies of all infected should be burned. Cremated on the spot! Don't fuck around with funerals. Resurrection time has been reported to be between forty seconds-four and a half minute! Blunt force trauma to the brain is the only way to put these infected down once and for all."

Everyone has questions, tons of questions! Nonetheless, General Worth was following his own script, so everyone read their email blast as he continued.

"The bottom line is, bites, scrapes and cuts rendered by the infected, infect! The infected go on to infect. Tulsa was ground zero! As of now reports of the virus have been monitored in El Paso, Nashville, Dallas, New Orleans, Portland, Boston, Phoenix, Miami, Atlanta, San Diego, New York City, Indianapolis, Hampton and Baltimore. You should have started seeing them in Chicago in roughly five hours ago."

Wynolla's mind's scrambling for the intel at her fingertips is beyond Sci-Fi, it's savagely cutting edge! Still to make matters worse, if this's the last Generation of the weapon. Colonel Lafayette could only imagine what the first five Generations are like.

General Worth continues the one-sided briefing. "In the first few generations of this weapon, the virus hits fast and hard. Most infected need medical care and die within twelve hours of contracting the disease! Nevertheless, variants of this weapon produced an effect on the infected with their eyes turning blood red and they're become consumed by RAGE. They process an increased strength and will be highly resistant to pain! These infected have been labeled RAGERS and they are beyond deadly. Treat like rabid dogs! Shoot them in the face, two times if you must. Just shoot to kill. Destroy them, burn the bodies for they too will RISE from the dead!"

That's it, thought Wynolla. The first Generations of COVID-MOMREL-6 function more like a focused tool, infecting the population as RAGERS, then whatever came next. She muttered the word and Monique looked up into Lafayette's hazel eyes. She muttered it as well, Zombies. Together they return to listen to Worth's briefing.

"Right now, cold weather cities like Chicago, Minneapolis, Denver and Ackerson Alaska are being set up as research and development of any vaccine model. For the most part the infected do not fare well in weather that falls below zero. However, we have nearly 4 ½ months before winter! As well as the last two winters have been produced less than wintrily wonderlands. Still options are limited, so Research Scientist and their families are being quickly swooped up and delivered to those locations listed in your email blast."

Colonel McKinney mutters to Wynolla. "This is clearly an extinct level event!"

If you thought General Worth's tone could not turn more somber, you were wrong.

"In response to this attack on our democracy, Sleeper Agents from our Intelligence community as well as S-4-COM, unleashed Generations 2-6 in thirty one countries labeled as possible enemies of the state...."

That was like the other shoe dropping. America had said, to its friends and foes alike, that death comes to us all! There would be no need for a nuclear war, a biological weapon with extinct level capabilities has been presented to an unprepared world. It was a giant double bird to humanity. It was simply us saying America first. Fuck you, fuck you and most of all, fuck you very much!

General Worth wipes his brow as he continues.

"Admiral Lee will be in command of the military response for this project in your theater. Right now, an entire area of Chicago is being considered a hostile zone, we will provide cover stories to start confusing the populace ASAP! We can't afford anarchy right now. Your task force needs access to the river and lakefront. Your mission is to reverse engineering a vaccine to the initial COVID-MM-OLE-R virus. It won't be long before samples of the virus will be probably attempting to kill you.."

He pauses for a brief second before saying in a somber tone.

"Be advised, soon you will experience a breakdown in all social services! To make matters worse, POTUS and the Vice President along with several members of Congress have been exposed to what we think are the first generation of COVID-MM-OLE-R while in Tulsa on the night of the blackout! Some non-exposed members of Congress are being shuffled away to ensure our government will Survive this day and those that follow."

Even if anyone in attendance wanted to say anything, the lump of raw emotion sticks in their throats allowing only gasps of air to escape, as General Worth continues.

"You have less than 20 hours before the internet picks this up and another 60 hours before it goes down, with pretty much everything else. Print up the intel, for once the lights go out again, we may not get them back for a long while, if ever! Hear this Admiral Lee, the sole function of the Military under your command is the protection of the Scientist working on what we have termed Project Salvation.

General Worth let his words sink in for several moments before continuing.

If they perish, so go we! Inside your email blast Admiral Lee, there's a list of scientists in your area. Get to them and secure these assets, their families as well. If they are sick, do nothing! Martial law has been extended until, well just until. Nonetheless, remember it's our job to serve. We will ensure Democracy goes on! I wish you all SUCCESS and go with God."

Chapter III:

YOU HAVE THE RIGHT TO SHUT THE FUCK UP

Two weeks ago, during the blackout of 2024, Indianapolis Indiana had been an area that the U.N would have labeled a war zone! Frankly, I could only guess that it was like pretty much every other city on the planet. Hell, even the smell of burning storefronts still permeates the air. It seems when the lights go out all the anti-social people in your community come out to play! Whether you consent or not. It was like a goddam 80s action movie, with some muscle bound mumbling manic murdering hundreds of people for his honor.

Thefts, murders and rapes rise one hundred-fold in less than ten hours. Still, Marshal Robin Aquila manages to sleep through the first eight hours of it in a serious drunk stupor!

When she finally awakes it's in utter darkness, Marshal Aquila's naked, sweating and thankfully alone in her own apartment. She has no answers or clue on what the fuck's going on. After a brisk cold shower, Robin towels herself off and applies an ample amount of coco butter and coconut oil to retain moisture. She throws on a pair of snug faded jeans, pulls them over her Nike purple cotton boxers, and puts on a clean black bra as well as a black t-shirt. Robin took a few moments to consider wearing comfortable running shoes, but passed and went with steel toed black Timberlands.

Then the tired woman puts on her bullet proof vest that spells out Federal Marshal, then hung her badge around her pretty neck. She holstered her trusty 9mm Smith & Wesson on her right hip. Then threw her 45. Caliber Colt in her shoulder holster and went to see what she had been missing!

By the time she gets down to the Federal building, Indianapolis was seeing how close it come to resembling downtown Bagdad in 2004! The sound of heavy machine guns fire fills the air much like a horde of angry bees preceded by bright long tracer rounds coming out of their collective asses. It appears Law Enforcement has been cleared to go Full fucking auto; your civil liberties be dam! Still Body Camera are ordered to be worn by all local peace Officers, to preserve the perception that Police were not on a nation killing sphere. At that time, law and order was paraded to everyone on Fox n Friends as being more than able to put society back on the right track.

The fraternity of Federal Marshall's has been reared in the traditions of saying "one Marshal one riot". As well as "a Marshal always gets their man!" So, when the shit finally hit the fan, each Marshal geared up with their choice of AR-15s, Street Sweepers and Auto Shotguns, all equipped with an assortment of scopes for better shot selection. Robin had even seen a big n brawny squared jawed, crew cut hair cut type lugging a .50 Caliber Anti Personal Sniper Rife! In the first eighteen hours of the world slipping into darkness Robin had more gun battles than in ten years of law Enforcement! It was truly a warzone, people were dropping like flies.

Truthfully, the breakdown of society comes quick! When the seemingly dominate hand of the rule of law is lifted, the ugliest portion of society, who has spent their existence been beaten down on a daily fucking basis. Will boil over and when they have had enough, their rage is unleashed in a tsunami of anger, hatred and pure fucking greed!

She has personally shot thirty people who were shooting at her. Even then Marshal Aquila didn't struggle with doing the right thing!

Robin was able to get the first two suspects' medical help. Probably saving their lives for at least the next few hours.

However, as the day turned into night Paramedics were spread thin and the last unlucky seven-would-be hoodlums that wanted to rumble with her, and the Federal Marshal Service. Slowly bled out on the garbage infused street of Martin Luther King Blvd!

That was two weeks ago, now something worse has hit her city and by all accounts it won't get better! Five days ago, the briefing at Marshal HQ pretty much spelled it out, buckle down because help isn't going any time soon.

That's when the ER started filling up with people bleeding from their eyes, mouth and literally their assholes! Robin knew now is the time to use her vacation time and take care of some long put off family matters. In the last two weeks she gathered as much water, canned food, antibiotics, booze, ammo, clean clothes, surgical masks and gloves as she could get her hands on.

She didn't leave her apartment after the all the news networks started mentioning something about a world-wide pandemic. That was five days ago! Robin had already had the news broken to her by the Marshal Services that shit was going to get worse before social and civil liberties could be restored. Technically Marshal Aquila was supposed to be helping IPD or the Indiana State Police right now.

Nevertheless, fuck that thought Robin! Whatever's happening was lethal, people who get infected die quickly and very painfully! Besides she has a date with a man that may or may not have let her down. So, she waited those five days, sobering up, getting her shit together so she can move out. By the third day, the lights began to flicker, and Robin knew time's running out. Still, she had the willpower to wait three more days until the gunfire began less and not so goddam close!

As Robin lugs her two backpacks to the door of her one-bedroom apartment, her eyes scan the room looking for anything she might have neglected to pack. And yep, there it was, Chap stick! As Robin grabs the cherry flavored lip balm from her countertop. She pats both her weapons to ensure they were in the proper place.

Marshal Aquila exits her humble abode, dragging the spare backpack behind her towards the elevator. She eyed the metal tomb, and she knew the power was out. Robin had no choice but hit the stairs, seven floors down, lugging her backpack and heavy duffle all the way. Yet, Marshal Aquila feels she is more than in her element. She was a girl scout, and her father was survivalist nut.

Once she opens the door to the parking garage, Robin came across a scene that should not be happening. The parking gate had been forced open and several vehicles have been recently vandalized!

Robin quickly flips into game mode clearing her Smith & Wesson from her hip. Leaving both her heavy packs by the stairway door, Marshal Aquila lowers her frame to a shooters crouch. As she can hear muffled voices. Each rough and violence driven voices.

Robin sticks to the shadows and uses parked various cars has cover. The head strong Marshal moves quickly, yet silently in the direction of her 2022 black Chevy Tahoe.

The air is thick and moist, with the underground parking lot having at least two inches of standing water due to clogged drain. Inside five grubby, pants sagging, Confederate Flag on hats wearing white males from the ages of 16-25. Were busy breaking into parked cars looking for god knows what. Marshal Aquila could hear the Meth-Heads discussing their plan.

1st Meth Head, "Man this is a fucking waste of time!"

2nd Meth head, "Look man, I just know one of these butt pluggers have to have some drugs hidden in their car."

3rd Meth Head, "We have broken into 20 cars and all we found is a little weed and maybe some X.

4th Meth Head, "Shut up your dumb ass up and work faster, I'm getting hungry fucker!"

Robin can see her vehicle's next on the menu, so she pulls her 45. Colt from her shoulder holster, and with both weapons raised she springs into action shouting.

"Federal Marshal Service! Raise your heads over your fucking head morons!"

The 5th Meth Head and youngest of the group's closer to Robin and for his troubles, he whirls around to find the black barrel of cold steel pressed against his hard head and dirty black hair.

He mutters, "What the fuc.."

He tries to reach up and knock away the weapon. When Robin shifts her weight so her right foot can impact the drug addicts exposed grimy ankle. A loud crack is followed by a louder scream and the sound of his fat body crashing into the wet concrete!

It takes his friends a few seconds to make sense of what's happening. Each is visibly armed with either a crowbar, baseball bat or some sort of melee weapon. Robin keeps her aim trained on the remaining four knuckleheads while making sure the one in pain doesn't try anything crazy. Marshal Aquila repeats herself, however, this time she put venom in her words.

"I said Federal Marshal you stupid crack heads! Last time drop your fucking weapons!"

It's a tense movement before anyone moved. The 1st, 2nd and 3rd Meth Head comply and do as instructed. Nonetheless, the 4th junkie feels the need to lip off.

"Fuck you, black bitch! I ain't no crack head. I smoke Meth! You're got dam Security guard, you fucking Nigg.."

He never finished his sentence as. Robin fires a 45. Caliber round into the loudmouth's left kneecap! It makes a sickening sound as the bullet races along tearing through the bone, his tendons and cartilage. Nevertheless his screams were delicious to Robins re-quite ears!

They greatly surpassed the whimpering of his young buddy with the broken dirty ankle. The smell of bowels releasing from the pain of having a kneecap blow out of a stubborn body in nasty. Still, it rushes along to mingle with the smell of piss, GASOLINE and spilled alcohol.

The remaining three vandals keep their hands raised high above their head in a non-threatening manner. The 1st Meth Head swal-lows hard before saying.

"Sorry, ah, ah Marshal, is it? Ma'am we meant no harm..."

The 3rd Meth Head chirped in. "How about we all just go our sepa-rate ways?"

Followed by the 2nd Meth Head. "We understand you have a hard job to do. And for the record you are one hell of American! I thank you for your service."

He gives Robin a fairly decent salute. Marshal Aquila scoffs as she holsters her .45 and points to the first two Meth Heads then said.

"You two, go grab the two packs by that door and bring them over to that Black Chevy Tahoe Go on now!."

As his bubbies hustle to the stairway, the last Meth Head must ask.

"Do, do you know what's going on?"

Robin has no real answer for the clearly frighten man. Before she can answer, he goes on to ask.

"Have you heard anything about people coming back? You know, coming back from the dead?"

Marshal Aquila didn't know if the man was crazy, high or a bit of both! She shakes her head no, before glaring at the two men wiggling on the ground in pain. Robin told their fellow Meth Head.

"You should get your friends to the hospital, if they are still open for business..."

Marshal Aquila uses her car remote to open the truck of the black SUV and start her vehicle.

All while keeping the barrel of her weapon trained of the two approaching pack mules. When they get the packs to Robin's Black Chevy Tahoe, the men marvel at the gold mined they never got!

Robin had several gallons of water, five cases of MRE's, five med kits, two AR-15, two Full Auto Mossbergs shotguns, two machetes, several firearms and a shit load of ammo! When she's all loaded up and driving away. Marshal Aquila looked at the would-be felons helping their wounded comrades and spoke. "Crime, gentlemen, crime never pays."

Twenty minutes later Robin was headed down I-65 heading to Michigan City Indiana to see her dad, who was sitting on death row. It's a four-hour ride on a good day and this's going to be far from a good day! Most of the talk shows on NPR have been busy debating who was responsible for the national grid going down.

It was partisan hosts looking to cast blame across party lines, arguing and never getting anything done. Robin ran her fingers through her hair and knew she should have washed it before she left home. God knows when she will get a chance to get it done professional ever again!

She might even be a wanted felon by the end of the day. She did fire her weapon, flee the scene and fail to report the shooting to IPD or her superiors. Marshal Aquila had certainly left the reservation! Robin fumbles in her arm rest looking for a CD to play. Even Satellite Radio went down 48 hours ago, and Robin came up with, **Sister Christian a song by Night Ranger**

"You're motorin, what's your price for flight. You're driven through the night. You got him in your sights. Sister Christian the time has come to say…."

It's nearly two hours into a four-hour trip, yet due to increased traffic jams, Marshal Aquila must travel ole country roads. Her GPS is glitchy, but busy working overtime, when Robin noticed she is six hours into her trip, and Marshal Aquila needs to gas up.

The next gas station's a few miles away, and the smell that dominates the air was smoke. The road's small, seldom used by anyone other than locals. There are no lights on inside of huge country homes, each space multiple acres apart. It's an area of pictorial farms growing wheat and corn, as lazy cows sit in the shade. While the world turns ever more violent around them! Nonetheless, Robin saw THEM a fraction of a second too late to do anything but bare witness.

From Marshal Aquila's P.O.V. an older heavy-set white farmer with the traditional long white beard and wearing overalls. He stumbles down an adjacent gravel road looking like he was in trouble. In the portly farmer's capable hands, he brandishes a busy pump shotgun! Steadily firing his weapon in the direction of several people who are engulfed in flames. Yet they steadily shuffle onward, moaning through the murderous gunfire and engulfing flames until they reach the doomed Farmer!

As Robin slows her SUV down, she has no way of seeing the other group of people racing through the cornfield. They wore insane looks, angry faces, yellow/grayish puss filled blisters don the faces of men, women and child alike!

In the future those infected by COVID-MOMREL-6 will be known as

RAGERS! At this moment they are known as, honey, baby, sweetie, mighty sons, aging parents, trans, pan, nonbinary and angelic daughters.

Marshal Aquila turns off her music as the numerous frightening screams will not be denied a captive audience. Out of the corn field descend fifteen angry as hell neighbors, church goes and friends descend on the shotgun wielding senior citizen with a vengeance! Beating the old man into a crumbled lump on the barely used gravel road. To top it off, several flaming corpses continue stumbling towards helpless old man, dropping their weight on the hopefully unconscious Farmer.

The smell of burning flesh's hard to mask, even when lined up next to stalls of pig shit! Robin's acute eyesight noticed the crazy ones don't fight among themselves. They simply snarl or growl before running off in the direction of God help whoever they find!

Marshal Aquila looks at her GPS and noticed the nearest gas stations about seven miles away, off a popular route. She hated to head back to I-65 nevertheless the nearest place to pick up petrol's, is Crawfordville! It took her about 40 minutes to reach the outskirts of the rural farming community of Crawfordville Indiana, population 1800.

Robin's Black Chevy Tahoe approached from the south side of the town. Slowly the Marshal's SUV rolls down the uninhabited main street. So far things seemed, normal. Citizens going about running errands such as getting haircuts, visiting the post office and buying groceries.

Robin pulls into Luke's Gas & Car wash and as she exited her vehicle there's no mistaking the humidity had gone up. For a brief moment, Marshal Aquila thought about taking off her bulletproof vest, then thought better of it. She noticed a young white couple pulling into the stall next to her, clearly nervous at the sight of a heavily armed minority preparing to buy gas! They didn't have to notify the local authorities, because the Crawfordville PD happens to be rolling down the street. The lone Police Cruiser pulls to a stop behind Marshal Aquila's Black Chevy Tahoe. It didn't stop Robin from calmly going about her business of trying her Debit Card to buy fuel.

A short heavy-set Midwestern woman with glasses and pudgy her hand on the butt of her service weapon slowly approaches Robin. The Crawfordville Police Officer stops several feet away from Robin and nervously inquires.

"Are you just passing through?"

Marshal Aquila looks down to make sure her badge was in plain slight before asking"

"Who's asking"

The heavy-set woman scoffs and replies in a huff.

"Officer Hindaburg, Crawfordville PD, Marshal."

Robin smiles she saw that the Officer did notice her tin, well now it was time to see whose dick is bigger.

"Well Officer Hindaburg, since you plainly see I am also an Officer of the Law. Much, much higher up the food chain that you are. Why the hell are you still racially profiling me? You enjoy getting sued?"

Officer Hindaburg used her left index finger to push up her wide frame glasses and asked in a worried tone.

"I, I, well NO. I'm sorry. I thought you were with those Army Trucks that sped through an ago."

Robin needs to pay with cash for her fuel. It's too early in her trip to use her reserves. So that means entering the small gas station. Marshal Aquila stares at the Crawfordville Officer who still had her right hand touching the handle of her 9mm Handgun. So,

Robin scoffed.

"Why is your hand still on your weapon in an aggressive nature, Officer, Hindaburg?"

She looked around nervously, before slowly removing her grip and whispered.

"Have, have you experienced anything weird lately Marshal? I mean, something strange. Something, something you, you, fucking well know shouldn't exist? Have you.."

Robin returned the nozzle and went over in her head what she wanted to say, instead replies.

"Have you?"

Officer Hindaburg swallows hard a few times, she opens her mouth, but she doesn't seem to know where to begin!

Nevertheless, it takes the screams of the female half of the ginger couple parked in stall number two, to bring Officer Hindaburg back to reality. From Marshal Aquila P.O.V she can see the tall Ginger Male struggling with two yellow-grayish blistered faced, red eyed looking people like she had seen even less than an hour ago.

It's not the same group of people, still the two Hispanic teenagers have the same apparent infection! In an attempt to protect his girlfriend, the lankly Red-haired man has picked up an oval rack of greeting cards and is using it as a wedge in attempt to keep them at bay.

The infected Hispanic youths, clothes are baggy, bloody and hanging off them as is the ridiculous style. However, their torsos are bloody and filled with cuts and stab wounds! Officer Hindaburg looks at Robin before drawing her weapon and running into the fray.

Marshal Aquila sighed. "Fuck me!"

End P.O.V. as Robin un-holsters her 9mm Smith & Wesson with extend barrel, fourteen in the clip and one in the chambered.

She takes a quick two steps away from her Black Chevy Tahoe before seeing a crowd of assorted ages, shapes and sizes running towards the gas station! Marshal Aquila can hear the blood curling yell and feel the vibration of nearly eighty people hell bent of committing mayhem and bodily harm! They are 300 yards and closing fast, Robin screams.

“Officer Hindaburg! It’s time to D.D MOW! Follow ME! Time too fucking go hon!”

Either the Crawfordville Police Officer either didn’t hear or isn’t about to allow what Is going on inside the store, to go any further. Either way the ginger couple wasn’t making it easy of themselves, the screaming girlfriend wasn’t a bit helpful!

She was dressed more like a hottie in cut off shorts that gave homage to her toned thighs and cute bottom. A tight white T shirt, which framed her perky nipples like life saviors for your soul and cute white gym shoes for looking like she’s a runner. Each item reveals she’s probably great in between their sheets, nevertheless, she is useless in their tussle!

Officer Hindaburg runs into the Red-haired woman as she is backing out the store. Causing both to stumble on to the piss smelling concrete of the parking lot. This causes the boyfriend to stumble as well. That’s when one of the two infected Hispanic teenagers sucker punches him in the jaw Knocking the Ginger out cold as a canceled comedian career! While the other infected teenager leaped on to the girlfriend, who’s laying on Officer Hindaburg and began thrashing, scratching and biting at their faces.

As he struggles with the two women, the yellow blisters on his face explode spraying foul smelling red puss on the female Ginger, as well as Officer Hindaburg face. The Crawfordville Officer struggled to take a shot around the struggling civilian in her lap. Sadly, the

Infected youth manages to bite down on her wrist. Ripping and grinding his dirty yellow teeth into her tender flesh.

Her vital fluids splattered like a plump balloon filled with blood hitting a wall going 55 miles per hour! Robin knew that they were beyond her help. The red-haired boyfriend is busy getting his brains bashed in as the rapidly approaching crowd is coming uncomfortable close for her comfort. All Robin can do is mutter. "Shit."

She hits the automatic starter, starting her vehicle and Marshal Aquila somberly gets in. She can plainly see their yellow, blistered faces and now Robin can smell them as well. For the first time, it dawned on Marshal Aquila she might need to find protection, from whatever it's that has turning people into rage infected assholes!

Several hours later, the lone Official still at her post at the Indiana State Prison at Michigan City has been alternating power between cell blocks for nearly 36 hours.

The prison has been running on its own generators since primary power went down seventy-two hours into the fall of civilization.

Prisoners in every wing scream and holler for guards and fucking answers! Some more enterprising inmates have managed to get doors to their large dorms to open. Still, they're hampered by the bars that are controlled by control booths. Booths for the moment are well out of reach of Convicted felon's hands. One way or another, most if not all will die behind those sturdy iron bars.

A few weeks ago, it started exactly like every other day, with the count. Followed by breakfast and a job if you had one. John Hammond or Inmate 997421 is on Death Row, he only has only one job and that's to wait. Wait, for the executioner's call! As are his tier mates former Sicario, Ernesto "Ghostface" Valdez and serial killer Earl "Chicken head" Gaines.

The three men make up and unholy trio of wisdom, deadly determination and sheer fucking menace!

John sat his 270 pound, 6'3 inch frame on the corner on his bunk in his 8 by 9, one man cell. His bald head needs a shave as did he, but without the ability to do, being on death row, Inmates only get razors once per week.

John can hear a shuffling from the cell next to him. The hut on his right belong to former Mexican Cartel hitman or assassin known as Sicario's. Ernesto earned the name Ghostface Killer, for if you saw him, you probably did it as the life faded from your eyes. Fun Fact it took Convict 997619, or Ernesto Valdez, nearly a year of being on their tier before he even spoke.

John had been on Death Row for nearly 15 years, not for the alleged murder of his wife. DNA evidence and cell phone records clear him of that on his last appeal. John Hammond the ex-Air Force Major and Genealogist has been repeatedly jumped behind bars. There had been three attempts on his life behind bars, even once while in protective custody.

The Warden at his last prison, wanted to keep John in segregation, deeming him a hazard to himself and others! Yet lawyers argued that is cruel and unusual punishment. That gave rise to the third attempt of Convict 997421, which came from a dirt bag Prison Guard attempting to escort John into a trap! He may or may not have known four members of the Aryan Cross- skinhead Prison gang- are waiting in a shower area.

Nevertheless, when Convict 997421 refused to move towards a darken hallway leading to the gate that opened into the shower room. The shit heel Prison hack stuck John Hammond in the ribs with his night stick! Handcuffed or not, Convict 997421 had been behind bars for nearly fifteen years. Furthermore, in that time, an inmate learns a thing or two about fighting up close and personal.

John stomps on the guard's foot, while pressing his thigh into the guard's knee, pushing it towards a very uncompromising position. The loud snapping sound is followed by a heavy thud and even louder wail of agony for the Prison guard. The man wiggles in pain as John takes a page of out Law Enforcement 101 and places his knee on the young dirty blond man's neck.

John growls, "Why? Why are you trying to kill me?!"

The Guard struggles, trying to grab hold of the inmate strangling him with his very mass. The young Prison employee might have thought it would be the quickest ten thousand dollars me would ever make. Lead a "scumbag" to a door and walk away, who gives a shit, right? That's all he had to do, didn't matter what the man had done. Someone wanted him ended and behind bars there's a price for everything!

John Hammond testified in court that he didn't mean to kill the Guard that was setting him up. However, since there was no evidence of a conspiracy to murder him, his Hired Defender urged that John plead insanity. He has been locked up in SEG for nearly six years and that would drive anyone bat shit crazy.

Nonetheless John Hammond would not hear of it, he pled not guilty. He reasons, self-defense. It took the mostly white Jury-looking at the widow and her two children- only about two hours to return a guilty plea. Numerous years later, here's where Inmate 994721 awaits the cold, uncaring hands of Lady Justice.

Ps, that BLOATED bitch is certainly not a fair mistress! Ernesto tried writing letters when there was light, yet this grew fruitless when his pencil broke. His 5'5 135-pound frame is ripped with stomach muscles from a regiment of 300 sit ups a day. And his biceps are rock hard from the same amount of pushup every day before breakfast! His bronze skin and eagle-like face, envoys the memory of a long-lost Aztec Warrior. Ernesto was quite and must warm up to a person and when he did, that person was John Hammond!

When a prisoner gets convicted of murdering a Prison guard, pretty much nothing goes right for them from the rank and file ever again! If any Guard even halfway believed his story, none would show John Hammond an ounce of mercy or compassion. Or risk being labeled a turncoat by their peers. The only upside the hacks don't attempt to beat Hammond now he's on Death Row.

Even so, they knew how to stick it to Convict 994721 every day to make his wait unbearable. The first two years, he could go days without food or water! Guards would find ways to write John up so he would miss his one day out of his cell per week. Instead of lashing out, Inmate 997421 found a way to document his treatment.

When a journalist came looking to interview Inmate 997421 on his conviction of his wife being overturned only to find himself on Death Row. John Hammond presented his life story, and it made national news! It seems Convict 994721 claimed to be an Air Force " Black Beret" one of America's Special Forces Warrior and he did offer genuine remorse to the family of his attacker.

Still, he stuck to his story and it's the way John handled it all that struck Ernesto as honorable! Ghostface had been around murders, thieves and coyotes all his life. He and barely survive being raped as a child and the only thing he hated more than pedophiles is American Football, gringo country music and fucking Catholic Priests!

Ernesto "Ghostface Killer" Valdez is a legend among his elk! The Indianapolis nightclub shooting that led to a five-hour running gun battle across the city, killing several dozens of people- including 10 Cartel members, over a dozen Police Officers and 16 bystanders- and causing over ten million dollars in damages made worldwide news. Earning him the title Million Dollar Man in the local newspapers!

Flash forward to the present, Ernesto is lost in the repetition of shadow boxing. Left, right, left, right, right. Left, left, upper cut. Endless combinations thrown from various angles, needless to say Ernesto probably would have made a good welterweight boxer. He calls out to his tier neighbor Inmate 997421.

"Hey John. What do you think going on, amigo? You think it's another 911?"

Frankly John's trying not to think, the air in this wing had been off for a few hours and the humidity's rising. He knew if they didn't get out of their cells, they would die in here! From starvation, or even heat stroke, yes their death was always in their cards, now it just seemed, possible.

The last cell of their tier's occupied by the last part of the unholy trio, whether they wanted to include him of not. Earl "Chicken Head" Grimes's mumming and sinning the words to, **DMX's Party Up In Here**, *"Ya'll gonna make me act a fool up in here, up in here. Ya'll gonna make me lose my mind up in here, up in here. Don't make me go all out up in here up in here.."*

When Ernesto heard Chicken head singing about losing his mind. He must stop from chiming in, "you did that years ago you tub of shit." Nonethless even Ghostface Killer knows it's not wise to poke an insane grizzly bear, unless you use a very sharp chainsaw!

Earl stopped singing and slowly rose from his sweat drenched mattress, allowing his 6'8-inch 300 pound frame to move in his snuggly built cell. His bald head and happy blue eyes give Inmate 997960 the appearance of an upbeat gentle giant and in some case that much is true about Earl Gaines. Still, Chicken Head could be jovial, jolly and jubilant while dismembering a still warm body!

By every clinical definition, Earl's, a true sociopath, a person who never sees how he is at fault for his tragic actions. Even though formally Earl Gaines only has a 11th grade education, he has the high functional ability of a real-life Hannibal Lector! Earl learned how to play Chess behind bars and if Convict 997960 had not been a person with deep abandonment issued. He might have made a career as a National Chess Champion!

Chicken Head doesn't have to work hard to foster the impression that's he's a crazed hulking giant. Nevertheless, Earl is a planner, it takes a lot of planning to dismember fifteen bodies and leave pieces across several states. The newspapers got it wrong, and Earl never clear up their bullshit story, because frankly he felt it made him look even more bad ass!

The newspapers claimed Inmate 997960 collected body parts to have sex with and maybe digest select body parts. That was crap! However, Earl figured out why he should tamper with the gold star on his resume! Really the only reason he kept hands, torsos and penis of his victims was to leave their DNA at other crime scenes to mess with Law Enforcement. Each of his victims had disappeared without a trace from either their work or their homes. Their cars, right where they left them and on one occasion, at least one victim had food still cooking on the stove! Earl has never told anyone his trade secrets, however, he and Ernesto do seem to enjoy trading murder tales! Furthermore, it seems, Chicken Head has a lot more than the fifteen the D.A. hung him out to dry on.

Nevertheless, for Earl to land on Death Row, he had to go beyond the murder, death, and kill limit the state of Indiana set as a guide-line to execute a felon.

Earl "Chicken Head" Gaines's the one Inmate you rather not turn your back on, even if he did like you! Some people have that one loose screw they can't get under control. Well, Inmate 997960 seems to pride himself on hunting what he considered bad people with no morals, class or shame. He acted like Hannibal Lector and was proud of it!

Plus, he had a voice of an angel trapped in the body of an offensive lineman, which made him very popular when the local bar threw gay or transgender karaoke night. However, Earl's speaking voice kind of resembled the boxer Mike Tyson on helium! He had a slow cadence to it and for your sake you better not dare laugh.

"Ya'll think when they find us, they will be able to recognize our skeletons. If I don't eat soon, I am going to die!"

Big John calmly said. "It's takes nearly thirty days to starve to death my friend. We may perish due to heat exhaustion long before that. Ernesto, you should slow down on all the moving around you will only burn energy faster."

Ernesto stops shadow boxing for a moment before saying.

"True, but why should I waste away when I can leave an excellent looking corpse?"

Back inside the main facility housing the Warden's Office was the Hub of the Prison's communication system and computer main-frame. Marshal Aquila slowly opens the door with the business end of her AR-15, because when she arrived at the Prison, the front gate was unmanned and there was no one at the front desk.

Garbage was piled up in containers and rats openly ran from feast to disgusting feast! The parking lot was pretty much empty except for six cars that sat in a lot that had room for over ninety.

Yet someone did buzz her into the visitor's lobby and Robin took the time to drag a nearly empty metal garbage can from the front of the room and wedged it in the door frame. Robin wanted to make dam sure not to allow herself to be entombed like others!

The main area that houses the visiting room and guard locker room expressed the sentiment of the day- from the number of personal items left lying about- it seems people left in an awful fucking hurry. When the news of infection hit the airwaves, many of the Prison's employees probably marched right off the job and into self-survival mode! Robin walked off the job, so she certainly can see others following suit.

Nevertheless, this's a Prison filled with many unaware souls! Maybe they're degenerates, even social and psychopathic waste of human DNA, pondered Marshal Aquila. Still to condemn all of them would make their jailers monsters, Fascist or even worse goddam Republicans!

However, she was aware some of these Monsters imprisoned in this tomb of steel and concrete may not deserve a second chance. It's up to Robin to make sure somebody gets what's coming to him!

The smell coming from inside the prison is part sweat, part fear, along with backed up toilets and 100% rotting flesh. The corridors of Indiana State Prison at Michigan City are semi dark, damp and somewhat slippery. Marshal Aquila entered through the front gate unmolested and seemingly welcomed by whoever buzzed her in.

The salt of Robin's sweat was embracing the cracks of her lips and she kind of wishes she could ditch the body armor. Yet the Marshal knew better, a gunshot today would mean certain death! Gone are the days of calling 911 for assistance or going to a medical center for needed attention. Let's face it when Prison guards and law Enforcement in general pack it on in, from that point everyday life is a big shit sandwich.

For there it was pretty much clear sailing all the way through the admit wing. With no Prison guards at their post, this part of the prison was eerie quiet, much like along-lost tomb! When Robin makes it to the Warden's office, she finds the door securely locked. Marshal Aquila gives the ole four knock signal, just about every kid learns while growing up. She waits a brief second before clearing her throat and proclaiming with the authority her title used to present.

"This's Federal Marshal Robin Aquila. Anyone alive in there?"

Slowly a rustling could be heard from behind the heavy wooden door and hesitantly the door opens. Robin can see a middle-aged heavy-set white woman with dirty blond hair and glasses. Her clothes have that I'll been sleeping in them" for days look. After a few seconds she mutters.

"Are, are you will some sort of crisis team?"

Marshal Aquila pushes her way into the cramped office-filled with can goods, gallons of bottled water, Peanut butter, crackers and microwave popcorn. The heavy-set woman quickly locks the door and her tone was filled with fear.

"My, my name is Abby Carpski, assistant Warden. Do you know what's going on?"

Robin turns to look at the woman, who has been hold up like a rat and started to say something rude or crude. Instead, her heart opened just a bit, so a real human being can see the frighten woman trembling in front her!

Marshal Aquila takes off her Chicago White Sox baseball cap and loosens her body armor. Taking it off so the sweat that was clinging to the olive frame, may lazily drip to the cluttered office floor. Robin pours herself a glass of water and does her best to explain what she knew.

"From what I understand a pandemic is sweeping across the planet. Just about everyone's going bat shit crazy! I've seen people with red eyes and yellow nasty grayish puss spilling blisters, doing unspeakable things! I mean, it's anyone's guess I suppose. Still, I, I've seen human beings rip each other apart like they were candy store taffy."

Abby's wringing her hands and her voice's soft and filled with dread.

"I, I know that. Ahh, but the dead, the dead, why are they getting back up and walking around?"

Marshal Aquila looks at Assistant Warden Carpski like the poor woman has cracked under the stress of the Apocalypse! Nonetheless, Abby must have seen the look on Robin's face and she shakes her head saying.

"No. No, NO. I'm not crazy. I'm NOT! We, we had sick inmates in our infirmary. Some sort of viral infection ah, ah, like a flu. Believe me I saw the pandemic part! Those inmates died and we put them in our morgue. Those inmates that survived the flu, have red eyes like you said. We sent many to Michigan City General Hospital... Then those in the morgue, they, they got UP. They came back and started attacking everyone. Marshal, they are eating, US!"

Robin put her empty glass down, cracked her neck and slowly places her body armor back on. Replaced her baseball cap then handed Assistant Warden Carpski paperwork and said.

"I need this, Inmate."

Abby looked confused, she muttered.

"What, why? The court system is done. We haven't had any Prisoner transport in ten days. We generally get fifty a day! Who, who are you here to get anyway?"

Carpski glanced through the paperwork, then said.

" Prisoner 997421, John Hammond's on death row. Marshal, this is highly improper!"

Marshal Aquila puts her hand on her hips and turned the tables by asking Abby.

"Why did you stay? Clearly your boss fled. So why did you stay?"

The middle-aged woman pats her dirty blond hair and tears flow freely from her brown eyes. As she cries, a bubble of snot plays peek a boo with her left nostril! Abby softly mutters.

"What, what could I do? We have over two thousand Inmates! With nearly five hundred women on our adjoining campus. Once the infection spread, people, people just started walking away, I, I couldn't, I just could not leave them all here to die! What, what would you do Marshal? Let them all go?"

Robin chooses her words carefully, knowing that Abby Carpski is holding on by a slender thread.

"Listen hon, may I call you Abby?"

She terrified woman slowly shakes her head yes, choosing her words carefully Robin goes on to say.

"It's beyond messed up out there. These Convicts, no matter how fucked up they are, trust me, there something going on that's worse. Death is on the horizon! I pity any family just trying to survive that would run into someone recently released from doing countless years in SEG.... Still not all these Prisoners have been sentenced to death."

Abby mutters, "Convict 997421 was. Why, why do you want him? By the way, this paperwork is garbage!"

Robins at a loss for words, she knew it was a rush-putting together the right set of paperwork during the Apocalypse is hard to do- yet she did not waver.

"He's my dad and I'll come to deal with him."

There's silence for several beats and Carpski, tries to find the right words to say, nonetheless she drew a blank.

"Ahhh, ahhhhhh,ahhhhhhhhhhh, I'm sorry Marshal I can't do this."

Marshal Aquila fills in the blanks. "My father's sentence to die. I will not allow him to rot in this tomb. No, I will do what the State of Indiana failed to do."

Abby mutters, "That's cold, even heartless Marshal. He's your father!"

Robin changes the subject.

"How many CO's are still on duty?"

Assistant Warden Carpski mutters, "Nine at last count. Once the power went out and we got down to the gennies, most just bugged out. I, I've had to turn off entire cell blocks for hours at a time. The air is off, and we are quietly running out of gas."

Marshal Aquila stuck a several protein bars in the back pockets of her loose-fitting black jeans and replied.

“You are indeed caught between a rock and a hard place Assistant Warden Abby Carpski. Do you behave as a loyal employee or the state or a vial mass murder? The choice is yours, now I need you to accompany me to Death Row. Garbage paperwork or not!”

Before they walked out the door, Robin glanced at the intercom system and asked.

“Does this thing work?”

Abby nods yes, Marshall Aquilla picks up the microphone and begins to speak.

“This’s the Federal Marshal Service...Here are the facts. A virus is spreading across the pretty much the entire planet. Anyone infected will have flu like systems, yellow and gray puss filled blisters accompanied with bleeding from the eyes, mouth and ears. These people are toxic to your health! This virus seems to be 100% lethal, anyone contracting this illness seem to go mad with RAGE...”

Robin battles with herself as she decides to include the information Abby provided.

“I cannot confirm this as being one hundred percent accurate! Nonetheless, it’s said the bodies of the recently deceased of returning and attacking the living.”

Abby can be heard saying. “Eating, EATING the living!”

Robin’s voice is without emotion when she said.

“Some of you have already been infected and there is no longer a system in place to properly execute your sentences. Furthermore, if it weren’t for the pandemic, I would support your transport to another location. So, the state could ensure your victims would not be cheated out of their due! However, we are all FUCKED! Still, I will not release you to rape and kill in these last days of humanity!” Robin pauses for a second, so she can measure her next words.

The Marshal continues, "If you manage to free yourself so be it! Nevertheless, I am telling the remaining CO's to go home or whatever they feel safe. For those among you that deserve to die, this place is about to be your earthly tomb."

After that, it took about thirty minutes to make it to the building that houses the only three Prisoners sentence to death at the Indiana State Penitentiary at Michigan City. Abby had told the Marshal that several wings had been comprised and attempting to cut through them was suicide! So, they had to take the scenic route.

The two women could hear the sound of screams as groups of Convicts look for someone, anyone to free them from their concrete and steel ossuaries! Prisons are made to keep bad people in under a watchful eye.

Nevertheless, when you remove that supervision, bad people will test the bounds of their captivity. Robin knew they had at most two hours before anyone that really wanted out would be getting out.

Abby was as nervous as a church mouse as she walked quickly to keep up with a hell bent Marshal Aquila! The thought of the Marshal killing her own father, shakes Carpski to her core beliefs. As well as corpses that rise and attempt to eat the living!

Abby had decided to leave the Death Row wing unguarded. She had not the manpower to solely guard three Inmates. From Assistant Warden Carpski perspective there's only one wing that needed guarding, S- as in she- wing.

Furthermore, the Death Wing, that is like the penthouse of the Prison system.

Inmates have their own private yard, private huts and no one real looking to meet death before it's legally prescribed. So, there is a truce, built on we are all sentence to die, why the hell would we want to rush it?

The air's thick, so when the door to the wing opened, the rush of fresh air must have made the inhabitants feel like they were skinny dipping on Mt. Everest! Assistant Warden Carpski enters the wing followed by Marshal Aquila. The sunlight forces the Inmates to offer shade to their eyes, not knowing whether to shout close the door or let me out.

Earl is first to say.

"Well, I do declare! If isn't Assistant Warden Carpski. How's it hanging Abby?"

Carpski feints a moment of calm and sincerely answers.

"I wish is better Mr. Grimes. Did, did you gentlemen hear the intercom?"

Ernesto replies. "No. You turned our power out and that means no power, until you just turned it back on. What the hell is going on?"

Abby's tone is apologetic, "Sorry, it cannot be helped Mr. Valdez, the world is falling apart around us! Frankly, gentlemen all of this is above my pay grade."

Big John said nothing, he waited for the other person following Carpski to step out of the sun. Robin slowly steps forward. Father and daughter lock eyes in an intense stare off, before John said. "Hello, it's been a while, Marshal. Look like you haven't been sleeping well."

She replied, "Are you telling me or asking me?"

By Marshal Aquila's tone, Earl and Ernesto automatically caught that their tier mate has some sort of emotional connection with the pretty, yet sweaty FED. Robin signals Abby to release Convict 997421 and she did. When Big John Hammond exited his cell, he slowly walked towards his daughter. He cannot gage the anger in her eyes, nevertheless he could feel it radiating from her skin!

Robin looks up into her father's brown eyes and fights back the emotions that flooded over her like a hot wave. When he holds his arms wide open, Marshal Aquila finally understands what she has been mad at. She has been mad at herself, for needing him, for absolutely missing her dad!

Ernesto smiles as he states. "I can't say I saw that coming."

Chicken Head replies, "Me either, but they do smell a like."

Ernesto shakes his head and mutters. "Sometimes mi amigo, you creep me out and you have no idea how very hard that is to do..."

Big John kisses Robin on the head and softly whispered.

"Thank you, for coming for me."

Both his tier mates clear their throats in unison, signaling what about us.

Robin forces herself out of her father's embrace and replies. "The world has lost its shit! The disease you kept warning me about is burning like wildfire! We need to go, NOW."

John looked at his tier mates and said. "Warden Carpski would you be a dear and let my associates out?"

Abby's went with her first instinct and shriek.

"Oh NO! I, I can't do that. Mr. Grimes is, you KNOW and Mr. Valdez is well, you know!"

These are the times that John Hammond was certainly glad he allowed the United States Air Force to pay for his master's degree in psychology, and this was one of them.

"I do understand your concern Ms. Carpski. Nevertheless, if any of us have any hope of surviving this plague. My friends cannot stay locked behind those bars. They are great at what they do. I suggest WE allow them to shine, and they will reward their liberator with at least their loyalty! RIGHT, gentlemen? Are we able to agree that Ms.Carpski has kept us at least, safe?"

Big John looks through the locked bars at Ghostface Killer and then to Chicken Head just to make sure they understand their contract. Both men nodded their heads that, they understood. John goes on to say.

"Comrades allow me to introduce you to my only child, my daughter Robin. Or Marshal Aquila as she likes to be called."

As Abby let the two out of their cells, both men nod their thanks, that's when Ernesto asks Carpski.

"Would you take me to see my wife, please?"

Instead of resisting Abby throws her hands up signaling, why not!

It's a short five minute hike across the prison yard, for the group led by Marshal Aquila to reach Building S. A uniquely foul wind has begun to blow and the smell of unwashed, unclean and undead was a hard smell to keep a bay.

Assistant Abby Carpski had placed the last of her CO's in S Wing for she feared what would happen if the larger male portion of the prison population were to escape. The men outnumbered the women nearly three to one, and Abby didn't want to be held responsible for mass rape. Or Mass murder!

The seven remaining CO's are comprised of five men and two women. Each appeared very tired, highly frustrated and mostly afraid! They smelled of too many cigarettes, too much coffee and not enough showers linger between the remaining employees. When the Robin's group walks into the intake, the CO in charge, a mildly obese, pepper colored haired white man named Fraizer aims his weapon at the group and said with a bit of anger.

"What gives Carpski? Why are these inmates not in their goddam cells? Hands up! I said put your got dam hands up!"

The group stops, Marshal Aquila makes sure her badge is in plain sight, when she said.

"Are you threatening a Federal Officer?"

The Officers are unsure what to do. Assistant Warden Carpski attempts to show some sort of leadership.

"Lower your weapon Officer Fraizer, the Marshal here is letting some of the Prisoners go.."

Frazier begrudgingly lowers his weapon a bit, still he doesn't break eye contact with Aquila, Chicken Head, Ghostface Killer or Big John. He spits and replies.

"Bullshit! This isn't a Federal Penitentiary; she has no goddam authority here!"

Robin takes two steps forward, so she can look up into Frazier's cold blue eyes and spoke with venom of a person twice her size.

"Listen fuck face! I guess you didn't hear when I told the entire Prison to fuck off! I 'm not the liberator to the masses, just a few fuckups and Nair-do-wells. Now unass the front door so we can get through, please."

From the look on the other CO's faces they had not heard the news. That's when Abby informs Robin.

"I didn't know you wanted to give that speech to S-Wing Marshal. Huh, sorry I didn't patch it through. Of the five hundred and ten women residing here, only one hundred and thirty are in for murder! The rest are here with low level drug convictions, forging checks or prostitution. Most are not harden felons like the men."

Earl scoffs much like the tone of a prissy sixteen-year-old school girl!

"Ah sister, you can shove that foolishness where the sun can't find it. Every one of those gashes in here could slit your throat or suck a dick with equal exuberance!"

Ernesto chimes in. "I guess you met my Celeste."

Frazier screams.

"You mean Calamity? Fuck that she and the rest of these bitches are going no..."

Frazier never finished his sentence as Marshal Aquila lowers her center of gravity so she may punch the CO to his 39 year old rarely used groin! The air goes out of Frazier's quickly as he crumbles to the floor. For her next trick, Robins kick is aimed directly at the white Officer's mouth and before her father can lecture for calm heads to prevail. Frazier catches a steel toed shot directly to his exposed chin! His head quickly jerks back in a violent fashion and his body slumps over onto his back.

Chicken Head holds out his hand to signal give me high five as he chants a scene from days long gone.

"Down goes Frazier, down goes Frazier, down goes Frazier. Muhamad Ali is still the champ, down goes Frazier!"

Before the other Prison Guards can choose a side, Assistant Warden Carpski said.

"As acting Warden, I am releasing all the female prisoners. We don't have enough food or water to continue their incarceration. You may all go home, or anywhere you see fit. If you choose to stay we will only be focusing our attention on the male Prisoners. Hopeful history won't judge us to be a pack of gutless mass murders!"

One of the female Guards, a slender chestnut brown-haired woman named Lmoot meekly offered a bit of information.

"Ahh, Acting Warden Carpski. One of the shrinks, Indigo Roberson went into the Block two days ago and she hasn't come out. Sergeant Frazier advised her not to. Still the asshole would not allow us to enter and search for her!"

Abby shakes her head that she understands, as she heads into the pit and releases the doors to all the cells in S-Wing, steps back and waited.

All while Marshal Aquila used the intercom to explain the facts of what is going on as she knew them. Furthermore, it took about ten minutes for the first inmates to poke their confused head out of the cell block door.

After they figured out, they would not be shot, groups of women run laughing and twirling in the area in-between wings. When Ernesto didn't see Celeste, his heart panicked. The Ghostface Killer asked the nearest CO.

"Which Block is my wife on, Inmate 997960?"

Officer Lmoot replied.

"We all know Calamity, she's originally in C block, now she could be anywhere inside."

Ernesto tells the group.

"I am going in there to find my wife. If you would like to come with me and be my guest. However, I ask you, do not attempt to stop me or interfere with our reunion.."

A few minutes later Abby follows Marshal Aquila, The Ghostface Killer and Chicken Head into the woman's Section of the Prison. By all accounts they had been just as destructive to their surrounding during the last 120+ hours of lack of supervision as their male counterparts. Garbage is littering the floor, old food trays mold in food carts and human waste smears the walls!

It doesn't take long before the sound of music can be heard coming from somewhere deep inside the block. Not the radio or a CD or even an audio file, but the voice of a woman. The sound reverbs of the cold gray walls, sending waves of head bobbling musical notes to even make Abby say.

"Someone, huh, well, I guess someone has some talent."

Earl huffs, "Like you never heard me sing?"

Carpski flashed a smile as she replies. "Mr. Grimes you have the voice of an Opera luminary, I could listen to you for hours!

Earl's oval face looked angry, nonetheless he slowly smiled and everyone in ear shot could literally hear Abby sigh in relief. Fun Fact most people would think the soundtrack Earl Grimes plays in his head was that of Slayer, or some other heavy metal band. Well Ernesto was shocked when Chicken Head, said his favorite sound he sings over and over to himself, was Frozen! Yep, that song from the Disney movie and if he ever sang it in front of you. There's a good chance Earl was probably dismembering your body!

Robin leads the way holding her 9mm Smith & Wesson at her side. Taking in everything as they proceed, Robin moves past a cell, a blur of movement catches her eye.

Marshal Aquila halts long enough to see three semi naked women kissing and fondling each other while drinking homemade prison wine! Big John whispers to his daughter.

"How long has your tempter, been, well you know?"

She looks at her father and the fury in her eyes begins to ignite once more as she said.

"How long has mom been dead?"

The tone in John's voice expresses concern and forgiveness.

"Honey, you know I had nothing to with your mother's death. I told you that for so many years and when the courts proved my innocent, I thought this nightmare would be over."

Robin grunts, "Then you had to go kill a Prison guard, so here we are. Plus, it seems some evil corporation or shadow government jagoffs whom we will never their know name has your work and WELL. Once again here we are, Dad... What do you want me to say?!"

Father and daughter continue their journey in silence, following the sounds of someone singing **Tina Marie's, I need you Lovin,**

"Love fever coming on strong I don't want the fire without the flame, no... Mother Nature gave me two hands to hold you, but the pressure of material gains, makes M'O'N'EY do a thing for L-O-V-I-N..."

As the group gets closer Ernesto smiles as he tells Big John.

"That's my Celeste, ahhh I've missed that voice."

The music fades as the beat switches to the **Wu Tang Clan C.R.EA.M..**

"Cash rules everything around, got to get the money dollar, dollar bill ya! I grew up on the wild side on that chemical high side ridin on 40 brick, constantly invadin the fuckin law. Shit got real son when I got my first gun! PLOW, PLOW, PLOW. Makin moves now, cause, cause CASH rules everything around me. Got to CREAM ya'll!"

Marshal Aquila's group now led by a jogging Ernesto turns the corner to find nine women, including Prison shrink Indigo Roberson sitting around a table playing what appears to scrabble, drinking and enjoying themselves. That's when the plump, now 150-pound, with waist long black hair and deep chocolate brownie eyed Celeste, sees Ernesto.

Well, fuck me! No one could imagine what would happen next, as the couple approached each other very slowly and cautiously. Like boxers sizing each other up, and as soon as they are within arm's length. Celeste shows why while at work, her professional name will always be Calamity! She throws a vicious right jab at her husband's nose, followed quickly by a left and a kick to his shin. Either Ernesto wasn't expecting it, or he didn't care because he took two of the three shots and shook it off. When his wife attempts to grab the back of his sweaty neck and pull him into a vicious knee, thrown into his toned stomach.

Ernesto responds by digging a wicked upper cut towards his sweetheart, just missing the sweet spot of his wife's chin! Calamity's toned calves buckle for a second, as her husband's next blow connects right in her fat muffin top. As Celeste collapses to one knee, Ernesto bends down to ask his love.

"Our we finished, my love?"

Mrs. Valdez punches Mr. Valdez in his family jewels, he certainly would have vomited, if he had any food in the last 24 hours.

Instead, her love joins her on the dusty prison floors, groaning in pain. Robin stepped forward to say something, nonetheless her Dad shook his head and said.

"No this' not domestic abuse. It's, it's a family thang."

Celeste has regained her composure, as she hisses.

"How could you?! You fucked that waitress punta when you said you were going to get coffee! You fucking asshole!"

Ernesto sighs as he tries to pull it together.

"Corazone, I, I didn't fuck that waitress! However, I did let her blow me for some coca. I, I could not see giving it away for free! I paid for our food with our money. She wanted coke, I had a baggie full, so I traded some of it... Look, I'm sorry! It's how do gringos say"

Earl with his slow Southern cadence provides the words, Ernesto lack.

"Like water under a bridge and if blood is thicker than water, why do we drink wine?

Everyone not accustomed to Earlism, kind of stare at him with that WTF look on their faces.

Celeste looked at Ernesto with fury and passion, her smile is planned, yet not forced when she said in a spoiled childlike voice.

"Well, I have TWO girlfriends now. So, I don't think I have time for you anymore! What do you think about that? Wait a minute, how are you even here? Who are they and why does that one look like a fucking COP?"

It took nearly five minutes for Assistant Warden Carpski to explain the facts as she knew them. Then the remaining Female inmates barricade themselves in their building and waved those that wanted to leave goodbye!

Outside it's the sharp eye of Earl that noticed several free birds.

"Looks like our fellow rats have found a way to escape the sinking ship."

The female inmates lingering on the grounds noticed as well, their male counterparts using ropes made of knotted sheets began shimming down cold gray prison walls. The women applauded and cheer as what starts as a trickle and soon turns into a blood drenched wave!

Once they hit the ground, various screaming men are running away from some of the inmates that had jumped from the prison roof after them. Much like water rushing over clogged drains, several dozen Convicts leaped from the building. Their collective roar sent tingles of fear down the spines of everyone who's not infected! Well, not including Earl and possible Calamity.

As the front doors of Building A fling open hundreds of non-infected Convicts flee from the building as Red Eyed convicts, armed with yellow and grayish puss blisters look to infect the those that are still, normal!

Seeing hardened felons, murderers, robbers, pimps and such getting stabbed, and body slammed by those infected by the COVID-MOMREL-6 virus was like watching a horror movie in 3D.

The RAGERs as they will be come to be known are running on pure adrenaline! Brains boiling with Ebola, measles, mumps and rabies, they do not heed towards reason or sympathy! Furthermore, the Zombie Virus has it will come to be known, is spread by the free-flowing puss and blood of RAGERS as well.

Each RAGERS is a virus in search of a host! Six to ten people who encounter the RAGE virus will not die from the infection. They will continue as carriers until their bodies are destroyed. **Fun Fact 29.8%** of the human populace that contracted the COVID-MOMREL-6 will die bleeding from all their orifices. Very soon after they will rise to as dead heads or Zombies**! Bonus Fact**, as their inside fester to a fetid smelling dark liquid, that toxic brew happens to be one hundred percent lethal and contagious to human life.

The smell of the RAGERS should have proceeded their vicious rights hooks and timely left jabs that were surprisingly devastating and effective against fleeing opponents! The COVID-MOMREL-6 virus seems to have given RAGERS superhuman strength! One O.G. Skinhead Inmate tries squaring up toe to toe with one of his attackers. The 6'1 220 Non-infect Convict lands massive haymakers to the RAGERS puss covered face! Only to send fresh infection airborne on to anyone close enough to be upwind of this brawl.

Nevertheless, the infected never went down, instead the RAGER grabs the Big Irish man's bald head and presses his thumbs into the Convict's eye socket while ripping out his jugular vein with sharpened teeth! It was from every prison dorm that RAGERs began pouring out into the large prison yard. It's only the various fences that kept the dorms separated, and have kept those standing by S-building, safe!

Indigo Roberson pushes her glasses-which are held together by tape- up the bridge of her dark chocolate colored nose and stammers.

"I, I, I don't think we are safe here."

Marshal Aquila notices a white flatbed truck parked forty yards from their location. She shouts a plan of action.

"The only way out is through the administration building. Which one of you can hot wire that truck?"

Celeste huffs in Spanish to her husband.

"I'll do it! When we are finished escaping mi Ernesto, you must tell me who is this chino looking Negra?"

From Big John's P.O.V he can see firsthand the properties of the virus he had worked on playing out in REAL TIME. The feverish blistered act like a launching system for their puss filled crates. Infected blood runs from nostrils, ears, mouth and eyes. The scientist in him can't help but analyze how long it takes for the infection to take hold of a host!

It took a few minutes for the would-be skinhead boxer to bleed out. Yet, it takes less than twenty seconds for the former Inmate to reanimate into a moaning hunger driven fiend! The smell of the infected is now hard to miss and the stench makes everything seem, sour.

Luckily Celeste's good as her word and got the flat bed pickup started using her very sharp nail file. Ernesto joins her in the cab followed by Marshal Aquila, Earl, John, Abby, Indigo and several of the other ladies and two CO's. Each of the newly freed, hastily pile into the back of the flatbed truck and hold on for dear life!

Why? Because Calamity had plenty of experience as a getaway driver! Yep, she drives FAST.

After they first got together, she and Ernesto use to rob banks in Texas then escape to Mexico laughing their young heads off! However, the bulky truck has logged well over 225k of mileage in the last nineteen years and it's not built for speed, still Celeste has gotten the black smoke bellowing beast up to forty-five miles per hour. Barely missing infected and non-infected alike, she shouts to her husband.

"Well Ernesto you are looking great, while I allowed myself to get fat! I look just awful I know it..."

Ernesto smiles and replied, "Honey, I know how we are going to burn a lot of calories."

Robin was curious, so had to ask.

"Why did you attack him?"

Celeste replies.

"Well boss lady! When we got captured, Ernesto, he shouldered all the weight. Instead of me getting death row with my love. I got life without parole, while he got die! How is that fair?"

Ernesto huffs, "Ah woman you are impossible! Don't you I didn't want to see you die?"

Celeste voice dropped, sounding nearly childlike as she replies.

"Why do you think I would what to live without you? Why would I choose to live in a cage? I, I sorry for punching you and to show you I am sincere, well, I left my two girl friends in S-Dorm."

Earl can't help but mutter, "Or dead back there."

Robin scoffs, "You fuckers are crazy! He didn't want you to die, so he took your weight. Then the first time you see him you punch him in the face and his dick?"

Celeste huffs, "Well, when you say it like that, my welcome might be a bit extreme! Still, he knows I get very excited when I feel I have been wronged. It's that ok with you, Boss lady?"

Robin exhales then said. "Look I need to get to visitors parking lot. There are enough vehicles here that people can go their separate ways."

Ernesto said. "Oh no, Big John foretold this day coming to us year after year. I thought he was going insane; no, he was fucking right! Listen, I know where we can get food, water, weapons and shelter! We are going where he goes and don't worry about Earl. He rarely if ever kills women. I mean in the fifty-two tales his told, the only woman was his mother and that was by C section! In these times, WE need a man like him on OUR side, trust me on that."

Marshal Aquila was fighting with her frustration as she scoffed and spoke. "OKAY! Just get us to administration building in one piece, please."

Outside their vehicle, RAGERS trample the non-infected in a race to see who gets to the administration building first. The remaining CO's which included the asshole Fraizer feverishly fired into the streaming screaming infected Convicts chasing their flatbed truck! Shotgun blast to the chest have some effect, still wounded RAGERS give chase like cheetahs hunting prey. Swift and fucking sure!

Inside the cab Calamity tries to push the envelope.

"When do we get guns? That's our right! As well as a change of wardrobe? Oh my god, I stink!"

As Robin looks at the carnage going on out her window, she must control her tone as she said.

"Right now, all you newly emancipated have the right to shut the fuck up, PLEASE!"

Chapter IV:

YOU DON'T GET TO FIGHT THE APOCALYPSE YOU WANT.

Unbeknown to the masses nearly 75 hours prior to the world finding out, pieces were being set in motion for the survival of humanity and of course the American way of life! After the sober General's conference call ended, everyone in the room at the Great Lakes Naval Base went into crisis mode. Calling superiors and checking on the status of their loved ones. With no hate towards their decision, some would bow out, leaving to return to their families. While others understood the gravity of their situation and are prepared to shoulder the line!

Lieutenant Colonel Lafayette was the latter, it took a few minutes before she could video chat with SPECFOR-COM. When she does, Wynolla can see the staff behind Major General Rochelle filling boxes with files, computers and charts. Windu informs her superior about her tactical needs.

"Sir from these reports, this virus is an extinction level event! Just how are we supposed to reverse engineer a cure before it ravenous the planet? General, has the nuclear option been discussed?"

Major General Rochelle looks weary and noticeably frustrated during the conversation.

"Colonel what the hell do you think we want you to do? Right now, you are standing in a room with scientists and doctors from the CDC and the WHO! You yourself are one of the Army's best when it comes to infectious diseases! Use the time you have to assemble and pull together any resource you deem goddam necessary. As it stands, we only have time to set up four cold weather stations. And to answer your second question, yes. The nuclear option has been discussed, sadly frankly it won't fucking help!"

Colonel Layette mentally puts events in order seeing this may be the last time they have any communication. Her request's simple.

"Sir I am the only regular Army in the room, requesting you send me some support. Simply a few A or B teams would greatly help my present situation."

Major General Rochelle frowns and asked. "Colonel, would you edify me on why you need teams of Operators? They're not doctors?"

Windu walks out into the hallway and towards a bay window, she said.

"Sir, if contact is lost with our superiors, Admiral Lee becomes ranking military officer in the entire United States. General, I have no clue what type of Officer Lee happens to be. As of now I'm a guest at his base, I'm Airborne. I'm supposed to be surrounded, just not by my own people SIR."

Major General Rochelle understood Wynolla's requested and replies.

"Colonel, I'll see what I can do about getting some support before this goes sideways. I do know that teams are being sent out to secure high target assets. I strongly advise you keep you SAT charged as long as possible."

Before he could sign off, Wynolla floats the idea.

"General, since we can't graduate another Special Forces class before this thing hits. Why not reassign me some of those Soldiers still in training? No Marines, Sir. I feel I will have enough of those around me when this gets started. Also, sir, if you could include some good old Regular Army Infantry NCO's and a few butter bars from any Engineers battalion. That would be greatly appreciated in my war effort. I could position them with a least one professional A team and that will get that force up to at least Platoon strength, sir."

Major General Rochelle grunts as he signs off. "What else you want, Colonel, a goddam tank. Like I said, keep your SAT phone charged. I've always thought you were a more than capable office Lafayette. You should go with GOD, Colonel, there won't be much left after this!. Hell of a way to see the end of civilization. Neverthe-fucking-less, at least the Russians, North Koreans, the Chinese and the entire Middle East will feel take the same bite from the shit sandwich as US."

Their conversation ends, Windu scans the room, she can see everyone having heated or animate conversations. She notices Doctor Littlefield texting near a stairwell. Colonel Layette walks over to Monique and inquires.

"What do you think?"

She looks up and the horror in her eyes could not be contained as she scans the PDF file sent by the military. Monique's voice trembles as she said.

"This is incredible. OUR government made this, they made this?"

Wynolla wanted to hold her, but knew she could not show such tenderness, not now. They would be working closely together for the time to come, and she doesn't want how she feels, conflict with the monumental task at hand! However, Wynolla does offer words of encouragement.

"Yes, it's horrible. Yet, we must investigate how to deal with this plague. No matter what it takes, I'll be there working right beside you. Trust me, together, I have faith we will see this through."

There's a twinkle in Monique blue eyes and forced a smile before replying.

"I'm going to hold you, to that, Colonel."

It doesn't take long before Admiral Lee's aid calls everyone back into the large conference room. While the crowd filters back into their chairs, Navy personnel are busy pulling together lists and graphs. Rear Admiral Jefferson Bullraguard Lee stands at the podium waiting for the various civilians and assorted military to have a seat.

Once they do, he clears his throat into the microphone being sent up by a Navy Ensign and spoke.

"Testing. I said testing, is this thing on?"

When the Admiral hears his own voice, he grunts, twice and begins.

"We have just been given unbelievably devastating news as well as a task which is responsible for saving our way of life. Each of you have departments that you need to report to and most of them may not have this information. Nor will you provide it to them..."

There's a lot of muttering and whispering among the crowd. Still Admiral Lee continues his briefing.

"We will not start a panic; I know some in this room the definition of duty is different from mine. Yet here we are, and the United States Navy will not turn away or neglect its duty in the trying times that lay ahead."

The crowd wasn't sure where the Admiral's going with his briefing, time is ticking, and a subpar motivational speech is not helpful!

Doctor Littlefield was first to speak up. "Hello, I'm Doctor Monique Littlefield from the CDC. If we are to work on some sort or cure or vaccine, we will need equipment that your base facilities might not have."

Admiral Lee scoffed as he replied.

"Excuse me Ms."

Monique would not be dismissed so easily, she interjected.

" Excuse me Rear Admiral, like I just stated, it's Doctor Littlefield from the CDC."

Once again Jefferson Bullraguard Lee huffs and scoffs. He isn't used to being denied and the sounds of frustration crept into his tone.

"Well then Doctor. You write down a list and we'll get It for you ASAP! Okay?"

Then, the Air Force Colonel McKinney brings up an important logistics concern.

"We can't have the research center here. Too many people on this base may already be infected, we simply don't know. That means we could be overrun even before real work can begin. This a non-starting factor if we are to be successful."

Windu's doing what she has been trained to do, watch and listen! Before she put her thoughts to the wind, Colonel Layette needs to know which way it's blowing. Monique agrees with McKinney by saying.

"I agree with the Air Force Colonel, we needed to get a lab up and running with whatever samples we can get our hands on. This COVID-MOMREL-6 must be studied and pulled apart at its molecular level! Each hour we wait, we lose our advantage."

Admiral Lee turns to the Marine Colonel Dunston and signals for him to come closer so he can whisper something. Dunston nods his head that he understood and turns and walks out the door. He comes back later with a large folding map of the base. Admiral Lee stated proudly.

"This base is capable of housing any band of scientist; we have plenty of space on these 80 acres of land."

Finally, Windu stands up and addresses the crowd.

"Hello, I'm Lt. Colonel Wynolla Lafayette out of Ft. Bragg, I represent Special Forces Command and I am an expert in infectious disease and weaponized viruses...."

She lets the last part linger out there for a few seconds before continuing.

"Admiral, to put this mildly sir, this base cannot be defended against infectious diseases. Once this virus hits every active-duty member living off base, will be scrambling to bring their family, here! Sir, with them comes the infection. We must find another location ASAP. One with sea and air access, which was just mandated by our superiors at the Pentagon."

The muttering continues and the whispering grew to something a bit more audible. Wynolla invoking the guidelines of their mission made an enemy of Jefferson moving forward, Admiral Lee lock eyes with Colonel Lafayette and never breaks contact as he said.

"I said, MY base is secure, Lieutenant Colonel."

Monique stood up, sharing the burden with Wynolla and threw her hat into the ring.

"This Officer is correct in her assessment! Admiral Lee our greatest enemy now is time and the general public. We need to be mobilizing and not bickering about whose right or even in charge. If we are to research a cure or even vaccine, we need not worry about infecting others or being overrun by the infected!"

It's the Air Force Colonel McKinney that came up with a plan of action most suited for their mission. He snapped his long slender fingers and said.

“The McCormick Place in Chicago! The structure sits on the lake has room for Air Support and a vast underground main parking lot that can hold a nearly six thousand vehicles, trucks, equipment and even people if need be.”

The room is silent, everyone waits for the Admiral to have an objection and he did.

“Excuse me Colonel, but you want to take this show to McCormick place? How do we pay of it?”

McKinney’s answer is simple.

“Ahh, the almighty United State taxpayers. Sir, we will rent the entire building for ten days and after that it will not matter....”

Silence blankets the room like a god-awful ugly Christmas sweater! Everyone in attendance is fully aware of what he meant and it’s upon each person to cope with what’s on their foreseeable collective horizons. That’s how it all came together!

In the first three hours a series of convoys comprised of heavy transport trucks leave the Great Lakes Naval Base under the cover of darkness.

Seeing thirty trucks hall ass down the freeway is a slight to behold. Now toss in an escort from Sectary of State Police and any bystander might think a problem is a foot! **Fun Fact**, the Navy convoy were able to do the trip in under 38 minutes. Which is a fucking world record!

Colonel McKinney has done what he said and used taxpayers’ money to rent the large convention center known as McCormick place for ten days. That’s all the property managers would rent, seeing a culinary convention due in four days after.

When McKinney puts his name of the lease and the United States Air Force as the lessor, he knew they wouldn’t be leaving in ten days! Deep down McKinney must wonder if even ever.

Colonel Kevin McKinney's a procurer, trained by the U.S government to spend taxpayers' money! Yeah, that was a job our military had to offer. Whether it was with defense contractors practicing in their own fortunate brand of socialism. Or worse Big Pharma! Kevin McKinney knew that his day had just begun.

As the Navy Seamen- wearing civilian clothes- lead the way, Kevin checks off the next place they would visit. How does one arrange for one million gallons of drinking water to be delivered in under 72 hours? Well, Amazon Prime got some of the order. Various Sam's Clubs, Walmart's, Walgreens, Menards, Home Depot and COSTCO received a windfall from the US government!

Colonel McKinney was one of the several procurers working for Homeland Security in attendance at Great Lakes. Others of his elk were given the task of going to several area hospitals and arranging for some very sensitive equipment to be paid for and picked up, before the day ended. This's one of the few times that the wheels of Government turned fast enough to face the problem that's in front of them! Instead of facing the problem that past them by.

What is McCormick Place? **Fun Fact**, it's the nation's largest convention center, comprising of four state-of-the-art buildings, the West, South and North Buildings and Lakeside Center. These buildings have a combined total of 2.6 million square feet of exhibit space, 1.2 million square feet all on one level.

In addition to expansive exhibition space, McCormick Place also features:

- 173 meeting rooms offering 600,000 square feet of space.
- 4 ballrooms ranging from 21,000 to 100,000 square feet.
- Assembly seating for 18,000 people.
- 4,249 seat theater (Arie Crown)

- 3 theaters seating 300 each.
- Ceiling heights up to 50 feet.

Easy access and 6,000 underground parking spaces. The entire McCormick Place campus is linked by dramatic pedestrian promenades and sky bridges, containing retail shops and other visitor amenities. Now military engineers must develop a system that would allow max capacity generators to provide electricity. Turning meeting rooms into medical centers, turning ballrooms into living quarters, and turning theaters in hydroponics labs

There's so much to do with very little time to get things done! Yet everyone in the know fully understood the price of their failure! When the infection hits, there will be no one to monitor mainframes, or satellites and all manufacturing will grind to a tragic halt. As well agriculture and mass production of all medicine. Humanity will simply return to whatever came before the fucking Stone Age!

Getting all the essentials into their shelter was in Lt. Colonel McKinney best interest. However, that still didn't stop him from treating his small team and drivers to a couple of deep disk pizzas and one glass of Goose Island Beer! He reasons with himself, that if this isn't the time to enjoy the little things, then when? No one outside the chain of command has any idea what's going on. Hell, McKinney's Navy escorts must have thought the Air Force Colonel's just being a great fucking guy!

By the second day it must have been someone in Chicago to see, nine Army helicopters landing of the roof of the South Building of the McCormick place. When Colonel Lafayette got the last call from her superior. All what is asked of her, was what your location!

Now, she stands on top the roof of the secure building and waited for thirty-seven Army Airborne Rangers who had been recently promoted to Special Forces Command. Alongside five Army Engineers, NCOs from the famed Infantry Battalion the Big Red One. Two Navy SEALs, with three Marine Recons, along with twelve Air Force Black

Berets to land safely! The force under her command represented fifty eights souls she could only hope will buy into the mission! This force includes four seasoned Army Green Berets, Soldiers Windu has worked with in the past hot zones.

Notably, Army Captain Lance Brown, who's a tall goofy kind of soul that generally will find a way to inject a bit of humor in his work. Not a class clown, the kind of guy with that dry observational humor that some self-involved women find strangely hilarious!

After their military formality- the salute- is taken care of. Captain Brown's smile is nearly contiguous. The tall light skinned African America man was born and raised on the South Side of Chicago and for the moment he's happy to be home. Even if he didn't know why! His greeting's warm and yet formal.

"Good to see you Ma'am. I see you haven't gained a few pounds. Must mean the Army's is keeping you busy."

Windu laughed and said.

"Yes, my young padawan. The force has been good to me, and I see to you as well."

Captain Brown sheepishly laughs.

"Ah we are still doing that Colonel. Okay. Yes, I have grown in the force as well."

Both Soldiers share a laugh, before getting down to the brass facts.

"Ma'am, if I may speak freely."

Wynolla nods her head yes.

"We all know something BIG must be up. I mean, the brass pulled these troops out of during hell week! Some with nearly five weeks left on their training. None on passed the course, so what gives?"

When Colonel Lafayette confides in the young Captain what, Lance looks like he might want to vomit! His mouth's fixed in a tight grimace and he appears like he need to sit down. However, Captain Brown didn't. He stands tall and listens to everything, and it's Wynolla that brought forth the Elephant in the window.

"I know your mother and brother are still alive and I know you will be tempted to reach out to them."

Before Captain Brown could say anything, Wynolla held up her hand to signal hold on, then he said.

"You brother is an X ray tech here in the city and your mom holds a degree in Chemistry. How old is she?"

Lance said, "She be seventy four in December."

He notices how Colonel Lafayette winched just a little! He didn't know what it meant, yet he was assured it wasn't good. Windu stood in front of the young Captain trying to figure out the finer details of this clusterfuck when it dawned on her.

"I am pretty sure we don't have a Chemist on site. However, we have a number of people that can learn. I need you to quietly go get your mother and your brother, bring them back here, and make sure you get a list of their medications. Captain bring no ex-girlfriends or current ones unless children are attached! I know that's messed up, only if they have children that need to be with their parents. We have an Air Force Colonel getting everything in bulk. We will have to confiscate anyone's phones for seventy-two hours then after that that cat is out the bag!"

Captain Brown wants to hug Colonel Lafayette, not only to save his life, but that of his last living relatives as well. The young Captain snaps to attention and gives Windu the proper salute of the day. The two soldiers gaze signaled a bound of mutual respect and camaraderie.

Nearly thirty-nine hours later the first reports of the virus sprung up from the ER's of every hospital inside infection zones. So many that Emergency rooms had to close their doors and turn patients away!. At Camp McCormick, Air Force Colonel Kevin McKinney is the ranking Officer on site and it's his command. Lt. Colonel Lafayette is ok with situation, for McKinney seems to be a man that takes counsel from others and isn't a raving fucking egomaniac.

The Air Force Colonel was also very forward thinking. It's Kevin McKinney who positioned for a quarter mile stretch of the major through way- known as the Dan Ryan or Dam Rayan- to be closed off. Not only entrance ramps but exit ramps as well! Commuters had to travel city streets that run alongside the route. It caused traffic to snarl up at traffic lights, nonetheless it keeps the area around the McCormick place undisturbed.

By the time the infection has moved towards the no coming back mode; this little defensive move will aid the cause. Colonel McKinney had giant shipping containers-like the kind trucks or trains used for hauling materials- to be taken from the underground parking lots and placed at the bottom of the entrance and exit ramps. As well as stretched across both lanes of the choked off throughway for a quarter of a mile.

This action's repeated on four separate streets that fed into their sanctuary's habitat, including Martin Luther King Drive, Cermak Road, Prairie Ave and Indiana Ave. The Mayor of Chicago must have been scratching his short afro wondering why the Federal Government is taking over his throughways without so much as a please or even a goddam goofy thank you!

The goal is to make it hard for the infected to get in and with that came an entirely different set of problems. They must wait until the infection is underway to get samples to work with. That meant capturing RAGERS or worse their counterparts. When news of Walking Corpses began to filter their way across multiple television and printed news outlets, worldwide, signaling the era of humanity was over. Signed Z!

No news station wanted to be the first one to shout fucking ZOMBIE! Nevertheless, by the 64th hour of infection, everyone who could scream was screaming, HELP. First came the gunfights caused by the greed of human's looting or those simply settling old grudges! They say when to comes to revenge it's best to bring a shovel and dig two graves. Honestly, it's not like the graves will work, but I could se using the shovel.

To anyone that engaged in such behavior, it quickly became a one-sided sort of gun fight. Bullets stopped being thrown at those still alive, to those that are infected and those that don't want to stay dead!

Nonetheless, the infection's fast moving, fast acting and its exploits will be known across the planet before the week is out. Imagine the anguish of the mother who returns home from doing a twelve-hour shift-including a two-hour commute- only to find your teenage son racked by fever, bleeding from his eyes nose and mouth. Plus, it appears he has just bashed his father head in. Sadly, he used the claw end of a stainless-steel hammer to finally change his little sister's mind!

Or the fire fighters who respond to reports of a house fire to find an entire apartment complex gulfed in flames. However, when they move in to offer medical assistance, they find themselves being attacked by flaming bat wielding psychos! The COVID-MOMREL-6 virus was built to be fast and hard hitting. By all accounts, it worked better than a fat baby Jesus!

As an airborne allegiant, the initial infections were designed to be released in a small yet dense area of human contact.

Places like a professional ball game or a concert, strip club, church, shopping mall or a dance club! One hundred sick people become two hundred sick people in less than four hours, and you keep doubling that number every four hour.

The virus was a one-of-a-kind cocktail designed to make it hard for

Authorities to get ahead of this plague. When the ER piles high with the dead and dying and they will have no hospital beds left to spare! Furthermore, a fresh wave of those sick and near death's door enter your establishment looking for medical assistance. Only the true professionals stayed on during their jobs in those first 30hours of this plague. After that those that stayed were either trapped, infected or the dead who didn't die!

The infection traveled on the wind; its maximum effective range's 350 miles. Here's a little know fun fact, half the population of the United States of America lives within a day's drive of the city of Chicago. The samples terrorist released on American soil were samples of the first generation. That meant it's still unstable and kills the target host right out, instead of infecting them!

That wasn't the desired effect the Military industrial complex had in mind. They wanted entire infected community to turn on each other! They wanted ripping, hacking, bashing, stabbing, shooting and strangling of loved ones before misbelieving eyes.

Military think tanks wanted word of mouth about horrendous, unspeakable crimes against humanity to get to the next town and the next town! However, the first generation of the virus hadn't been perfected, yet. More than half of the infected die, nevertheless MOST don't tend to dead for long.

So, when the dead began to rise, it is not with a whimper. It's with a blood curling roar! The amplified moans of several of the recent dead can echo off walls making it sound like hundreds instead of dozens.

Like in vintage horror movies, the dead stumble, bumble and claw their way towards the living. Never tiring, never wavering in their pursuit of warm flesh. In under five days the city of Chicago's Morgue has over eighteen hundred bodies in a place than barely held five hundred. They had so many bodies that the city of Chicago began storing them in shipping containers in the South Loop, West Side and far South Side of the city. The Mayor left places like Lincoln

Park and the Gold Coast alone, nevertheless the North Side out hit hard as well.

Somewhere around day the fourth day one of the attendants came down to investigate loud moaning coming from inside the cooler! The unaware city employee must have thought several people had been mistaken for dead. Flash-forward a few minutes later when the living dead are stumbling through the facility, spreading the virus on American soil. Probably never anticipated by the people that conspired in its creation! Or maybe, the wave of domestic terrorism that had been crafted during the last several years, might have been a COVERT OP to get the America in the flow with the here and goddam now!

There's a small variation between first and the remainder generations of the COVID-MOMREL-6 virus. In the first version, every third person or so who contracted the RAGER virus, upon death, would turn into the living dead! Small, yet important fact. In the first generation, the living dead was a fucking fluke, a simple mistake. However, in the latter versions, it is a goddam requirement!

The citizens that caught on quickly destroyed the infected brain. They didn't waste time or ammo shooting to wound or aiming for center mass! Those that caught on quick, are bashing in skulls and blowing heads clean off shoulders! It's not the time for the timid or the unsure. The single question everyone faced was how badly do you want to survive?

When the infection hit, the lights first went out. Lots of people reacted like it was 1991 and the Chicago Bulls had just won their first of six championships! Most of the rioting and the looting was just Chicagoans reacting to what they didn't understand. To others it was an opportunity to feed their personal greed and otherwise petty emotions! Nevertheless, that's before the first RAGER hit the scene and probably 4-8 hours before the first Zombie shambled up to an unprepared soul and moans HHELLOOOOO.

By the time the populace finally got up to speed on their present situation, foes had quickly become allies.

Ordinary citizens were forced to fight side by side, house to house, street by street, if they have any hope of survival! When COPs and Gangsters, Blacks, Hispanics, Asians, Natives and Whites, Gays, Queers or Straights stand and fight side by side, back-to-back without a bit of hesitation. You know the shit finally got real!

Frankly, there is only one good thing about the COVID-MOMREL-6 virus. It plays no favorites, and in the end, it will wipe every ISM of the face of the planet! Life will consist of three groups. Small groups of Non-Infected Humans, large groups RAGERS and nearly endless number of hungry, shambling Zombies.

Inside McCormick place, the two hundred and eighty assorted civilian and military personnel fall under the command of the Air Force Colonel Kevin McKinney for all of six days! For on the seventh, Rear Admiral Lee and what's left of his command land two Navy helicopters on the unconcealed roof of the North Building.

Eleven, eleven people on a base of four thousand managed to escape the horror of Great Lakes Naval Station! **Time Stamp the first night:** that's when the first dozen recruits and several DOD family members hit the base hospital. After that the virus pretty much quickly spirals out of the bases control! Admiral Lee had not briefed his base physicians on the nature of the pathogen, in fear a leak would alert the locals, or the news and cause certain mass panic. A costly mistake maybe, nonetheless who the fuck's left to judge?

His quarantine had not worked, Great Lakes Training center was one of the three military installations devoted to training medical personnel. Nonetheless it was grossly unprepared for what would be later known as the "**Red Death** or the **RAGER** virus."

Instead of going down with the ship! Rear Admiral Jefferson Bullraguard Lee doesn't think twice about self-sacrifice. He boarded his Navy transport and never looked back.

He fled with his Provost Marshal, Colonel Dunson and a few support staffers along with a detachment of eighteen Marines-five made it to their Helios-, escorted their commandeering Officer as his escaped fate. Leaving thousands screaming in his wake!

Admiral Lee had not understood how rapidly the virus replicates, and his decisions were based not on the worst-case scenario. Instead, Lee relied on mantras' like, we are well trained, we are professional, we are the United States Fucking Navy! Fuck, he was so wrong.

When Camp McCormick had gotten the heads up, they prepared a decontamination tent sent up for the arriving refugees from Great Lakes Naval Station. Yep, Admiral Lee attempted to pull rank, doing his best to do an end run around the mandatory nine hour stay in tent city! However, to his credit Air Force Colonel McKinney never faltered.

He stood by regulations set in place by the CDC and Ole Bullraguard must cool his heels with the surviving base personnel that managed to flee alongside him. Sadly, that placed him and McKinney on the path to never being on the same page.

In the ninth hour, Rear Admiral Lee also stood on regulations when he assumed command of Camp McCormick as ranking military officer! He quickly installed Colonel Dunson as his XO, even though McKinney outranked him! This's when the struggle for power takes route. While McKinney and been an effective base commander, Lee's an overall walking two-star cluster fuck of an officer!

So far Doctor Monique Littlefield and the rest of the team have had no luck in isolating the many different variants of COVID-MOMREL-6. Namely because the new commanding Officer will not let them get off their collective butts and do their job! Live specimens are needed and that means suiting up in M.O.P.- air tight rubber suits and oxygen tanks- gear and going outside their secured area.

One day before Admiral Lee arrives, former base commander Colonel McKinney authorized Colonel Lafayette and seven of her Green Berets to escort Monique and a team of four Doctors outside their haven. Their route, the major artery that leads from North to South, is now a clustered parking lot, for as far as the naked eye could see.

The closing of ramps and blocking off the entire section of the Dan Ryan Freeway with metal shipping containers did help. It's the only reason nearly a one-mile area of the Chicago's Lake front was infection free.

Once the Red Death hit those stranded in traffic, it kind of resembled a crowd doing the WAVE at a football game. One moment a Parent of four could be coughing as their head hurt while driving their family home from kindergarten. Only to go into a coughing fit, throwing their body into conclusions as their fever spikes, shutting down their major organs and slamming their car into the one in front of it.

Suddenly the infected Parent opens their now bleeding redeyes and exits their vehicle running, only to dive headfirst into the rear windshield of the car they rear ended. This's when life takes a turn for the cinema themed horrific!

Week One of Admiral Lee's Command:

It's a sunny and humid day as Captain Brown escorted several doctors to the edge of their safe zone, he made only one decree.

"Everyone makes it home safe."

For their effort they did not find RAGERS in the vast parking lot that laid to the North or South or their positions. Oh, they did find Zombies and at first the stumbling, haggard looking figures are not at all any different from sleep deprived drunk toddlers! Walking a bit, falling on their behinds, only to struggle to stand up and do it once more. Their constant moaning tend amplified when it mingles with one another. And those hellish moans that seem to be a dinner bell to any Dead Head in ear shot. With stained teeth chomping, broken fingers clutching and shuffled feet moving, they will answer that bell! The army of the dead will follow the sound of their associates.

Even so, Captain Brown's team of Rangers and Berets quickly and quietly- by using suppressors- place three still moving specimens in body bags and towed the living corpses back to the makeshift elevator the Engineers rigged. Only for Rear Admiral Lee to show up and order the Zombies put down before he understood what the Doctors were working on.

Week Three:

Admiral Lee's fond of meetings, he seems to rather enjoy sitting at the head of the room and staring off into space as Base personnel reported on their resources and their situation.

Monique flips the light brown hair out of her blue green eyes and speaks with enough vigor that her breast jiggles when she spoke.

"We can't keep sitting around doing nothing! We have been dispatched to find a cure for this plague. Why aren't you allowing us to do our jobs, Admiral?"

The crowd murmurs as Marine Colonel Dunson had placed himself in lock step as the strong arm of Admiral Lee. Dunson's cold blue eyes squint hard at Doctor Littlefield.

He would have love to give the smart mouth, stuck up bitch a much-needed block of instruction on when to shut the fuck up! Jesus, he thought, are you trying to get us killed? He wondered solely to himself.

On this day, Admiral Lee has something to say after all and his Western drawn made his every word sound like Jefferson stepped out a redemption of Gone with the fucking Wind!

"Doctor, Littlefield. We are but at the inauguration of this scourge. From what I've read the first generation of COIVD-MM-OLE-R6 has a half-life of one year..."

Monique couldn't believe her ears, she felt like someone was stuffing her head in a bag and tossing her off a cliff. She mutters.

"Wha, what? In a year's time we could map out this bug out. In a year's time we might have a cure or even a vaccine Admiral! We must make progress; humanity deserves that much."

Windu has to admire how hard Monique fights for what she believes in! She's intelligent, attractive, funny and a Martial Artist from birth. It's their conversations about Chinese Internal martial Arts that helped catch each other's eye.

Monique had been classically trained by a daughter of a Taijiquan Grandmaster! She had not met many Americans who have read the I Ching and understood it. Nor had she met many African American women who could speak fairly decent Cantonese.

Yet the more she talked with Wynolla that first week, the more Monique felt a deep and personal connection. Lieutenant Colonel Lafayette had been watching her new commandeering Officer since his arrival.

Being that 95% of all Military personnel originated from Great Lakes Naval Station, Wynolla is on the lookout for any the type of behavior that may transpire when a Post is cut off from the Command Structure.

It's too easy for a Commander to want to take on too much responsibility or become so sort of misguided father figure who can do no wrong among those under their command! This behavior may include denying the present, for fear of the past.

Rear Admiral Jefferson Bullraguard Lee runs his right hand through his thinning salt and pepper hair and replies.

"Ma'am, you have not seen what those, those things are capable of. One infected person in these walls, get us dead. When you witness a teenager of a man you called friend, who that morning appeared to be normal. Yet an hour later, is cutting his father head off with a Swiss army knife in the J.A.G. HQ. Then, then you would know Doctor Littlefield that being cautious is better off that ending up very, very, dead!"

That's when Windu slowly stood up and addressed the forum. One block of instructions taught by Special Forces Command has to do with how to deal with Assets and their destructive behavior. In the onset of this infection, from her first meeting with Admiral Lee, Colonel Lafayette's gut told her that the lanky man was a bit, odd.

Positively, his behavior since setting foot in Camp McCormick has been downright confusing. Hands on one minute, intense and moving, the next moment, followed by distant and unsure how to lead! Wynolla has seen this before, even in herself. Simply Admiral Lee was suffering from PTSD. Whatever he witnessed at Great Lakes Navy Station stained his very soul!

"Good morning, Admiral, staff and room. In this time of great need, we must possess the courage to do what's right. Self-preservation generally moves the common human being to do what's needed." Anyone know who said that?"

She pauses for a bit, as people in attendance mutter among themselves, nevertheless no one speaks up, so Wynolla continues.

"Ben Franklin. WE, need to be the Ben Franklin's of now! Sir, what you've seen so far is nothing compared to where this is going to end up. I hate to use this ole movie cliché. Listen up people, life is about to be a huge shit sandwich and we all have to take several big ass bites before it's finished!"

Colonel McKinney stood up and interjected. "Admiral Lee, as this week continues, we are firmly headed for another bronze age. Next week, the internet, cellphones, satellites, mass production are about to be a thing of the past.

Without constant care by millions of people, civilization will go away! Sir, these doctors need to get to work before we hit the Stone Age. Because after that we are all the dinosaurs. And whatever is happening outside these walls will be the dominant species."

The mummer grows louder as the civilian population of doctors and civilian scientist who only number forty-nine,-most with familes- react with passion! THEY are the reason Camp McCormick came into existence, their mandate came from the DOD, Assistant to the Joint Chief of Staff and one can assume the President of the United States! Why they are sitting on their asses, they wonder out loud.

The more they talk, the more Jefferson Bullraguard Lee mind wanderers, he needs his form of release. For their words were falling upon on deaf ears and it has been too long since he has used his slave for personal twisted desired. Admiral Lee was attempting to recall his last session, not out of sexual desire! More like an attempt to block out the images of dead people eating the living.

When he snaps back to reality, all eyes are on him. Rear Admiral Lee is caught off guard and he grunts.

"Well, my decision stands for now. We meet next in 24 hours, until then. No news is good news, you are all dismissed!"

People mumble as they filter out of the room. Unsure if their situation is better or worse. The Marine Colonel walks over to Monique, McKinney and Windu, flashes a quick/fake smile and said.

"Look, I agree with you. In a sense we should be doing something. However, you, you didn't see what happened at Great Lakes. I mean right now, no one's sick. Isn't that a win?"

Monique does her best to appeal to Colonel Dunson's sense of patriotism, his sense of duty and most of all his common sense.

"Colonel, what do we do if someone gets infected? How do we deal with the infection when it lands in our laps? Simply, what happen to know your enemy?"

Wynolla noticed how Dunson's eyes were bulging, his outside tone registered under control, yet his entire body language screamed TIME BOMB! Monique sensed it as well; she didn't need to have Wynolla slightly usher herself at bit in front of her. Yet, she felt pleased that Colonel Lafayette thought she had to.

Colonel McKinney does his best to defuse the situation by delivering Dunson a report.

"XO, we might have a slight problem with garbage in the rear future. Seeing we can't use the toilets we are bagging up our waste as you well know."

Dunson shook his head, placed both hands on his hips like a square head Captain America then said.

"Yeah, I can see how that might be a problem. I understand it's a hazard that can't be thrown over the side of the building. I guess it's just another problem that needs to be put in its proper place!"

The words might not have been directed at Doctor Littlefield, yet she fielded their intentions.

Colonel Lafayette goes on to say. "Snipers say they think they might have seen survivors signaling S.O.S in a building several blocks to the east."

Dunson huffs. "Well, that sucks to be them, right."

He pauses for a brief second before saying.

"You know all my life I trained for some god dam terrorist son of a bitch to be on my plane. Or in front of my rife sight! Look, at me now, I'm stuck surrounded by godless fucking Zombies and scien-tist! Ladies and Gentlemen, WE don't get to fight the Apocalypse you want..."

With that Colonel Dunson walks out of the room.

Chapter V:

IT'S THE APOCALYPSE, WHY NOT REINVENT YOURSELF?

129 Hours into infection:

Once they freed themselves from the prison in Michigan City, Marshal Aquila wanted to ditch everyone except her dad. Even so, Big John would not hear of it even though Earl took up the entire third row seat! However, this allows the Valdez couple to cuddle together in the back seated next to ex-Assistant Warden Carpski. With Robin driving, her dad's in the passenger seat with the plump Prison psychologist Indigo Roberson riding in the middle.

Ernesto had floated the idea of a Cartel safe house he had known about before they got caught. He felt it would be stocked with, weapons, water, food and extra transportation, so they went with it. It should have taken less than 28 minutes on a good day-unless traffic is back up due to several Semi-Trucks flipped over- instead, they have been in the black Ford SUV for nearly three hours!

Freeways are packed with discarded vehicles sitting bumper to bumper. To make matters worse, what started as a major traffic jam heading west towards Chicago and East towards Detroit; rapidly downgraded into a slaughter fest! When this all started, RAGERS must have exited their vehicles looking for any noninfected person to spread their joy with! Which leads to parents being pulled out of their cars and stomped to death in front of their crying and confused offspring.

Or screaming infants being bashed against steel girder by enraged red eyed parents to the delight of fellow RAGERs! The traffic jam snakes its way along for nearly fourteen miles, only to open for two-three hundred feet and then grind to a quick snarl. From inside the safety of your vehicle, it might look like groups of people fighting. Only for someone to smash your window with a piece of concrete and stab you in the neck with your own windshield! Yes, one could say, road rage that leads to homicide is pretty the norm.

It has taken a lot of driving down city streets, traveling on old country roads, passing through burning neighborhoods, and even through a goddam cornfield. Just to end up seven miles from their intended location! An East Chicago Strip Club, that serves as a cartel hideout, yet they have to get reach their destination, unharmed.

Currently the sound of gunfire's random and in far off clusters. Nevertheless, the air quality's thick with lots of humidity and the putrid smell of burning tires easily makes a person's eyes water. The breeze that's blowing is coming in from the South and it brings nothing but warm coastal air into the plains of the Midwest. Finally, their vehicle was nearly out of gas near an industrial park a few blocks from an old steel mill.

Side note from 1942-1980ish Northwest Indiana was a hot bed of passion for steel Mills, Labor Unions, White Christian Families, Bowling Halls, Fireworks stands, Strip Clubs and 4H Clubs!

Not to mention, High School football, cheer competitions, Various church groups, the Indianapolis Colts, DA Chicago BEARS, Chicago Bulls, Chicago White Sox's, Chicago Cubs, Indiana University, Purdue Boiler Makers and Norte Dame Fighting Irish pride! All had been the backbone of this region for far too many decades to count.

Flash-forward forty years and this depressed area had been dry cleaned by urban blight and commercial storefront development. In the sleepy summer sun several similar office complexes stretch out before the group, much like cookie cutter houses in the suburbs! While multicolored Semi-Tractor Trucks lounge in a large lot much like giant dragons waiting for their time to ponce.

As Marshal Aquila exits her vehicle, she looks at all the resources she will have to leave- AR-15 x 2, Mossberg Semi-Automatic shotguns x 3, 20 gallons of water, 2 cases of MRE's and a case of Cognac for her and her dad- if they didn't find replacement transportation and fuel.

She scans the area and saw only a few mid-size compacts and hybrid Mini Coopers. Certainly nothing big enough to carry this lot. When Robin noticed Calamity and Ghost Face Killer eyeing her stash, she let it be known.

"For reasons we all can contest are more important than just being trapped together. WE will have to TRUST each other, just as WE have to work hard on not get each other killed. I'm going head over toward those Semi trucks to see if there's something we can travel in. I need someone to watch my back..."

Before she could finish, a Valdez's volunteered, and it's Ernesto whose first to say.

"I would be honored, for you saved our lives. No one was coming for us and I'm certain assistant Warden Carpski would have let us die! Not because she's cruel, just bland and unimpressive. Being we were on Death Row; it was the smart move I assure you. Yet here WE are, yes we owe you our lives. Bonus, you reunited me with my heart and my moon!"

Calamity smiles, licks her husband's cheek and replies. "What he said... Nevertheless, I will not go anywhere unarmed. I saw what those, those plague carriers can do."

For the first time Indigo speaks to the group and her voice's strong and upbeat. A professional analyzer of feelings, dreams and thoughts. Even though she was only transferred to the prison in the last few weeks. The plump dark-skinned woman with the twist tie braids has a stake in what was going on!

"Ahhh, listen I know we just met and have not gotten to know each other properly. Still, wandering off would not be a great idea at this time Marshal."

Big John watches as his daughter scans the road for signs or life or trouble. She has grown so much in the last dozen years, he thought to himself. What he said out loud boiled down to:

"Robin knowns what she's doing, like my friend Ernesto pointed out; my daughter is the reason why most of us are still alive! I would be thankful if you kept her that way."

Earl always the master of the quip, replied. "Besides your complexion, I still don't see the family resemblance. Honey child, your mother must have been an angel!"

Marshal Aquila allowed her escorts to pick up their own weaponry. Celeste choose twin 9mm Berta's and hunting knife. While her husband frowned at first, then picked up an AR-15 and begins to load four clips. As Robin told the rest of the group.

"I don't know what's going on, but I do know I won't stop anyone that feels the need to arm themselves. As long as we are clear, don't bite the hand that freed you. That means me and your former Assistant Warden! I assure you, she had your best interest in mind."

Big John asked. "You sure you don't what me to tag along?"

Robin flashes a smile as she states. "When's the last time you or Earl had to fun run for two hundred yards while being chased by a mob?"

Earl squeals in schoolgirl like delight as he said, "Honey child! That's my lifelong dream of mine. As long as they are sexy 18-28 year old transgender queers who can keep a secret, or even not."

Flash forward to sixty seconds later. Robin and the Valdez's have skillfully found temp cover behind a large empty green garbage container. The sound of thousands of buzzing insects becomes the rhythm of all background noise. The trio must place one careful step in front of another, trekking through pools of drying blood and the stench of rotting flesh! Sadly, the area that holds the Semi Trucks was bare of all civilian transport. However, there's another cookie cutter complex to the left of that.

The humidity makes the entire ordeal even fucking worse! Warm saltwater beads down Robin and Celeste's forehead. As the shirt on Ernesto's back has wielded the sweat to the middle of his semi hair-less torso. When they reach the outskirts of the complex, yellow puss faced RAGERs are staggering around the parking lot. Bumping into and off each other as if they are acid tripping in a mosh pit!

The smell that RAGERs produce reminded Robin of going to the gym and smelling the sour body expulsions of a dozen steroid us-ing gym rats. Ernesto counted in Spanish until he reached fourteen and whispers.

"It will be tricky; I think if everyone goes with head shots we might be able to pull this off with drawing too much attention. Which ve-hicle you have in mind Marshal?"

Robin scans the lot, there are two late model min vans, one Ford F-150, one Ram Silverado, and one Lincoln Navigator. She calls for the Navigator, still it's Celeste who said.

"Why not roll two of three?"

Before anyone can contest, she whispers to her husband.

"I could be sucking your pena in that big rojo truck right over there while you drive, Ernesto."

He whispers back, "Just like the old days, mi Corazon..."

Before Robin can contest, family Valdez surge forward doing what they do best. The Ghostface Killer and Calamity are back in the goddam game! From the RAGER's point of view the non-infected most smell like steak, or even hamburger! For they quickly rush howling and screaming towards their own destruction. Nonetheless, the Valdez's are professionally trained killers, Cartel shooters and Mucho, Mucho horny! Every well place shot from either of Calamity's 9mm Berta's caused brain matter of her intended targets to rise in the air like kites on the southern wind.

The sound of gunshots brings more RAGERS out of their hiding places. The constant sound of three round burst coming from Ernesto's AR-15 kept pace with the weapons Robin's wielding. Yet their success brings unwanted results towards the south of their position.

The smell of the staggering undead is far different from that of the RAGERS! Maybe it's the deterioration of their skin? The decay of the dark colored blood that is dried at the corners of their eyes, mouth and various wounds that's sickening to the senses. If you have never smelled the dead rising, consider the smell of rotten fruit, mixed with an overwhelming stench of Sulphur, mucus, iron and vast amounts of vile puke and of course human shit.

The smell's overpowering and to make matters worse, the "Zombies" didn't seem to give two shits about the RAGERS! They will shamble past the infected with their broken bones and missing limbs. Not even paying them as much as a never fucking mind. For hunger drives the dead into constant action against the non-infected living!

Marshal Aquila isn't going to let any of those things get close enough to identify what ethnic group they might have hailed from. All she had to see were the gaping wounds and rotten flesh to know they were flesh eating Dead Heads! She fires a 9mm hollow point into one of her attackers' kneecaps.

Just like she had done so many shitheads and assholes over her ten years on the job! It was easier than killing a suspect if you really didn't have to. The paperwork was less, and you could always fall back on, "did you want me to kill the suspect or bring the piece of shit in?"

Nonetheless, the dead don't play fair! The bone and cartilage that exploded out the oily deceased cadaver flew across the rock and pebbled parking lot, yet that didn't stop it.

The milky eyed Zombie doesn't scream, doesn't cry or beg for medical assistant. It simply moans, grinds its blood-stained teeth, never stops its air chomping and biting.

It's a gray skinned reminder that the world has indeed descended into utter fucking madness!

Slowly the would-be corpse crawls towards Marshal Aquila who doesn't blink as she aims her Colt .45 directly at its filthy broken nose, then fired. It takes four minutes to clear the area and the smoke from the constant gunfire forms its own cloud. Quickly blanketing the area like a snow cap on a distant mountain!

Celeste heads to the big red Dodge Silverado, hops into the truck bed and climbs through the window. Cleverly unlocking the doors without smashing anything.

Marshal Aquila quickly heads to the White Lincoln Navigator and snatches up the door. She is shocked as she is forced to take back as a struggling Zombie infant is trapped in a child's car seat! The toddler snarls, growls and shits its pants in vain as it crawls towards her! Robin felt sick to her stomach at the sight, she must fight back the urge to vomit across the expensive Italian leather. Slowly she mutters more to herself than the Valdez's'.

"I might be a borderline alcoholic and a rogue Marshal operating way outside the constraints of what I thought was even goddam possible! Nevertheless, goddam it I am not a child murder! Maybe, I should have brought Earl Grimes along?"

Robin chuckles at her inside joke as she strikes upon another way to deal with the problem. Carefully using her knife, Marshal Aquila cuts the restraints that hold the baby carrier in place. Even more carefully, Robin picks up the moaning and screaming infant's soiled pink carrier and placed it on the ground next to the vehicle.

She bends down and stares into the ghostly pale-gray face that attempts to bite her cute little nose. Only to see the tiny little teeth of a two-year-old gnawing and grinding until vile blood pours from its dead lips! That's one of the most frightening things Robin had ever seen, yet the day was still young.

Ernesto's drives up in the red Silverado and shouts out.

"It's time to go back to get the other's, are you coming?"

Marshal Aquila stands up and turns to say something, when she notices Celeste winking at her; as her head disappears from sight!

Robin replied. "Yeah, I'm coming, I coming and I guess so are you."

Ernesto smiles as he grunts, "Yeah well it's been a very long time for me and trust me I'm trying hard not to!"

It isn't long before the group is back on the road. Earl rides with the Valdez's and Robin drove the rest of their group. Ernesto's vehicle is in the lead, slowly maneuvering on sidewalks, through front yards and even through a cemetery. While all around them mayhem's in the making. Inside the Valdez's' vehicle a tender conversation was under way.

Celeste cuddles up under Ernesto's strong right arm, as her feet rest on the window. She floats any idea.

"How long are we going to play nice-nice with this Marshal Aquila? Look around, there's no more LAW. Fuck there's certainly no more order! What are doing, I am not saying kill her. I mean why are even allowing anyone to follow US?"

As Ernesto scans the street, he saw the reason why spelled out in huge, red letters. Small groups, battling for the right to be among the living! Men, women and child clubbing, bashing, stabbing and in most cases shooting other survivors. Survivors picking up dropped weapons and firing it into their attackers! He's hoping, his love saw that now their lives can have purpose.

Yet it's Earl, whose deep insights are as simple as Forest Gump, still so less deadly than a hot knife to your still beating heart!

"You know before I, I went inside. I loved vanilla ice cream and one day I smoked the best marijuana I ever had it was called Ghost Cookie."

Celeste cosigned, "Oh, yesss. That Indica, it puts you on your ass!"

Earl smiled and replied. "You are so right Mrs. Valdez."

She counters with, "What's this Mrs. Valdez shit? I am Celeste and sometimes I'm Calamity. A woman has many different personalities..."

Earl nodded his giant oval head you're right, wiped the sweat from his brow and said.

"On that night, I was feeling blue."

Celeste sighed and asked, "Ahhhh, why?"

Ernesto wanted to tell her to please stop interrupting him. Earl would take two days to tell one story if you let him! His slow delivery and commitment to details would make a simple I got high and fell asleep tale, EPIC. Mr. Valdez decided the best way to keep his wife occupied was to let his fingers do some taking.

Like the itsbi spider crawling down the waterspout, out came the labia and spread her wings out! When fingers found the intended spot Mrs. Valdez shuttered and let him in. The fingers find the mark allowing Earl to continue and everyone wins!

"Once I felt I had to strangle this wonderful white bubble booty bottom escort... Bottom line is I misplaced some money and a few ounces of primo medical grade mushrooms and I figured he was trying to rip me off! Ahhh, it wasn't until I watched his twitching corpse expel gas, did I remember I sold the mushrooms a few towns over."

Mr. Valdez's fingers have not pleased his wife in nearly four years, nevertheless he has not lost his touch! While Mrs. Valdez and not been celibate behind bars, like she said, "I have two girlfriends."

Still, that's didn't dampen the pleasure felt by Celeste as her husband feverish works his index finger and thumb in tiny circles around her clitoris! All while avoiding burning vehicles, staggering Zombies and death dealing RAGERs. The man's a true goddam professional!

Earl goes on to say.

"So ,when I find the poor bottoms weed, I have to smoke it. Right? Then I go on to eat two quarts of Soft Churned French Vanilla ice cream and a warm apple pi!. I went to sleep happy, nonetheless I woke up the next morning sick to my tummy. I stuffed myself so much I never wanted to see French Vanilla Ice Cream or warm apple pie again!"

Earl looks at the face of a puss filled red eyed manic, sawing off the head of a screaming middle-aged man with a hearing aid and he sighs.

"That's what all this means, it's just too, too much! For me, this takes all the joy out of being labeled a homicidal maniac. For me, this is like living in a bad Italian B movie! You know I took real pride in my work."

FUN FACT; In what was the present, the city of East Chicago located in Northwest Indiana's economy had revolved around Various Casinos. As well as dozens of strip malls for small business reaching for the American dream and of course a shit load of strip clubs! One of the largest in the area was built in early 2018.

During the mortgage meltdown of 2006, a converted bankrupt strip mall was purchased by front men for the Sana Malonia Cartel!

Their club was built with over twenty-five thousand feet of loud music, flashing colored lights, disco balls, private dance areas, discrete VIA lounging, expensive to cheap booze and of course, all that ASS, ASS, ASS and Tiddies!

At any given time no less than forty seminude dancers could be found parading perfumed booty cheeks and fake smiles to the hundreds of men that toss their hard-earned money over a rail or into a G-String. Semi naked women pretending to find men interesting if only for a few moments, was a worldwide past time long before Jesus was a baby!

Sadly, when you think about it, if some of those misguided men had only tossed those badly needed dollars to their own women, maybe their relationship would not be fallen apart. Or maybe if those misguided men's love interested and been in the best shape of their lives like these strippers, they would all still be alive. Who knows?

Moving on, the Cartel knew it had a money maker right off the bat! The old strip mall easily contained a refurbished night club, adding a decent steak house and a coffee shop to the property only attracted more people spending money. A customer pays an entrance fee to enter the location, where they are free to engage in all its trappings. You could continue on and enter a real high-end Gentleman's Club- properly named Candy Land, where it cost you a C-note just to get through their fucking door!

The safe house Ernesto has led the small ground to looks like a Tire shop at the far end of this refurbished strip mall. All around the parking lot an assortment of vehicles sat with either their doors wide open, or overturned and smoldering in the later afternoon sun! To make matters worse a High School football team of RAGER's- around twenty in uniform- wander aimlessly among the wreckage.

Approaching quickly from up the street, Ernesto brings his red Silverado to a halt, so his driver's window faces Marshal Aquila's.

He points over to the open bay doors of the Tire shop, where no less than eight Zombies stumbling and roaming throughout the ransacked lobby. The broken-down sign reads. GABE's Tires and Alarms.

"Inside Gabe's tire there is a door, which leads to an underground chamber that runs alongside the sewer line for two hundred feet of this city block! Amazing right?"

Robin scans the area, and she knew they had to get off the street before it got dark. Before, she asks. "Your Cartel owned all this?"

Celeste leans over Ernesto and replied happily. "My husband and I were more like freelancers; however, WE won't work for certain cocksuckers and will with others! As for this place, we had planned to rob it, before that strange night in Indy. And for the record I can now see how stabbing that fat, ugly, cartel cunt with a broken beer bottle, jumped everything off that fucked our life up... Fast forward, here we are!"

Robin's head is hurting, she wants out of her bulletproof vest, and she really needed to pee. Nevertheless, she calmly asked. "Do we, in which I mean YOU, have a plan?"

The Zombies wandering inside what's left of Gabe's Discount Tire & Alarm Shop were mostly ordinary employees. No real Cartel members, just regular guys, some ex-cons, and one store Manager who knew about the hidden door, the ladder and a series of rooms that lead to the area outside the fabled CANDY LAND-Gentlemen's Club!

Mr. Valdez noticed that both bay doors where open, however only one is empty. He instructs Marshal Aquila to bring her big body Lincoln in hot and heavy. She didn't have to be told twice, running over two beefy Zombies in the process. Pinning their snarling carcasses into a cinder block wall! Forcing what's left of their guts to go splat over the colorless concrete walls. The Valdez's came in just as fast, throwing their big red truck into reverse getting up to 45 miles an hour. Before coming to a screeching halt and parking mere feet from the open bay door.

The sudden sound caught the attention of the High Scholl football team of teenage RAGERS. That's when The Ghostface Killer and Calamity quickly exit their transpo ducking into the garage. As agreed, the rest of their group sat tight in their vehicles, until called upon, just to make sure none of them caught a stray bullet.

Celeste possessed a firearm like a world class Chef Brandishes a stainless-steel carving knife! Allowing Chicken Head and Ernesto a chance to close the bay door, all while his love places double taps into separate Dead Heads.

After blowing what little brains they have left across the garbage laden floors. Calamity picks up a black metal pike and drives into the rotten skull of an older Mexican man. His skin's gray and he smells like cat urine, soot and smoke. His chattering red teeth only stopped moving when the metal pushed deep into its eye socket. While the Ghostface Killer snatches up a heavy wrench and bashes an approaching Zombie in its ankle.

With a heavy thud, the decaying mechanic crashed to the concrete! Using one might swing Ernesto smashes the heavy metal into the face of the Zombie until a deep purplish foul liquid mingles with broken bone fragments.

The RAGERs quickly approached the now closed bay door, slamming into it and banging on it as they tried to get inside! As Earl moves around towards the driver's side of his vehicle, he looks at a one-armed RAGER with maybe a broken back crawling towards the truck door. Earl picks up a screwdriver and with one push of the thin metal wand, Chicken Head punctures the skinny female Zombies frontal lobe!

Big John exits the passenger side of the Lincoln Navigator, standing mere feet from the snarling mechanic that was pinned to the wall.

His dull milky eyes display no thought, no emotion and no intelligence at all. Just a drive, a craving for warm human flesh.

Robin mutters, "Dad, put it out of its misery."

Big John turns to his driven offspring, he has so much to tell her in such little time! That's when Earl walks over to the clawing Zombie, its red teeth never stopping in its pursuit of fresh meat. Chicken Head eyes his surroundings and puts his big meaty hands around a heavy rubber mallet. Before he can bash its exposed skull in.

Indigo Roberson, followed by Abby Carpski exit the Lincoln Navigator. Indigo shrieks, "Nooo. Wait!"

Earl's puzzled, he looks at the Zombie straining to break free from the ninety-thousand-dollar vehicle that had shit slammed into a wall. Then he looks to the ex-Prison Psychologist, scratched his big clean-shaven head before replying.

"What do you think you hope to accomplish by sparing this creature? It has no compassion for you, no desire to learn about your pitiful one-bedroom apartment with free cable..."

The room gets quiet as the real Monster in the room breathing became hard, Earl's eyes burn with anger and the malaise that pure madness brings to the table! His massive chest's huffing and flexing as Earl fought to control his wrath, his very nature! His friends see they must calm the water, Big John goes on to say.

"She means THEY are US, so how we handle them shows respect for ourselves."

He looks at Indigo, she sorts of flashes half a smile as a way of saying thanks.

Instead, Indigo takes a deep breath before saying. "Mr. Grimes, it's the Apocalypse why, why not reinvent yourself?"

Nonetheless, Ernesto goes on to say. "Listen my friend, if we find any living fucking member of this Cartel, feel free to act out. They're all puntas!"

Fun Fact; The Sana Manolia Cartel put down roots in Indiana in late 1990s buying up vacant store front property and opening business that catered to cash only customers.

The Cartel's found out that checking cashing places, used car dealerships, tire repair shops, taco stands, Dollar stores, liquor stores, Dry Cleaners and Strip Clubs were, like MOO, as in cash cows! They had even built a trap door under an out of commission stall in the woman's bathroom inside a store directly outside the fabled CANDY LAND. Fortunately, the Mexican Cartels are more effective than the ole school American Mafia or the Russians. South American and Mexican Drug lords have always proved highly resourceful and good at digging long fucking holes!

A generator sat idle near a banged-up shell of a 1998 Toyota 4X4 and once it's started up, the noise dove the RAGERs outside into a killing frenzy. Their bumping into the closed bay door, quickly turns into pounding, kicking and throwing items like concrete slabs to break that shit down!

Once the shell of a car's lifted, they turned off the generator and Ernesto used his pocket knife to unscrew four screws that reveal a control panel. Mr. Valdez smiles as he flicks the white switch. The floor underneath the Toyota rumbled as Ernesto jumped out of the way, a five-foot-wide hole opens in the middle of the floor. Revealing a single ladder leading down into a semi dark tunnel. Ernesto takes the lead followed by Celeste, Robin, Big John, Abby, Indigo and finally Earl.

For Earl it's a tight fit for his massive three-hundred-and them some frame, he has to suck in his stomach and chest until he's fifteen, maybe even twenty pounds thinner! They descend the equitant of two flights of stairs, navigate a short humid hallway before emerging into a goddam Narco Traffickers wet dream. Alongside their birthday, rolled up inside Christmas day with a vibrant blood red cherry on top!

There are duffle bags, upon duffle bags filled with gallon size zip lock bags of clearly labeled medical grade marijuana. Duffle bags with several different colored pills and a shitload of dried mushrooms. Hundreds of bricks of cocaine and heroin rest on opposite sides of the spacious concrete room!

However, that's nothing compared to the countless bundled up crates upon crates, upon crates of greenbacks, money. Plus, there were assault weapons, 50. Caliber Sniper Rifles hunting rifles, handguns, shotguns and even US Military grade hardware! Such as night vision glasses, Frag and Concussion grenades, as well as several Russian made RPGs.

Robin is taken back by the amount of hardware as well as the work bench for modifying weapons to full auto. She even notices the required materials to make pipe bombs scattered about. Marshal Aquila's scowl is hard to hide as she growls.

"What the hell was up with the pipe bombs? I clearly see drugs coming in and money and weapons going out. But why the pipe bombs?'

Ernesto replies with a hint of emotion.

"They boobie trap their trucks, in case someone hi jacks them or the driver gets cute and runs away with a shipment. However, no one has any knowledge that they are sitting on bombs. Or that there may or may not be a disarming switch...."

Celeste signals as she whispers "BOOM."

Dam, whispers Abby Carpski.

It doesn't take long before personal weapons are selected alongside knock off blue jeans, Nike shoes and sports jerseys.

FUN FACT, Mexican Cartels found that manufacturing bootleg designer sneakers, sportswear and jeans in Mexican. Then flooding swap meets from Coast to Coast with their merch made up for the huge loss of their marijuana business that North American Legalization created!

Earl found a double-breasted black suit coat that fit him and eight ounces of Indicia he stuffed in the inter breast pockets. He wasn't really a cocaine type of person; it made him paranoid. Nevertheless, he did load up on X-pills and mushrooms.

Robin wanted to say something when she noticed Calamity stuffing a brick of cocaine inside her black, spiked motorcycle jacket and decided why fucking bother! Marshal Aquila looked down at the table of illicit narcotics and she settles for a several bags of Sativa- labeled to reduce stress and add to creative thinking- and quietly stuffs four ounces inside her back pack!

Big John follows Ernesto over to the armor's bench and instructs him on simple items they would need.

"Ernesto a capable man such has yourself must know how to make suppressors', right?"

Calamity finishes rolling up some loose Sativa using a cigar as the casing. She lights it up and smiles as she blows her husband a stream of motta. Ernesto coughs a few times, looks very serious before saying.

"No problem Hefe, I will put few together for the AR-15 and for a few handguns. But we won't be able to test them down here."

Calamity takes another toke of the blunt before handing it to Big John, then turns and walks over to the bens of clothes. Big John takes a long drag and doesn't flinch or cough a bit.

He blows three large rings of smoke into the ceiling and hands it to Abby Carpski. She refuses and passes it on to Indigo, who panders to the do and don'ts for a few beats.

Nevertheless, the strong smell of good marijuana to many brings to mind the smell of good coffee and she decides, why not! A short drag of the marijuana filled cigar made Indigo cough several times, feel warm, then calm.

It took nearly ninety minutes before Ernesto was able to use pieces of pipes, washers and black tape to fashion several make-shift suppressors.

Four for AR-15s, three for the 9mm Rutgers's lying about, two for the twin 20 gauges, lever action shotguns and one for Marshal Aquila's 9mm Smith & Wesson and another for her Caliber Colt 45.

Nonetheless, for his Celeste he made two special suppressors. Calamity found something right out of for the 80's Miami Cocaine Wars! Twin midnight black UZI's and just like that, Death is about to become CHIC.

Each person has found empty backpacks and made sure they pack enough dry socks, MREs, bottled water, toilet paper, emergency medical kit, and ammo they could carry. When it came to party favors, Abby asks Celeste why's she loading up on male enhancers, acid and cocaine.

"Excuse me, Mrs. Valdez."

She replies. "No please call me Celeste. Why so formal Abby, it's the Apocalypse. Oh, and you, I'm not calling you Marshal anymore. No offense, but it is the end of the freaking world! I'll either address you by your first, last name or hey you. The choice is yours."

Robin scoffs, but before she can say anything Carpski goes on to ask.

"Thank you, Celeste. If I may, why are you stocking up on all those, drugs?"

Celeste smiles as she replies. "Don't worry I don't plan to take this today! I do plan to slip Ernesto one of these blue pills.... I don't want him tiring on me too early! If you know what I mean? Men are all bluster for about 2-6 minutes. Followed by a few smelly farts and lots of loud snoring. Even so, I do love that man!"

She lets her words sink in before continuing. "Plus, this stuff is better than money because money doesn't mean shit now! Dope and pussy are worth their weight in gold. It's best you remember that in the incredibly hard times that lie ahead. Abby, you better learn how to either kill without hesitation. Suck a pena or at least do fucking anal!"

Robin chuckles as she stands at a table filled with ammo crates, loading thirty round clips for the AR-15s. Big John joins his daughter at the table and begins to load 9mm clips alongside her. He smiles at his stern looking offspring and said softly.

"I'm so proud of the woman you have become."

Robin slams her hands to the table and lets out a bitter laugh.

"HA! You have no idea the person, not alone the woman I am.."

He holds his hands signaling that he doesn't want to fight. The father can recognize the anger, pain and sadness in his daughter's eyes.

As much as Robin might have wanted to let her emotions run wild, she feels all eyes weighing heavily on their family reunion. Calmly she tells her dad.

"Let's just focus on not getting infected by whatever's turning people into raging maniacs."

That's when they noticed Earl eating a bag of microwave popcorn, staring at them.

"Sorry, I was missing my daily soap opera and you two were filling in nicely. Please, do not stop on my account..."

He does a slight turn and said, “I’ll turn around and only listen if that will help?”

Robin puts her hands on her hips, then up in the air signaling she doesn’t have time for this shit! She walks away, allowing Indigo to move on in and do her best to console the father. Indigo’s soft charcoal toned hand hesitates before moving in to gently rub John on his broad shoulders. She does her best by saving.

“I guess you two have some unresolved issues your both need to work through?”

Big John Hammond let out a nervous, stress filled laugh and replies.

“Yeah, yeah I missed out on all her formative years’ -he laughs a nervous laugh, before saying- and here we are today.”

Indigo Roberson uses her Professional voice when she states.

“Well dad, you better figure out what needs to be said. For from my professional standpoint, you daughter is a ticking time bomb waiting for a signal to detonate.”

John glances at his traveling companions and mutters more to himself than Indigo.

“Sadly, we are all a float in an ocean of gasoline, fertilizer and C-4. What a wonderful way to experience the Apocalypse, huh?”

Abby looks at the gun being placed in her palm and shook her head no. Ernesto asks her, “what are you shaking your head no about?”

Carpski opens her mouth and for a brief second nothing comes out. When she pulls it together, Abby’s voice breaks up and off as she replies.

“I, I don’t know if I can do this. I, I’m not a good or even a decent shot. I, I can’t do this!”

Ernesto snatches the gun out of Abby's hand, cracks open the breech to make sure the .38 Caliber sub nose revolvers indeed loaded. He hands the weapon back to the nervous woman. His tone's gentle, yet fierce as he explained.

"Aim for the knee, put them on the ground. Then if you have to."

Celeste comes up beside her husband, he flips his arm over her neck as she interjects.

"You will have to shoot, Abby. Our lives depend on you as yours do on us. I mean I wanted to gut you and leave you for roadkill! However, Ernesto has grown a heart to go with a pair of big hairy balls. A bit salty, still very hairy just like I love them!"

Mr. Valdez leans forward and kisses his wife softly on her lips then said.

"Shoot them in the face once, conserve your ammo. Remember this weapon only holds six shots."

Earl walks over picking popcorn out of his teeth then said.

"Like the prison shrink told me. It's the Apocalypse, time to reinvent yourself Carpski."

Chapter VI:

PARADISE AND SKY, BFF'S OF THE APOCALYPSE.

Two Hours Before Infection:

The smell of Casa Erotica or CANDY LAND to the gringos is one of money, hi-lighted by expensive cigar smoke, various perfumes, baby oil, suntan lotion, undiagnosed HPV and liquor! Lots of lots of alcohol is served hourly in this Cartel controlled enterprise. Of course, there are after-hours rooms for Cartel members and high rollers alike. Where anything goes if the price is right and your means of paying is in hand. The Mexican Cartel's had taken a page out of Italian and Russian mobsters' playbook when they invested in legal business in the land in which they wish to launder their money.

The bankrupt and nearly empty strip mall in East Chicago Indiana was a great front for Cartel business interest! The influx of immigrates from Central American and Southern Mexico meant neighborhoods were in the stage of ethnic change. Instead of the Cartels thinking small, they thought big! Their investments turned an entire vacant strip mall into an entertainment complex. With two dance clubs, a five-star strip club, two three-star restaurants, an expensive cigar store, one lingerie store, a gourmet popcorn shop, one take out taco stand, one tire repair shop and a cellphone store.

The Sana Molina Cartel spent nearly fifteen million dollars making this property presentable. What made it profitable is it sat directly in between two Casinos and the toll Road running through that part of the state of Indiana, towards Chicago Illinois. The Cartel smartly hired locals, mostly young white twenty- to thirty-year-olds, some blacks, yet few if any Hispanics to work in their store fronts. If you saw a Hispanic gentleman in a black suit and cowboy boots, he was muscle and he's Cartel!

This kept most if not all their legal business below the prying eyes of I.C.E. The only place you will find Hispanics working in mass numbers on this property are in their tire shop at the end of the property lines. That left no need for I.C.E, to enter the real money-making portion of their property looking for ILLEGALS. The Mexican Cartels are much better organized than most and knew that playing the game, is done better away from prying eyes!

Placing this complex between two NW Indiana's Casinos makes a good night out even better for the winners. And to the losers, well no one rarely loses at the West of the Rine- Entertainment Complex. The Cartel's makes sure there is so much to do, that no one ever suspected what's going on under their feet!

Inside Casa Erotica the sensual blue and white lights were still bouncing of the glimmering disco ball high in the ceiling. Casting a rainbow of colors across the dance floor. Sky was on stage two, her tanned membrane amalgamates rather well with the tiny pink see through lingerie she's wearing, it casts a sense of pure sexuality!

She slow crawls across a marble stage towards a group of slightly drunk and leering Japanese businessmen. One of the men has his blue necktie, wrapped around his forehead as his friends chant him on. He gleefully tosses a wad of one-dollar bills at the alluring Sky, as she uses the heel of her foot to push him back into his plush metal chair.

The smile in her green eyes, hid the distain Sky feels every time she must allow some low IQ, privileged, asshole to fawn over her toned thighs or tender brown nipples! Nonetheless, Casa Erotica's the only place- not Magic City in Atlanta, the Crazy Horse in Detroit or Las Vegas- where a dancer could request two thousand dollars for a private dance and get it! That just covered one dance, for yes; there are extras in the champagne room.

However, the Japanese tourists were so drunk that a lap dance would not be needed! They are throwing hundreds of dollars at each dancer. Each man gets up saluting his peers before tossing a hand full of money at whatever entertainer who's on stage.

When Sky hit the side stage **Trina No Panites-** was playing.

"No BOO what's the deal, you got cash to enter in here? I know you be packin that steel, but I'm not gonna suck your dick and get my lipstick smeared...No panties cumming off, my love is gonna cost, no way you gonna get this pussy for free! Skank you don't have to like me, but's it's clear your man likes me. You better respect, it's my job to break your husband for his check! Remember I'm the bitch that had your man in my car, with his hand on my bra, whispering TRINA. Uooo no panties cumming off..."

Sky lays on her back thrusting her toned hips in the general direction of various drunken Japanese tourist. Sky seductively runs her left index finger across her top lip. For some reason that seems to drive men out of their goddam minds! Sky rolls over to her stomach, slightly raising her ass up to assume the dog style position.

This is her finishing mover, the performer in Sky knew she has about 45 seconds of song left and here's where she put the Sexy in Stripper! Hiking the tiny G string as high as she could around her round tanned buttocks, she focused the gyration of her hips to resemble a cup of Jello riding a rollercoaster!

As she twerked in the general direction of the paying customers. Sky isn't focusing on the men reaching into the pockets of their eight hundred-dollar suits and making it rain. Sky feels that's a given! No, she saw her current BFF, plus two sitting in the crowd.

Paradise Hunter, the twenty-three-year-old transgender youtube.com star that's been the brother and little sister Sky has always wanted! Hailing from the mixed heritages of a Thai mother with a bi-racial Korean and Caucasian father. Paradise's the type of male to female transgender that can only be sired in the cradle of Brazil or Thailand!

Dressed in a black and white revealing sun dress and white heels- which gave her two inches. The 5'8, one hundred and forty-five pound, 34C-28-35 is a true Asian beauty. Paradise's hips have a way of captivating to the men she passes on route to the stage!

She leans over the railing and hands Sky a stack of hundred-dollar bills. Turns and winks at one of the businessmen- who pretends to have a heart attack as he falls drunkenly into his companion's arms- and walks back to her table.

As soon as the song ends, Sky gathers her assortment of bills, making sure to thank each and every man with her classic manufactured smile and gentle caress to their hands, necks or faces.

It's the same most nights, the plan is to get in and get out! That's Sky approach, she works the times most girls won't. The 12pm-5pm shift could be feast or famine! A dancer doesn't know if the place will be packed or a regular ghost town. It cost one hundred dollars just to get into the **West of the Rhine Entertainment Complex**! After that most clubs inside are free to the bearer wearing the admission wristband, except CANDY LAND where it costs an extra 100 to gain entrance.

That's the beauty of the Cartel's business plan of the **WOREC**- as it's known by the locals- it opens promptly at 12pm and closes at 4am six days a week- Thursday through Monday. Tuesday it's closed for cleaning and as well as various Cartel-related business.

Sky knew that making at least 800 hundred dollars a day three days a week was just a matter of finding the right guys and the right songs. She's a performer, a fucking artist done to her pretty toes.

She's an artist who would rather be painting, however Sky understood on any given night the stage should be her canvas!

Frankly it turned out to be a better Thursday afternoon than she expected. Before the tourists showed up Sky had made about two hundred dollars in three hours. However, when the Japanese businessmen showed, they shelled out a collective twenty thousand dollars in under three hours! After it was all said and done, Sky made a total of thirty-one hundred dollars. Mostly in big, faced twenties!

Fifteen minutes later dressed in ultra tight fade blue jeans, a white T shirt- tied in a knot exposing a pierced belly button- and white K Swiss tennis shoes. Sky joins her BBF Paradise at her table flanked by two people clinging to Paradise for her attention and even her fame!

Anyone can shave an otter down and put it in a dress, nevertheless it's still a hairy man in a dress! Another person can try to grow a horrible goatee, lift a few weights and put on a lumber jack shirt and cowboy boats. Nevertheless, they're still an over weigh woman trapped in a woman's body! Who's probably loving the strip club experience more than the chubby man in the purple dress seated next to Paradise- she refers to them as her BASE!

Sky sits down and orders a round of whatever the table is drinking and bottled water for herself. Paradise is first to say.

"Girl, you look marvelous, as per-usge! Oh, you know the BASE."

Sky dons a quick smile as she nods to Fredda and Barry, they nodded back as the waitress arrives with two waters and two 7- Ups, Sky tips the seminude co-worker twenty dollars. Then she turns and slides the wad of hundreds her friend gave her back across the table.

Paradise nose crunches up and she half sticks out her lip in a pout then said.

"I had a great day, that's why I am here! What? I thought house rules is $2000 equals I get to see a private dancer; you mean I don't get to have all that puss in my face? Bitch, please pop that pussy for me, please, please, please.."

Paradise sticks out her bottom lip as Sky pauses for a second and waits for Paradise to keep a straight face. It took three seconds for she cannot contain her upbeat laughter any longer. Paradise took a one hitter out her purse and casually takes out a prescription bottle with nearly a half a gram of Sativa and packs the bowl.

One of her base, quickly produces a lighter and lights Paradise's fire! She touches the woman posing as a lumberjack's face and Berry responds just like the dunked men Sky just danced for! The Trans man seems to melt in Paradise hands. Not in a sexual way, no in finally I've gained acceptance, I've found a peer and hopefully a friend kind of way!

After Paradise exhaled the one hitter, she quietly went on to repack the bowl for her BFF. Paradise didn't exhale until she handed Sky the tiny bong that resembled a cigarette. She snaps her manicured fingers, and the base in the lumberjack shirt- Berry hands over the lighter, so Paradise can do the honors for her bestie- Sky. Who said before partaking in the gesture.

"You know we are not supposed to be doing this in here?"

Paradise smiles and replies.

"What, I have a prescription and a disability! Plus, you know I can't handle rejection, it makes me want to go shopping. Now please can we go do some shopping? I'll take my lap dance down at the lingerie shop, thank you very much!"

Sky exhaled and said, "So, you are serious about that? Ok let's do it!"

FYI, inside the WOREC, there are several trendy unisex clothing stores, one woman's shoe store, a tanning salon, unisex steam room, nail shop, a cigar store, a pretzel/popcorn stand and ice cream pallor.

Sky and Paradise walked side by side, as Freda and Barry gratefully followed behind much like servants following their hi-born benefactors!

For the in-tow Trans man and Trans woman, the flow of following toned thighs and bouncing booty cheeks are an easy target to follow even when fully clothed.

The WOREC wasn't crowded, not this early on a Thursday. There were the customary businessmen out of Chicago, the professional athletes- millionaire bench riders- that no one ever heard of, private Security and assortment of Single women, men and couples on afternoon dates, hidden from the public eye.

The West of the Rhine Entertainment Complex caters to just about all sexual preferences and entertainment choices. Except country western of course, the Cartel felt more COPS listen to Country Western and they didn't want their traffic. The smell of fresh popcorn freely mingles with the aroma of baking pretzels, fresh brewed coffee, cotton candy and the co-mingle in the effort to entice guests to spend as much legal tender as possible.

Their first stop was at the Northwest Indiana Greedy Pretzel Company for four slightly salted and hot buttered pretzels, with a twelve oz. crafted beer! The sound of laughter, song and people otherwise enjoying themselves is the theme of the moment. Few if any inside the WOREC are prepared for what will happen in under thirty-two minutes!

The next stop for the unlikely foursome is the Soft & Sweet Lingerie shop where Sky noticed one of her fellow coworkers. Claire "Cherish" McGill whose another vision of loveliness crafted in the great melting pot of the **U.S of fucking A**! Standing all of 5'5 1/2, weighing 135 pounds of 34-26-37 ½ inches, she was the color of sweet, deep dark chocolate, an extremely moist brownie. Everyone figured she's how God spelled, Delicious!

The West Side of Chicago native has stripped her way across Florida, Louisiana, Georgia, North Carolina, Las Vegas and Los Angles. Yet, she was only 24 years old. The cute but street tough Cherish had grown up the hard way. In and out of foster homes, barely finished High School, yet did manage to attend two years of college!

Clarrie Cherish McGill, has been a Cheerleader, played basketball like a tomboy, ran track, has been devilishly sexy since she turned sixteen and knew how to make men and women spend their hard-earned money. To any bystander when she walked, Cherish's buttocks behaved like twin bee hives buzzing with excitement!

The Afro wearing Cherish, dons a tight pair of white Levi's with slits to expose her toned thighs. She wore a blue silk top which framed her pea shaped nipples like their a gift just for you and black stylish two-inch come fuck me pumps! When she saw Sky come through the door Claire lit up with a genuine smile and asked.

"Hey hon, how's the crowd tonight?"

Sky walks over and gives the dark and lovely Claire Cherish McGill a warm hug and replied. "Pretty good,giiiirllll there's about eighteen Japanese tourists inside and they are tossing money around like they invented the stuff!"

Cherish wiggles her hips with glee and cooed. "Mama needs some new ice for her wrist!"

Paradise cleared her throat and Sky turned to introduce her needy best friend and her of course her entourage.

"This is my BFF, Paradise and her, "base". Freda and Barry!"

Cherish complemented Paradise and her friends. 'Ohhhhh snap.

You are simply breathtaking, look at you! My goodness, honey child, I would kill for those nails."

Paradise smiled and replied. "Oh, I would pay a King's ransom for those dimples."

Sky's next line could be considered flirtatious, nevertheless it's just one co-worker talking about another.

"You should see the ones in her booty cheeks, they are the size of dimes! It's hard to resist putting one in your mouth."

Cherish flirts back. "Remember, you can't eat just one. Hey, I need to try some new gear out for work! Would you ladies and gentleman mind if I try something on? Let me know which one I rock better."

Sky followed by Paradise shrug their shoulders signaling why not, and Freda and Barry follow suit. They have a seat near the discrete mirrored dressing area. Paradise orders a bottle of red wine from the unisex Salesperson, and they wait for Cherish to give them a show.

It took a few minutes, yet directly after the chilled wine was served. Cherish exits the dressing room wearing a see through purple and white teddy that clung to her quarter size nipples like early morning film on your teeth! Cherish saunters out doing a quarter turn as her ebony booty cheeks can't help but jiggle pretty much signaling to anyone watching, HELLO. Get in here and stay awhile!

She smiled and asked, "So, what do you think?"

It's Freda who speaks more out of awe than anything else. "You're beautiful."

Claire smiles flashing her pearly white teeth with the slight gap in the front and replies. "Why thank you hon."

Just then the streak that Sky hated in her friend rears its ugly head, jealously! Paradise enjoys being the light or life of a group. Just as long as you don't distract from her shine, you can be in her circle. If not, she will throw you shade! However, she doesn't take that approach with Sky, just with anyone who happens to like her more.

Paradise said in a passive aggressive way. "I think you would better in red, it would mesh better with your wonderful skin tone. Besides, Sky looks better in purple!"

Cherish tilts her head not knowing if she should take offense when she notices her coworker slightly shaking her head, signaling just forget about. Instead, Claire flashes a fake smile before saying.

"Ok, I thought we were having a "girls" moment, I should get dressed now."

When Cherish returns to the dressing room, Barry can't help but sigh loudly. Like he's missing out on the best show ever! Sky flashes Paradise a look of being disappointed with her funky attitude. That's when the first signs of trouble erupted outside the Soft & Sweet Lingerie shop. The two unambiguous store employees exit the store to see what's going on and that happens to be their last fucking mistake!

The best way to describe what was happening is suddenly a riot kicks off in the throughway! WOREC Private Security are busy pulling people off a guy whose kicking and screaming on the ground.

However, when the Security personnel turn to grab another troublemaker, they too are attacked! People were acting strange, extremely crazy and they had hideous yellow puss spewing mumps all over their bodies. They bash the helpless Mall Rent a Cops with garbage cans, for sale signs, feet and fist alike!

Armed only with Walkie talkies and pepper spray, the two dozen Guards are quickly over run and done for. Curiosity gets the best of the 'base' as Freda and Barry blindly walk towards the entrance and out the front door. Both probably went to use their phones to post what's going on to their social media sites such as FaceBook, Twitter or X, TickTock and Instagram.

When Claire Cherish McGill exits the changing room, she is not caught up in the awe of the moment. Instead Cherish whispered in a worried hush.

"Is there an active shooter out there?"

From Sky's P.O.V she witnessed Freda getting viciously punched in the face by a skinny man wearing denim, breaking his/her nose for sure! The hairy man in Freda came out rather quick as hm/her attempted to fight one of the attackers. However, the sight of the bleeding eye felon was very frightening. Sadly, Fred/Freda curls into a ball and accepts the kicks and punches being thrown her way. The last thing Freda saw before being dragged off was fellow member of the BASE- Barry getting stabbed in the face with broken glass. Over and over and over again!

Cherish reaches into her purse and pulls out a steel colored 32. Automatic, seven shots with one in the chamber. She mutters.

"What the fuck is happening right now?! Hey, listen, somebody needs to go lock the door!"

Paradise looks her up and down and reminds Claire. "Honey, you got the gun."

Cherish replies partly in anger and partly in fear.

"Damm right BITCH I got the gun. Plus, I'm getting tired of your shade!"

Sky looks at them both like they are crazy and runs over to the store's entrance and slammed the gate closed, making sure the bolts are firmly in place.

Slowly she backs up towards the partially enclosed dressing room area. Cherish and Paradise slowly follow suit until all three are safely hidden from view.

Paradise mutters, "Oh my god! Freda and Barry did you see what happen to them? Should, should we call the police?"

Sky pulled her phone out of her back pocket, placed it on speaker and dialed 911, but she got a message that said.

"The East Chicago Police Department is currently experiencing high call volume. Please leave your name, number and nature of the crime and we will get back to you as soon as possible. Have a good day..."

The confused trio just stare at each other, as the sounds from outside their sanctuary begin to include gunfire and the continuing cries for motherfucking help! This is one of the few times that your ethnic background, your educational background, sexual preference or religious zeal no longer mattered. When you fear for your life all you want to do is feel safe! For the moment this is as safe as they'll be for some time to come.

It takes ten hours for the noise outside the lingerie store to somewhat die down. The gunfire has stopped. Even so, isolated screaming and shouting goes on for several more hours!

Every time one of the girls got brave enough to stick their head from behind their cover to grab a peek on the mall. All they could see were people walking around bumping into each other, falling, getting back up and doing it over and over again.

Cherish mutters, "Shit, shit, shit! I am supposed to pick up my sister's twins from my play aunt's house after my shift hours ago. I, I can't stay here any longer."

Sky is first to say. "No, honey no. It must be some sort of terrorist plot has been unleashed out there. I, I don't even see any COPs! "

Paradise hesitates but said. "Not even the Fire Department, which is strange because they love to throw water at the problem making everything, wet."

Even so, Cherish wasn't letting go of her sense of duty, just because she is frightened right down to her purple and white thong!

"I'm, I'm sorry, I've got to go! I have to go! You, you should lock the door behind me."

As Cherish stood up, three figures stumbled into the closed outer gate nearly making the trio shriek in fright! The stumbling figures look battered and bruised, one has at least a broken wrist as the bone is sticking out. Another is missing an eye and blood drips freely from the wound!

Claire Cherish McGill slowly sits back down and softly cries to herself. Sky scoots forward so she can hug her co-worker and soon to be close friend. Paradise not to be left out, moves so she can come around and complete the group hug.

Six days later, the crowd of stumbling people in the mall had grown nearly one hundred times its original number! Cherish, Paradise and Sky have been surviving on the bottled water and assorted healthy snack choices from the Honor Menu Box.

By day two the water in the toilet stopped working and they could no longer flush. Now the trio must relieve themselves in trash cans for pee and shoe boxes for poop!

The time had come to make a decision! Furthermore, it was Paradise of all people, who led the charge.

"We need to arm ourselves, it's time to find our way out. I don't want to die here!"

Cherish mutters, "Like I said I only have two clips and that's only thirteen bullets."

Sky cannot help but say. "There are a lot more than thirteen people wandering around outside."

Paradise's about to say something when she tilts her head, like she's trying to investigate a sound. She whispers.

"Do you hear that? Voices, I think I hear voices from behind the mirrors?"

Cherish looked at Sky then Paradise and muttered. "Girl, you, you're creeping me out."

Then came the light knocking, resembling the sound of knuckles making the sound of, "Knock Knock, Knock , Knock."

The trio was so frightened they nearly jump out of the safety of their enclosed area! Catching themselves only by the gnawing fear of what they have seen, was a bit greater than the fear they have not encountered!

The muffed sound of a voice attempting to offer some sort of instruction is at first frightening. Then liberating for it signals to the three survivors, at least other people somehow survived whatever the hell is going on!

It takes nearly twenty minutes before, Sky, Cherish and Paradise figure out how to unleash the mechanism that opens the secret hatch behind the mirrors. The first person to enter the room was Ernesto, followed by Celeste, Robin, Big John, Abby, Indigo and Earl. Anyone that has ever heard the term "crazy knows crazy", would have recognized that look when Earl and Paradise eyes lock into a quick gaze. It was a look of where have you been all my life?

All is missing are twin winged chubby Cupids shooting flaming arrows of lust and a stranger's acceptance free of lingering self-doubt into each of their shielded, yet fragile heart! Cherish points her tiny pistol at Ernesto who smiles as he said.

"Mines bigger."

Before Celeste could turn into Calamity, Robin enters the area and said.

"Look, please you lower your weapon, we mean you no arm. My name's Robin. What's yours?"

"Claire but most people call me Cherish, said Ms. McGill."

Celeste replies. "Even without a shower at least, smells like at least five days' worth, I can see how you earned that nickname! I'm Mrs. Valdez. Friends call me Celeste and enemies call me Calamity. If they could call, because they can't... I am sure most if not all my enemies are all dead, probably."

Sky goes on to say, "I'm Sky Harrison, who are you guys? Please tell me you are with some sort of Rescue, SWAT type of thing.... Right? No?"

Big John steps forward and his tone has a tender side to it. Much like a loving father or protective uncle. "How long have you three been hiding here?"

Paradise mutters, "Two hundred and eight hours, thirty-two minutes and forty-nine seconds and counting..." She shrugs her slender feminine shoulders and stated." What? I used to be locked in a box and had to count each second so I wouldn't go crazy. Sue me."

The room was silent for a few seconds before Earl, just like right out of a romantic rom/com steps forward, takes a sort of bow and said with Southern charm.

"My name is Earl, Earl Grimes and it's my pleasure meeting you. I am so glad we all have managed to so far survived the Apocalypse."

It takes an additional twenty minutes to clue the trio in on how the world they knew fell apart. Robin and Ernesto stared at the figures bumping into the store front window and knew they are indeed Zombies. Not the infected Bleeding Eyed fiends beating and pouncing their way across the several states! No, they are surrounded by the dead or still dying, Robin asks the one known as the Ghost Face Killer.

"Ok Mr. Assassin, how do we move this lot out of here and to where?"

Enestro scoffs, "How do I know, I only knew to come here! Because Celeste and I had a contract to hit the bastard that runs this place. Where we go from here, you better ask him."

She doesn't have to look; Robin knew the infamous Ghost Face Killer has gestured to her father. She sighs and re directs the question.

"Like I said how do we move this sorry lot, DAD?"

Before John could answer, Ernesto turns to Robin and offers what little advice as he could.

"My wife and I never saved anyone before, this is all new to us. As for Earl, well Earl is a man of many surprises! Yet I don't think he's the type that will run into a burning house to save an old lady and her various kittens."

Marshal Aquila chuckles, "Yeah, I don't see Earl Grimes running to put out fires. Start them to hide evidence, but certainly not put one out."

If anyone was looking, they would have noticed that Earl and Paradise hit it off like two Love Birds sitting in a tree! She complains about how she looked; he complements her on never looking beautiful. It is an old school courting going on and it frankly intrigued Indigo as she could not help yet stare. It's Big John who made his way over to her and offered some advice.

"Try not to stare, Earl might take that has you consider him a freak.

Frankly, it's better to get on his good side until he gets to know you better."

Indigo doesn't pull punches as she replies.

"As you did? I mean you shared a wing with many accused men, all tried on multiple homicides. Authorities suspected Mr. Grimes is responsible for dozens, maybe even a hundred unsolved murders."

John sighs as he mutters, "we were all on Death Row for different reasons and when you are waiting to die, you can't be too choosey about the company you keep. Muck like now."

John Hammond looks at the Doctor long and hard before saying.

"We have never met before, yet I can feel your burning anger every time I speak to you. What gives?"

Indigo's taken back and she takes a few moments to gather herself before saying.

"I'm, I'm so sorry. I was a victim of violent spouse in my past and I am somewhat similar with your story."

This time it's Big John who is caught off guard, yet he recovers smoothly by saying.

"Then you should know that my conviction was overturned. I didn't kill my wife!"

Indigo chews on her plump bottom lip and quickly nods that she understood. Robin approached her father and asked if they could speak privately. He nods yes, as Doctor Roberson wanders off.

"Huh John, I know I've been a real buzz kill. Still, I need to know the plan. Where do we go from here?"

John Hammond can see the fear in his only child's eyes, and he didn't raise her to fear any woman or man! However, they aren't facing ordinary humans. It isn't time to come all the way clean, yet father did his best to ease his daughters' worries.

"Long before I was sent away from you, I purchased some land down in St, Charles Illinois. Not far from the Saint Charles River, a nice size lot of 27.5 acres of land. What most people didn't know is that land was an abandoned Korean War Era, never fully operational Air Force Silo. It was never more than a big hole in the ground. With several floors of unfinished rooms."

Big John moves in closer, so he can rest his hands on his daughters' shoulders and said.

"Over the last fourteen years, I sunk every dime I made that wasn't ear marked for you, into a safe place when the time came....."

Robin pulled away and looked deep into her father's big brown eyes. He is still that man that taught her how to ride a bike and catch a fish. Still the same father that told her Martial Arts was a gateway to knowing one's limitations!

The same man that helped her get over her fear of heights. As well as the same man that got mixed up in something that got her mother murdered! Marshal Aquila went with the old wise saying when it comes to considering how do you if a Convict is lying? The answer to that question is simple from law enforcements perspective, is the Convict or felon breathing?

Robin stares at her smiling dad hard and long and before she could say anything. Abby interrupts their happy moment with breaking news.

"Ahhh. Hi, huh look one of the other survivors wants to leave. Something about checking on her family members on the West Side of Chicago."

Robin removes herself from her father's embraced and scoffed. "That's suicide, let me go talk to her."

Ernesto and Celeste look out of the secure front door. Yet all they could clearly see were the outline of blood stained figures stumbling in the dark. It's Celeste who first broached the thought.

"I wonder if our target is in the Strip Club?"

Ernesto stated a fact. "Maybe, maybe dead or one of those puss faced maniacs. It's been so many years since we had the contract. We simply will never know."

Celeste reaches down and strokes Ernesto's big hairy balls and seducible states.

"We could know! If I remember right, we are two hundred and fifteen paces from the front door of the Candy Land, right?"

It didn't take Robin long before she saw Cherish pacing by the trap door in the wall. Attempting to work up the courage to see where it leads and hopefully to freedom.

Robin looks at Ernesto like why you aren't trying to talk her out of it and then she remembered their earlier conversation.

Claire has her weapon down by her side and her legs seem to be shivering. Sky is standing next to her attempting to be a voice of reason.

"Hon there must be a better way, right? Claire, you shouldn't go out there. It's not safe."

Cherish let out a bitter laugh as she replied.

"Not safe? I grew up on the West Side of Chicago! I am used to not being safe! But my play aunt's not. She's nearly blind! All she has is me and my no-good foster sister. Dumb Ho doesn't have enough game to strip, she gives pussy away like its potato chips."

Robin walks over, overhearing part of the conversation as she walks up.

"Hi, my name is Robin, Robin Aquila. I used to be a Federal Marshal and I am being honest with you. The roads are parking lots. It took us four hours to get thirty-four miles. You going to the West Side of Chicago, on foot, even not in those shoes, it's pure suicide."

Cherish jumps to her feet in deviance. "I'll figure it out! I must! When they said I couldn't ball, I went and worked on my handles and in my senior year my team went to state! When I was told I wasn't fast enough to anchor the relay on my track team at FAMU. I ran on the beach sporting five-pound ankle weights for eight weeks. After that I blew the doors off my competition. Lady, I don't quit!"

Indigo asks, "did, did you finish Graduate from FAMU?"

Claire lets out a bitter laugh as she replied, "no, no I had to turn to stripping my sophomore year when my scholarship got pulled over a fight, I had with a ratchet ass bitch and I, I did quit. So, I can't quit now, people are depending on me, I just know it...."

Robin shrugs her shoulders signaling I get it as she replies. "Nor will those things out there! They never tire."

Earl was busy telling Paradise about the secret rooms downstairs, when Big John breaks the news to all.

"Downstairs are supplies, clothes, weapons and other items that you might find useful. I suggest you venture down that ladder and see for yourself."

In a matter of minutes everyone moves back down into the Cartel's most prized secret. Sky, Cherish and Paradise took turns.

Sky's asks, "Whose stuff is this?"

Cherish's response is, "Oh shit, we have been sitting on a stash house this entire time?"

Paradise went with, "I am going too slipped into a pair of those knock of Levi's..."

Carpski hesitates before asking, "How do you know they are knock offs?"

Paradise frowns as she shows the name on the label, "When did Levi's start spelling its name Levitt? Anyway, next I think I would like some cocaine. Yes, yes I would very much like some cocaine and maybe even smoke a primo. Anyone have any rolling papers?"

Big John said, "I advise anyone wearing cute shoes to change into a pair of those knockoff Nikes, I mean Bike's."

Cherish laughed as she replied. "Bikes? They have bootleg everything! Look there's even pink bottles label estrogen. Oh no, I don't know if I would trust that shit!"

It took about seven minutes before Robin noticed that the Valdez's are missing. She has chalked it to them taking off to screw in one of the changing rooms. However, that's before a Dead Head comes tumbling down the open stairwell, breaking its legs with a sick crunch!

It doesn't scream, it never begs for help. The Zombie just clawed at the air moaning, then it was followed by another and yet another. Everyone stood in silence for reality just fell into their goddam laps! The smell in an enclosed space was so overwhelming.

Abby vomited on the head of the Zombie crawling towards her quivering legs. The first two ex-members of the human race fell down the hatch breaking limbs yet never wavering on their obsession to feed! When the third and fourth Zombie hit the ground, they landed on their brethren, rolled off and moved on moaning towards warm human flesh.

The Zombie that attacked Big John was mostly naked, missing part of his right cheek and his chunk of flesh out of his left thigh. His body's gray and his flesh's flaking and shedding. White crusted over eyes search for a prey it can't ever get enough of. The creature's cracked and dirty fingers slowly reach out for Robin's father.

Big John quickly picks up a ball point pen from a wooden clip board and rams the blue ink provider directly into the Zombie's exposed skull. It shudders for a brief second before collapsing to the ground.

Robin pulls her Colt 45 "Peace Maker" and fires the first round into the face of an approaching ex twenty-something wearing soiled skinny jeans and a blood strained ripped open sweatshirt! The force of the shell explodes bits of infected brain matter across the room. The sound in their enclosed area only seems to assault the ears of the living! Chicken Head ushers Paradise behind him as he picks up a box that reads, Microwave oven and bashed the head foul smelling creature in its disgusting face.

The sick sound of the skull being crushed cannot be heard, as the ringing in their ears from Marshal Aquila's Peace Maker was still going strong. Sky and Cherish cuddle together pressing themselves into the space between a well-stocked refrigerator and a big screen television, each holding the others hand in fear.

It takes a few moments before they are able to clear the room and the group can safely make their way up the ladder and back into the lingerie store. The picture is plain to see, the front gate's up, the door unlocked and the Valdez's nowhere in sight.

Robin's first to say. Great! Looks like our killer couple has finally flown the coop!"

Big John rubbed at the salt & pepper stumble on his chin and countered with.

"They have not gone far; trust me Ernesto has no reason to want to be out there alone."

Indigo comes up behind the duo and injects. "He's not alone, he has Calamity."

Four Minutes earlier;

The Ghostface Killer and Calamity carefully open unbolt the door to the lingerie shop. Starting the show off, Celeste calmly pushes the tip of her hunting knife in the base of the skull of the Zombie hanging out by the front door. Ernesto places the barrel of his silenced 9mm Rugger in the mouth of a moaning Zombie and quietly closes the door behind them.

Creeping as they go, the couple noticed the once clean mall, smells of human decay, sweat and blood! Moving silently like the professional killers they are, the couple cautiously hide behind overturned garbage cans planning their next move.

Celeste notices the yellow puss filled, Red Eyed fiends are mostly hanging around the entrance to Candy Land and over by the Coffee Express Shop. The Zombies on the other hand happen to be sprinkled all over the place.

She whispers to her husband. "Yo, those red eyed fuckers are hanging around those areas. I bet you there are sorry sacks of frighten poo, hold up in both of those places."

Ernesto winks and replies. "No bet, for you are more than likely right. Now, which one would our target be hold up in? If he were still alive that is."

Celeste kisses Mr. Valdez on his lips and replies.

"I think that piece of shit would be getting a lap dance. Shall we direct him towards his next one, in hell?"

That's when Calamity stood up to go to work, it must have felt like slow motion as her Silence MAC-10 rattles and tears through infected and dead skin alike! Ghostface Killer follows his lovely spouse, by dispatching Dead Head that didn't have the common sense to stay dead from Calamity's assault with full metal jacket to their foul faces.

It took less than three minutes to work their way to the entrance of the Candy Land Strip Club. A mixture of infected and Zombies mingle by the locked entrance, with their backs conveniently to the approaching Mr. & Mrs. Valdez

As the couple reach into their tactical vest and change out ammo clips, Ernesto pulls out a small pipe bomb out of his sack and smiles.

"Will you do the honors?"

Celeste smiles and replies. "You do know how to make me smile and wet!"

The survivors can feel the explosion down in the lingerie shop, causing Paradise to sheik.

"Oh my god! What the hell was that?"

Earl sort of pouts as he replies. "Well, that blows, I think my friends are having a swell of a time without me!"

It isn't hard for Robin, Earl and the rest of the group to follow the carnage left by Mr. & Mrs. Valdez. The smell of sulfur from freshly fired guns fill the nostrils of the survivors. Cherish and Sky are frightened and they hug each other as they step their knock off athletic shoes/Bike's over puddles of cold urine and dried blood!

Paradise follows behind Earl and not with Sky and her black beauty of a friend. She's not sure on why she's following the mountain of a man. Nevertheless, in her mind she's way too cute for hand-to-hand combat with flesh eating monsters. *Yuck!*

Abby and Indigo are lagging in the back, doing their best to stay close to walls and anything they could use for cover.

Their path takes the duo directly in front of the trashed cigar shop. Unfortunately, it's Abby who's creeping closest to the open front door! As they passed the broken door frame, together, the terrified look on Abby's face will forever be framed in Indigo's psyche.

Regrettably, Abby Carpski never identified the foul odor coming from over her right shoulder. She never saw the creepy gray colored fingers appearing out of the dark doorway, followed by the moan of a heavy-set woman until it's too late! The Dead Head had chucks of flesh missing from both arms and her left foot had nearly been chewed off. She drags her massive decaying frame from the dark into the soft mall light investigating the sounds of prey afoot and indirectly found lunch waiting!

Effortless, the reanimated flesh latches on to Abby's backpack and drags her kicking and screaming back into the depths of the dark cigar store. Indigo hesitates for a few moments before backing away first in fear, then in utter shame! For she does nothing to help her one time coworker.

Nonetheless, the poor woman formerly known as Assistant Warden Abby Carpski- lover of the Dave Matthews Band, town festivities, white wine and chicken fingers- died like she lived, with no one noticing and few if any people even cared! Indigo runs to catch up with the rest of survivors. For she understood it's no longer wise to be alone.

Robin slowly enters the huge, jagged hole where the front door used to be! She found various body parts littering the area.

A Zombie with its legs blows off, locks eyes on her, before allowing a dry hollow moan to escape its grimy throat, while it struggles to boogie its bloody hump across the dance floor! Ex-Marshal Aquila fires one clean shot from her suppressed AR-15 and continues on her way.

Big John doesn't have to guess what has driven Ernesto to act out like this. Hell has no fury, like a crazy ass woman! John trains his lever action 20 gage shotgun on the bodies littering the floor. He just hopes he reaches his friend before he does something bad.

On the other hand, Earl's trying to have a fact-finding conversation with Paradise, however she's way too freak out by all the death and destruction to be social!

"I said, you read any good books lately?"

"What, what?"

"What kind of music you like to dance to?"

"I, I, I versatile."

By the time Indigo catches up to Cherish and Sky, she has huge tears in her eyes and her face is covered in sweat.

Sky asked, "Where's your friend?"

Indigo was shaking like a leave in the wind, it appears like she wanted to faint. Cherish put her arm around her shoulder and asked with a genuine motherly concern.

"What, what happened?"

It's like a light goes off and Indigo straightens herself up, compartmentalizes the event and replied calmly. "She's gone."

With that Indigo walks off leaving Sky and Cherish not sure which direction to aim their weapons at! The sound of a man screaming allows the group to focus tracking Ghostface Killer and Calamity.

When Robin turned the corner leading to the rear office, she saw the Valdez's standing over the twitching body of an obese middle-aged Arab or Hispanic male.

Keeping her weapon trained on the couple she shouts.

"Hey, fuck heads! You want to tell us why you left our location exposed?"

By the time Big John hit the room he can see the powder keg in his daughter and the matches standing in front of her. He quickly places himself in between his daughter's and the Valdez's line of fire. His calm steady voice advises,

"Let's just calm down. No harm no foul, right? Ok? Ernesto what's the deal bro?"

Ernesto sighs as he spins a tale, he hopes sooths everyone's sense of hurt or mistrust.

"This piece of shit was named Pablo Contreras, and we had a contract to put him down. So, playing a hunch, me and Mrs."

Celeste injects, "It's the Mrs. and I, my love."

He smiles, nods his head and continues. "Yes, Pablo's, he's a rapist. He raped one too many and the power structure above him defended him even though he was bad for business."

Robin countered with. "Bullshit! You two have been on death row for years. If the Cartel wanted him dead, he would have been dead by now!"

Celeste lowered her gun and steps forward; her voice is attempting to hold back the pain as she states.

"It because I am one of those this piece of shit raped! Me. He was the coyote that my grandmother paid to bring me across the first time I ever crossed into America."

The room fell silent, until Cherish and Sky entered the room and saw three of their coworkers huddling in a corner, too frighten to move or speak. The two women rush over to check on the ex-Strippers as Indigo wanders up to John and spoke.

"Abby's gone, those, those things got her."

Then she goes and sits at the bar. Big John looks at his daughter, urging Robin to holster her weapon.

Begrudging, she does as her father goes over to have a one on one with his friend. They sit at the bar, as Celeste plays bartender to anyone that needs a drink.

"What are you doing brother? Your actions got one of our group killed."

Celeste asked, "Who?"

Indigo picks up a bottle of Grey Goose from the bar and takes a drink straight out the bottle, then said.

"Abby. They, they dragged her away and I, I didn't even hear her, her scream. But ,but I didn't go in there after her. Could I, I mean should I have gone, right?"

Indigo ponders her own questions as she takes one more drink before pushing the bottle away.

Celeste scoffs, "Carpski! I had plans on strangling Abby myself! She left us locked away, like, like, like sardines while the world was crumbling around us.."

Robin pours herself a drink and states. "No you're wrong, Assistant Warden Carpski made sure the women's dorms were protected. She didn't deserve what happen to her, none of do."

Robin bitterly slams her whiskey neat, as John whispers to Ernesto.

"My friend I told you what's at stake, I need you on board. I can't do this without you!"

Ernesto looks up at the man that help him turn his mind from that of a cold-blooded monster. To one that's at least evolving! John taught him how to read, how to resist the Guards looking for a reason to beat him down. Even on Death Row, a Demon may gain kinship with a Saint!

Earl and Paradise seat themselves at the bar, while Celeste takes their order and serves them up with a smile. Robin is still pissed off and she needs some answers.

"What do we do now, dad?"

Celeste said. "Well, you should probably go your way, and we'll go ours right Ernesto?"

Ernesto took a deep breath and did his best to explain why they needed to dial it back some.

"My Corozone. If we leave these good people, we will be dead in under a week."

She looked at her husband with confusion, yet he held up his hand to signal let him finish.

"Before this WE only survived because the Cartel had use for us. We were wild, unpredictable, nonetheless we always got the job done, always! Remember they paid off the Policia, they paid for our medical care. Today we have no network and no support. All we have is each other and these good people!"

Mr. Valdez allows his words to sink before going on.

"Left to our own devices, we would fuck, get high and put ourselves in a position that gets one or both of us DEAD in under a week. For so long we have been like wolves on a constant hunt! From here on out we must be the Shepherd, if we have any hope of surviving this terror. We MUST find out how to save people, not harm them!"

Cherish and Sky walked over with their three scantily clad coworkers.

A thick white Stripper whose stage name is Passion. A short part Mexican and Venezuelan hotter that went by Destiny and a tall buxom red head that went by Dawn. Everyone needed a place, however, Cherish still has a place she need to be and that would not wait!

She said. “Thank you, and I wish you all well. But I got to get home and check on my nephews. Will you look after these three ladies, that’s if they are interested in your help of course?”

Ernesto claps his hands and signals. “We’ll all go. There’s a party bus located near the rear exit. I don’t think it’s been moved since all the patrons are more than likely dead.”

No one said anything for a few moments, before Paradise who didn’t want to sound bitchy and needy, yet does anyway, some may feel she pulls it off rather nicely!

“How are we supposed to drive to Chicago? The roads are jammed packed! I don’t want to die today.”

The sound of moaning let everyone in the room know they are not safe. Big John did what he does best, critical thinking. He replied. “The Gary Airport is seven miles from here. We should head there find some sort of aircraft and land it in the nearest possible place to rescue her nephews.”

It’d Paradise who said. “Wow that’s some real Mission Impossible type shit. No offense, I really hope you don’t get me eaten.”

Earl smiled and stated. “Me either, still I guess it depends on the connoisseur.”

Celeste scoffs, “Earl please, nothing’s killing you but old age!”

Book Two

Chapter I:

THEY WERE ON US FASTER THAN STINK ON SHIT.

1-138 hours into Infection.

Imagine starting your day off as usual, two eggs sunny side up, a piece of wheat toast, three strips of bacon and a pumpkin spice latte! You jump into your 2022 Subaru Forester and begin your forty-five-minute trip into the city from the Northern, or Southern suburbs. Traffic's bumper to bumper as predictable, it is 8:45am and traffic is sort of moving. Sort of...

Each dawn the sounds clattering in any given city in the U.S of A are typical, ringing of doorbells, honking of car horns and yelling of children on playgrounds. Mingles with the smell of car pollution, a freshwater lake, and the scent of simmering Midwest barbeque still fill most waking hours. Crowds of shoppers begin their day looking for deals as they stroll down Michigan Ave. Some Boaters may even take off for a day of cocaine with mistress or femboys for a bit of yachting on one of America's largest freshwater lakes!

It's a normal day at both nation's 4th and 10th largest airports. Long lines at TSA have travelers parting with keys, phone, and computers. The whiff of hamburgers, hotdogs and Italian beef do their best to catch the attention of hungry travelers on their way to somewhere else.

The protocol followed by operatives that unleashed the first generation of COVID-MOMREL-6, as well as the following generations of the virus; was to release the deadly disease inside various airports worldwide. The first generation of the virus is strictly an airborne entity! It could not be active by water, only carbonatites in its immediate atmosphere.

Cigarette smoke's a key factor in spreading the virus quickly among smokers and non-smokers alike. The COVID-MM-OLE-R latches on to harmful elements already being breathe in by humans every day. Imagine heading into your local airport seeing people smoking outside and not thinking anything about it. Do you ever see anyone spraying themselves with air fresher or hand sanitizer and not think anything about it?

That's why the first generation of this noxious plague was design to be delivered in that fashion. It's considered that for the most part, we humans are disgusting creatures! So small teams of operatives were sent to expose a nation's weakest spots. Sending the "**Red Death**" to spread across lands for all to behold a biblical sight for the senses!

The COVID-MOMREL-6 infects the host like a normal influenza virus, hitting you fast and hard. This was followed by raging fevers which boil your brain inside your skull! This will be followed by body drenching night sweats and soul crunching body aches. The first clue that something's amidst, will be the smell of cooked food, makes all that infected vomit out some sort of dark foul-smelling bodily fluids. Like clockwork, every minute and every hour infected hosts looks to spread the disease by acts of violence, spit, blood and of course motherfucking semen!

However, further generations of the virus are designed to be activated by either exposure to dirty air or by H2O. A simple rainstorm at an outdoor soccer tournament could infect fifty thousand people, who returned home or to work and infect anyone they came across! Thus, giving the gift that keeps on giving and so on and so on and so on.....

In the city of Chicago, the first sign of infection showed up at 2pm at O'Hara Airport on the Far Northwest side of the city. And at 3:49pm at Midway Airport on the South side of the city. The first reports cited mass fights breaking out in main terminals as 911 calls from frantic city dwellers needing help with a sudden illness, jam phonelines!

In two separate sections of the city, nearly four million people succumb to the feeling of the onslaught of the flu. Towards the end, their bowels empty, followed by their bladders and any thought of getting better withers in their own bodily waste. Even so, there was a small percentage of infected hosts that died on contact yet refused to stay dead! It seems that's a bonus factored in further generations of this man-made plague by some other asshole in a lab.

At the onset, law Enforcement would respond to what they might have considered to be Domestic disputes or even large brawl. Only to become unwittingly infected by flying blood, puss or saliva! During the old days, police always like to use their fallback slogans on why they had to use deadly force. Words like the suspect acted like he's on PCP or Angel Dust or they were a Rapper or simply they fit the description. AKA, black!

First Responders would say, the suspect had unbelievable resistance to pain, acted aggressively, would not respond to police command. Frankly, it felt like they were on some sort of drug. Nonetheless, this time Cops were fucking correct, for that drug is RAGE! It fuels their Adrienne, giving the infected a greater degree of pain tolerance. It clouds the infected person's judgement and exposes the raw emotion that most "civilized" human beings mask every single day of our existence. ANGER!

The smell of barbeque on the South Side has been replaced by fires of recently abandon vehicles. The city went up in a series of small, followed by larger gun battles erupting from house to house, block to block and finally neighborhood to neighborhood. At first people have no clue on why their loved ones are attacking them, stabbing them, shooting them or using their cars as battering rams!

The Red Death moves from neighborhood to neighborhood much like the fable of the Angel of Death descending upon ancient Egypt during the reign of Pharaoh Rameses. Like a tidal wave, large groups of yellow puss faced, red eyed fiends find each, Much other like long lost friends on the soon to be defunct, social media!

By four pm, roadways and train stations are filling up with people attempting to get back home. Some may have heard about the civil unrest; others are simply too caught up in listening to their music files or playing Candy Crush on their phones. That's when traffic comes to a sudden halt because people are walking on the god-dam freeway!

The first thought must have been another misguided protest aimed at waking "white Chicago" up to the plight of the poor and not so fortunate. Nonetheless, the truly unaware promptly find themselves being dragged out of their vehicles or tossed on the third rail of the Commuter train tracks!

Up on the North Side of the city, people stood in line to attend a Major League baseball game and came in face with the full brittle fury of the Red Death. At about the same time a fleet of city garbage trucks ran over several dozen screaming people, before smashing into the side of the fabled Wrigley Field!

The sounds of baseball were quickly replaced by breaking bones, snapping of spinal cords and running over screaming toddlers. The heavy men with yellow puss faced, red eyes fiends begin leaping from the driver's seat to promptly curb stomp anyone their heavy trucks failed to injure. Time to PLAY BALL!

Around that time, Camp McCormick was barely up and running before the outbreak began. Inside their semi secure location, the sound of police scanners provides the early play by play. One of the most revealing conversations heard early on; came from ONE POLICE PLAZA or **Chicago Police HQ**. A field commander was attempting to tell the Deputy OPS why his thirteen Policers had to open fire on a group of Hispanic teenagers.

"They were on us faster than stank on shit Chief! I mean they; they wouldn't respond to our verbal commands. And get this when we fired on them, they, they didn't stay down either. Hell, they didn't even show pain sir! I got five Officers on their way to the ER with bite marks on their faces, necks and arms. Yes, sir the dirty Beaner bastards' bit us!"

By day five there are no longer such conversations, or any conversations heard by the personnel inside Camp McCormick. Even the sound of organized gunfire didn't resonate anymore! Camp McCormick was much like an island in an ocean of shit, blood, pain and fucking Zombies! Inside everyone had to quickly come to grip with the emotions of having survived what their loved ones probably didn't. Those thoughts weighed on so many that major depression would have strangled the base if it wasn't for Colonel McKinney. For most being alive was a wrenching gut punch that will only be dulled by the mission of preserving humanity. For a few, it may be a reason to self-checkout! It was still early in the game, yet the option was always on the table.

Outside the base, the smell of the city was still of fire, or smoldering lots of mayhem because the Fire Department was dead or worse! This bouquet seductively combines itself with the smell of garbage rotting in the streets and clouds of lingering sulfur from countless hours of gun smoke. Even with all that, no survivor could stand the smell of decaying flesh and festering feces without getting sick to their stomach! With that, the first sight of the dead lumbering on both side of the main road heading north to Wisconsin and East to Indiana, resembles a long, long, long highway of worker ants!

The only thing that keeps the dead from converging as if they were a giant school of fish, was the block section of freeway Colonel McKinney had the military Engineers put in place.

To the dead and to the RAGERS there's no notable reason to flood down the embankment and attempt to force their way into the building. So, for now, those inside have safe harbor.

However, the living must be very careful to keep the noise down and their movements restricted too indoors. So, when the sight of a lone Russian Helicopter lumbering in from the East heading West caught the eyes of the Army Snipers concealed on the roof. They radioed what they saw down to the base Commander Colonel McKinney.

His only response was, "you only saw one?"

It wasn't until the fifth day, when Rear Admiral Lee relocated his command to the Camp, did any real problems start. With the infected, with those left behind and with the few that have no faith in the leadership abilities of a madman!

Chapter II:

COME WITH US IF YOU WANT TO LIVE.

180 hours or 7 days & 12 hours into infection

It was a great stroke of luck or timing for Robin and her rag-tag band of survivors, for this had been the time of the yearly Air & Water show! The city of Gary Airport was the usual staging point for the aircraft preforming on holiday weekend. That meant, there are plenty of vintage aircraft on site waiting for the weekend of shows that will never happen again in anyone's lifetime.

The highway-**I 8O/94**- heading North to the city of **Chicago** and East to **Detroit** Michigan was a valley of abandoned vehicles. A splattering of open doors, and blood-stained windshields adorned the landscape like a sad ass abstract painting! Several thousand or so Zombies wander aimlessly among the long line of parked cars. Not sure in which direction the mass should be traveling. Held at bay by only the embankment of the highway and a modest chain link fence.

The Gary Airport was mostly used by private pilots in small planes most months out of the year. However, there is one month, where Military style aircraft take over the airport, in order to provide the people of Chicago and Northwest Indiana one hell of a patriotic show!

The city of Gary had some of the worst property values even before the Red Death virus reshaped the status quo! Now it's no less dangerous than before, just the brakes have been taken off.

A mass gun battle must have gone down before Robin's party bus filled with survivors rolled down the burnt-out streets of this less than prominent American neighborhood. The one good thing about the Party bus was that it came equipment with a fully stocked bar! As it passes every home in the area, survivors had to notice every window either shot out or in jagged pieces. Parked cars smolder as a city bus rest in the living room of a once modest framed home!

The smell of decay, sewage and heavy smoke linger in anyone's nostrils that dare be walking around. Zombies lumber, stumble and gnat towards the Party bus as it must travel using front yards to continue its trek to the airport. The Zombie herd's moving too slowly to catch a vehicle going 38mph. However, Dead Heads won't stop until they get you!

When the Party Van makes it to its destination, it's not Zombies that they are facing, but RAGERS. When the virus hit, Pilots had been busy landing vintage aircraft from across the country. World War II Mustangs, Vietnam Era Huey's, even a vintage- Shot down in their Afghanistan era- restored Russian attack Hellcopter. Mechanics, P.O.L-petroleum, oil and lube- personnel, alongside uniform Security personnel, were paid to endure a rather hot and humid day, for the show to go on!

Everyone was more than likely busy working hard to make sure the Air & Water show went on without a hitch. No one probably wanted to notice the constant coughing of nearby coworkers. Still most people probably arrived unaware they have already been infected. Some may have felt like they have the flu, nonetheless they need their job! So, they reported to work as usual. The infection spreads quickly from co-worker to co-worker with every sneeze, expel of mucus and emptying of bowels on public toilets!

Several days later there's no Security stopping the party bus from driving directly on to the tarmac, barely missing the RAGERS emerging from out of blooded stain parked aircraft. As others appear brandishing wrenches, others with crowbars and a few have flaming axes.

Inside the party bus Big John gives last-minute instructions.

"With any luck, the Russian IS-791 attack helicopter's large enough to transport twenty-armed people has been fueled and ready to fly."

Cherish said, "Huh anyone of you know how to fly a, what did you call it?"

Big John looks at his daughter and smiles before saying. "I think I got that covered. I mean I was trained when I was in the Air Force to fly Army Helicopters, if needed. I mean I've only been a co-pilot, twice."

Cherish sits back and mutters. "Okay."

Sky looked out the tinted windows and saw the ripple of angry people converging on their position. She mutters, "Huh, what, what happens if there's no fuel in it?"

Silence befalls the party bus as the thought makes its way around the six degrees of separation. Robin takes control of the situation by giving direction to their dread.

"We can't travel on the roads to Chicago or anywhere. We need to go airborne! This is an airport, a refueling truck must be on site. You're all armed, it's time to get with what's going on for we don't have time to hold your hand..."

The rescued white stripper Passion slowly raised her hand and spoke. "Sorry, but we're not armed."

Robin sighs and replies. "Well, then don't get off the bus and pray we get this right. As you can see there is nowhere to go, but up!"

Celeste raised the next good point. "Just where are we supposed to go? I mean after we land a helicopter on what, the West Side of Chicago to find a couple of young boys?"

Big John slams on breaks and the party bus lurches to a stop, he turns and tells everyone in a hurried voice.

"Listen I know a place, now we will work together, we will pull this off! Earl with his new friend and Indigo exit the Bus and provide fire at anything approaching from our rear. I need Ghost Face Killer and Calamity to protective my front. While Robin and I head straight for the cockpit. Everyone fights, everyone lives. You got to believe that!"

Seconds later the first RAGERS crashes into the Bus doors banging on it with bloody fist and metal pipes.

Paradise mutters, "No, no, no. I'm not going out there! Gun of not FUCK THAT."

Earl sort of frowns, like he just bit into something sour, he softly stated.

"How you perish, is never as important as how you lived. I know we just met, still have a little faith in yourself and me. Trust me when I say, the world is finally in my element!"

Outside there's a Heavy set RAGER attempting to pry a grimy metal bar into the party bus doors. And it has been joined by four red eyed fiends with yellow puss barring pores, all doing their best to rip the goddam doors open! Even if that means tearing off their fingernails in the process.

Once the door sprung open, Big John aims his sawed off 12 gauge armed with a slug followed by buckshot, into the chest of the first attacker. BOOM, BOOM! John stood up so he could aim directly down the stairwell and allow the spray of his buckshot to be absorbed by the heads of at least two of the remaining RAGERS.

It didn't take long before the more reasonable parties involved did has instructed! Robin followed her father directly towards the aircraft as Ghostface and Calamity flank them. Less than seven feet from the restored Russian aircraft RAGERS rush towards the party of four; howling and hurling sharp instruments!

Even though they stocked up in the Cartel's secret stash spot, Robin knew she didn't have enough ammo to fight all these things. So, she aimed for their hideous faces or the grimy knees! When Big John climbs into the Pilots chair, he just sits there starring at the controls for a few seconds. He closed his eyes, took a few deep relaxing breathes before exhaling, then saying.

"Robin dear, please climb into the co-pilot's chair. Before you say anything, I know, I know you don't know how. Please, just, just allow me to help you, ok?"

The first of many breaks happens to the group transpire when Big John turns the mighty aircraft on and finds the tank near full! He asks Ernesto to get the others and without suffering further casualties, the group manages to break the hold of gravity and escape the moaning and clashing of teeth that awaited them. For at least the next dozen miles that is.

Twenty minutes later the West Side of Chicago showed the segregation built into a city that prided itself on having broad shoulders!

Most of these neighborhoods presented undervalued habitants. Historic Gray stoned and red brick building at the turn of the 18th century. A marvel in their day were those three- and four-story apartment buildings. Now they sit in ruin and were neglected long before the Red Death!

Several Blocks further north, the same style of property would have cost you 1.5- 2.4 million dollars. For of course White Lives Mattered, so much more!

This's the area where Cherish had grown up, was one of those oppressed neighborhoods. There are as many patches of brown grass as there were broken bottles and used condoms! However, Cherishs' family lived in a high rise, on the ninth floor, in a twelve-story building rent controlled property.

At first Robin might have been nervous in the copilot chair, nevertheless not after five minutes in the air. It gave great delight to John to see his beautiful daughter filled with childlike joy. Yet their view of the city reveals the horror of seeing what happens when the system breaks the fuck down! It was a lot like Humpy Dumpty, except no one is coming to put the fat fuck back together again, maybe ever!

Not like anyone's left to notice, but in Syria after the Russian back extermination of Assad's enemies, now looks a lot like Chicago, or vice or versa. Some buildings are still smoldering with thick black smoke rising from structures much like volcanos attempting to decide on whether to awake from distant slumbers! When the helicopter approaches the location Cherish provides, John lands the loud Russian machinery as slowly as he could on the roof. Before he sets the heavy helicopter down with all its weight, Big John winches as he swore, he heard the roof groan. "GET THE FUCK OFF MY BACK ALREADY,ASSHOLE!."

Big John exhaled and then said.

"I can't leave, neither can Robin, for we are the only ones to fly this heap. I need someone to volunteer to get this young lady to her door."

There's a brief silence for a mere second before Sky said. "I'll do it."

Paradise let out a loud dramatic sigh and said with fright. "NO! I'm sorry, but, Really? Ok. OKAY! Sky if you do it, I guess I will too..."

This act of semi selfless devotion caught Earl's attention and he spoke in his slow southern cadence. "I'll escort these ladies to their destination. It's the least I could do. Ernesto, would you mind taking a stroll?"

Ghostface Killer looks at Calamity and she smiles before saying.

"Oh, I'm not going. I'm going to stay here sharing a bottle of Tequila I lifted from that party bus with those three dancers. When you return, I'll tell you which one we'll be sharing when you get back. Ok my love? Listen Ladies I left my girlfriend for my husband, buuuttt... I still love a little inhouse pussy now and then!"

A few moments later the roof top stairwell door opened and the area's pitch black. Ernesto takes each step very slowly, while holding a mini flashing in his left hand and a 45. Caliber Browning with homemade suppressor in his right! Ernesto's' backs pressed to the wall as his brown eyes attempt to adjust to the arid smell that presses into the very fabric of their eyeballs.

Cherish was slowly moving down the wall in the same fashion as the man in front of her. Instead of a flashlight, she used her now useless cellphone for something it wasn't designed for, precious light. Ernesto instructed her to keep her weapon pointed at the ground, he would rather get accidentally shot in the foot, than the back of his head!

Sky cautiously follows behind Cherish, her cellphone has the flashlight app which flashes every twenty-five seconds. Turning itself off before asking if you wanted to rate the app. Frankly, in the eerie darkness of the effect is bone chilling. Paradise followed Sky like a younger sibling not wanting to get left in a haunted house on Halloween night!

She doesn't have a flashlight, so Paradise must rely on Earl bringing up her rear, with his emergency tactical flashlight aimed over the railing, helping lead Ernesto floor by floor. The stairwell was wet with humidity, steeped with garbage and dried blood or human waste smears just about everything that needed to be touched! Ernesto stops on the eleventh floor because he thinks he heard something bumping against the door he's about to pass. Ernesto held his arm out to halt the group and it encountered Cherishes' plump Levitt jean clad hips.

She could not feel his smile yet Cherish sure thought she could feel his delight! Instinct tells the Ghost Face Killer that each floor could possess dozens of infected. The key to this operations to insert quietly for as long as possible.

Ernesto checks his silencer making sure it's properly equipped for immediate service. Earl clears his throat to get Ernesto's attention, then shines his light further down the stairwell. The point man can see an obstruction of wooden furniture, mattresses, tables and sofas. Ernesto nods that he understands, the group must cut through to the other stairwell.

Ernesto turns his head so he can whisper to Cherish.

"We need to cut through to the other stairwell. I need you to open this door so I can clear whatever's on the other side. Once I clear this door, remember don't shoot me in the back of the head for my Calamity won't be happy."

She nods her head she understood.

Sky leans forwards so she could whisper supportive words in her co-worker, turned ally's ear.

"Don't worry we'll get through this. I grew up a Navy brat, in an NRA household, I won't be shooting you accidently or otherwise."

Paradise fights down her fear of the darkness that has engulfed her entire life. It feels like she's suffocating, making Paradise ready to quell over at the knees and take a header eleven floors down for the ultimate time out. Just when she feels herself ready to take the free fall of fame!

Chicken Head's strong hands grab Paradise around her shoulders, pulling the radiant transgender back from utter destruction. He whispers to the one-time YouTube star.

"Don't go falling for anything, but me. Head back up three floors and wait with the others."

Paradise vigorously shakes her head no, clears her throat and replies.

"No, no I, I'll be ok. Thank, thank you for, being there. I, I owe you my life, yet again."

Earl smiles and nods his huge head melon head signaling you're welcome.

Cherish holds her breath as she tightly grips the doorknob leading to the eleventh floor. She snatches the door open and the Ghost Face Killer clocks in for work! He flows around Cherish once again slightly brushing her against her exposed heavenly backside.

The first RAGER was banging a severed arm against a locked door. It's an elderly man by the look of it. Middle Eastern, red eyed and spewing vile dark black blood! Ernesto fires one shot in the skull of the infected fiend, its body slams into the closed door and slowly slides to the ground. Much like a cat strolling through its habitat, the Ghost Face Killer's gracefully! He's a death ballerina, Ernesto's focus was busy spanning all things up, down, left and right.

As he passes the next apartment the door's slight ajar. Day's old, dried blood stains the doorframe, Ernesto slides over to the entrance and sticks his weapon into the unknown, tapping three times on the metal door frame. Then waits for a response!

When nothing happened, Ernesto gently closed the door and moved on down the hallway. Every other door's closed and posed no immediate threat. Nevertheless a few doors remain open and one rest right next to the upcoming exit. Ernesto approaches each as he has done the first, weapon in door well, tap on door frame wait for response. Two apartments investigated, luckily for all, both yield no response.

On the way to the third and last open doorway, the stench of death roared out of the dwelling like a race car on an inverted wet dream! Ernesto gagged as the bile rushes up into his throat and he fights the need to expel the inside of his intestines.

He stops in his tracks for the Ghost Face Killer ears, pick up loud grunting and laughing! Cautiously Ernesto approaches the door-frame, before he taps his weapon of the door frame. Ernesto peeked inside the apartment where he noticed a heavy set formerly African American male; a RAGER stomping around in bloody boxers' shorts.

A pile of dismember corpses litter the inside of the filthy low rent apartment. Yellow puss filled blisters form a braille map all over the out of shape, red eyed, blood leaking bodies scattered across the dirty floor!

Ernesto motions for Chicken Head to join him at the door. Earl does not hesitate and for a big man he quickly moves into position. As the Ghost Face Killer's hand moves to grip the door handle, a blister filled hand reaches out and snatches the door open.

That's when Ernesto freezes! The sight of a Toddler covered in foul yellow puss filled blisters and a dripping shit filled Pamper was a bit much, even for a seasoned assassin.

The infected toddler probably had just recently learned how to walk. It's young face was etched in sorrow, hemorrhage dark red blood from the corners of its bloodshot eyes and bleeding ears. From the color of the diaper, the child was a boy and at time of infection probably around age three.

For the record, it seems the Ghost Face Killer's indeed human after all. Before death row, he had shoot up cars with families in them! Even killed witnesses in front of their crying parents.

Now, Ernesto can't even shoot a little infected child- that is intent on killing him-, in the face. Thank goodness Chicken Head tagged along for the adventure! Earl places his silenced 9mm Browning automatic on top of the struggling toddler's head and quickly pulls the trigger.

The infected baby expelled a foul smell in its overloaded pampers and fell to the ground. That's when the sudden thud catches the attention of the stomping and ranting RAGER in bloody underwear! It turns and whether it saw a grinning Chicken Head or not through its blood-stained eyes, will be debated later. Nevertheless, Earl saw him and with one squeeze of the trigger. A single bullet puts down the obese West Sider RAGER down for the count. Bonus, for it wasn't heard by a single living or dead soul! Chicken Head closed the door and patted Ernesto on his back before returning to his position at the rear with his new friend, Paradise.

As they work their way down the next few flights of stairs, Sky tries not to ponder long on what happened to all the people that lived here! She figures at least two hundred people live in a building such as this and they have encountered less than a dozen so far. So much blood makes Sky think that her co-worker's family might not have survive this after all! Then her mind thought about her own family and Sky quickly pushed those ideas out of her head. She knew this isn't the time or the place to get into touch with her feelings.

On the other hand, each step Cherish takes consumes her with fear, then anticipation, followed by an impending sense of apprehension. There is so much blood! The taste of iron attaches to her tongue much like a frozen pipe on a frigid day. The taste of blood was so intense Cherish must ponder did she bite her tongue and just failed to realize it.

Nonetheless, none of that has transpired and Cherishes' eyes can't help but pick up on the slaughter that has taken place. The absence of body parts makes the entire scene even creepier, nevertheless the small group presses on. After ten minutes they make it to the ninth floor. Cherish prepares to open the door, allowing Ernesto to follow his own protocol. As he held up his hand signaling, wait, they peered into the small window and both noticed the hallway is littered with Zombies.

Cherish realizes they are jammed packed in front of her play Aunt's door. She mutters, "Shit, shit, shit they are in front of my Auntie's door."

Ernesto tells the group, "There are at least thirty Los muterous standing in that halfway. Chicken Head and I call handle the first dozen or so before we need to reload. If for any reason something comes up behind you, shoot them in the knees then the head! Until then don't expose our position. Any un-muffled shot will draw more attention."

Each one of their small group understood the stakes and nodded their worried brows signaling, yes they wanted no unwanted attention. As Chicken Head passes Paradise he cannot tell if the worried looks for him or that she had for the moment lost her security blanket. Nonetheless, he falls in line with a shooter's stance as the Ghost Face Killer leads the way.

As soon as the duo hit the floor, Ernesto skillfully trains his twin 9mm targeting shots into any Zombie or RAGER in his path! The main mass of the group was wedged in middle of the hallway in front of Apartment 915J. Dozens of bloody hands and shoulder prints are smeared across its exterior. Chicken Head like the cold-hearted professional he's, uses one shot kills to clear an area of infected. Gracefully, Earl steps his heavy frame over the twitching bodies of the recently dispatched, much like he has done once or maybe even several dozen times before!

In under twenty seconds the deadly duo has done away with half the herd when the biggest RAGER stops pounding on the door as he turns to see Ernesto and Earl standing a mere few feet away. Before a moan can escape its parched throat, the Ghost Face Killer place a bullet right between the RAGERs eye! The force of impact drives the corpse back creating a bowling ball effect as it crashes into its cohorts.

Seven of the remaining twenty zombies crash to the already blood-stained floor. The remaining slowly turn to face Chicken Head and

Ernesto. Most appear as if they just stepped out of the cult classic film, Night of the Living Dead. The deadly duo stood side by side and allowed their guns do their talking!

Deep red blood flows from holes exploding out the back of skulls. Spreading disease and bits of the virus anywhere it touches. When Earl's silencer fails and his muffled shot echoes between the walls. Ernesto knew they better hurry this rescue the fuck up!

After a combined four clips later, the area's clear and Ernesto signals for the group to move forward.

Cherish let the lump in her throat grow bigger as she slowly walks to the woman she called her play Aunt's front door. She swallows hard, she knocks on the door as she calls out.

"Auntie, it's, it's me Claire. Auntie are the twins in there?"

The silence in the narrow blood-stained hallway's palatable as the gun smoke, bodily fluids and infection! Earl politely asks Cherish to move to the side so he may place his size 15EE on the door and press forward. Within seconds the doorframe explodes inward as the wood gives, however it's blocked by furniture from the inside.

Earl and Ernesto gave the pile a mighty push and the obstruction is dislodged allowing access to the modest dwelling. When the door gives, Cherish squirmed her hips in between the two men before they could offer resistance to halt her progress! The smell of death's hard to miss, even with the numerous corpses all around them.

The odor from a decaying body or bodies in a closed space's very hard to stomach! Still Cherish slowly raises her pistol, as her toned dancers' legs can't keep but shake in dread. However, she has the will needed to press forward! Ernesto slowly uses his hand to force her unsteady aim down as he moves past Cherish to take the resume the lead. He gives a nod of respect to the young woman, signaling its ok, I got this.

It doesn't take long before they soon find the source of at least one of the smells in the humble dwelling! A middle-aged woman sat dead, resting up against the stove. She has two knives sticking out of her chest and a small frying pan sticking out of the base of her skull. Claire "Cherish" McGill's play aunt rests in peace in a dried smear of her own middle-aged waste!

A series of Zombie bites on her arms, breast and neck, explained the poor woman's cause of death. All while Sky remained in the apartment doorway with Paradise partially breathing down her neck! Earl stood firm guarding their path making sure no unwanted visitors wander into the hallway.

Cherish follows Ernesto's tracks as he slowly pushes open the first bedroom door, to find the bed unmade and the room thankfully empty of dead people. Cherish found the courage to peek into the bathroom, only to notice the shower curtain was eerily closed! At that moment she nearly returned to the unsure young lady that was Claire before she found the calling of stripping game.

Nonetheless, the woman that is Cherish finds the backbone to extend her weapon and use her free hand to pull back the curtain. When she finds the bathtub empty, Cherish can only let out a large sigh of relief.

Ernesto approaches the last bedroom door, and he finds it locked. He whistles to Cherish, she glances out of the bathroom as the Ghostface Killer gestures to the door. Cherish quickly heads his way, she lightly taps on the door before saying.

"Hey, it's me Nef, anyone in there. Open, it's ME, Nefertiti!"

There was silence for a few beats, before the sound of shuffling of feet followed by the scuffling of furniture being moved from the sturdy breech. Next the sound of the tumbler turning was followed by the squeak of hinges as it nearly pulls the remaining breath out of Cherish' heaving chest! She inhales quickly and deeply attempting to ready herself for danger.

Yet what she saw from her P.O.V. make her heart swell and eyes weep with joy!

The next-door neighbor James Johanson Jr or Semaj- because the nineteen-year-old plump, City college student in' transition- was clutching Cherish' two foster nephews! The boys are dirty, tired, and frightened, still they're gratefully alive.

Ernesto enters the room, quickly scanning the area. He noticed the cases of used juice boxes, carton of finished Goldfish, an open load of bread, half a container of Peanut butter and one of jelly, several finished cans of Pringles and one gallon of water left out of three. A trash can had been set up in the opposite side of the room for them to relieve themselves and from the smell of it, it's nearly full!

The boys were the cutest little brown skinned, doe eyed, skinny 9 and 7-year old's left in the Apocalypse!

The duo ran crying and sobbing to Cherishes' side. Gripping her thick thighs and struggling not to topple her over. Semaj's last to come jump on the hug Cherish train bandwagon.

Even through Semaj might practice on his voice being feminine, in times of stress, he sounded just like a regular guy name James.

"Oh my god. Oh my God. Thank you, sweet baby Jesus! Thank you Ms. Cherish, I really mean it. Your Aunt she got bit, and she went, you know, I'm so sorry, I, I, I had to."

Cherish stops the young Pan gender, shaking her head signal she understood. Ernesto tells the group. "Come with me if you want to live. Oh, I've waited so long to say that!"

It's Paradise who heard a door opening down the hall and she softly calls out to Earl.

"Excuse me, Mister. I just heard something from down, THERE."

She points behind her as she scoots inside the room. Sky quickly follows suit. As Chicken Head walks by he said in his slow southern drawl.

"My friends call me Earl; you don't want to know what less than friends call me."

Earl glances around the crumbled door frame, and he can see a RAGER standing in the hall holding a shotgun. Coughing up body and dragging a broken foot, the RAGER limps its way towards apartment 915J. Earl isn't a gun guy, but he knows how to effectively use one. Nevertheless, he isn't a total expert shot like Ernesto. So, Chicken Head must steady his aim, his first muffled shot's a bit off and hit the infected male in his filthy neck.

The force of Earl's 9mm hollow point tears through the grey ashy skin, this action causes the infected to let go astray blast from its shotgun. The sound echoed between the narrow hallways and caused a rippling effect. Slowly other doorways opened and for the first time Earl's voice went up several notches in surprise and maybe even fear!

"Oh MY."

Back up on the roof, the passengers of the Russian escape express have little to no knowledge of what was happening a few floors beneath them. Celeste's busy making small talk with the new travelers.

"So, you blanca. You got someone needs rescuing?"

The thick white stripper replied. "Naw, just an asshole boyfriend, but I was thinking about breaking up with him anyway. I'm just a girl , her dreams and the end of the fucking world."

Celeste smiles and replies. "NICE. What about you, chica?"

The tough looking Hispanic stripper clicks her tongue ring at the room of her mouth and with much attitude replied. "What's it too you?"

Celeste frowns and states. "Because I saved you! Plus, you might look decent in tight jeans, I'm not taking no attitude off any of you. I've killed to many people to end of sitting right here next to you funky behind to take shit today or any other day. Do YOU got that?!"

Up in the cockpit Big John has been busy doing his best explain what led to all of this.

"As you know I have been many things in my lifetime. I was in the Air Force, I am a scientist and an inventor. My job as a freelance geneticist paid well and I invested in a never completed Missile silo from the fifties down near Saint Charles River about eighty miles from here."

Robin mutters. "You manage to do all that from Prison?"

Big John held his daughter's left hand and somberly said.

"No, I. I started this process before, before you were even thought of... Then I met your mother and life made a little bit more sense."

An unease silence fosters between them as Robin slowly withdraws her hand from his. Nonetheless, the father continues.

"I sunk nearly every cent of what I made into the proverbial hole in the ground. It uses to drive your mother crazy, but I knew it would come in handy... Five years into my conviction construction was complete."

Robin clears her throat and mutters.

"That was twelve years ago. How do you know the place is still every there? Furthermore, how do you know construction was completed? They could have just shown you photos of some other doomsday shelter?"

Big John chuckles as he replied. "I hired an Independent Property Management Company to look after the near fifty million dollars I invested into what I consider would be a brighter tomorrow."

Celeste interrupts their bonding moment when she popped her head into the cock pit and asked.

"I am not one to judge. Yet don't you think it taking them a long time to find a couple of dead children?"

Soon, RAGERs and Zombies began flooding out apartments blocking access to the stairwell going up! Ernesto was at the lead, he unslings his AR-15, leading their way towards the other stairwell. Cherish followed by Semaj- and the boys- fall in behind the Ghost Face Killer and in front of Sky and Paradise. Leaving Chicken Head to bring up the rear.

The moaning and clattering of hundreds of teeth clambering for warm human flesh was unnerving to everyone; even the serial killers and mass murders alike! For the stank odor of decaying skin, musk, vomit, blood and shit, made the survivors want to stop and empty their nearly empty stomachs all over the already filthy floors.

Two floors later their group begins to get squeezed between converging hordes of RAGERSs running up the stairs and Zombies shambling down their intended escape path. Pretty much leaving Ernesto's with limited choices. When he opens the door to the seventh floor, the Ghost Face Killer can see only a few stragglers lingering in the hallway. He pulls his silenced handgun from his waistband and calmly fired two rounds into the back of the head into RAGERS standing closest to the nearest open door.

He quickly leads the group into a vacant apartment heading to the windows to get a better glimpse of their position. Allowing Earl to silently as possible closes the door behind them. Paradise huddles shaking with Sky, but once she latched eyes with Semaj, she only thought of how she has found another Freda.

Cherish does her best to get her nephews to stop whimpering and crying, however currently that is pointless! Living in horror for the last five days have their nerves burnt out and maybe beyond repair.

From Ernesto's P.O.V. he can see a small roof one floor down. Nonetheless is angled more under the next apartment than the one they occupied.

He mutters, "Shit."

Earl joins his long-time tier mate at the window and asked. "You got a plan?"

Ernesto exhales before saying. "Oh, I got a plan. Look, I'm saying it's a great or even good one! However mi amigo, it's the best one I have. You know my friend, rescuing people is a lot harder than murdering them!"

Earl grins as he mutters, "Tell me about it, I was thinking about killing the Asian Tranny for being a self-center prick. Then she shows courage and compassion for someone else. Then we go rescue two children, now we are doin God's work mi amigo!"

Earl pauses a bit then continues, "plus behold you get a series of strippers to test drive with the misses. While I get rewarded with a plump chocolate fem boy ready to fall into my lap. I call this day a two'fer."

Ernesto shakes his head and replies. "It's great to focus on the little things...Now, I am going to unscrew the gas pipe and it there's any fumes let in it. Blow a hole in that wall.."

Earl holds up his hand signaling wait a second as he digs into his shoulder pack and produces a couple of pipe bombs and a stick of C4! Ernesto grunts and smiles, even jumping up to kiss the Earl's bald head.

Sixty seconds later a rather large explosion destroys the wall separating apartments. The group rushes coughing into the exposed hole, as Sky notices the door to the apartment was open and she rushed forward to do her part. Attempting to slam the door in the face of approaching RAGERs. Her small frame cannot hold the breach and cannot force the door closed.

Once again Paradise hesitates, refusing to place herself into the fray. Another selfish act, yet humanity finds a way, for James Jr. didn't. Semaj propels her/him 180-pound frame on a 5'8 inch frame into the fray. Slamming the door shut!

They duo looked at each other and Sky nods thank you. Then she looked at Paradise and for the first time in their brief friendship, felt disgust and shame!

She and befriend a person nearly three years younger than her all because of her internet fame. Over the last two years they had partied together, gone on road trips together, dined out in five-star restaurants over all the country; yet that's what made up their post-apocalyptic friendship! Even so, Sky finally got what her Father used to tell her.

"Real friends show up when you are in need! Fake friends talk about how much they wanted to help but didn't."

The Ghostface Killer finds the window directly overlooking the floor that hosed the buildings AC unit. Ernesto places another modest size piece of C4 on the floor and said.

"Fire in the hole!"

The Ghost Face Killer takes several steps back, aims his AR-15 at the blasting cap and fired one round.

With a BOOM, the shaped sharp blows a jagged hole leading down to the apartment. Ernesto looks down to find a group of Zombies starring up at him. Their infected hands reaching towards the ceiling, calling out for a hot meal.

Ernesto drops a pipe bomb taped around a box of 45. caliber shells, with a blasting cap as a cherry on top right in the hungry Dead Heads lap. The explosion shook the floor and rattled some to be forgotten photos off the wall. Seconds' later wet, foul, slimy blood, bone, brains and bile plasters what's left of the apartment's shabby walls.

Back up on the roof, Robin tilts her head and asks. "Did have one else feel that?"

Celeste jumps out of the Helicopter and runs to the edge of the hi rise, using the medium scope on her AR-15, she notices a group of people running across the street towards the only structure close enough to provide cover. The burnt-out shell of a neighborhood convenience store.

Her mouth drops in horror when Calamity realizes it's indeed her Ernesto! Much like flies to shit, his group is being followed by an ever-increasing crowd of RAGERs and Zombies.

When they hit the ground, Ernesto scoped that it was the only place around that wasn't a Hi-rise apartment. Was a looted out two-story weather worn neighborhood convenience store. The second floor was clearly some sort of living area and there was at least some sort of roof still intact. Ernesto hopes the explosions signal to their group that they are on the move!

Even with Earl's hurling pipe bombs- like a major league baseball catcher attempting to pick off a runner stealing second base- in the direction of approaching hordes and at parked cars. The mass of infected only grows larger! Frankly the only way one could tell the difference between RAGERs and Zombies in the thickening crowd's that RAGERs hold an assortment of weapons. Baseball bats, crow bars, swords, machetes, Robar, bolt cutters and chainsaws! Rushing past their slow moving Dead Head counter parts, the RAGERs make a beeline for the fire damaged shell of that one time neighborhood convenience store.

Explosions from Earl tossing pipe bomb did do some damage if they fell among the dense masses approaching with intent to do grave bodily harm and dismemberment! Infected body parts are ripped from Zombie and RAGERS alike, nevertheless it doesn't affect a Zombies desire to reach the intended target.

Once the group of survivors approach their last hope for protection.

Chicken Head notices a smashed-up delivery truck resting at the base of a crumbled fifty-foot oak tree nestled next to the badly damaged shell of a neighborhood convenience store.

Ernesto doesn't stop long enough to check if any one left anything he might find useful. He just keeps low and kept his aim trained in front of him.

The stairs were dark and covered in dried blood and grime, nonetheless that doesn't matter for the violent smell of the crowd's almost upon them! Woefully, the upstairs apartment door is swinging off its hinges. It will not offer one bit of goddam sanctuary.

Earl sought to buy every second of time he could, when he rigged a pipe bomb across the splintered door frame.

Ernesto's keen eyes searched for a way to the roof as he turned towards the kitchen, the backdoor's nailed shut, however a hefty Zombie stood aimlessly in the area. Only noticed when Ernesto carelessly nearly ran into its molding back!

As the Deah head turned, its grimy hands and jagged nails, nearly clipped Ernesto's nose. Luckily, he quickly maneuvers to the opposite of the flesh eater as it turns to lunge at Cherish and her nephews. Luckily the Ghost Face Killer's quicker, he placed the barrel at the base of the creatures' thick skull and fired. It went down like a sack of wet cat shit! Smelled like it to.

The pretty hairs of the back of Sky's neck were standing straight up and she doesn't know if anyone of them would survive. The trampling feet of the oncoming crowd cannot even be masked by the pounding of her rapidly beating heart!

The fear in the air's as thick as the sweat beading down everyone's foreheads. Everyone could taste it, along with the bile filling up in their throats! Ernesto could see the huge tree that the truck crashed through the opposite side of the roof could be used as a makeshift stairwell leading up. Calmly, the Ghost Face Killer lead his wards up the last area of retreat without bothering to check for any signs of life or otherwise. Simply there's no time, death was quickly rising from the shadows to strangle the life out of their bodies if they do not move!

These are times in life it's necessary to be aligned with someone that is truly GREAT at their job. For that would be the constant planner that's Earl "Chicken Head" Grimes. He places another boobie trapped rigged in the path of the only way leading up to the roof.

When he made it up the big broken log, Earl places another pipe bomb at the top of the landing and backs up to the middle of the roof. They had barely moments before the approaching moaning, screaming and cussing from the Zombies and RAGERs overtook them all.

It is certainly not just another hot day in July! True the air is humid and filled with various hazards smells and everyone's breathing hard. Nonetheless, everyone was extremely frightened and wondering what the next move is! That's when the first pipe bomb goes off. Blowing a section of the first-floor kitchen wall with it, taking out a dozen flesh eaters in the process. However, that's merely a drop in the meat bucket!

Below the survivors, await an angry ocean of RAGERS and Zombies washing over the area like a toxic flood of puss and pestilence.

A moving mass of contamination fighting, nudging, shuffling and stammering just to get close to the warm flesh of noninfected hosts. The first several that found the kitchen stumbled into the room unaware of the explosive at their ankles.

BOOM went bloody bones fragments and infected puss across already stained floors! Even so, the sound made by the explosive devices only drove the RAGERs even more angry-if that was even possible. Soon the crowd might number in the tens of thousands or more! The kids are crying, as were Cherish, Sky Semaj and Paradise!

Ernesto and Earl are breathing hard, and everyone has their weapons trained down on to the barely concealed floor. By the time the second pipe bomb goes off, the kitchen wall collapses blocking the path for some of the less than agile stumbling Zombies.

However, that doesn't deter the more agile RAGERs lurching about. Leaping on to the crumbling wall and bouncing over to tree branches embedded in the roof, they seem as nimble as a derange circus troop! The first RAGER that ran up the earthen wooden column's brandishing a bloody sledgehammer was unlucky. Because before IT could hit the rooftop sanctuary, the small band of frighten survivors lit it up!

Ernesto and Earl might have been using ammo conservation with their shot selection, but the others certainly were not! Two more yellow puss bearing, red eyed- fiendish RAGERs rush out to the roof, both carrying box cutters. They rush towards Sky and Semaj and this time Paradise empties her entire clip in the general direction of the RAGERs. Hitting one in the hip and nailing another in the chest.

Earl steps forwards and fires one shot in the wounded RAGER's face, before turning to nod to Paradise, good job! It's getting tight, more and more RAGER's are attempting to leap up the crashed support column.

It wasn't until the sound of the approaching vintage Russian helicopter does the crowd of infected momentarily halt their expansion. Only to find Celeste happily providing cover fire as Indigo lowers a ladder to get their people off that goddam roof! It takes a painstaking two minutes and two hundred rounds to clear the LZ. Nevertheless, when then did, it's Cherish who said.

"Thank you, thank you all! I owe you for our lives."

She hugs her last remaining relatives tightly as their journey has just begun!

Chapter III:

THE ENEMY WITHIN, IS ALWAYS WORSE

Five Days- Twenty-Five Days into Infection

During the first several days under the leadership of the Air Force's Colonel McKinney operational functions as with life flowed in an orderly an enjoyably predictable manner. Colonel McKinney had done a rather excellent job of spending taxpayer's dollars in stocking Camp McCormick.

A whooping seventeen million dollars in as many hours! Everything that was needed had to be ordered and had to be in one days driving distance. That meant unaware enlisted Navy recruits would experience a rare day trip transporting bulk goods to their new location. At least nineteen tankers filled with twenty-two thousand gallons of fuel have been bought and stashed in the east wing of the underground parking lot.

Nearly a million bottles of water; to go with eight hundred cases of different types of American and German beer. 150 cases of scotch, rum, gin and tequila. Not to mention items like sixty -one generators, 200,000 rolls of toilet paper, 10,000 blankets, 5,000 cots, 1.4 million bottles of sweet tea, 75,000 assorted batteries,100, 000 cases of Ramon noodles, 850 portable showers, 7,000 water purifier tablets, 37 big screen televisions, 65 dvd players, 25 video game consoles, 450 video games, 200 microscopes, 4500 Petrie dishes, 18,00 DVDS, 25 radio-telemeters, 15 x-ray machines , 21 ventilators, and 9 MRI machines all from local hospitals. As well as just about anything that's not been labeled a banned narcotic for their stay in the upcoming Apocalypse! All courtesy of the soon to be sick or dead, U.S taxpayers.

The day before Rear Admiral Lee showed up at their base; Monique and Wynolla enjoyed their morning in a makeshift bed. They didn't have to share a quarter, they choose to, even though Camp McCormick has room for over five thousand souls. With its huge overflowing empty bays that house most of the Navy recruits. Which made up the majority of the base's military personnel.

Nevertheless, some of the Civilians and most of the Officer's weren't interested in reliving by gone days of their youth! There's plenty of vacant office space for private quarters and Colonel McKinney got the biggest since he's the ranking officer, which made him base commander.

Colonel Lafayette could have taken the next biggest suite, but she insisted that room is best serve as the base' briefing room. So instead Wynolla took a decent corner office overlooking the Lake Michigan shoreline; directly below the area where the helicopters are secured.

Wynolla, being the ever-clever old soul she was, managed to appropriate a number of items; including two air mattress and a single compressor out of one of the trucks loaded down with incoming materials.

She also snagged a personal computer, an assortment of blankets, two car batteries, three 48 packs of AAA batteries, three packs of 48 AA batteries, two back up chargers and a AC/DC converter. A 32-inch television, PS5, an assortment of DVDs, music CDs, various books and various video games to pass the time away.

To go along with two cases of wet wipes, six cases of Ramon noodles, seven family size bags of M&Ms, a case of 46 cans of Pringles, seven cases of 12-ounce water bottles, three cases of juice boxes, one box of condoms and two cases of menstrual pads. There won't be any way to recreate or manufacture anything, so Wynolla knew it's get it now, or never! Monique kept a cot in her quarters for appearances sake, still she pretty much has woken up all of the last five mornings in Windu's toned arms!

It's 4:43am and the ticking of the old fashion alarm clock had Wynolla awake for at least twenty minutes. She finds Monique lite snoring was cute in that, AWWW, sort of way. However, Wynolla knew there's only two minutes left before reality ruins their day. Still, Colonel Lafayette always found the early time between twilight and dawn, rather peacefully.

It's the slender moment between what people need from you and what you are prepared to give has not transpired yet. You are free to have no agendas, duties or personal ambitions! It's the time when Windu could lay pressed up against another wonderful woman and rejoice in the fact that she must have at least some redeeming qualities.

She softly removes the hair from Doctor Littlefield's slumbering face, in order to get a glimpse of her angelic slumber. Wynolla marvels on how Monique could just slide into rim sleep. Even after dissecting infected bodies, Monique could drink one- two glasses of red or white wine, snuggle up against a pillow and welcome sleep like a farmer welcomes life giving rain!

The feeling of her butter soft flesh pressing firmly into her lions, made it hard for Wynolla to sleep. Nevertheless, she doesn't believe in forcing herself on anyone. In their sleep or if they've had too much to drink. Her right hand slowly slides down to her counterparts hips, cupping it as she breathes warm air on the back of Monique's neck.

Wynolla cannot get help but get a whiff of their nighttime bouquet! The sweat of two bodies sharing proximity is hard to conceal. When the alarm goes off with a metallic sounding ring, Colonel Lafayette reaches over the stirring Doctor Littlefield to turn it off. Her elbow accidently brushes her tender nipple poking itself up through the tight t-shirt that read, UCLA.

She groans, "Ahhhhhh. Time to make the donuts."

Wynolla chuckles on Monique's ability to raise obscure slogans for television commercials from by gone eras! Doctor Littlefield always chalked it up to playing a lot of beer pong while in under grad.

As she draws her hand back, Wynolla' s fingers do the itsy bitsy spider dance down her thigh and towards the growing fuzz on her peach. The *California Girl* nestles deeper in the gape of Colonel Lafayette's bosom and softly exhales. After a short hike, her fingers encounter an obstruction. So, she whispers.

"Knock, knock."

She purrs, "Whose there?"

Windu licks the base of Monique's salty neck stopping at the top of her ear before replying.

"Little freak, little freak let me in and I promise you we'll both win.."

There's silence for a few beats, before Monique bursts up laughing, even with a bad case of morning breath, Wynolla' s still pleased to hear her joyful voice.

"Really? Little freak, little freak let me in? Excuse me ma'am, I have never been a little FREAK."

"You would, you want to be and still can't help yourself," replies Wynolla.

Colonel Lafayette gently pried open Doctor Littlefield's sweaty, consenting thighs. Allowing Monique to burrow her neck into Wynolla's soft kisses, all while the Colonel's fingers moved with the nimble power of the *Force*. She teases Monique by running her long middle finger inside the folds of her moist vagina lips. The soft moan that escapes Monique's full lips is one of utter pleasure, nothing like that of the Zombie horde!

Wynolla's stroke was busy sending tingles of sensations down Doctor Littlefield's spine as she presses her passionate and sweaty booty cheeks into Colonel Lafayette thrusting pelvis. While Windu's finger interacts effortlessly with her hungry clitoris, Monique's body bucked like she was struck by a bolt of God's own lightning!

She reaches up using her right hand to touch the side of Wynolla' s face as her mouth clasps the back of Monique's neck.

Monique whispers, "I need you to fuck me like you love me..."

As any good Solider should, Wynolla did as lawfully instructed! Fully awake and motivated by hormones stirring in her still manicure bush. Doctor Littlefield turns her body, so she can face Wynolla. Their first kiss of the day is right out of a fairy tale. Passionate, unapologetic and totally done to drive the other out of their minds with unadulterated lust!

She rocks back and forth as their legs embrace and intertwine allowing direct stimulation to their longing areas of pleasure. Their combined breathing becomes rushed and swallow as tongues fence inside hot morning mouths and tender lips place gentle kisses wherever they are fucking able.

Still, neither of them needed to attend the morning briefing with hickeys on their neck like they are so sort of high school knuckleheads! Their mission is to save humanity and most of all that comes first, or second this morning, but who's counting. Nonetheless, Wynolla stops kissing Monique on her neck and began massaging her back as she pulls her ever closer grabbing hands full of her wonderful ass cheeks in the process!

Doctor Littlefield's body motion had picked up steam and she must fight the feeling of moaning too loud or screaming out from the pleasure from Windu's night saber like fingers lovingly massage her amenable citadel.

Monique head's resting on Wynolla' s left forearm as her right-hand dangles by her gaping mouth. Wynolla quickly pops two fingers in her lover's morning mouth to keep the sound level to a bare minimum.

Doctor Littlefield sucks down hard on Colonel Lafayette's fingers matching the stroke of their bodies. Lust has overtaken them both, Windu must fight the desire to scream out as well. Plus, she's trying hard not to pull a calf muscle! For this couple, it starts out a good morning because their moans are driven by lust and the feeling of being FREE. Not that of being hopelessly and utterly fucking dead!

One thing about the ***Apocalypse***, everyone's free. No more cell phones, social media or FAKE NEWS! Being here, driven by the smell of Wynolla's sweat mingling with her own is enough for Monique. Even among all the death, it made her feel ALIVE, free to hope, to dream, even to LOVE. HOPE that the fate of the world will end with one of the teams finding some way to battle this horrible goddam plague!

Monique had been milling over in her head how to propose they slip away, take their chances, somewhere cold. All they know so far is the virus itself might go dormant in cold weather. For in the aftermath, there will still be RAGERs, and they hope far less active. Most might even freeze to death; however, come spring they will reanimate into- wet skin falling off their rotten bones- Zombies.

However, right now having another human being in tune with her needs and desires was good as the day will get.

After thirty minutes of bliss! Monique and Wynolla part for the next several hours, each heading their separate ways. Colonel Lafayette to do her morning workout and Doctor Littlefield to the female's shower area.

It's a short jog up over to the south wing, where the helicopters are positioned facing the lake. This portion of Camp McCormick is currently being used solely as a staging area for nonperishable resources. Two guards sit lazily around the crates until Colonel Lafayette jogs into the area. The duo quickly leaped to attention as Windu slows to a stop.

Bothof the young enlisted personnel are no older than nineteen years old, and Wynolla has made it his business to get know as many of the enlist personal and Officers she could in the last five days. She strives to establish a rapport with those under her command.

This outbreak, this Red Death was no joke, a true extinction level event! Even with some of the most talented people left in the world working on it and with a limited road map of the virus, they still have a tough if not impossible task at hand! Windu jogs in place as he asks the first Seabee.

"Rough night?"

The Sailor that Colonel Lafayette addresses is a freckled face, red haired kid with crooked teeth and a scar on his forehead. He nearly shouts.

"No Ma'am!"

Wynolla nodded, having to remember the base is staffed with far more recruits right out of basic training than seasoned military personnel. The next sentry is a bit older and a Marine of Hispanic descent, he stood at attention and replies, but didn't shout.

"Besides the moaning of the dead, Colonel not much to report. Two of the doctors came down and signed for a case of waxed candles. Other than nothing else. Ma'am."

Wynolla stares off at the surf smoothly rolling in off the lake and said.

Wynolla replies. "At ease then. It's probably going to be hot and humid once more. God, I wish we could go jump in that lake, don't you?"

No one answered, the recruit out of fear of being wrong and the Marine out of fear of sounding less than bad ass. Wynolla looks at the young people and sighs.

"Get a hot meal and enjoy the short time off. I will be down here for the next hour. Report back in in fifty eight minutes.."

Both men smile, do a quick salute and about face and take off to do whatever men do when then get fifty-eight minutes to themselves!

It took about fifteen seconds for Colonel Lafayette to jog up the cold metal stairs that lead to the highest place on the roof. Her journey takes him past eight Army Helicopters lazily basking in the rising sun. Each's positioned facing away from the lake just in case anyone was left alive in the city to spot them.

Plus being up this high allows anyone to peer over the top of the South structure into the army of the dead. With the sun rising over Lake Michigan and at just the proper angle to reflect upon the freshwater lake. It kind of resembles a glowing disco ball to anyone left alive to notice.

Wynolla's' daily workout included some rigorous stretching she learned from a Hindu Military attaché she met in London several years prior.

He was handsome and insanely limber! He also felt Wynolla should be as well. Together they spent the better part of a month exploring the meaning of the Karma Sutra. The best three weeks she had spent since she was thirteen and found out she was going to summer camp with her two best friends!

Which in fact turned out to be the worst two weeks of her life because one of Windu's companions caught a serve asthma attack in week two. Which sent him to the ER, then home for the summer. While her other friend, well it wasn't until Wynolla was older that she would reflect on that she left her friend to be molested at the hands of an older student/ Camp Counselor.

Flash back to sixteen years prior, Wynolla and her other best friend Randy Ballard are in a rowboat with a nineteen-year-old white male with long dirty blond hair named Ted. He wore thick black glasses and he just felt creepy! As Wynolla remembers Ted was rowing them towards a small island at the edge of the swamp. As the boat got further from land, Wynolla got a sick feeling in the pit of her stomach!

She didn't know what it was, maybe it was how Ted always smelled sour, like expired milk. Nevertheless, she knew she didn't care about the candy promised by strange looking, scurvy beard wearing, older teen. Windu remembers trying to signal to her friend that she was going to jump. Knowing they both weren't great swimmers, Wynolla was hoping for misery loves company as they both laugh while they doggy paddle back to shore. Windu patted her husky friend on his back and quickly stood up and sort of belly flops in the cool water.

Wynolla remembers swimming as fast as she could, never looking back, occasionally swallowing cold nasty water, gagging for dear life. Even so young Wynolla never allowing herself to stop! When she finally makes it to shore, she must struggle to pull herself exhausted frame out of the water. In the end Wynolla collapsed out of sheer exhaustion. Nonetheless young Windu's yet to be defined muscles, ached and she didn't move for nearly an hour!

It was only the smell of meat cooking over open coals that forced Wynolla to finally open her brown eyes. She heads off to his eight-person cabin for a well-deserved shower, then a change of clothes. She didn't give it a second thought at the time, nonetheless Wynolla didn't see the tall skinny creepy Ted or her friend

Randy Ballard at dinner. Hours went by and she didn't see them at lights out!

The next morning during the headcount an alarm was raised signaling a missing child. Adults were pacing about all day and most of the night. At first the blame's cast on the night shift for not doing a proper head count. Followed by the night shift blaming the day shift for getting all the qualified personnel. It wasn't until East Baton Rouge Parrish Sheriff's department began talking to Randy's bunk mates that a clear picture is formed.

Wynolla told of her encounter with long dirty blond-haired beard wearing Ted. Sadly, it wasn't long before Randy's naked asphyxiated corpse was found left partially buried in a small swamp bog!

Later, it came out in civil court that the camp failed to uncover that Ted was a registered sex offender working under a phony name and social security number. The identity Ted Figgins, used by the pedophile under was barely nineteen. While in real life the rapist and murderer Lloyd Moore was fucking twenty-seven!

The Sherriff's office pieced it together, figuring when Wynolla leaped overboard and got free, that set the tragic events in motion. What the pedophile had planned as a simple blow and go from one or both. Turns into a full rape and murder, either way the pedophile knew he was going down for his third strike! Lloyd Moore must have felt murder was his only recourse. That day scared young Wynolla with the reminder of that bad feeling in the pit of her stomach! In turn Colonel Lafayette hones that feeling into a sort of sixth sense that seems to appear when things were generally about to go from bad to fucking worse!

Nonetheless, it's all due to the rape and murder of her friend Randy Ballard which has stuck with her to this day. Wynolla had come to understand a bad feeling in her soul means something and she has one brewing in her gut right now.

Time to train; Wynolla assumed the Horse stance, her right foot positioned directly in front of her hip. While her waist faces straight, and the back foot faced the ten-o clock position. She holds her right hand over her right knee and her left hand under her right elbow. Slowly Wynolla turns to the right allowing the hands to extend outward as they pass each other.

When Colonel Lafayette reaches an apex to her turn, she slowly contracts as she turns to the left, generously opening tendons and ligaments throughout her entire core. Each turn includes a rigorous example of deep inhales and deeper exhales.

After five minutes of that, Windu performs two hundred kicks a combination of outside crescents, inside crescents, front kicks, and karate style front kicks. Twenty-five of each kick, done by each leg. Followed by two hundred assorted palm strikes and or punches! As true Wing Chun practioner, Colonel Lafayette has strived to learn the ways of what was Southern China's fabled marital art.

Inspired by a nun, promoted by quiet champions and made famous by a cultural icon. Wing Chun was Wynolla's base art, yet like most serious martial artists, she doesn't keep a closed mind to other martial disciplines!

Windu has sparred with 7th Degree Karate Masters, whom which have enjoyed the sharing of techniques and ideas with a fellow martial artist. She has shared sparring sessions with Aikido practioners as well as practioners of an obscure Korean art form known as Hu Hrang Doo! Each collaboration with fellow martial artists left Wynolla feeling more connected to the universe as a hold.

Still, nothing compared to the humid night she brought Monique up here and the stars bore witness to the couple as they experimented in Wing Chun sticky hands and then found themselves playing Taiji roll hands. Wynolla could tell right off Doctor Littlefield has been formerly trained by a superior Martial Artist for sure!

Her waist was full and alive with hidden power. Every time Windu attempted to press her advantage, Monique would expertly neutralize the incoming force. By quickly readjusting her frame and allowing Wynolla most times to nearly stumble by her. Colonel Lafayette had rarely encountered true Taijiquan practioners before! Quan means fist, and there are few if any genuine Taji fighters in what was the American Mix Martial Arts circuit! So, it wasn't very popular in modern fighting circles.

Even so Monique Littlefield's the real deal! She knew how to use her art form to defend herself against an aggressive opponent. Wynolla didn't want to hurt her, and she certainly didn't want to get hurt. That night neither fighter pressed the competition to a painfully conclusion.

The approaching sound forces Wynolla to look up, towards the noise that nearly encompassed the complex. Colonel Lafayette scanned the cloudless blue sky, getting a good look at a at the undercarriage of a vintage Russian made helicopter banking over the facility. Before shooting out over the city and finally lumbering out of line of slight.

Windu has the same feeling in her gut, just like the day when her friend Randy Ballard failed to swim for it. She looked at his ole fashion TIMEX watch and thought to herself it was time to hit the showers.

Into their seventh day of infection, among that being the day of Rear Admiral's Lee arrived. Something else to be considered S.O.P. Standard operating procedure - happened. Even though the day started out exactly as the previous six. A squad of volunteers of Marines, Rangers, Black Berets and Green Berets would use the sewers to escort- everyone's decked out in M.O.P of course - science team members in search of fresh cadavers for much needed experiments.

By the end of their daily outing, Army Ranger & Green Beret, Captain Brown reported back, he swore he saw an S.O.S. signal coming from a building a mile north of their position! Yet, getting to it would take planning, nevertheless the young brash Officer was sure it was an S.O.S. and not summer sunlight playing tricks!

Then base commander McKinney, had been listening to the young officer's report when Jefferson Bullraguard Lee arrives with the nature of a goddam tornado! Yes, a big loud rush of air that disrupts and dislodges the nature of things with no hope of putting it back to together again. Yep, that's Admiral Lee alright! Followed by his constant fucking shadow; Marine Colonel "Dick Head- as he will be called by some" Dunson!

First, let's consider his aircraft never followed the protocol set by Colonel McKinney. Lee's Navy Helio didn't approach Camp McCormick from the lake.

Lee's craft didn't bother heading out towards the Lake a quarter mile before circling back to not attract the millions of Infected that wander without thought of direction!

Oh no, instead the loud aircraft makes a beeline down I-40 from Waukegan Illinois straight to the lake front on the South Side of Chicago. Well, fuck me stupid!

Lee's escaped from his base, bringing with him the unwanted attention of any RAGER of Dead head in a 34.7 mile ratios. For the second time Wynolla is glad she has chosen an office off the beaten path. When Admiral Lee arrives and installs the Colonel Dunson as his XO. Meaning Colonel McKinney had to move, he discussed moving in down the hall from Colonel Lafayette, however Windu advised against it by saying.

"We should not keep all our eggs in the same basket. Unless you trust the Admiral with your life? So far, I can't say I've seen any reason for me to do so."

As for the command structure's pecking order; as the ranking Special Forces Officer on site. All SPECFOR-COM, Army Rangers, Green Berets, a few Force Com Marines and all the Air Force Black Berets were still under Colonel Lafayette's direct operational command. Tactically she made sure that this force was spread out throughout the Camp. It is a security precaution and a safety precaution as well; they needed to be able to address threats immediately!

Under Colonel McKinney's leadership the first six days were surprisingly calm, and people understood their role in their critical mission to save the human race. Four days later under Lee and everyone has the feeling of walking on rusty needles and jagged broken glass!

Lee's curt, cold and sometime abrasive demeanor made it hard to gage whether it is all an act. Or maybe Jefferson Bullraguard Lee was just a massive self-absorbed prick!

It's the ninth day and tempers are once again flaring up in the morning briefing. The smell of freshly brewed coffee mingles with the odor of confusion and cigarette smoke stuck to the skin and clothes of numerous base personnel.

For the fourth day in a row the Civilian Scientist entrusted to save the world must argue why they need fresh specimens for their research! Admiral Lee's use of dark glasses provided the effect of an Italian Mafia boss sitting at the head of table. Giving the appearance of either sleep or barely listening as his underlining discuss family business.

Marine Colonel Dunson's short buzz cut hair style doesn't flatter his huge doe like eyes. The dimple in his chin, provides the appearance of character. Yet, his allegiance is to the chain of command= Read Admiral Lee. And not necessarily the Military Code of Justice shows his real worth as an officer and human being!

"I understand your frustration, HOWEVER, we just arrived days ago, and I still need time to study your Operational awareness projections."

Wow, that's when it hit Colonel Lafayette like a slippery fish full in the face. Most if not all the Military Personnel assigned from Great Lakes naval station are either support staff, AKA, pencil pushers, raw recruits out of basic training or are from the medical field.

Besides the 48 Ronin- as they adopted Army, Air Force and few Veterans of battle Marine personnel under her command began calling themselves- no one else has ever provided cover fire or fired a round at a determined enemy to save their life! Not alone a living dead one. Maybe that is the reason, present command was dragging their feet?

The Army pilots got the skinny from the two Navy Chief Warrant Officers that flew the last flight out of Great Lakes Training Center. At first the Admiral didn't want to leave his base, even when it was being engulfed in flames! He clearly didn't understand the rapid nature of this infection and once contact was made the base fell quicklier than you walking up the stairs while scrolling on your phone.

Now, he sits stone like, allowing his XO to hold most of the briefing. As Commander of the "Operators", Colonel Lafayette was responsible for Project Security, so it is in her realm to address what Army Ranger and fellow Green Beret Captain Brown discussed. Wynolla stands up and addresses the room.

"One mile to our north, a series of S.O.S. signals have been flashing for the last two days. It happened twice, the first time at 745am and the next time a quarter of a mile closer at 815am."

Wynolla tries her best to ignore Monique trying not to smile at her, so she let the words linger before continuing.

"Admiral, obviously, someone is attempting to get our attention."

There's a muttering brewing among the Civilian attendees. Colonel Dunson casted eye daggers at Colonel Lafayette, much like his squint was straight out a Clint Eastwood Spaghetti Western. Even so, Windu doesn't back down, for she knew her force was much bigger and stronger! Nevertheless, it's one of the rare moments that Admiral Lee speaks up. His Southern cadence makes his curt tone and cold demeanor seem out of place.

"I suspect Colonel you are requesting to mount a certainly hopeless rescue mission, resulting in getting some of our people killed. Or worse bringing the infection back to base camp...Anyone out there is as good as dead and we don't have the resources to.."

Monique is tired of this melodrama she stands up, interrupts this weird opera by saying.

"Excuse me, I'm so sorry. But what's our mission? What were we assigned to do here?"

Doctor Littlefield knew the only way to make any sense of the stagnation is to address the function of the Camp.

Out the corner of her eye, she would swear she saw Wynolla wink at her in appreciation. She paused, yet didn't give the Admiral time to dodge or deflect.

"Sorry Admiral but, like many in attendance, we thought we were dispatched here to save humanity from certain extinction. We were told the fate of our planet may rest squarely on our shoulders, OURS. Please allow us to get off our collective butts and do our very necessary jobs!"

Air Force McKinney stands up to offer sound Military advice.

"Sir, we could attempt to plot the next location the S.O.S will be sent from. We could dispatch one gunship for close support and the Navy Heli as transport. We then find whoever's sending that S.O.S, we can also grab and bag three specimens for the Docs. Have no fear Admiral, we can get it done! This is what we do, sir."

The room goes silent as Colonel Dunson looks at Admiral Lee for any sign of direction. He can see the back of his superior's jaws clenching and actually heard his teeth grinding as Lee said.

"I will grant you permission to attempt to locate the position of any so-called survivors."

He pauses for a brief second like he's still trying to figure out his next move, when the Admiral said.

"As for your request to bring back test, subjects, that request is denied. This meeting is over."

With that Admiral Lee rose- as did his XO, as did everyone is the room- and exited the command center followed closely by Colonel Dunson and three Marine enlisted men. Colonel McKinney huddles next to Wynolla and Monique he exhales.

"I really thought we had him that time."

Monique doesn't try to, even so she subconsciously she stuck out her bottom lip and pretended to pout as she replies.

"This is like being stuck in kindergarten when you belong in third grade."

Windu kept a straight face, as her lips barely moved as she spoke.

"Meet me up by the Helio's in five."

Five minutes later, the trio are sitting on a crate clearly marked, missiles. While looking out over the lake, each held a cup of morning coffee or tea. McKinney said.

"You think we will find any survivors?"

Colonel Lafayette takes a slip of his coffee, then replies.

"Captain Brown is confident he can narrow down to seven to ten blocks. Being up in the sky, it will be easier to find the signal that inserting from the sewers."

Monique takes a sip of Green, ginseng honey flavored tea, affording herself a second to savor the taste before saying.

"Yeah, but without getting access to new specimens, we are just playing summer camp on borrowed time. If Lee actually thinks the infection won't end up here because we don't go out, he's sadly mistaken."

Wynolla confides in her two closes friends on base, which the exception of Captain Brown of course.

“I think Rear Admiral Jefferson Bullraguard Lee is suffering from PTSD. Whatever happened at Great Lakes Naval Center has him afraid and maybe incapable of leadership.”

The Air Force Colonel McKinney tenses up as he said.

“Whoa, hold your horses.”

The Army Colonel replies.

“Kevin, I’m not saying the man needs to be replaced, yet. Nevertheless, you cannot deny Lee is acting strangely! He’s very distant and it looks like Colonel Dunson is actually running day to day OPS. We need to find out just what happen at Great Lakes, don’t you think?”

Monique wanted to interject her thoughts; however, she knew that a discussion between Military personnel. Nothing would be aided in anything a Civilian would have to say. Not when the hint of munity may be raising its complicated head.

Kevin McKinney has been in the Air Force for nearly eighteen years, and he’s seen all kinds of Officers. Those that have been squared away to those that have been pure *Shit Bags*. Still, it’s the ones like Colonel Lafayette that truly baffled him. She has the looks; she certainly has the smarts, and she had the Brass’s ear!

Nevertheless, with SPECFOR-COM gone or at least gone dark, Colonel McKinney feels that an Officer like Wynolla, needed a strong Commanding Officer to keep her for hurting her career. Officers like Lafayette are willing to risk it all, not for glory! But in the assumption, they prepared for all the angles. Kevin McKinney does his best to gage Colonel Lafayette’s intention.

“Look, Colonel you may be right, however maybe you’re wrong?

We are all under stress and I don't know how Lee handles his. Even so, we need to give him the benefit of the doubt. Right?"

Wynolla takes a sip of coffee before replying.

"Same question I pondered to you earlier. Are you willing to bet your life on him, Colonel? Because whatever happened at Great Lakes, Lee is wearing that shit! It's clouding his judgement and making it difficult for him to make a command decision."

Kevin stands his ground with a bit of grit, replying.

"We must remember this is still the United State Military, Lt. Colonel. It is best we do our duty, until a time and place that may or may not come. If change is warranted, we will address it then."

Monique attempts to change the subject by saying.

"WOW. What a view, right? The lake looks so calm and peaceful."

Fifteen minutes later Monique is in the lab she shared with two other infectious disease specialists. Both older females, one was a sixty-year-old woman with a Hindu accent and the other the other a fifty-year-old of pure Bostonian descant. All three were dressed in hazmat gear right down to the rubber boots.

The room was sterile as an operating room, thick plastic sheeting covered every inch of the converted area. Their movements mimicked Astronauts on the Space Shuttle, slow and deliberate! The older Hindu woman looked up from her microscope and proclaims.

"Well, that does it for me. I can't use have more of these useless specimens. What good is it if we can't isolate any live enzymes?"

The younger- yet older than Monique by a decade- red haired Boston Native replies.

"It' just an exercise by men in power, without the god given sense to ask a woman what the heck to do!"

The Hindu Doctor pushes her chair away from her workstation, looks at Doctor Littlefield and inquires.

"Speaking of women in power, why not tell us about that swaggering Colonel you seem to spend all your non waking time with?"

The Boston native chirps in by saying, "Yes Doctor, inquiring minds need to know, is she you know..."

Monique fought the urge to devolve into a teenage girl, kicking up her heels and telling her older friends of wistful carnal knowledge. Instead, she allows herself to divulge one steamy detail.

"For some reason I have yet to discern, she smells like warm vanilla flavored hot chocolate, and I find her absolutely delicious!"

At 01300 both Lafayette and McKinney join Captain Brown as well as the XO Dunston in the command center. Captain Brown explains his theory to his superiors. A large paper city map rest of the table and the four men are gathered around it.

"Well, I've spotted the S.O.S twice for sure and now that I think hard about it maybe three times. The first time, I probably mistook the last part of the message as random light infracting of jagged glass."

The Marine Colonel Dunson arms are resting on top his heavily defined chest, he breathes in deeply for a few moments then said.

"I don't see how you will be able to pinpoint the location of the next so-called signal Captain?"

Brown glances to Windu for support who nods to the young Captain to just tell it like you told it to me.

"Huh, well sir. Each day the sun's position changes and whoever's sending this is moving. They're sending the same message at the same time of day, but from a different location. Making this not an anomaly, it's a pattern, sir."

McKinney points to the map and offers his thought-out advice.

"If Captain Brown is correct, the next signal should come from somewhere around, here."

The Middle-aged Air Force Colonel points to an area just west of downtown Chicago. McKinney continues with, "All we need is to invest two aircraft allowing the detachment to leave twenty minutes before sunrise heading a quarter of a mile out into the lake before swinging back and approaching the city from the North. This will put the team in place by sunrise."

Colonel Dunson scoffs, '" What if you're wrong? That dam herd of infected just started moving on."

Colonel Lafayette frowns and nods her head signaling for Captain Brown to take off. The young Captain snaps to attention, then excuses himself. As soon as he leaves Wynolla takes the kid gloves off with David Dunson.

"Colonel what the hell are we doing here if not to authorize the mission we thought was already authorized as a go?"

The Marine Colonel's eyes betrayed what he fought hard to conceal. You know the look of I have no use for you, I consider myself better than you and I was born for this shit, not you! Colonel Dunson was the only one Lee's staff that has seen so sort of combat, even if it was in a limit role.

Fun Fact; before he has been with Rear Admiral Jefferson Bullraguard Lee since he was Commander Lee. He and Dunston served on the USS. Shelton, a light Cruiser which came attacked by Iranian speedboats in the Straits of Hormuz in 2017. Lee was acting ship surgeon and Dunston was a young Provost Officer, a military police officer. When three Iranian floating match sticks felt the awesome brunt of American firepower, Dunston never fired a shot! In the end, thirteen Iranian Sailors died for their god and their country and Lee and Dunston got battlefield medal to wear on their dress whites.

In the here and now, in his mind, David Dunson so wants to punch Colonel Lafayette in her big fat black mouth! He had a hundred pounds on her and Dunston wonders if the Army bitch could take a fucking punch!

However, he read her DD-214, and even before earning the right to be called Special Forces, the woman standing in front of him had been a hardcore Martial Artist. So, Dunson hid his distain as much as he can.

"We are here Lt. Colonel for me the fucking XO, to see that you two! Have your goddam shit wired fucking tight."

McKinney generally attempted to be the voice of reason and this time is no different.

"Well? Is shit wired tight for the OP?"

Colonel Dunson bitterly nods his head yes, Wynolla quickly gives a mock Salute and exits the room leaving McKinney staring at David who said.

"Why the fuck does that gal always act like she was a stick up her ass?"

McKinney replies with a chuckle, "Well she does. That Officer has a P.H.D and she's a fucking Green Beret, that makes her among the cream of our crop Colonel."

Twenty minutes later, Wynolla is picking the team that would go on this probably wild goose chase. Captain Brown was a bit hurt that he is being left off the starting squad.

"What gives Windu has your pandwua displeased you?"

Brown knew the Star Wars reference is always going to find a soft spot in Wynolla, for she fancies herself a real-life Jedi warrior!

"No, no, no my pandwua! You are still strong with the force."

Captain Brown dropped the act and he spoke like he was kind of hurt. "Then what gives ma'am I mean; I'm riding the bench on this one?"

Colonel Lafayette pulls the young Captain to the side lowering her tone.

"I need you to look after and by look after I mean shadow Doctor Littlefield."

The young Captain was taken back and he asked permission to speak freely, which Wynolla granted.

"Colonel, you want me to baby sit your girlfriend?"

Wynolla tried not to smile, she could see how Lance Brown might have taken her request.

"Lance, something is strange going on with command. These civilian scientists are our top priority and if something happens to them, our world might never recover from an event worse than the Bronze Age Collapse!

Windu let those words linger for a moment before continuing with; "So, yes! I need you to watch over my girlfriend and all the Doctors while I'm gone. Pull seven Operators and get ghost, let no one see your team until we get back. By all means keep those scientists safe, and yes, especially my girlfriend. Give me the names and I will include them with yours in my duty roster. Is that cool with you Captain?"

Captain Brown forced a smile and nodded that he understood.

It is 2100 hours and one lantern, and one strawberry scent candle illuminate the personal quarters of Colonel Lafayette. Monique was sitting at the makeshift desk, dressed in tight yellow yoga pants and a loose-fitting t-shirt that read CDC. She's busy typing on her laptop, when three sharp knocks are followed by one single one.

That is the code to unlock the door for Wynolla, who slides in wearing a flatter less robe and flip flops. Her brown curly was hair still damp from her nightly shower. Monique had dated some women that only showered once a day, she personally found that gross and never dated them for long! So, she was surprised to see this tough Green Beret enjoys taking warm showers and she confessed even long warm bubble baths.

Once she explained her rational, it made perfect sense to Monique. Wynolla told her if you ever had to sit in the waste of a farm animal so you're not discovered by enemy combatants, or you can't shower because you're in the field for a grueling twenty-one days.

You kind of develop a deep appreciation for some of the trappings of civilization. Things like a hot shower, a clean bed and soft pillow make all the difference- whether you want to accept this or not- those luxuries made a person feel wonderfully human!

Monique greets Wynolla with a deep, passionate kiss. Their tongues met in a whirl of fury and passion that when they parted, Wynolla's face was kind of wet and frankly she didn't mind a bit. New love is like discovering that high school wasn't all bad! Wynolla noticed the open bottle of white wine and knew Monique had been relaxing.

"I would have been here earlier, but I worked up a real sweat getting our T.O.E. really for tomorrow."

Monique heads back over to her computer to shut it off. She bends over forty-five degrees and her left foot leaves the ground, flirting as she replies.

"I don't mind a wee bit of stink on my gal, it's kind of cave womanish! Besides, I have toes you can take care of, so win, win."

Her foot just happens to reach, Colonel Lafayette's robe covered vagina.

Monique gently uses her purple-colored manicured toes to massage the awaking face of Windu's clit. The smell of the strawberry scented candle and the glass of wine Monique had been slipping on had her feeling rather bubbly!

Wynolla stood firm allowing her robe to open, the cold of her feet caused a proverbial stirring of her womanhood. Which's more than willing to respond to the occasion, as Wynolla offers hushed whispers. The ones we suggest when lust is busy weaving the tapestry of our psyche!

"Yes, I can feel how these toes are, perfect. Sadly, I was speaking on our tactical operational equipment that the team will be taking with us tomorrow."

Monique brings her foot back to the floor and from Colonel Lafayette's P.O.V. her well rounded butt cheeks resembled an artist depiction of a Valentine 's Day heart! The yellow yoga pants really hugged her twenty-seven-year-old hips just right.

Monique bounces up, turns around and from her P.O.V. the sight of her mocha lover, standing oiled up- and nipples clearly motivated by the statement in front of her- entices Monique to step into her arms. Their kiss was just a prelude to the carnal favors that await them! Even in the best of times love is always fleeting. Yet even in the apocalypse, love could be fostered.

Wynolla's firm hands roam freely over her loves willing body. Monique's tan lines might be fading, still her skin still's baby soft. Wynolla pulls her as close, helping her shimmy out the yoga pants to reveal a complete shaved vagina in much needed oral consumption!

When Monique starts to pull off her L.A Chargers T-shirt, Wynolla signals for her to leave it on. She allows her robe to hit the cold floor as she guides them both over to the air mattress. Wynolla lays on her back so Monique could straddle her defined frame. She sits on her soul mate, running her capable fingers along Wynolla's pear shaped breast. Monique smelled it again and this time she had to inquire.

"Why do you always smell like, like warm vanilla?"

Colonel Lafayette chuckles as she replies.

"Coco-coco butter and vanilla lotion combination, I perfected it myself."

Monique nods her head like she's impressed, as she leans to the right to pick up her cellphone. Windu's fully aroused clits rubs gently across Monique's'. Wynolla really loves that Monique had a brilliant mind, then again, she silently thanks the heavens above Doctor Littlefield had a great ass! Monique scrolls through the music files- downloaded on her phone long before the world went to shit- and whispers in a sultry, yet playful voice.

"Oh, that's how the attractive, bi curious Army Doctor turned Green Beret, pampers herself! Do you care to see how I spell relief?"

Monique starts her playlist and the first song's **Aero Smith's I don't want to miss a thing,** begins as she gently slides the hair from in front of her face and leans forward. The feeling of their kiss stirs emotions neither thought possible a few days ago! Maybe it just maybe it was something more. Only time will write their tale.

" I could stay awake just to hear your breathing.. Watch you smile when you are sleeping, when you are far, far off dreaming."

Maybe it is their hormones or maybe it's just the end of the world?

Whatever the case, Monique's heart was unable to contain the way it feels when they are together! Doctor Littlefield's clever tongue licks Wynolla's mocha skin and Wynolla shudders as her grip on Monique's hips secures their mutual fondness of Doctor Littlefield's round bottom! It showed commitment to personal exercise and Wynolla could only wish she had a third hand to pick up the slack of booty spilling out of her greedy grip.

Wynolla's hands caressed Monique, drawing her closer still, allowing her strong yet tender grip to guide her flowing hair away from the base of her neck. It's Wynolla's turn to kiss Monique's strawberry scented skin as the music plays on.

" I could spend my life in this sweet surrender.. I would stay lost in this moment forever. Every moment we spend together I treasure."

Doctor Littlefield's little hush moans were a byproduct of their fervor, once again passion has completely overtaken them both! Monique was so aroused, her lovely almond-colored nipples woke up, poking Wynolla's excited heaving blossom. Nipple paly further excites the passionate couple to further heights of ecstasy.!

Monique adjusts her hips, so Windu's clit sits on top of her own, each woman's steadily falling in love with every single thrust to their absolute being. Monique attempts to curtail her moans, as the woman she embraces, lightly digging her nails into she back. Just as Wynolla fights to keep her grunts from being heard outside their quarters! Monique adjusts her palms, pressing down into Wynolla as her hips begin to match her upward motion.

Wynolla's feelings towards Monique soar as she's consumed in the valley of two women seized by lust and a moment in time, they both share!

Windu's resourcefully massages Monique's melon size breast, which fit snugly in the palm of her hands as the music sums it up.

"Don't wanna close my eyes, don't want to fall asleep, cus I'd miss you babe and I don't want to miss a thing. Because even when I dream of you, the sweetest dream will never do, cause I still miss you baby and I don't want to miss a thang!"

Wynolla cannot take her eyes off her newfound, love! From the tiny beads of sweat forming between Monique's eyebrows, to the way her sweat forces her thin night shirt to helplessly clung to her athletic frame! It's been a number of years since Wynolla has felt this way, and she had to admit it felt great!

Doctor Littlefield's head rolled back as her downward stroke nearly exceeds that of the bearer. When Colonel Lafayette capable mocha hands clamped down on Monique's cream-colored hips, finally their rhythm became as one!

At the same time in the seldom used West side of the Camp, the one that faces the urban sprawl that used to be the 4th largest city in the nation.

Fun Fact; this area happens to be more than a bit depressing to the majority of survivors inside what was once the McCormick place-the nation's largest convention center. Rear Admiral choose one of these bigger conference rooms as his personal quarters. Colonel Dunson moved into the next room over and moved four Marines out of the common bay, gave them their own room on the first floor and placed them at the bottom of the stairs to act as Security. No one was allowed to the Admiral quarters without express permission of the XO or the Lee himself!

That left this entire area isolated and off limits to anyone below the rank of base commander. Inside Jefferson Bullraguard Lee's quarters a black light provides the only illumination. Their light bounced off hundreds of boxes MREs functioning as a makeshift chair or throne depending on your perspective.

The shadows bouncing off the walls made sad impressions off the large plate glass window facing the city. The only light for miles came from inside Camp McCormick, even though a strict light ordinance extends to all base personnel. Only in areas without windows were any light permitted at all. To the causal observer JBL's personnel quarters have all the trappings on a person not looking for creature comforts or a person who no longer gave a fat flying fuck!

Besides the king size air mattress and air compressor, many of the other items seem to have been crafted especially for pain. The smell of sweat mingles with rope and baby oil. The L.E.D clock projects the time onto the ceiling, it read 2217 or 10:17pm. Jefferson Bullraguard Lee for an older man, was still lean. Chalk it up to clean living for the Admiral is merely a social drinker, an adamant golfer and only a social cigar smoker.

He rarely eats red meat and before the Apocalypse Jefferson used to run ten miles a day five a week! JBL would run among the recruits at his Naval Base and like a wolf in sheep's clothing, he was always on the scope for prey. Surprisingly he found one in his current Xo.

Inside Lee's chambers, Kevin Dunson the scrapping jarhead, knelt nude, bounded with rope around his wrist, allowing for his arms to be roughly restrained behind his back! The Marine Colonel's muscular body has been covered in baby oil.

His vision had been restricted by a thick black mask! Kevin's hairless chest has several burn marks- probably from a cigar- and a pair of clothes pin pinch both his accepting nipples.

Rear Admiral Jefferson Bullraguard Lee's, floppy Dong rests on his inner thigh as he goes over what needs to be done.

"What is there is no cure? What if the best we are able to do is batten down the hatches and ride this out? Self-Quarantine ourselves until help arrives or this plague passes? Move closer swine!"

Dunson may not be able to see, but he is still able to move. He uses his oiled-up knees to scoot across the large green tarp on the floor. Once his face rest inches from Lee's hairy thigh. Only then does the Admiral continue.

"Doctor Littlefield represents the civilian faction and their pursuit of something that might not exist is dangerous to my pursuit of happiness... You may begin, you fucking worm."

At first glance, it would seem Kevin should have been a difficult slave for Jefferson to acquire. Yet when the Marine reported to Great Lakes Naval Center, Lee noticed he had all the trapping he was looking for. Moderately young, white or Asian, in good shape, no personal commitments and could keep a fucking secret! Then had served together once before, but Lee didn't need a slave. This time it started with them running together and it took a few months before the Admiral allowed himself to trip and fall.

Skinning up his knee very bad, Dunson felt duty bound to help his commanding Officer back to the base commander's home! Inside Jefferson instructed where to find the needed medical supplies, towels, green alcohol and Band-Aids. After retrieving the items from the Admiral's bathroom, the new Provost Marshal reenters the living room to find Jefferson Bullraguard Lee's sweaty naked frame laying on his back on his Italian leather sofa. Dunston could have walked out, nevertheless he didn't and that brings us too today!

It was once said, that to be famous in Hollywood you have to do some weird gay shit. However to be in the United States Navy you are constantly eating, sleeping and showering with seamen!

Kevin Dunson's tongue licks his way up and down Jefferson's right thigh. The obedient slave, requests permission to move closer.

"Master, shall I advance to the objective?"

JBL grunts dispassionately "Affirmative."

Dunson scoots a few inches closer and begins placing soft kisses on his Masters semi smooth thigh. JBL is a sadist, even so he's certainly not a foolish martyr!

Not after seeing the way his base fell to the infected, he had no use for those that cannot or will not get with his fucking program! Jefferson Bullraguard Lee intents to live, even if that price must be paid by others.

"We must rid ourselves of the unclean. Of those that wish to promote a system where a White Man must listen to anyone but almighty God! I will no longer foster my allegiance to, to this, farce. There is no cure! The world WE knew is gone, now it's time to reinvent our environment."

The Marine Colonel's tongue finally reaches its intended target.

Kevin sniffs the purple mushroom head of Jefferson's veiny cock before allowing his pink tongue to lick the rising white stalk. When the tip of Admiral Lee's cock touches Colonel Dunson's pink lips, it's sucked into his mouth like the sun's gravity latching on to a stray moon!

Master grew inside of Slave, never touching him, just allowing the warm rapid growth to swell in the mouth of a very capable cock-sucking Marine! The purple mushroom cap is engulfed by a greedy slave, salvia gleams as Kevin's head moves back and forth. Jefferson leans forward and grabs Kevin by his windpipe and gives a firm squeeze. Lee watches his slave struggle to keep the hard appendage firmly wedge between his cock sucking lips and his greedy gums while attempting to continue fucking breathe!

Kevin Dunson coughs as his Master watches him squirm, the baby oil on his forehead makes the sweat bead into tiny balls. The slave must fight the urge to squirm, to fight back, he must surrender himself or perish under his own foolishness!

Lee said. "The Enemy Within, is worse than the Enemy out There! When that bitch Lafayette takes her Army boys on their mission. I will deal with that pompous Air Force shit heel McKinney. Camp McCormick is a naval base now. All non-Naval personal will unass my A.O!"

In the background Dunson IPOD was playing the 1970s rock band, **Boston's More than a feeling**. Still, it takes Jefferson Bullraguard Lee supplying his own lyrics as his slave inhaled his hairy cock to sum up their experience.

" I woke up this morning and my world was gone, I told my slave to play my favorite song. I closed my eyes, hoping all would fade away.."

The music seems to move them both, because the slave's tongue darts around Lee's purple mushroom top as his breath becomes swallow, but Jefferson's words still ring true.

"It's more than a feeling, when I think about all the things that use to go my way, it's more than a feeling to have my cock sliding inside your jowls, it's more than a feeling to kill some Army pukes today! I won't be dreaming when I teach that CDC bitch some manners, in my own goddam way..."

Chapter IV:

WELCOME TO SHANGRI-LA

200 hours – 17 days into Infection

Two weeks prior, when Ex-Marshal Aquila's group of survivors landed their Russian made vintage attack Helicopter less than fifteen miles from the Saint Charles River- about 80 miles outside Chicago Illinois- there should have been at least a crowd of curious onlookers. Traffic should have come to a snarl when the lumbering silver aircraft flew across the nearly cloudless August sky!

Nevertheless, the only eyes cast upward were those of the infected and the recently dead! The Hunnfield farm had been in Hank's family for nearly six generations. It had been through the Civil War, the farm survived Black Monday, The Great Depression, as well as three so-called once in a generation floods. Even including the same number of Saving & Loans or Banking and Wall Street meltdowns!

Still the Hunnfield farm could not survive the RAGER or the COVID-MOMREL-6 pandemic. If historians were still a thing, they could scribe how Hank Hunnfield had been a farmer like his father, and their fathers. It all started in the spring 1843, when Hank's Great, Great, Great grandfather along with other whites settled- or forcible relocated or killed the local Native Americans, it solely depends on whose side you identity with- over five thousand acres of unforgiving frontier land!

Over the next several generations, parcels of lush green farmland were sold off for numerous undertakings. Including an Army Corps of Engineers project to monitor the flow of Carp in the St. Charles River. Or so as it was pitched to Earnest Hunnfield in 1949; mostly because the Air Force wanted to put a clandestine Missile Silo outside the city of Chicago!

Fun Fact; the Air Force under the disguise of the Army Corps of Engineers purchased two hundred of the remaining three hundred acres of Hunnfield family farm for the then whooping sum of 475, 000 dollars. A small fortune by 1950 standards! Sadly by 1963 the Air Force project never fully got off the ground, the covert Missile Silo idea was moved further downstate closer to Springfield. Amazingly, in 1975 it only costs the American tax payers another $1,250,000 dollars to buy four hundred acres of land further downstate!

Instead, the original area purchased was used by the Army Corps of Engineers as a staging area for monitoring local flooding. Nonetheless, when the 1980s, Saving & Loans scandal hit the press and banks were caught with their pants around their ankles again. Jerking off all their investors' hard-earned money on bad investments and of course real good cocaine, again!

Once more people lost their entire life savings, their pensions, their jobs and their lives. Entire neighborhoods of new construction sat idle, with no way to be financed!

And that would be the third time and next to last time the Hunnfield family farms would sell off parts of their heritage just to keep some of their family legacy intact. However, in 2008, the same thing happens again to the American homeowner! Their local "trusted" banks got caught in another round of poor investing, excess paying of bonuses, wild trips to exotic conferences and once again very good cocaine!

Back in 2004 the Government was busy selling off assets like Army Corps of Engineers substation, which rested on two hundred acres of unincorporated land. It was Big John Lawyer who purchased the entire parcel for 1.5 million at auction. If his daughter only knew why he worked so many long hours and stayed gone for so many weeks a month, maybe she would have grown up less angry. Nonetheless, Shangri-La took nine years to build, at a cost of an additional forty-three million dollars!

Right before the last bank meltdown, Hank Hunnfield had hitched his hopes of a good growing season of his lime green soybeans and yellow corn to make ends meet. However, when the market crashed, so did the price of his merchandise! Now saddled with nearly five million dollars of debt, he was on the verge of losing the rest of his family farm. His six children- ages ranging from 5-17 years old. - would be homeless! Hank lived in constant fear that the bodies of his ancestors would be dug up to make room for a Super Store or goddam low-income housing complex.

At that time Hank was so depressed, he figured he was worth more to his family dead than as a failure! He had even considered running his pickup truck into the river, in an attempt to make his apparent suicide look like a foolish accident. It wasn't until an envoy for the Construction crew working at the old Army Corps substation delivered Hank a sealed envelope that his day got somewhat brighter!

The proposal was simple, yet straight forward and for his cooperation, his debt would be paid off to his creditors. As well as a monthly salary as caretaker to their hidden task. At first, Hank Hunnfield wasn't sure if their offer was legal or even morale! As of date nearly 24 states had voted in favorable medical marijuana laws. Even so, he never had any thoughts on the subject, until Illinois passed their own favorable marijuana laws.

Furthermore, if someone wanted to pay the $150,000 dollars in state licensing fees, as well build a grow house on his property and pay him to manage it, why shouldn't Hank milk that green cash cow? The private corp. wanted to build a private airstrip, and an access road to the outskirts of the old Army Corps shack. Hank was ok with that as well.

It was 2009 and all the father of seven is certain of, he didn't want to join the growing mass of homeowners losing their property! Bankers weren't going to jail and to make matters worse after ruining the economy, they still got their bonuses! Well then, why shouldn't Hank Hunnfield accept questionable earnings? The Hunnfield farm had grown an assortment of crops in their 178-year history, and he figured marijuana would not be their last!

Ten miles from the road from the Hunnfield family farm, Shangri-La was built to sustain being submerged up to 250 feet of water for up to three hundred and twenty-five days!

It's a six story circular hole that's three hundred and fifty feet in width and nearly hundred and eighty feet in length. From the outside the field of eight-twenty foot high- windmills, might appear as a forest of giant metal sunflowers basking in the post-apocalyptic sun! Each's painted white and located in the middle of one of these steel giants is a metal door which's can only be accessed by a twelve-digit keypad.

Fun Fact: when air travel was still an everyday occurrence, only the astute air passenger would marvel how the layout of the windmills stretched high towards the cosmos resembling Orion's Belt! Furthermore, to the bearer of the correct access code and key card, the entrance would open preceding to a ladder that leads to the first level. There a freight elevator awaits the processor of a key card and another access code combination. The contractors that worked on this are probably dead, infected or undead by this point and there's no way anyone outside the bearer of the code and keycard could enter. So, it sat untouched, like a homely virgin in an airtight dungeon!

John made sure he hired a company from down near Springfield Illinois, they marveled that someone would foot the bill to import a crew of eighty workers and sport for that major overtime. When he could have easily hired locals and saved a lot of money. The total for the entire project would be- windmills included- over forty million dollars!

Before and even after being incarcerated, John always planned the long game. He had formed several corporations, LLCs and two-family trusts. Before his run in with the markers of the RED DEATH, or at least the cabal that knew the COVID-MOMREL-6 was a possibility. John Hammond had managed to make and stow away nearly twenty-five million dollars on his own.

Luckily when President Obama attempted to usher in a wave of green energy companies in his first term. John bought in! He used one of his LLCs to apply for a grant when he purchased the Army Corps property through a straw corporation, he set up pre murder charge. Little that Hank Hunnfield knew, he was key to getting the pieces John needed in place, for their families to survive.

Hank was in need and while sitting on death row, Hammond learned from his talks with Enestro that the cartels were worried about the legal marijuana trade ruining their take. Frankly, that meant vast amounts of legal money was on the table to be made! Pot was becoming legal or somewhat legal until laws were passed to make a confusing situation less confusing and solely profitable. Even so, there was big money to be made by the bold!

When the lawyers John used to approach Hank Hunnfield offered him a golden ticket to escape his crippling debt. Hank didn't hire keen or astute attorneys on his behalf. Hank didn't read the fine print on several of the documents that set up the grant for the windmill farm on the old Army Corps of Engineers property.

There was much Hank Hunnfield didn't know about life, for he strove to be a simple church going man.

A farmer by heritage, a minor league baseball player by choice and a deeply religious father of seven who simply needed a break! Hank may have been a plain farmer, nonetheless his wife Joanne, was not.

The US. Army helped the tiny, red head with the brave heart get her Nursing Degree at Saint Regina's online College. At the time Joanne was 18 and had been working at pizza hut! She had been taking online courses when she saw an Army recruitment commercial that changed her life.

The soon to be nineteen-year-old St. Charles native looked around her place of employment and the smell of pizza sauces, grease and her low expectations weighed heavy on her!

It was 2004 and America was at war and the bonus for enlistments was awesome. Fifty thousand to the brave souls that pledge their allegiance, plus the need for health care professionals was dire! Joanne Patterski heard the call, and she left her dead end job for the lore of the United States Army!

After a year of combined Basic and Advanced training, Joanne was finally stationed at Fort Meade in Maryland. Sadly, never leaving the country in her four and ½ years of service. Joanne was bright and a fast learner, obtaining the rank of Specialist before her enlistment was up. Returning home in 2009, Joanne had been armed with a Nursing Degree and a sort of worldly experience that only the military can foster in a young adult.

It was a warm, yet humid day, the sun shining brightly, and the flowers were in bloom when Joanne meet Hank coming out of the bank. Growing up in the small community of Saint Charles Illinois meant most people seemed familiar. The shy duo had a few classes together in High School, even though Joanne was one year older. She still kind of remembered the shy, blond and blue-eyed hunk that is Hank Hunnfield!

Fast forward two years, the madly in love couple were married and expecting their first child. Bless for their patience, Mother Nature consecrated them with quads! Two girls and two boys, and most couples would stop there. However, in 2015 Joanne got pregnant once again and nature once again blessed Hank with another set of daughters.

Flashback to 2010: Hank was drowning in debt, still John Hammond's foresight helped funnel federal grant money from various projects including monitoring clean water, clean energy production- including solar panels and windmills-, and wetlands. Totaling a whopping 8.5 million dollars in federal grant money!

Even with the over twenty-five million dollars John sunk in of his own money, he knew well beforehand that capital would need to be raised. As fate would have it, that's when the state of Illinois passed their first medical marijuana laws!

From a prison cell John Hammond had used his offshore shadow companies as a means to an end, long before anyone understood what that end was.

The Hunnfield family farms devoted seven acres of land for construction. That construction included a greenhouse the size of three football fields and was no less than twenty-five feet deep, along with three industrial generators, all built on his property. With the licensing for the greenhouse came four dispensaries!

One in the popular Chicago neighborhood of Pilsen and the other in Hyde Park. Another dispensary was granted in downtown Saint Charles and the last dispensary near the border of the state of Indiana in Alsip Illinois**. Fun Fact**: Indiana was one of the last states to stop prosecuting its citizens for marijuana. As true Republicans these elected officials took Prison Lobbyist money to the grave. Even through a former Governor of theirs who went on to be Vice President to a whack job had been caught with a shoe box full of pot when he was at Indiana University. Yep, his rich lawyer/donor father made it all go away! Ps, we all know that any college student with a shoe box full of pot is a fucking dealer.

Nevertheless, John listened, he had already understood the message Ernesto tried to install in him so long ago. It's more profitable to own the factory and the dealerships than lease them! The Hunnfield farms grew over forty thousand medical grade marijuana planets per year. With the estimate worth of over twelve million dollars per yield-retail. 2022-2023 would have been their tenth year in business!

Flashforward to the here and now; John was impressed as he circles the Russian made Helicopter around Hank's recently built 7.9-million-dollar home. You know the kind, ultra-modern, 12 bedrooms, 7 bathrooms, equipped with a giant 15-foot American Flag in the front yard! Followed by a tennis court, one archery range, a small pond and a professional restaurant quality outdoor meat smoker.

After circling the main house once, Hammond did not see any signs of life. At the first location or at the greenhouse complex near the small airstrip which John landed the restored Russian aircraft on semi level farmland. Robin was first to jump from the helio, to her feeling the crunch of the firm ground felt real good under her soles.

It doesn't take long before the rest of the aircraft exited, stretching and wondering what was next. Several smells, hit aware noses all at one time. Some smells that could be factored was the dead. However, the next is the deep rich scent of marijuana! The other's that of the river, rushing several miles away.

Calamity is first to say. "Ohhhhhh, mi dios. Where is that smell of motta coming from?"

Indigo Roberson asked a question that is on everyone's mind.

"Why are we here?"

John stretched his toned arms and cracked the bones in his neck, his stern gaze scans their surrounding before slowly answering.

"Simply we are home. I was fortunate enough to prepare for this day, this farm, is part of a network of investments I had before and during my incarceration."

Earl whistles and said. "Big John, you never cease to amaze me with the secrets you hold. You did all of this while wasting away on death row? Imagine what you could have done as a free man?"

Ernesto grins, then pretends to pouts. "You mean all those nights I talked and talk and talked about drug trafficking you were actually listening? Fucker, you already knew as much as me."

Cherish, Semaj and her two eight-year-old nephews aimlessly wander towards the Hunnfield mansion. Unaware of the dangers that wait to unfold.

Paradise follows Sky has she walks towards Big John Hammond waiting for him to explain what their next move is.

Sky inquires. "Huh, are we supposed to live in that place?"

Paradise chips in, "It's HUGE, still kind of tacky!"

Robin adjusted the AR-15 shoulder strap, allowing her weapon to slide behind her back. She held her gun hand on her weapon holstered on her right hip and asked.

"Come on dad, what are we doing here?"

John wanted to answer their questions, even so, he knew there would be time for that. Still, he must give them something.

"I own, what you may call, a doomsday shelter. Inside that house we'll find the keys that will allow us entry to Shangri-La."

Indigo frowns her nose and inquires. "Shangri-What?"

She never got the words out. Suddenly the front bay window of the Hunnfield mansion explodes outward! The sound causes the survivors to tense up for various amounts of time. For most it seems like slow motion as several RAGERS leap from the newly formed hole. Each is armed with either butcher knives, hunting knives or bits of metal pipes.

They run, yelling and screaming alerting all infected or Dead Heads that game is a foot! Destiny and Dawn sheik as the piss smell of the yellow puss bearing psychos invaded the entire area! Proper training has it that Robin and Ernesto draw at the same time. Robin's 9mm hit a few targets high in chest and arms, yet that doesn't put the infected down. All got up screaming and cursing to the heavens. Murder is his call to arms and the Ghostface Killer answers, for his AR 15 spits! PAP, PAP, PAP, PAP, PAP, PAP.

Even though he had been imprisoned for nearly seven years, that doesn't stop Ernesto from having a tight shoot grouping!

Three of the infected, one short man, a heavy-set woman and one child race towards the back peddling Cherish, Semaj and her nephews. Calamity follows Earl as they move towards the RAGERS.

Shooting as they run, Earl thinks to himself that has not had this much fun in nearly nine years, thirty-four days and several seconds! Calamity is yelling as her MAC-10s spun a tale that ends the rage in the approaching RAGERS. Danger may have passed for now, nevertheless tension still rides high!

Paradise looks at Earl with a bit of interest and at least admiration! Sky's worried about Cherish and her family. While Indigo quickly points out.

"You mean, you want us, I mean you want to go in there?"

The group huddles near the entrance to the thirty-four hundred foot grow house which is fortified from the inside. Apparently, someone thought it was the best place to make a last stand! That means the dead are probably inside as well. John knew the route to his planned escape hatch awaits in the prescribed area twenty-three feet down. He turned to his daughter Robin and then said.

"We have a two, no three-prong problem. First, we need to gain entrance to this building, second; we have personnel that are not combat effective. And last, yes, I have to go into that house, because we need to get that door open."

Robin opened her mouth to voice her displeasure with the plan.

At that moment she reminds her father of the little girl that still resides deep, deep down inside.

"Why can't I come with you?"

Big John smiles, for he still heard the little girl in the grown woman that stands before him.

He softly replies," Because those that can't fight as well as you and I. Or our pair of love lore assassins and of course my good friend Earl, will need your protection, Marshal."

Earl and Ernesto walk over to Big John looking to know what's next. John starts walking to the Hunnfield mansion and his cohorts feel in step.

Ernesto must enquire, "So what's the plan John? Why are you heading into a house of horrors?"

Earl chirped in, "Better yet why are we following you into the lion's mouth?"

Big John huffed and said, "What else would you want to be doing? Or should I ask you who would you rather be doing?"

Earl said nothing, even so John offered some advice. "May I offer a word of advice? This's a brand-new world my friend, full of possibilities. It's best you approach your romantic relationships differently this time around. I suggest a bit more compassion and honestly over whatever leads you down your dark path."

Still Earl said nothing, as the trio approaches the step of what was the Hunnfield mansion. A series of screams come from behind them, forcing the men to stop and turn towards the mayhem.

The strippers Destiny and Dawn, along with the kids begin screaming when a gaggle of Dead Heads come from around the corner of the grow house. First it started as a trickle, one, two, then five and twenty, no thirty shambling Zombies descend of the group catching Calamity and Robin off guard!

Ernesto shouts. “Celeste!”

As he takes off running back to the group, the Ghost Face Killer clutches his AR 15 not firing it for the fear his aim may be off by a fraction of a hair. Big John and Earl bring up his rear, but both are heavy set men, and they cannot keep up. Big John’s scared for he can see the ring of Zombie trying to encircle the band of survivors. A lump of fear lodges in his throat as he loses sight of his daughter in the crowd!

Earl has been around death all his adult life and he is rarely frighten. Still as he charged into danger, John’s words stung him deeply.

Chicken Head could see Paradise and Semaj attempting to shield the children from the gashing teeth and clawing hands of the dead! Still for some reason Earl could not fathom, he kind of cares if these strangers live or died. For the first time in a long while, he’s experiencing good emotions.

The smell of the Dead Heads should have alerted the survivors that hell was on the way! However, once that signal’s missed, the small herd of thirty Zombies had already wandered in from the corn fields on the east side of the grow house. Generally, the Hunnfield farm hired twelve full time employees and forty-five part time employees six days a week.

The thirty that descends upon Marshal Aquila’s group were once part time marijuana pickers hired to clip and groom plants. It seems they must have been late to work for their shift never started! Now each sported fresh bite marks, milky pupils and blood dripping from most of their orifices. Plus, the screaming of the Cherishes nephews didn’t help matters! Calamity swung her machete with brute force or a woman twice her size. Catching one of the Zombies in the neck and nearly cutting off its rotten head in one fatal swoop!

Even so, the hell spawn kept its onslaught of chattering teeth and shambled forward. Forcing Celeste to unload one of her MAC-10s at close range, blasting away at Dead Heads before they can grab one of the shrieking children! One by one the rambling shapes stagger from around the corner of the industrial size grown house. It was like each heard an invisible dinner bell ringing only for their ears.

The speedy Ernesto arrives swinging the butt of his AR-15 like a bat! Impacting the dome of any Dead Heads facing him.

Cherish, Sky, Paradise and Semaj press the children into the door well. Kicking and screaming the four do their best to keep the Zombies at bay. Ex-Strippers Destiny and Dawn have no choice but to press their big booty backsides to the door or succumb to infection! They must kick and scream for dear life, if they want to live!

Indigo kicks a Zombie in its knee before it can reach for her face, sending it crashing to the ground, then quickly stomps what's left of its brain matter into the dark fertile soil of the Hunnfield farm. By the time Big John and Earl made it to the rear of the crowd, the ring of Zombies had quickly enclosed the survivors.

Big John raises his BAR-Bowning Automatic Weapon- shouting. "Get down!"

Cherish clutches at one of her nephews allowing them to slide down into a tight ball in the door well. Semaj grabs the remaining child, as Sky and Paradise slide to the ground holding their ears. Marshal Aquila was fighting hard with a foul-smelling Dead Head, just to keep its teeth from her face! Robin's right hand holds her trusty .45, as the weight of the undead collapses her to one knee. That's when Robin aim finds the sweet spot of the Zombie's forehead. With one well-placed shot the Marshal ends her fight, yet the battle rages on!

Earl, Big John and Ernesto have no choice but to level their assault weapons face high and empty their collective magazines with the professionalism of weathered warriors. A volley of NATO quality rounds impact, then separates diseased brain matter from harden skulls.

The stench from the dark red infected blood running from head, neck back and shoulder wounds is nearly overwhelming. Mostly the Zombies received a dose of hot lead instead of a hot meal. Even those Dead Heads who are gravely wounded show no signs of pain or even free will.

Every Dead Head is singularly motivated by the overwhelming urge to feed! The only thing louder than the screaming of the survivors being pressed back in the door well, was the continuous gunfire from their concerned companions. Gun smoke was as thick as Northern California wildfire! Yet when it cleared, the majority of herd of Zombies are now truly fucking dead.

A few had bloody spines blown out of diseased backs or mangled hips shattered by buckshot. With that said, Dead Heads still drag their bloody stumps across the grass, never once showing an ounce of pain, only the chattering of teeth! Robin stood up and stomped on the skull of a one-eyed skinny Zombie toddler crawling towards her left ankle.

The Ghost Faced Killer rushes forward stabbing Zombies in the head with his trusty bowie knife, as his Calamity uses her machete to finish off any Dead Head foolish enough not to stay dead! Ernesto runs and picks Celeste up and twirls her around, pulling her in and hugging her tight before slowly letting her go. He brushes the hair out of her eyes and Calamity smiles before saying.

“You act like you were worried about me?”

Her Ghost Face Killer replies, “Woman, every single moment we are apart.”

She can’t help but giggle, then give her husband a subtle, yet sexy hip bump. By the time Destiny and Dawn separate their shapely buttocks off the grow room door, both notice the teenage face staring at them.

It takes some doing, nonetheless Big John convinces the older offspring of Hank Hunnfield, Isiah Hunnfield to open the door. A child from a previous relationship with Hank's first love a, middle school sweetheart. Now nineteen years old, Isiah has lived with his father ever since his mother died of a heroin overdose when he was only eight years old.

Eleven years later, Isiah works the family farm, over in the field that still bore yellow gold. As in stalks of eight feet high corn! Today, the lanky and thin dark haired teenage is frighten out of his goddam mind. Flash back to when the infection first hit the Hunnfield farm, it started out just another day.

Fields of corn and soybeans were being irrigated as is their daily experience. Cows were being milked by hand as the smell of manure and hay filled the air. Inside Hank's extravagance home, two of his live-in house staff had come down with some sort of flu that week.

That leaves Mr. Hunnfield to run his own errands. It was midday when Hank Hunnfield returned in his Black Range Rover from making a run to his local post office. He noticed the usual armored SUV parked near the grow house rear loading bay doors.

Four of his employees were busy loading compressed gallon size bags of various strains of high-grade marijuana into shipping bins. Two of the men loading the large, sealed bins of grade A cannabis; sneeze and cough as they go about their daily tasks. At least one of the workers loading the bins of marijuana into the SUV coughs up and hacks up globs of dark red phlegm!

After driving past the grow house loading docks, Hank's Black Range Rover powered its way up the circular driveway and towards his double wide front door. As Hank parks and exits his vehicle, he's quickly taken back, because to Hank it smells like someone's barbequing some horrible meat in his expensive smoker!

Slowly Hank approaches his front door, and to his surprise he finds it jar. Usually, his home is a whirl of movement, between house staff, kids and a more than capable wife, the Hunnfield' s home was always noisy!

Nevertheless, it's just 1pm, his wife Joanne should have gotten their twins- Jennifer and Helen, seven-year-old blue eyed sprites- from kindergarten by now. Hank's fourteen-year-old triplets should still be at St. Charles Prep. While his oldest son from a previous marriage- Isiah should be down at the east farm- making sure the daily requirements of water to the fields of cows and corn are met. That's their daily routine.

The remaining house staff should be cleaning and straightening up for the fundraiser the Hunnfield' s were sponsoring for their triplets- Karen/16, Hank Jr/16 , Sarah/16 years old- class trip to Six Flags in Gurnee Illinois.

Hank was hoping he could find a few moments to catch his wife Joanne and get some tender kisses and warm hugs before they had to devote the rest of the night to being grownups. Joanne had given him the best years of her life and not to mention five wonderful children. So, yeah Hank loved his wife a lot!

However, when Hank pushed open his front door, he knew something was terribly, terribly wrong! Furniture's broken, a glass table has been smashed, plants were overturned, and fresh blood, dripping down stained walls immediately capture Hank's attention! His mouth hangs open in disbelief as a highway of blood stains their white carpet all the way from the 3,400 square foot living room to the 1,200 square foot kitchen. Hank grabs a large knife from the stainless sink and mutters more to himself.

"Oh, my. Ohh, my! Where's Joanne? Where are my children?"

He thought about calling out, nonetheless decided to head to his office upstairs by the master bedroom. Where Hank like most Americans kept his trusty 12-gauge shotgun and his capable 45.

Caliber Ruger! The floor was sticky from ground coffee, cracked eggs, blood and bacon grease. Smoke's busy rising from the skillet left unattended on the stove and from what he could see dark clump of crimson blood stains everything!

Hank turns off the fire under the smoldering skillet and turns on the overhead exhaust fan, in hope of staving off the sound of the fire alarm.

The smoke made it hard to see, even so Hank would swear he saw something moving up ahead, back towards the rec room and pool area! Before Hunnfield can move forward he heard something moving behind him. Like some unknown question, fear fills Hank's thoughts, parlaying his actions!

The footsteps are moving fast, that's when Hank heard his oldest son Isiah's voice call out. "YO, Dad? Anyone in here?"

Hank sort of low crawls under the smoke and back towards his front door, bumping into his oldest child. Doing his best to keep it together Hank grabs hold of Isiah and frantically said.

"What' what happen here? Have, have you seen Joanne and the kids? Oh my god where are the twins?"

Isiah shakes his head no. This's the first time he has ever seen his father frighten and that single emotion has a snowball effect from father to son! Isiah licks his nineteen-year-old parched lips and looks towards his dad for direction. Hank's eyes are darting, looking for answers! He strains to make out the figure bumping into the nook in the downstairs hallway. Whoever it's, moves off further down the hall, out of line of sight.

Hank knew he needed to get to his gun safe upstairs, and nothing would keep him from it. After he arms himself and maybe even Isiah, together they will search the house for his wife and kids. Shit! Hank thinks to himself, he only has two hours before someone has to pick up his triplets from High School.

Tall and lanky for his age, Isiah nearly trips over one of his stepsisters' cute little Barbie dolls, resting at the base of the stairs. Son bumps into who father, who turns with a scowl on his face, Hank whispers in a harsh tone.

"Hey, watch what you are doing back there."

Isiah just nods his head and meekly mumbles.

"I didn't do it on purpose.."

Slowly father and son do their best to silently creep up the two flights of stairs to the spare bedroom/office next to the master bedroom. At the top of the staircase, Hank slightly turns his head so he may whisper to Isiah.

"In my desk, there is a black notebook filled with all my codes. For the computer, to my bank accounts and the greenhouse secure room. You get that while I get us a couple of weapons out of my gun safe. Stay quiet, stay safe son."

Hank fumbles with his keys as he crouches down near the railing. He stands up and slowly heads to his office, taking a few seconds to peek into his bedroom. Finding only his unmade king size bed, Hank quickly takes two steps into his office and walks right into an infected Joanne. The stench of his once lovely wife resembles stale cat urine, and that stench should have met Hank at the doorframe long before his wife did!

Hank's mouth dropped in horror, and he freezes in his tracks when he noticed the yellow puss filled blisters, that weren't on his wife's face when he left home three hours ago. Joanne's once chestnut brown hair is matted with dried blood and Hank can see some sort of bits of flesh imbedded in his wife's front teeth!

Let's just say, her husband was beyond confused because his wife didn't even mention being sick. Joanne only mentioned something about two of the live in Nannies needing bed rest ordered by the

Hunnfield family doctor. Nevertheless, deep red blood drips from his once charming soulmate's now milky corneas, as well as her ears and mouth.

A dry scream gets stuck in the back of Hank's throat as he backs up into an equally terrified Isiah. Father and son stumble backwards out into the hallway as Joanne groans, swinging her arms trying to grab hold of a confused Hank.

He mutters, "Jo, JO, isn't me, oh my god. What's going on, hon, can you hear me? I, I, I'll call Doctor Lewis again..."

The COVID-MOMREL-6virus was built to be a powerful tool of regime change. The instinct to protect your loved ones is strong, even when they are being harmful to themselves or others. This tool was designed to overpower your basic will to survive!

Hank the devoted husband tries to reason with Joanne- his always supportive wife- while back peddling, yet he's unaware how rapidly he's approaching the second-floor railing. Isiah moves to his father's right, doing his best to this time get out of his way.

Except, the sight of his stepmom, covered in dried blood, with a gash on her neck kind of looks like Joanne has a second mouth! Honestly, that freaks the teenager out! Nonetheless, his father didn't move fast enough, and Hank didn't navigate the door frame well at all.

When the plague-ridden wife lunges at her husband, his heels snag on the carpet as his infected wives' bloody fingertips clutch at his bare throat. Hank's hands can't help but press the borrowed butcher knives into Joanne's mushroom cap shaped belly! Still the wife's face presses into her husbands for one last kiss. Unfortunately, his former love bites off Hanks' top lip, allowing the splattering of blood to adjoin their bodies. It was just like they fell in love, for together the couple went tumbling over the marble railing.

Hank's screaming frame made a horrible splat as their union impacts the already jagged glass table mostly used for only holding mail and car keys. Isiah's speechless, he runs to the railing only to witness three of the house staff shambling into the room. One had his back ripped and chewed up beyond repair. Strains of yellow and black puss oozing flesh hang from the Dead Head's torso.

Isiah shakes his head no, as the Zombie rips his teeth into his father's pants leg and tore out a chunk of flesh. Isiah backs into what was once Hank's office, where he heard soft sobbing coming from the closet. Slowly he knocked on the door and said. "Knock, knock.."

He whispers, "Jenifer, Helen, is, is that you?"

The two eight-year old's, sob from the safety behind a locked cedar door that protected their parents walk in closet. Isiah was stuck for a moment trying to consider which he should do first, head to the closet and check on his half-sisters, or should he go get his father's guns?

The moaning coming from the bottom of the flight of steps is getting louder, as is the shuffling of lumbering feet coming up said stairs. Isiah may not always be a quick decision making, but it's at that instance things changed!

Picking up the keys from where his father dropped them in the doorway, the son runs to the gun safe. Unlocks the gray steel cabinet door and removes the 12-gauge pump shotgun with pistol grip!

The moaning's getting louder as Isiah franticly gasps at the box of 25- OO Buck Shot slugs, he manages to load five rounds into his still twitching daddy's gun, when the first reanimated corpse enters the office. Isiah chambers the first round, when he notices the face of the fifty-year-old Hispanic maid Mora.

By the way her head can only look up towards the ceiling, clearly her neck has been broken. Her moan turned out to be a beacon to her kindred. Isiah's sweating and he stinks of fear!

Raising the weapon face high, Isiah really doesn't want to shoot

Mrs. Gonzales, but he can't stop thinking about his stepsisters crying, huddling together in fear in the other room.

He thought about his others three sibling at high school and Isiah could only wonder if they are still alive. The dead head seemed to be listening for Isiah's breathing or something for when he moved, so did she! Isiah saw three more stumbling into the tight office, and he knew it's now or never.

The thing that was once the middle age Hispanic maid, reaches out towards a trapped Isiah, he places the shotgun directly on her twisted neck and pulls the trigger.

BOOM, the impressive sound temporally drowns out the moaning as infected blood splatters onto the rest of her elk flittering into Hank's office! Isiah quickly jacks another round into his father's shotgun and takes aim at the next moaning disfigured face to shamble his way.

Isiah's breath steadied a bit as his next shot took the top of the head off the one-time personal Chef, Javier. Now feeling the false sense of courage that only a bottle of whiskey or a fully loaded firearm can bring! Isiah racks another round in the chamber and gladly shoots the one eyed, missing part of her jaw, Polish nanny Helga in her dead twisted face.

Isiah never liked Helga! She caught him jerking off and told Joanne, which gave her a reason to look down her nose at him even more. Three twitching corpses lay in the doorframe, forcing the next Zombie to stumble over its brethren.

Isiah mind set was calm, he felt more in his element with every passing second! Much like the ***Resident Evil*** *and* ***Black Ops*** *games he grew up playing, Isiah wasn't running out of ammo any time soon.*

He walks up to the Dead Head stumbling to get back to its feet and places the Mossburg to back of the dead head that use to be Rick- the Production Manager down at the Green House- and with one pull, Isiah for once was able to change Rick's fucking mind about something!

It took about three minutes before Isiah could clear the room and staircase of anything that wasn't actually alive or friendly. When he reaches his stepsisters, the look on their tiny little faces is part unspeakable fear and another part unquestionable joy!

Back to reality, John looks down at the tiny faces of the children, mingling with each other. Each were doing their best to process the events that have driven them to this spot. Compassion rules the moment, when the wards under Semaj's care lend their extra toys to the shaken Hunnfield girls.

That act of tenderness among the youngest of the lot, forced even the hardened among the group to examine their lives.

John turns and asks Isiah, "That book of codes, is it still inside, in your father's desk?"

Isiah shakes his head no, he hands John a sealed manila folder with the words written in black bold letters, **Shangrl-La.**

Isiah's still a bit stunned when he said. "I was never allowed to go deep down in the maintenance section of the greenhouse. I heard there's a cabinet with a strange keycard lock. My dad never touched it though, he said it wasn't ours to investigate."

Everyone waited while Big John tore open the seal on the envelope, and into his large hands a black book landed. Along with a silver coded key card! Big John handed his daughter Robin the key card as he scans the thin black book looking for the information it held. Once extracted, John hands the book to young Isiah and then said.

"My good man, the rest, belongs to you and your family."

It took only a few minutes to reach the obscure hatch hiding in plain sight. Father nods to daughter and she sticks the wafer-thin key card into the slot. Without much fanfare the cabinet door popped open, and a computer console was presented! Most of the group tried to look over Big John's broad shoulders with no avail. While Ernesto, Celeste, Sky and Paradise were busy investigating the merchandise. Because the grow house was filled with blooming plants! Celeste calls to Isiah.

"Hey farmer boy, how many plants are in here?"

Isiah replies with a bit of irritation, "My name is Isiah, not farmer boy! My father, my father grew thousands of plants here. Now would someone explain how you people are?"

Big John replies in a gentle, yet powerful nature.

"Isiah, I'm the BANK. The company that paid for all of this! The person that helped your family get out of debt. As well as, put your family on the road of forever financial security, that you were on. It's totally up to you, for your family may join our, family. In these times I sincerely feel the living need to stick together! Give me an amen if anyone feels that's right."

Earl hums, AMEN.

With that John punched in the ten-digit code and within seconds the sound of the floor moving startled everyone including Isiah-well everyone except Earl of course. For it's hard to frighten a serial killer, unless you have them strapped down in the gas chamber!

The floor opens to reveal a short staircase, which leads to a long concrete and metal hallway- back lit by sensor activated L.E.D lights. John takes the lead as the survivors walk one by one down a tight winding hallway, leading straight down into mother earth.

Earl had to hunch over so his bald head wouldn't scrap the cold concrete ceiling which was a humorous sight that everyone missed. Finally, after a four-minute hike the survivors reach a dead end! A huge gray pipe was embedded in the hallway, which lead to seemingly no fucking where.

Big John said, "Robin, hon, I need you to use the key card one more time."

His daughter stepped forward and handed her father the envelope holding the thin key card/computer circuit. Big John traces his big fingers across the nearly seamless surface until he finds the slit just behind the oval pipes molding. As soon as the circuits' touch, a console pops open for the input of the nine-digit code.

John does his part, allowing the wall behind the pipe to slowly crank down, disappearing below the floorboards. He smiles, winks and signals the group onward, right to the open arms of a large gain elevator. Everyone in the group had many questions, yet it was Celeste who asked first.

"Are we just going to leave our badass Soviet Helicopter just sitting out in the open?"

Robin replies, "If someone can fly it, they can have it."

Celeste pretends to pouts as she said. "Really, but, I,I want it."

As the last of the survivors enter the elevator, Big John closes the metal gate and then said.

"Celeste my dear, once you enter Shangri-La, there won't be need to leave for at least, well until we are prepared to meet what await us outside these walls."

That's when the questions start flooding in, first from Indigo.

"How did you manage to achieve all of this from Death Row?"

Big John's rugged yet handsome face smiles as he replied.

"Madame, I started this before, I was on Death Row, thank you very much."

For whatever reason Sky raised her hand as she asked, “Were you sort some of tech millionaire or something?”

Isiah’s trying to get his head around all that’s happening, as he clutches his tiny frightened step sisters, he muttered.

“I, I never knew this was here. Did my dad know?”

Big John slowly shook his head no and said, “Oh no, I could not let anyone know about this. At times, I made sure to hire construction crews from states away just to ensure secrecy.”

Cherish must know, “How, how did you know all this was going to happen?”

The elevator’s slowly moving downwards, and the inhabitants waited for Big John to say something. However, before he could, their short ride up is over. John pulled open the metal gate and lead the group to their new home. He leads the survivors down a short ramp towards another wall that seems to lead nowhere, and it took Paradise to mention.

“You really must be into Batman or James Bond with all this discretion.”

Big John just smiles as he uses the last thin key card and slipped it into a tiny slit in the wall and then replied. “I was taught discretion is always the better party of valor.”

The wall slowly cranks below the floorboard and John lead the survivors into their new home, **Shangri-La**. The survivors’ mouths cannot help but hang open in awe as they look up into the spiral sphere which resembles a cloudless blue sky, being projected on the roof! As they walk into the entry level, motion sensor L.E.D lights illuminate their path until John finds a panel on the wall. He flips a few switches and dim lights pop up all over the complex, John gives a brief block of instructions of what they are in store for and what their living conditions will consist of for the time being.

"Welcome to Shangri-La ! A six-story doomsday proof, utopia that was been design to withstand a 50 megaton Nuclear warhead, Various viral Biohazards, floods up to 250 feet and now the Zombie apocalypse! We have the making for everything we need for 700 people to survive for the next two decades."

From the movement John when into business for himself, this was his dream project! ***Flashback before September 11th 2001****, and terrorism had not been a primary thought of the American populace. Even though the Federal Building in Oklahoma City had been destroyed by an act of domestic terrorism in* ***1996.*** *America generally will turn a blind eye on the* ***right wing*** *Citizen who feels his country didn't try hard enough to reach out to them as well as respect the time honored values of; White Men, a White Jesus and owning a fuck load of guns!*

By 2006, the year John was discharged he had spent twenty seven years in the United States Air Force. Sadly, like a number of Veterans at that time, he had spent the last two years in a "forced hold"- meaning the government would not let them go- for their MOS were deemed strategic national assets! John could have spent another eight years to get 100% of his Air Force Retirement pension.

However, his skill as a freelance Geneticist was in high demand, so he gladly accepted the 70% the Air Force offered and joined the civilian work force! Finally retiring has a Lt. Colonel who worked in Special Forces Command. This allowed John to keep a security clearance. Which turned out to be a perk in his field of work!

It wasn't long before suitors came knocking on Big John's employment door. He remembered his first "Consultant" job took him to the South Pole's Amundsen-Scott Station.

Ice samples were dredging up samples of bacteria and other unidentified organisms that ended up dating back in some case billions of years! John remembered having earned more in a week, than he had in his first ten years in the Air Force.

Since then, just about every penny he made was spent for the construction and development of **Shangri-La**. *That included cultivating Hank Hunnfield as an asset! His farm had been one of the keys to getting all this done. If Hank had not been heavily in debt, maybe none of this would have been possible. John silently thank the heavens for the decease's poor money management!*

The total cost was nearly forty million as John envisioned. Federal grants dealing with issues such as clean energy, protecting wetlands and earthquake monitoring only chipped in for nine million taxpayers' dollars.

John split his original nest egg in acquiring the property and bailing Hank Hunnfield out of this debt before his hand that held his shotgun in his mouth, slipped! The rest came for the cultivation and distribution of medical and legal marijuana in the state of Illinois.

The deceased and now probably Zombie Hank had no way of knowing that four of the seven dispensaries his marijuana was sent to, was also owed by a sub company of the shell company that loaned Hank his seed money in the first place! Big John covered all the angles, this utopia was partly powered by a field of a half dozen-twenty feet high windmills. As well as one hundred and twelve solar panels raised on thirty-five-foot pikes to keep safe from the probability of local flooding. Still the local river did provide hydro-electro power, around 30%.

The bottom floor in which they entered via secret passageway, was the second maintenance level housing areas such as storage units, water purification controls and waste removal center. Each of the survivors are marveled at the sheer size of the facility.

Walking up a ramp towards another cargo style elevator, the group walks past the first of five hydroponics bays. As they reach the next elevator, Big John informs the group.

"It's surmised that all it would take is near eight hundred people to restart civilization. So, I built this place with that in mind."

Robin huffs and said, “Well, I don’t see that happening any time soon, so we have room to spare.”

Ernesto smiles as he replied, “That’s going to mean we are going to need to do a lot of procreating.”

Celeste laughs as she chimes in, “Ha,ha I’m not having eight hundred children! although, I could see myself with tres.”

Big John opens the grain elevator, allowing the rest of the survivors to filter in as he explains.

“There are bound to be some survivors in the area...”

That’s when Isiah mutters. “Huh, sir I need to go get my other siblings. Will, will someone watch my little sisters Jennifer and Helen?”

There was silence among the group as the elevator started its trek up to the main lobby. Cherish was first to speak up when she said, “I, I’ll gladly watch your sisters, but, but it’s really messed up out there.”

Jennifer and Helen are clutching on to Isiah’s pants legs, sobbing, confused and very, very frightened that he will leave them and probably never return! Indigo does her best to comfort the young man.

“Listen, you have no idea what’s happening, if we didn’t have that helicopter, we never would have made it.”

Isiah stated with anguish. “Then take me there! I know the rest of my family is waiting on someone to rescue them.”

Big John knows the matter rests in his hands, his is the pilot and engineer of this entire complex, so he said.

“I will take you to go check on your family, I understand your need to rush into danger. Allow me to start the computers that run this place and we’ll head out.”

John looks to Ernesto and Earl, and they don't seem to want to take up the mantle of road dogs, he frowns at them. Robin sets up, when she said.

"I'm with you dad, you're not getting rid of me that easy."

Big John smiles a deep heart felt smile, then cast an even harder look to his comrades, before each man nodded their heads in compliance. Once the elevator reaches the desired floor it stops, and Big John opens the gate allowing everyone to exit.

The room that housed the main control center was as large as a one-bedroom apartment without the kitchenette. The overall oval shape of Shangri-La made the area look and feel even bigger! The room's divided by two sets of four mounted Video monitors. One group of Video monitors reveal the various cameras located inside the complex. And the other group, show what the environment is doing outside Shangri-La.

Either side of the room contains either five Dell Towers Computers or serval Apple Laptops running everything in, above and under Shangri-La. Big John turns on each of the devices and with each turn on, a part of Shangri-La came to life! The kids among the survivors' marvel at the many different colored lights strung out through various levels.

As soon as Big John finishes his startup process, he calls to Celeste, as he points to one particular video screen and then said.

"Celeste dear I need you to monitor this screen. This is the only the second time since the environmental controls has been started. Any problems with register with this needle moving into the red. If that happens, hit this switch, fast!"

Celeste let out a nervous laugh as she nods her head yes, while saying.

"And run like hell, right hombre?"

Big John turns and tells his traveling companions, "We are going to need to change into something a bit more suitable for this mission."

***Fun Fact Flashback**, before European immigration St Charles was the location of the Native American community of the Pottawatomie tribe that inhabited the area for countless generations! After the Black Hawk War in 1832, the entire area of the Fox Valley was opened to American settlement. Evan Shelby and William Franklin staked the first claim in what is now St. Charles in 1834.*

They came like most settlers back in 1834 with their scraping families from Indiana and were joined by over a dozen other adventurous families later that year! The township was initially known as Charleston, but this name was already taken by the downstate city of Charleston, Illinois. Some have suggested that S.S. Jones, a Lawyer from Indiana came up with the name of St. Charles, which was later adopted in 1839.

St. Charles became incorporated as a city February 9, 1839 and reincorporated October 17, 1874 (under the 1870 Illinois Constitution). Which is an important fact, for during the American Civil War, St. Charles Illinois was one of the homes of the "underground railroad".

Several "stations" of the slavery-era Underground Railroad were in St. Charles homes, complete with tunnels and false doorways; there was also an open abolitionist group called the Kane County Anti-Slavery Society, founded in 1842, with about 180 members.

Most accounts lead back to a local blacksmith who set up shop in a building now known as 305 W Main St. This was most likely "the hub," and this address was the easiest to visit from the dozen still standing known "stations". As of 2015 a fine dining establishment holds residence at that address bearing a name in honor of that Blacksmith.

Five streets over, **Saint Thomas of Assisi**-the only Catholic High School in the city- had been on lock down since 10:30am and for good goddam reason!

For St. Charles, lies roughly 40 miles (64 km) west of Chicago on Illinois Route 64. According to a U.S. Census Bureau estimate in July 2019, the city had a total population of 34,627. Forty miles used to mean something before everyone had personal vehicles that go 0-60 in under nine seconds!

Before, a week ago forty miles was nothing when your personal vehicle gets fifteen miles to the gallon, and you have a full tank of gas and forty dollars in your pocket!

The official city slogan was ***Pride of the Fox***, named after the Fox River, that runs through the center of town. Nowadays after infection, only the sly and shrewd are still alive to talk about the origins of the area!

As it happened, good ole Route 64 was jammed with stalled, emptied or wrecked vehicles taking up both sides of the thoroughfare. The smell of overturned fuel trucks mingled with flipped over garbage trucks and the blood of thousands of goddam dead people. As well as the Dead who couldn't stay dead even if they fucking wanted to!

The COVID-MOMREL-6 virus, RAGER virus or simply Red Dearth was designed to be 99.7 % contagious. The reason that .03 percent persist, circled above the Catholic school looking for signs or life. However, the sound of the hoovering Helicopter was bringing out the dead for sure as well as the murderous RAGERs! John doesn't have the luxury of inserting a team on the roof and leading the herd away, fuel as well as time were a consideration.

So, he did what he does best, find a way to make it happen! If the school has been breached in any way John should have been able to make it out from the air. When he couldn't one, John skillfully set the heavy Soviet Helicopter down hoping every second the lumbering beast didn't crash through the school roof. Luckily St. Thomas was an older high school built in the 1950s- during the fear of Soviet attack. It's a sturdy three story building the size of your average Home- Depot.

Once that feat of landing the lumbering craft has been accomplished. The thoughtful father won't take no for an answer, about his daughter staying in the aircraft. While Big John, the Ghostface Killer, Chicken- Head and young Isiah Hunnfield venture into the belly of the beast to put in some work.

The trio were decked out in black welders googles allowing the Night Vison glasses to rest on top their heads-, blue painters overalls, Major League Baseball approved knee-ankle and matching forearm guards, NFL shoulder pads, body Kevlar, black leather gloves and black steel toed Wolverine boots! All compliments of Big John's apocalypse approved fallout shelter along with a small tank of pure oxygen equipped with its own mask.

John threw Ernesto a brand-new iron crowbar as they exited the aircraft.

Which he used to pry open the roof door to St. Thomas of Assis, even so not even the thick surgical mask could camouflage the smell of decay, shit and death! It was strong enough to nearly make the Ghost Face Killer puke.

For a brief second Ernesto reflected on how in the past he might have shot someone under his employment if they even gaged at such things! How times have changed, he thought, as he pressed forward. When the door opened the air was suddenly a whirl of dust, dirt and soot. The only light that's provided was that by the flashlights each man carried. Carefully Ernesto leads the way, stepping over decaying headless corpses or piles of chewed over bones.

Books, backpacks and molded over Lunchables litter classrooms and hallways a like! Not so **FUN FACT**, total darkness can be suffocating to the petrified and the non-terrified equally.

All the frightening aspects of your childhood are quickly put on display and without balance, fear will overtake most people. The deeper the four would be rescuers venture into the building, the more the stale smell of the enclosed area was hard to ignore.

Death reeks like a soiled infant in a pasture of cow shit! In these times if anyone doesn't lock in on the horrendous smell, then they are probably already hopelessly, dead.

Each of the men, take a room, opening or trying to open the soiled door handle of classroom doors. When anyone of their group found a door locked, they placed a few soft knocks on the stained wood. If nothing happens the men regroup before heading down the stairs.

Isiah definitely felt the need to move faster, nevertheless their task was a slow process. Because the seasoned assassin, serial killer and military minded people leading him would rather be safe than sorry.

Isiah whispers more to himself than the group, even so in the eerie silence that blankets the group, they all heard his concern.

"Oh, oh my god, what if we are too late?"

Ernesto did his best to ignore Isiah's concern as he silently made his way down the blood crusted stairs, moving with the effortlessness of a sleek alley cat. When he turned the corner leading to the second floor, the Ghost Face killer's keen eyesight catches movement. He quickly lowered his flashlight, turns his head and whispered.

"Mi amigos, it's time to go all cyclops and shit?'

Ernesto turned off his flashlight, pulled down the Night vision glasses and waited for his eyes to adjust to the greenish-grayish images. The stench of dead fruit and vomit was still wavering in his nostrils. However, the Ghost Face Killer sees it again, at least two yellow puss faced RAGERs talking to themselves- much like mental patients are known to do.

As point man, Ernesto could not help but notice there are eight and ½ Zombies scattered directly in front of the bottom of the stairwell. He screws the silencer into his brand new- right out of the box-, 22. Ruger and his companions follow suit with their own personal weapons.

Ernesto chooses the 22. caliber Ruger as his silenced weapon for the simple fact it allowed him to carry more clips for the AR-15. The Ghost Face Killer's 22. Ruger holds ten in the clip and one in the chamber and that makes eleven, his lucky number. As well as the use Night Vision Glasses makes it easier to see in the darkness of what use to be Saint Thomas of Assisi and that's a tactical bonus! As he carefully moved to the next soiled step, Big John's doing the same as over watch- that makes it John's job to catch anything that Ernesto may have missed.

Big John makes sure the back of Ernesto's head isn't lined up with his silenced .32 Berta.

He picked this as his silenced weapon of choice for it holds nine in the clip, one in the chamber and is nicely balanced. For his P.O.V. John can see the carnage that the *Red Death* has unleashed upon the unaware populace of St. Charles Illinois and the world!

The lump in his throat could not be contained as his mind attempted to ponder his role in all this madness. A severed torso drags itself across the filthy floor towards a teenage RAGER who mumbles to herself; and she kicks the Zombie in the face instead of trying to step over it. Must be no honor among thieves, John thought to himself.

His left hand was on Ernesto's shoulder letting him know he was in place. Next up was Chicken Head, who's closely following his two amigos. John was backing up the Ghost Face Killer and he surely didn't want to get accidently shot in the back of his head. Nevertheless, from his conversations with Chicken Head, he understood that Earl hadn't accidently shot anyone since he was eleven years old!

Back in his hunting days, the serial killer in Earl liked to carry a sub nosed ole school .38 Police Special. Simply because it never left shells at the scene of any of his crimes. From his P.O.V. Chicken Head can witness what happens when the lid is taken off sanity! The dead should not be rising and eating pimply skinned teenagers. The dismember corpses of what looked like teachers should not be crucified in front of classroom doors!

It made him feel fucking sad. Earl fancied himself an artist, a painter of death! And if you found your way on to his canvas, there's a slim chance you might have had it coming. Besides that, nothing felt worse than wearing all this protective gear, or lugging nearly five hundred rounds of personal ammo. With no air conditioning Earl's huge hairy balls are sweating big time!

Isiah Hunnfield didn't want his hands to shake. Nevertheless, it didn't matter for they had a mind of their own! The big bald black man instructed Isiah to watch their rear and they would hopefully find his family.

And for his credit, Isiah was doing his best not to run past the three men and find what's left of his kin! He didn't know them, nor did his father. Yet what choice did Isiah have, the three men at least volunteered their help. All he wanted to do was find his kin alive! Then get back safely to that James Bond/Batman style mancave and see if any of those hot women are single.

Isiah's mind slightly ponders on how he always wanted Night Vision glasses, but never bought a pair. Now the thought of having to battle these, these THINGS in the dark without the NV's is beyond frightening! The very thought of having his glasses ripped off his face's just as disturbing to Isiah as the smell of festering human waste.

Earlier John did his best to calm Isiah's fears, nonetheless he can only hope the young man can keep it together. Isiah was indeed brave, nevertheless the valor needed to constantly stare death down had to be earned through skirmishes, such as what is about to happen. Isiah's fear wants him desperately to haul ass down the trash laden stairs and splatter every got dam Zombie on the second floor of St. Thomas of Assisi!

However, all three of the serious acting men he was following told him to basically shut, up, don't shoot until we and never let anything creep up behind them! Isiah feels none of the men really trust him. More troubling to Isiah was why should he trust men who have a secret underground doomsday bunker stocked with weapons, on his family farm? His father's views were somewhat Conservative, even though he hired anyone, and he would pray with everybody. Nevertheless, father never built a super complex under their home to meet the end of the world!

Meanwhile back on the roof, Robin and Dawn nervously wait, hoping nothing runs out of the breached roof door. A week ago, Dawn was a thick- 36C-27-37- white girl whose only care was about how many creepy guys she had to talk out of their hard-earned cash- without actually allowing them to touch her of course!

Now she sits in the door of the still running aircraft, doing her best to hold the fully locked and loaded Soviet 7.62 mm aircraft gun pointed at the breached entrance. Eight hundred rounds sit ready and wait for anything not human that wanders out the entrance to the creepy school, turned into slaughterhouse!

Robin not one for making small talk does her best by asking, "Hey, it's Dawn right?"

Dawn the sexy redhead wore the same gear as the rescue party, she nods her head yes and replied. "Yeah, people thought that was my working name, but nope. I was born to trailer park parents without much imagination. Yours is Robin, right?"

Marshal Aquila knew her title carried little to no stinking weight in a Zombie Apocalypse. Everyone is pretty much now on a first or last name bases, over the roar of the aircraft she asks.

"So, Dawn why did you volunteer to come on this mission?"

Dawn never let her view leave the doorway as she replied.

"I don't know, I felt his pain. I, I hope someone would have checked on my father, he is a nursing home out in Oklahoma, sad to think of how we haven't spoken in years. And my mom, my MOTHER, I wish a Zombie ate her years ago, real fucking slow like!"

Robin let that conversation slowly fade off, she can hear the pain in Dawn's voice, and she doesn't feel the need to bring it out any further. Robin goes on by saying.

"I used to date a dancer. I think it took me about two weeks to find out he was more gay than bi."

Inside the Catholic High School, Ernesto was nearly at the bottom of the stairwell leading to the second floor. The rescue party so far was still unnoticed, the Ghost Face Killer nods his head giving John the signal, it's a go! Ernesto keeps his shooter crouch as he fired his first shot into the bloated skull of the crawling Dead Head.

The low pop from his pistol was barely louder than the impact of the .22 slug crashing into the Zombie's skull. He waited to see what the response of her cohorts would be. Luckily the Dead Head on the far in of the hallway didn't seem to notice. However, the five closest to the sound, did!

As they started to moan, the Ghost Face Killer stands up and moves into action. With steady aim Ernesto fires his .22 Ruger in a quick session as he moved straight towards the small crowd. Each round splatters the soft decaying flesh of intended target. Nevertheless, on this day the Ghost Face Killer shot selection wasn't perfect.

A few of his bullets didn't register clean head shots, two register as neck and upper shoulder wounds. The remaining undead still not dead, belong to Big John Hammond who briskly moved down the stairs behind Ernesto.

He carefully aimed silenced his .32 caliber firearm at any corpse his companion happens to miss. Their execution of the small group of Dead Head was so swift, the rest herd at the end of the hall hardly noticed!

Well, that's until the two RAGERs that had been walking up and down the hallway turn to see the men standing among fresh Zombie corpses. Both RAGERs probably were members of the High School football team, for they are HUGE! Pink chubby faces sporting ugly yellow puss marks.

The chubbiest RAGER's high school shirt was ripped and drenched in dried blood, deep red blood drips from his ears and the corner of his lips. Its screamed, grabbing the attention of twenty Zombies standing at the other end of the hall. Their shuffling and odd gnat propels the smell that signals the death of humanity!

Chicken Head hauled his hefty frame down the stairs to join his co patriots, for they shouldn't have all the fun! While both his friends are busy reloading their weapons, the serial killer that is Earl Grimes. Stepped forth and professionally dispatches the screaming RAGER and the first five Zombies that got in moaning distance.

Earl took a step back in order to pop in a speed loader, when Isiah comes down the stairs and he witnessed the remaining of that un-dead herd being gun down by steady handgun fire. The horror in Isiah's eyes wasn't hard to miss for the shooting of- middle school and high school kids- even as Dead Heads was a horrendous sight to behold!

Gun smoke made the already rancid air harder to breath. Everyone was craving fresh air, so they replaced the surgical mask with the ones carrying pure oxygen. Big John turns and tells Isiah.

"You need to check the bodies for signs of any of your siblings. I know it's a shitty job, nevertheless, sad to say it falls all on you young Hunnfield."

Isiah wants to shake his head NO; however, he knew the man is right! Nonetheless, the sight of mangled and chewed upon 14-18-year olds was having a negative effect on his stomach. Isiah must stoop down, so he can look at the broken, battered and bloody faces. It can't be helped as young Isiah raises the flap on his mask to vomit up the rest of his empty stomach upon the already fucked up floor!

Big John, Ernesto and Earl continue their search, each finding only empty rooms. There are no signs of any living creature, just ripples of sheer violence. Human teeth impaled into a teacher's desk. Half chewed limbs scattered across grimy floors. A beaten corpse lies embedded into a classroom floor! When it comes to the locked doors the process is the same, knock and wait to see what happens next.

The last door Chicken Head knocked on, slowly opened revealing a fifty-year-old woman with an olive complexion, baggy eyes and dirty clothes, who's frighten yet alive! Nabila Hussein opened the door holding the chopping half of a century old paper cutter.

***Flashback to 1987**, sixteen Nabila's Iranian family in all sense of the world sold her to a Kuwait man for a 1981 Ford Tauru with bald tires! That's right, literally sold to a Kuwait man with the last name Ami. Who was a fucking Magician! A showman to Princes', Emperors, Oil Magnets, Presidents', and Kings. Amir collected erotic looking females and transsexuals- Transgendered males- to distract his audience from his sleight of hand and visual illusions!*

Nabila's belong to him and for the seven years she toured with Amir's traveling harem. Which performed more than magic for any Prince or Ruler who was not accustomed to taking NO for an answer. In some countries she had visited a performer's answer might influence whether the entire group could even leave that country, or not!

For his credit- if you can say that- Amir never forced himself on any of his "assistants". He managed fifteen women or almost women, making sure their hotel rooms were paid, they ate in the finest restaurants, flew on his private jet, and made sure their beauty shops tabs are always picked up. Nails and toes freshly polished and each wore the newest designer clothes worth dying for!

Nonetheless, it took Nabila five years to figure Amir was no more than a balding, portly middle-aged pimp! As well as a third-rate magician.

The magic show was just a front to peddle exotic girls or Transgendered males from around the world. It seems Asian and bronze Brazilians transwomen draw a big purse in Arab and Persian palaces! Depending on the performer, up to one hundred thousand a night would be deposited into Amir's silk lined pockets.

Amir- like him or not- hit upon a gold mine of an idea, Billionaires in the Middle East for all their so-called religious bullshit, are still men, super rich men that are accustomed to having anything they want. No matter what the price! And behind closed doors that anything is generally fucking sexual.

Amir crafted his magic acts with tricks he lifted from Las Vegas magicians. His brilliance laid in the use of over a dozen drop dead gorgeous human beings in little to no costumes! As she got older the lack of clothes made no sense to Nabila. From 17-24 she would perform with her pear-shaped buttocks hanging out the back of her skimpy thong. Yet in those same countries, Nabila could not go outside her house without wearing a total beekeeper's outfit! What kind of male dominate bullshit is that?

When Nabila opened the door, from her P.O.V. she might have thought, finally the CDC had arrived. The surgical masked wearing induvial was at least human! A very large human. Earl shined his light into the room and asked in the gentlest voice he could muster. As he learned early on, his slow southern draw generally helps lull people into dropping their guard.

"Hello, I'm Earl Grimes and we are looking for the Hunnfield triplets."

Once Robin got Dawn talking, she didn't stop! Mind you she never took her eye off the doorway or her hand off the trigger of the mounted gun. That didn't stop Dawn from telling Robin about dropping out of college, falling in love with the wrong guys, an abortion and her current obsession with Hot Yoga and Reggae. When Dawn noticed a dingy white towel waving in the doorway, she tenses up, her index finger ready to apply the needed pressure to make the Soviet made weapon sing!

Luckily for all Chicken Head escorted the Middle-aged woman and three high schoolers- two girls and one boy out the door. Earl hustled his massive frame up to the running helicopter, leaning in the fuselage and said.

"We've mange to clear the third floor, and some of the second. We're heading to the first floor now."

Dawn asked in earnest, "Where do you think any survivors be hiding at this point?"

Earl pointed out, "I heard Private High School cafeterias have food to die for?"

It didn't take long before Chicken Head rejoined his comrades in arms. The Ghost Face Killer, Big John and Isiah are perched at the top of the flight of stairs. Big John whispers.

"It sounds like a whole lot more of them down there! We really need eyes on the terrain."

Earl holds up one finger signaling wait, his massive frame back pedals up the stairs showing more agility one would think a man large as him could possess.

Chicken Head back pedaled until he disappeared around the corner, much like a phantom. Forcing Isiah to mutter to himself.

"It looks, like, like he, he just melted with the wall and is, gone."

Ernesto whispered, "Yes, Earl is a man of many talents. Oh, by the way, don't extend to him any bad manners. He's kind of, over sensitive about stuff like that."

Big John turns his head to whisper to Isiah. "Just don't get on his bad side, until he knows you better. Ok."

Isiah slowly nods his head yes. Earl makes it up to the killing field of what is the second floor. He had noticed several female handbags scattered among the thick muck and human waste of what was the small Zombie herd. Earl checks some of the backpack, finding contents and wonders Chicken Head wasn't even expecting!

A tin of what parents might have considered could be breath mints. A pity they never took the time to sample one and found a hidden treasure. That's right motherfucking ACID! Some enterprising student or worse a hippy teacher was roaming the halls with a tin of wonderful ACID. Whoever said Catholic High Schools was lame can go fuck themselves! Well, what comes next when one of the malicious as well as industrious Serial Killers America has ever produced, unexpectedly was about to trip major BALLS?

Earl might have been locked up for over a decade, but still he knew the feeling of good drugs as it roams his body. It took a few moments, still after taking the three breath mints, Earl was high as giraffe pussy!

Luckily Earl was a big man and those three TABs-, just took most of the edge off the murderous rage he's dealing with. The smell of iron from the amount of blood in puddles attempting to dry in utter darkness was weighing on him! Combine it with the smell of mold and brownies, Earl swore he can smell brownies over the smell of decaying flesh and rotting wood, made him hungry. God, he felt hungry, no he feels famished! "Why do I want brownies, thought Chicken head.

He felt like life was moving in slow motion as Earl found a female's compact makeup kit with mirror in the bag in which he found motherfucking acid. For whatever reason, he made the classic rookie mistake in looking into the mirror while tripping on acid. A big NO-NO! Yet Earl has been locked up for a long time and he wasn't thinking safety. Only enjoying the moment, primo acid is hard to find!

As he stood up the floor began to change into a thin long white line against the backdrop of putrid darkness. Earl's feet clutched the lines, like he was walking a tight rope and one false move would plunge him towards certain death! Sweat beads down the shaven head of the acid tripping escaped serial killer.

Earl's breathing was coming short and fast, he attempts to slow down and put things in order.

"This isn't real, it isn't really. All I have to do is turn around and walk back up the stairs."

Then he heard the voice, he feels like it's something out of his past or maybe his future? It's so hard to tell when you are on acid!

"Earl, my lovely, lovely Earl."

Earl's bottom lip quivers as he mutters, "Is, is that you, mama?"

"I'm, I'm sorry baby, I never should have died, leaving you with my parents."

Earl cries like a newborn baby as he sobs and then said.

"I really didn't mean to kill Me-maw, I, was, I was, I, I was just angry. Pop-Pop did deserve a hammer to the back of his head for he made me kiss his private place! I'm so sorry mama, MAMA, MAMA! I broke everyone's heart, but you are, dead! What's. NO.NO.NO...."

Earl was whispering screaming! You know not loud enough to be LOUD, but enough that Isiah creeped up the stairs to check on him. Why Big John or Ernesto didn't move faster, might play into one of the greatest tragedies of Isiah's rescue mission. They had been busy discussing how to break the news to Isiah that his rescue mission maybe over. When neither bothered to address Isiah wandering back up the stairs, on his own!

Once he hit the second floor, Isiah saw the bald giant, sweating and crying, like Earl was going through a mental breakdown. He didn't know what to do, Isiah tried calling out to Earl.

"Mister Earl, mister, HELLO."

Earl had his eyes closed, as he slowly cracked the bones in his thick neck. The voices inside Earl's smooth cranium are screaming at each other about the direction of his life! He had been given a new lease, no longer on Death Row. Now, who should he be? The Shepard or the Wolf?

In his drug induced state of thought, the thin white line represents the good that is somewhere buried deep, deep- maybe a bit deeper still- inside Earl Grimes. Compare to the vast swaths of darkness that swirl like malevolent waves of evil, splashing against the edges of what's left of his goddam sanity!

Like an unaware swimmer caught swept up in a murderous rip tide, Isiah struggles with all his might! Yet he will never be able to break free of Chicken-Head's deadly grip.

Poor Isiah was no more than a rag doll being flung about by an angry toddler! When Earl does open his eyes, everything feels surreal, he looks at his hands only to find himself strangling the life out of another struggling innocent young man! Isiah's feet dangled nearly two feet off the floor as he fought in vain to break Earl's vice-like grip.

Young Isiah smacks at Chicken Head's face as his eyes plead for his life! Earl can feel Isiah's life draining away as his eyes bugle out of his soon to be lifeless head. He wants to stop, yet he just doesn't know how!

The snapping of Isiah's neck wasn't loud enough to draw attention, nor is his body hitting the floor of St. Thomas of Assis. Nonetheless, it did strike an accord, deep inside what's left of Earl Grime's soul!

Chicken Head looked at the crumpled body of Isiah staring up at him from the debris, the eyes seem to beg to know, why me?

Earl exhaled, steps over the body of his last innocent victim and jogs down the stairs to rejoin his comrades. When he gets there, he hands Big John the tin of Acid and the makeup mirror. Big John hands the mirror to Ernesto, then looks inside the tin.

Before he can take one Earl Exhales and said.

"No don't do that. It's Acid, I found out the hard way. I accidently took three!"

Ernesto chimes in, "Acid, OK, maybe later. Wait, THREE? Mi amingo, you're trippin balls? Now? No, really..."

Big John looks over Earl's shoulder and asked. "Ah, where's Isiah?"

Earl exhales a deep long breath, "Like I said I found out that is acid, the hard way."

Big John feels like he has been hit by a truck. They had come here to rescue Isiah's family and it appears young Hunnfield died for nothing! Now for the first time Big John was angry with his large comrade and Earl can feel it as he attempted to explain.

"I didn't do, that poor young man with malice in my heart! John, you must understand I had no knowledge that was acid, I thought it was a breath mint. I, I didn't even know I was strangling the poor lad until his neck snapped... Didn't either of you hear me down there screaming MAMA?"

Ernesto injects, "Yes, but I thought you were just, working out some issues as you, put in some work. I had no clue you were killing the young blanco."

Earl mutters more out of shame of his actions than fear of what his friends thought about him.

"I had no reason to hurt that young man, I never even thought it possible, I bore nor anger towards Isiah. It, it was just one of those tragic moments in time. I, I reached out to grab my dear departed mama. I just wanted to hold her and I, I grab out to Isiah and strangled him to death. I am so sorry for my actions. Plus, this acid is boss!"

John Hammond sighs as he asked in a weary tone. "You up for this? Earl, we owe it to that young man to search the first floor. I was about to call this off, now we can't head home without knowing what happened to his family. Right?"

Both men look to John for direction and has much as he tries, it's hard for him to think and behave like a criminal or even a convict. As much as it is for his comrades to act and behave like civilized non murderous human beings!

It's Ernesto who said.

"Even though his family is probably dead, we will press on, in honor of Isiah!"'

They move down to the first-floor lobby. Ernesto covertly uses the makeup mirror to peek around the 1nd floor stairwell. The stench wasn't as strong, which Ernesto sums up to not as many Dead Heads. However, he saw, what looked like RAGERs. At least ten members of the former baseball team have bashed out every glass trophy.

The Ghost Face Killer noticed a variety of RAGERs, football players, Band members, Teachers and Theater Kids!. Now all sport yellow puss filled blisters with dark crimson blood dripping from their ears, nose and eyes.

His whispers. "I see a sign, I, I think it reads, Cafeteria."

Earl mutters, "I knew I smelled brownies. Oh, now I really want some fried chicken and a Ginger ale."

Up on the overcast rooftop, Robin was sitting in the pilot's chair, and she was beyond impatient. She wanted to turn off the running aircraft, and head inside! Nonetheless, one look at the four people that Earl escorted to safety tells her everything she needs to know. Things could go haywire and if that happen there would be no way to quickly start up this Soviet made beast. All the worried daughter was able do was sit tight and wait until her father and the others made it back safely.

Down on the first floor, fifteen RAGERs and Decaying Dead Heads are loosely scattered throughout the cluttered hall. The Ghost Face Killer uses his silenced AR-15 in the fashion it's design. Ernesto deadly eye has been trained with over thirty confirmed cartel hits.

When he was young, Ernesto would walk right up to his target and expose their gray brain matter to the wind! That's what earned him the nickname Ghost Face Killer- plus he loves the Wu Tang Clan and played their music on the regular.

He silently crept up to the first Zombie, standing at the water fountain with its back turned, and placed the muzzle near the base of its putrid skull. The single muffled sound resembled no more than a PIFF! It was slightly louder than the sound of the round of Ernesto's 22. Luger dropping to the floor. The NATO quality parabellum slams into the Dead Head, dropping it like a sack of walking shit! The Ghost Face waited to see if any of the other Dead People Walking turn towards the sound and thankfully none did.

All while Big John was doing his best to keep an acid tripping hulk of a man, calm. Big John knew he can never show once ounce of fear around a predator like Chicken Head. The only one that truly understood the rhyme or reason of who, or why he murders was Earl! What can you do if a 297+ pound man was tripping on school high chem lab Acid? Earl was seeing all his biggest mistakes in 3-D!. While sitting on the bottom stair the silently sobbing Giant mutters to his, friends.

"Look at me, I can't stop sobbing like a heart broken schoolgirl.

John, what, what do you think of me? I know I'm a bad man, I don't even know if I could change... But I really what to!"

Big John without hesitation drapes his arm around Earl's shoulder, his whisper was filled with concern, he asks.

"Do you want to be a friend? Do you want to turn over a new leaf? If so, it cost nothing to be a kind human being Earl. There are so few of us left, we can't go on killing without at first seeking peace."

Earl Grimes, the serial killer others patterned their craft after, was going through an emotional upheaval – if only the Prison shrinks had offered him acid! As Ernesto silently dispatched the few Zombies close to them, Earl's sobbing began to cease, he said.

"I swear I did not mean to harm that young man! You're my friend and if you are right about it not costing anything to be a kind human being. Well John, now it's time for me to pay up."

Ernesto crouches as he moves back to their position, and he asks.

"Are you two ready or not? I will need your help to go any further. A mass of those things are gathered around the kitchen door."

Fun Fact.; St. Thomas of Assis was built in the 1950s and like most schools of that time -whether public or private- have a giant concrete, no window lunchroom that could easily serve as a school gym, a school auditorium or a makeshift fallout shelter. Even a school whose students' number in the lower four hundred, could manage to shuffle and juggle their students in and out of this area throughout the course of a day.

The kitchen has a metal partition with a heated countertop, with a rolling shutter that could be locked down at the end of the night. At the entrance there was the type of thick swinging doors that can be locked at the top, in the middle and at the bottom.

Ernesto was still on point, and he used the mirror to peer into the hallway leading to the cafeteria. He dares not risk standing up or moving any further, still all the borrowed mirror can reveal are the legs of RAGERs who are banging into one another. Ernesto was busy formulating his next position to move towards.

While a Chicken Head on ACID rears its head once more. Earl slowly stood up from his crouched position. As a look of revelation flashed in his eyes, as he preaches.

"I finally understand my purpose... The tragic death of young Isiah showed me DEATH should no longer be delivered to the living from the living. Only in the most extreme cases, for life. NOW is, indeed, precious! I am sorry for what I did. Yet, not for what I am about to do!"

Before his friends can object to those words, Chicken Head jacks the bolts back on the BAR- a 5.56 mm Browning automatic rifle which houses a 300 drum magazine- stepped around Ernesto and begins unleashing righteous fire down the trash ridden hall!

The first group of RAGERs look like rag dolls as 5.56 NATO rounds blowout ankle bones, impact lower spinal cord, rupture spleens and blast infected brain matter into open lockers and across dully painted walls.

Big John and Ernesto may not understand the words Earl's muttering. Yet his actions need no interpretation! The Browning Automatic rifle or BAR as it's known, is the weapon that changed the way **20th century law enforcement** went about doing its job. During the Great Depression, U.S. Veterans managed to return from WWI with an assortment of weapons used to wage total war!

The end of the war paved the way for US companies who were nicely humming with War time contracts, to scale back their work force. Factories laid off scores women and minorities to make room for returning the onslaught of white, male Veterans.

At the time America was tolling with Prohibition and that law unleashed a wave of crime upon America, which had never been seen before! **Fun Fact,** the lower class will refuse to simply starve! Violent crime went through the roof, entire shipments of BARs, Thompson- Tommy Gun- Submachine Gun, Winchester .306 sniper rifles, frag grenades and 45. Caliber big frame handguns found their way up to most city streets!

Just like one summer day, on the morning of **June 17, 1933**, a grisly mass murder committed in front of Union Railway Station in Kansas City, Missouri shocked the American public into a new consciousness of the serious nature of the changing face of crime in America.

On the morning of June 17, 1933, the killings that took the lives of four peace officers and their prisoner which came to be known as the "Kansas City- Missouri- Massacre" shocked and frightened all the nation. Before that day, armed criminals like Bonnie & Clyde, Baby Face Nelson, John Dillinger and Pretty Boy Floyd were Romanize as the Jesse and Frank James of their area!

Still, it was that fateful day when despicable bank robbers, thieves and murders of four law enforcement officers and a fugitive who was being delivered to prison at the Union Station railroad depot in Kansas City Missouri made history. The kind that wakes a nation from its slumber!

The flashpoint occurred as the attempt from a gang led by Vernon Miller to free Frank "Jelly" Nash, a federal prisoner, from incarceration.

At the time, Nash was in the custody of several law enforcement officers who were returning him to the U.S. Penitentiary at Leavenworth, Kansas, from which he had escaped three years earlier.

What happens next is a thing of public record and Hollywood frame! The Hollywood version and the FBI version pretty much match. Most historians of the Depression`s gangster era agree that the modern-day Federal Bureau of Investigation was born June 17, 1933, in a hail of machine-gun bullets that was dubbed, the Kansas City Massacre!

Historical fact, Raymond Caffrey and five local law officers were viciously gunned down in the midst of a stunned crowd at Union Station.

The populace screamed that something like this should not happen in the 20th century! Not even the days of the old West have five Peace Officers been killed in one shootout. The late J. Edgar Hoover branded the crime with great fanfare when he blamed it on one of the eras' most notorious bad man. Oklahoma bank robber Charles Arthur "Pretty Boy" Floyd, and several of his henchmen!

Jim Esposito the special agent in charge of the Kanas City Office, noted that public outrage over the massacre prompted Congress to pass nine separate crime bills in 1934.

These bills included the first provisions that allowed FBI agents to make arrests, gave them the power to ***carry guns*** and-most important to Hoover`s career-established the FBI as a separate office rather than a subdivision of the Justice Department!

Charles "Pretty Boy" Floyd was identified by the FBI as one of the gunmen. However, there is some evidence to suggest that Floyd was not actually involved.

A pre-apocalypse- of course- investigation by the Kansas City Times produced long-concealed internal FBI documents suggesting that Hoover ordered field agents to frame Floyd for the massacre because he needed a famous criminal case to generate the publicity that forced Congress to create the Nation's first national police force!

Being white, poor and uneducated didn't stop part of the controversy, it fanned it, for the controversy centers on complaints that the FBI manhunt was elitist and unfair!

There were 135 homicides in Kansas City that year, critics note, and none has received a fraction of the same attention, as the death of those local law enforcement in 1933.

Alvin Brooks, a former Kansas City police officer and president of the Ad Hoc Group Against Crime, said his organization`s hot lines had been swamped by callers who are angry that the FBI was pouring massive efforts into a crime involving a middle-aged white man when street violence continues to run rampant, particularly among young black males. For it seems, the real plight of America always circles back to blame the fucking black guy!

"We get many, many callers who just think this is completely unfair," said Brooks.

Officer Brooks stated. "They say that if the police agencies had done (years ago) what they`re doing for one white man NOW. We wouldn`t have the crime problems we have with the darkies today!"

And with that, the Browning Automatic Rife helps usher in the era of a national police force that was intent of preserving the elite social structure, even among its own elk!

Today it rests in the hands of a Serial Killer on a roll coaster high of acid and remorse. The sound of the BAR barking in tight hall space catches the attention of the hundreds of Zombies loitering near the drawn shutters of the kitchen counter.

It seems like the virus caught most if not the entire school unaware. The reek of rotten chunks of flesh falling from the bottom of dead bare feet as they shuffle across cracked tiles was hard to ignore.

The metal clang of bullet cases hitting and bouncing of the trash on the floor, does little to drown out the constant moaning from the lumbering dead heads doing their best to exit the lunchroom.

Acid trippin Earl was single handily dealing with the lunchroom problem, when suddenly behind the trio. The door of the school principal's office explodes outward! A heavy-set man, equal to the size of Chicken Head runs out of the room, infected with the COVID-MOMREL-6 virus. Thick yellow puss runs down his face as blood drips from his ears and eyes.

Big John had just enough time to whirl towards his right and get a quick shot off that luck has it, caught the RAGER directly under its left eye. The force of the round explodes out the back of the heavy-set man's head and he crashes mere feet from John much like a wounded rhino! Other RAGERs followed, forcing John to step back-to-back with Earl as he unslung his suppressed AR-15 off his shoulders and into business mode.

Ernesto understood it was now or never, still the would-be rescuers were too far away from the sealed-up counter area! The Ghost Face Killer moves forward and tosses two shock grenades, shouting with all his might while his comrades kept up the onslaught.

"HEY, HEY, IF YOU CAN HERE US. RUN, RUN TOWARDS THE STAIRS!"

The zombies whom the gunfire had only damaged and not destroyed, limp, crawl, stumble or shamble towards the trio. Who were making a Custer like stand near the base of the first-floor stairs!

Big John could see a mixture of Zombies and RAGERs filing down the stairs like water running down a slope. He mutters,

"Oh NO.."

Ten, twenty, thirty of them followed the sound of gunfire and the hopes of a free meal! John shouts out ,

'we are cut off!"

That's when Earl's weapon goes dry, yet he kept pulling the trigger as if he was unaware what the sound of an empty chamber means. Ernesto shouts.

"Earl. EARL, punta! Snap out of it!"

The acid has Chicken Head by the balls and wasn't letting go, he drops his BAR, while freeing a brand-new razor-sharp machete from a holster on his hip. The first Zombie that approaches Earl gets a size 16EEE though its rotten chest! Nevertheless, it's a horrible time for Earl's foot to get stuck in its gapping cavity!

The doped up Serial killer tumbles forward the machete falling into the chattering Zombies mouth, Earl's weight forces the razor-sharp blade though the creatures' jaws serving most it's head off. John must ditch trying to place headshots to go full auto. Just to stem the tide of death rolling towards their doorstep!

Even with destroying half the horde, the reminder doesn't stop, seek cover, shelter or seem to fear the thought of full metal jacket bouncing off the faces. Ernesto screams one last time as he helps Earl out of the Zombie mess and to his feet.

"PLEASE, COME OUT IF YOU WANT TO LIVE!"

Big John has no time to reload before the first RAGER is nearly on him. Instead, he dropped the AR-15 and pulled up his silenced Berta and is very lucky to get the shot off.

Still, shooting a target exactly where you aim takes skill and his first three shoots impact the chest of the first the targets he lined up on. Nevertheless, the tide of dead and soon to be dead kept advancing!

By the time Ernesto got the emotionally distracted Earl on his feet and headed towards the stairs; that's when the metal doors of the sealed lunch roof counter explode outward!

Five dirty teenagers ran screaming, crying and frightened out of their young minds.

The horde of foul-smelling fiends heading towards the stairs were confused about which direction them should be going. The horde descending the stairs received silent surprise in their rear; in the form of Marshal Aquila and a suppressed AR-15 coming for their ass! Robin uses one 30-shot magazine to rid herself of anything standing between the stairs and her father.

Unfortunately, most of the five students didn't fare as well. The first to go is a strapping stocky lad, who must have been on the football team or wrestling team for he tore out of their hide out with all the steam of a runaway train!

He's a good forty feet away from the stairs, even so, most of the way was covered with something that wants to eat you! Yes, this would-be survivor had armed himself with two cast iron skillets! The blond youth swung his Thor like hammers, connecting with such force the clang from the impact of metal on bone was like making loud fucking heavy metal music!

However, it is his one missed attempt that spun the blond-haired teen 180 degrees around into the arms of a former peer turned RAGER. Who not so politely shoves a large knife into the teenagers' tone belly. He slowly mouths something, but the RAGER fucking didn't care! He gladly slits his former classmates' throat before kicking him to the Zombies that are waiting for any meat they can get.

The next two would be survivors are a bit heavy set or chunky and even armed with butcher knives they're not swift enough to outrun a half dozen RAGERS with baseball bats and way too much attitude! Their horrible death peeled off more Dead Heads who are more interested in the meal that's in front of them.

Enestro, John and Earl laid down intense cover fire, so the last two teenagers have a chance. They keep low and moving, holding hands, the two chestnut haired girls sob loudly. Large globs of snot run from their noses as they maneuver themselves through trash, feasting dead heads, blood-stained floors and remaining RAGERS.

The teenager girls were nearly at the stairs, having avoided the hands of the dead that lurched up from the task of eating their recently decent classmates. The end of their tunnel seemed attainable, that's when tragedy generally steps forward to kick you in chin! Tonight, tragedy was 2-3 and no strike outs.

Big John and the rescuer squad would later find out the two twins running towards them were indeed the Hunnfield daughters Terri and Kerri. Their younger brother Hank Jr was eaten by Zombies on the first day!

Terri, the older and more dominate of the two was leading the way, when the same RAGER who knifed football star Ned Plauson in the belly; even with two bullets in his chest manage to grab hold of Terri! Snatching her down into a whirlpool of gnashing teeth and pounding fist.

Thank heavens Earl snapped out of his acid trip long enough to step forward and snatch hold of Kerri, ripping her hands out of her sisters'. Or death would have gotten its claws on another Hunnfield! At least they manage to save a few people, while regrettably losing a young man who deserved better on this day.

Book Three

Chapter I:

I DON'T KNOW ABOUT YOU, I DON'T PLAN TO DIE HERE!

Four Weeks into infection, time 0730- date 07-01-2024

Chicago Illinois, had been labeled the city of big shoulders. Fancy steakhouses were once the flair of the Midwest, now sat idle with only the hollow sounds of the dead to resemble paying customers. The Chicago Stock Exchange, where hundreds of millions changed hands daily, is now no more than a rave filled with RAGERs. Tens of thousands to be exact, one-time traders, runners and hedge fund managers bump into one another while mumbling some sort of mad lingo too themselves!

High end stores along the famed *Michigan Avenue/MAG MILE aka The Gold Coast* were primed for infection when sneezing employees, mingled alongside paying customers. Each totally unaware there was more going around than summer allergies! Now the smell of the dead, dying and RAGERs cannot be concealed even among thousands of broken bottles of expensive perfumes.

All around the city nearly five hundred thousand Dead Heads crack their diseased ears to the wind when the sound of helicopters broke through the chorus of their fateful moans! Every road in the formally windy metropolis happens to be jammed packed with stall vehicles of every make, year and model. Damaged fire hydrants expelled the last of their contents, flooding out entire viaducts and streets. As the burnt-out shell of high-rise apartment buildings, government offices and private own businesses still smolder in the glow of another Post Apocalypse sunrise!

The morning of Colonel Lafayette's team inserted into an ocean of moaning infected, started out for most inside, as well as outside of Camp McCormick. Among the hustle and bustle of various Military personnel loading, unloading or moving equipment from one designated area to another. Wynolla and Monique find time to share a Lukewarm shower and a cup of warm coffee, per use.

The night before, base XO did his best to flex his authority by limiting the scope and T.O.E.- tactical operational equipment- for Colonel Lafayette's mission. The conversation was tense, for whatever reason the Marine Colonel Dunston, much like the new base commander one Rear Admiral Jefferson Bullraguard Lee were not behaving like sound military men!

The only time David Dunston makes the mistake of getting chest to chest with Wynolla Lafayette. Windu made sure she response was only for Dunston's ears when she whispers.

"Should we need to take this discussion to an empty room, Marine?"

For the look on Colonel Dunston's face expressed to Colonel Lafayette that indeed her force was so much bigger. Colonel Lafayette may be an infectious disease specialist, nevertheless she's an Army Special Forces command infectious disease specialist! Even in the middle of the fucking apocalypse, that shit still means something.

In their parting words that morning, Wynolla reminded Colonel Dunston that the Admiral's private Heli's still be gassed up and ready just in case they needed to abandon ship for a second time. Certainly, that was a dig to what's left of the Marine's ego!

Late the previous night, while holding Monique in her arms, Lafayette lays out her reasons on why she should stay at the base and out of sight until she returned. She even laid out the plan to have Captain Brown shadow Monique in her absence.

However, she will not hear of it! Doctor Littlefield has been in the Amazon rain forest and the slums of Somalia! She knew she was more than capable of handling herself and doing her job in the process.

However, Monique's heart was struck with emotion for Wynolla felt she had to protect her! Even though in their only so-called sparring session, Monique had gotten the better of the Army Officer. Thankfully, the end of the world tossed each other into a shared horizon. For now, one of the safest places for them to be is together! Both doing their best to hold on to whatever humanity they have left.

That same night Army Ranger/ Green Beret Captain Brown takes his 12 operators- consisting of nine Army Airborne Rangers NCOs and three Air Force Black Beret Warrant Officers- high air among the rafters of their makeshift base.

Here's an obscure **Fun Fact** base command probably wasn't aware of. The McCormick place in its heyday housed many different types of conventions and all types of equipment as well of merch must been hauled in and out of the massive showrooms! There are walkways which span the entire complex and most rest secure out of line of sight. Around 30-60 feet above unsuspecting eyes.

Twenty-four of the base's Operators are involved indirectly and directly in the morning mission. Without Doctor Littlefield to watch over, Captain Brown's three-four- person teams lay in wait providing covert recon on base command and the medical staff in their care. That left the remaining twenty-four Operators to perform whatever daily duties that have been previously prescribed.

The night before it was considered best if everyone on the mission wore surgical masks, painters' goggles, long sleeve BDUs and of course BDU cargo pants and surgical gloves. Armed with Captain Browns map, their goal- besides everyone returning alive- find the source of the mysterious S.OS.

The following day the warmth of the morning sun was just starting to make its presence known over Lake Michigan. When the siege of humid air upon the roof of Camp McCormick forced sweat from the brow of Air Force Colonel Kevin McKinney. He was standing with Monique, and Windu as three Army Helicopters are being prepped. The twelve-person team prepare themselves for what awaits beyond the safety of their base.

McKinney states, "All successfully Ops need a good Code Name."

Windu grins as she said, "you are so right, the force is strong with this one."

Colonel Kevin McKinney has always been a self-described goofy fuck. He stood stone faced as he flatly stated.

"Sorry, I'm more of a Vulcan, you know a Star Trek kind of guy. Anyway, what's the Ops name for the official record of course."

Colonel Lafayette looked to Doctor Littlefield, and she stated.

"This will probably make Lee happy. How about, Operation Goose Chase."

While Wynolla interjects, "at least she didn't say wild."

It took a few seconds before all three share a nerve releasing laugh. Wynolla did explore a thought with her fellow officer before hoping aboard waiting helio.

"Colonel we might need to explore a backup sight. We have all are eggs in one basket here and if anything in here goes bad..."

Windu lets her worlds linger as she does a proper salute and McKinney tilts his head to signal, he hadn't been thinking along those lines. Nevertheless, the new base commander's bizarre behavior should have been a concern! McKinney quickly approaches the running helicopter so he may catch up with Wynolla to ask.

"What do you think is going to go wrong Colonel? We spent a lot of time and effort setting this up. Besides were could we even go?"

Wynolla looks her fellow officer in his blue eyes and wondered why he didn't feel the feeling on impending doom since Admiral Lee's arrival. Instead, she answered by saying.

"Hey, I don't plan to die here McKinney! Twenty-one years in this here military has taught me a few things and one of them is always have an area to perform a quick organized forced maneuver to your own rear. Ponder it, Colonel."

With that, Lt. Colonel Layette hops on to the Army Helio, landing right next to Monique. Colonel McKinney turned to see two Sailors walking up to him carrying a message. He follows them into the base as the three helicopters rise off the roof top, back out towards the lake and fly directly into the approaching horizon.

By now every major city and most if not all the minor ones are rivers feeding into oceans of dead people! If the world were flat, like some of the now gone Hipster Anarchist used to ponder, the dead would have tumbled off by now. Finally, those assholes smell like they sound. Honestly just about everything any Hipster or Conservative ever said was all bullshit anyway! Dead Heads and RAGERs have no use for mass transportation, so the sound of air travel got the attention of all. Even those without a pulse!

To their credit the Army pilots effortlessly flew their crafts over the still lake, climbing to four hundred feet before banking and cresting over the city.

It was like the three Army Black Hawk Helicopters were a trio of pterodactyl who didn't understand their time was over!

RAGER began swelling out of their dwelling to shake their fist, as well as throw numerous amounts of office furniture, household items, bricks, bottles and of course human shit towards the sky.

The vibrant city that was, is no more. Now the Dead and their close cousins are the rule of law! Approaching from the North, the Army Helio's were following in the direction of the sun. Yet on this day, the sky was a bit overcast making tracking the movement of that giant fireball in the sky much more difficult. Not to add the numerous broken windows made the colossal skyscrapers appear more like gapped tooth goliaths, than living quarters or former places of business.

The air was hot, humid and the smell of death was very hard to miss even when you are descending from high above. Inside the lead Black Hawk helicopter, Colonel Lafayette confided in Doctor Littlefield they might not ever solve the mystery of the light signals.

"It's been sunny for three days and today, it's overcast. What are the odds of that?"

Monique replies, "I have placed the Weather Channel down to 151 of things I missed before the Apocalypse. Now, I think it just made its way up to number thirty-nine."

Wynolla plays along by asking, "What's thirty-eight?"

Monique smiles as she whispered, "Disney+."

Windu always seems to have the right response when she whispers back, "That's my number fourteen."

The Pilot called out over the roar of the engine, "Taking it down to three hundred feet and would everyone cast all eyes to the nine o'clock position."

As the aircraft moves among the shells that once were home to world renowned restaurants, law firms, investment companies, sports agents and museums. Everyone looks towards the left side of the aircraft, scanning for signs of life.

The once proud CNA Center- was a 600-ft, 44-story high-rise building – stood at once what was 333 South Wabash Avenue. In what was the central business district of Chicago, Illinois. The CNA center as it was once known, opened its doors in 1972 and its original Height: 600 feet (Architectural)

On this day, the building has as many missing or broken windows as it holds unforeseen dangers. Nevertheless, just as Captain Brown predicted. The sun rose right over a mostly damaged set of floors and that's where the signal revealed itself. The first blast of reflected light hits the pilot in his eyes, and he squints while shouting over the roar of the engines.

"Looks like we have a positive sighting."

Windu frees her SF binoculars, scanning the floor and it doesn't take long to see a huge piece of glass is positioned to catch the rays of the giver of light.

Even so that doesn't explain the S.O.S. signal they have been seeing over the last few nights. Nevertheless, the mere presence of the iron dragons calls all the RAGERs and their dead elk, to arms! Out of broken windows many carelessly foes hurled themselves, only to meet the ground at a pronounced pace!

Monique also sported a pair of field binoculars and she's first to make out what looks like a man, holding a jagged piece of mirror one floor above, the huge slab of mirror's facing the rising sun.

She quickly nudges Wynolla and shouts.

"One floor down!"

Colonel Lafayette adjusts her field of vison to find a man trying to get their attention by using his mirror to capture the rays of the sun in his attempt to signal, HELP. In the background of office debris and numerous cardboard boxes, Wynolla can make out a haggard woman and two children desperate to survive! The woman's holding a red ax, she has positioned herself by a barricaded door waiting for the horror of what's bound to happen next.

The wily Army Helio pilots are doing their very best to keep their whirling blades from making contact with the semi-intact CNA center, moving as close as the aircraft will allow! However, there's not enough room to position the aircraft close enough for the SF personnel to disembark. That's when the doors inside the room shatter in a loud crunch. Allowing RAGERs to swarm into the area like flies to shit!

Monique looked on in horror as the woman holding the ax backs up with two terrified children huddling behind her. What happened next was right out of a fucking comic book! One floor above the hollering Black Hawk helicopters, some of the few remaining windows in the CN building explode outwards with RAGERs dead set on rushing headlong to their death!

When the pilots caught sight of tumbling RAGERs barely missing the rotary blades of their aircraft, frantic shouting can be heard through the speakers.

"What the fuck?! They're jumping out the got damm windows!"

The three Army Helicopters back off, as two Helios rise to meet the threat head on. Special Forces were the elite of the old world and 50mm cannons are still the unofficial rain makers of their day. Consider that one hundred years from now their firepower will be described as breath of a dragon! The Army Sergeant manning the dragon's deadly breath let out a loud whistle in his headphones and then said.

"Wholly mollie! There are a lot of them..."

From the Army Sergeant's P.O.V., most of the RAGERs are staring at him, breathing hard, most ranting and all resembling a street gang waiting for a brawl!

When a Cannon photo copier comes flying towards the front windshield of Windu's helio, all the survival instincts in the task force present themselves and that's when the breath of dragon finally exhaled!

The rain caused by two 50mm cannons fell several hundred feet to the now crowded street like hot drops of hardened metal. The heavy slugs tore into flesh, concrete, steel, plaster and office furniture with the regard, it was simply unforgiving.

Hot lead dismantles skin much like acid rain! All infected flesh was blasted from bone and the blood of the dammed runs ankle deep. The poor embattled woman with the ax manages one swing, which connects into the side of a young skinny RAGER with a mullet. After that the mob exacted their revenge! Monique can only gasp in horror as one of the RAGERs snatches up a computer tower and bashes the screaming woman's face until her bones broke. It kept pounding until the brain matter resembled strains of fresh cooked pasta, with mama's homemade marinara!

Even with the effort of the other two Helio's cover fire, debris was still being hurled towards the rescue craft. The man was screaming for help, as the two scrawny, eight year old girls ran to his side.

A few of the SF warriors in Colonel Lafayette's transport, quickly use their AR-15 as designed. Even so, the crowd moves closer to the man clutching the two children, the trio have no choice but to back up towards the gaping and broken hole in the wall of the forty-first floor of the CNA building; at what once was 333 South Wabash Avenue. In what was the central business district of the city of Chicago, in what was once the state of Illinois.

The desperate man looked at the people in the Military Helicopter with spite, anger and at last a glimmer of hope! Without saying a word, he picked up the first of two-chestnut haired, young sprites, gave the child a rushed, yet gentle kiss on her tender forehead. Before using all his might, to toss the weeping child towards the open door of the Army helicopter, then quickly repeats said action!

Windu's hand and eye coordination were tested when the first child comes sailing towards her chest. She barely had time to shuffle the child off towards Monique when the next air borne package was making its way for delivery. The last look on the man's face's that of one of accomplishment, the one of a job well done! That was before the mob of RAGERs moved forward to overtake him. Yet, as in slow motion the grinning man, gives a proper double bird salute to the world! Flipping his assailants off, while allowing himself to fall out the gaping hole. For that effort, transformed himself into an oversize lemming! Either way it's time for the task force to leave.

The two Army Helios ceased their cover fire and back off allowing Colonel Lafayette's helicopter to move away with its cargo intact. Conversely, fate, life or just the cruel joke of the day always strikes when you are least prepared! As the aircraft does a forty-five degree turn to follow its flock, RAGERS leap out of the CNA towards the tail end of the helio.

The first RAGER- s the luckiest or unluckiest depending on your outlook- impales itself on spinning rotary blade, causing Windu's transport to go into a tailspin. The pilot was heard saying.

"Mayday, mayday! This is Tango Fire One, we are going down! Repeat we are going down!"

Chapter II:

SOME THREATS ARE FROM WITHIN.

Ten minutes prior back, at Camp McCormick, Colonel McKinney found himself standing in Admiral Lee's personal quarters. Which at the time he should have thought odd, since the Rear Admiral has never invited anyone except Lt. Colonel Dunston to his living space. Even that should have seen as odder, however, Dunston was the base XO.

If Air Force Colonel McKinney had been in combat ops, when he entered the candle lit room, his military sixth sense would have kicked in! Even when he heard the crunch of heavy plastic under his feet, still Kevin McKinney didn't muster a fucking clue! It's clear his views on survival have been dulled by easy living. McKinney must have stepped into Lee's quarters expecting some sort of questions about the OP.

Instead, he receives more than he should have had coming to him! As Kevin McKinney moved into the room, he could barely see the figure sitting on the makeshift crates. Nonetheless when he did get close enough, the Air Force Colonel can see Rear Admiral Lee's completely naked. The Admiral was covered in some sort of glistening oil, while holding an old fashion navy cutlass!

A song is playing softly on the IPOD and as much as Kevin McKinney wanted to turn and leave, he felt the need to inquire on his commanding officer's mental state. If one look wasn't enough, McKinney sought answers.

"AH,ahh,ahhhhhh, SIR. Is, is everything, alright?"

Rear Admiral Bullraguard Lee said nothing for several moments, it was like he's letting the look set in, before saying.

"What we have here is a failure to communicate, Colonel! See in this brave new world we find ourselves blessed to be a part of. Your kind, which I mean goddam liberal do gooders! Frankly, I don't see you as part of our current or future landscape."

Finally, Colonel Kevin McKinney could see Admiral Lee was indeed not fit for command. Furthermore, for the first time since setting foot inside Camp McCormick, he was sacred.

He mutters, "Sir, you need help. This, WE are still the United States Military, WE have been tasked with finding a cure.."

Lee cuts him off with a scolding laugh, "Cure? Cure, there's no cure for this... This's God's wrath to the wicked and the pure alike Colonel, this is resetting the clock on humanity. No longer will the weak govern the strong. No, no, no this is a reckoning!"

McKinney can't help but say, "Colonel Lafayette was right, you are insane! Rear Admiral Lee you are being relieved of your command. This base is too important to be left in your hands..."

As Lee rises from his makeshift throne, his naked frame glimmers in the candlelight. Slowly his lankly frame bends over and turns up the volume on the IPOD to high. That's when McKinney makes out the song **2008s *Drowning Pools- Let the Bodies Hit The Floor!***

"One, there's nothing wrong with me, two nothing wrong with me, three nothing wrong with me, four there's nothing wrong with me! One something's got to give, two something's gonna give, three someone's gonna bleed! Make it me, no YOU!"

Lee SCREAMS and takes off running swinging his collector's 18th century American Navy cutlass at McKinney's exposed neck as the chorus kicks in.

"Let the bodies hit the floor, let the bodies hit the floor, let the bodies hit floor!"

His blow was clean and sure, like Lee has performed this same action once, twice or possibly four times before! Air Force Colonel Kevin McKinney was an affable, goofy kind of fuck who didn't deserve to get his head loped off in the first month of the Apocalypse. However, there he was watching his world turn upside down! As his head slipped off his narrow shoulders and on to the thick gray plastic tarp.

Colonel McKinney's body dropped to the tarp with a thud, as Lee wiggles his toes in Kevin' warm pooling blood.

Jefferson Bullraguard Lee's slow Southern draw mutters more to himself than the corpse in front of him.

"While some will deserve a bloody death on this night! Here's why Colonel you lay in Dishonor, for you deserve this McKinney. You dishonored yourself as white man Colonel and you lay in its price!"

Around the same time Captain Lance Brown's Special Forces team has been noticing strange movements going on among base Security. Two of the four SF 4-man strike teams have been surrounded by Navy personnel and forcible placed under arrest! It's a confusing time for all of Camp McCormick for sure.

Lt. Colonel Dunston had issued an order to round up all Special Forces Operators and by force if necessary. From high in the rafters Captain Brown's team can only watch as their fellow Operators are being forced to decide on whether they should fire on fellow Americans! It's a tense situation for both sides, base XO Dunston knew he doesn't have enough season Marines or Sailors to tangle with SF. So, he put a weapon in just about every Sailor's hand, right down to the fucking cooks! The atmosphere was tense, everyone must have been expecting a breach. Not an unprovoked civil war!

The doctors assigned to finding a cure were taken back to see every

Sailor sporting assault weapons and side arms Nevertheless, not all threats are from outside some come from within! As they must witness in shock and bewilderment as what's left of the Military seems to be turning on itself. Captain Brown had to move fast and the orders to the twelve men under his command are simple.

"Teams B and C move and secure the landing pad. Don't kill anyone if you don't have to. Just make sure Windu has a secure LZ upon her return. I will lead Alpha to secure the lab and Delta team you will find a way to free our people they've just detained! I don't know what's going on, even so Colonel Lafayette will have a better gage on what fuck we are doing here, once she gets back."

Back in the Admiral's quarters, David Dunston wasn't sure how he became so enthralled in his master's insanity! Right now, he's using a bone saw to hack up the body of the former Air Force Colonel Kevin McKinney. In order for it to be rolled into the tarp and disposed of. After that will be Lee's purposed bloody night of purging all nonwhites from under his command!

David allows his mind to drift away from the task of dismembering a man he at least was civil with three hours ago. The smell of the human waste and internal organs forces the Marine Colonel to vomit all over the body his master commanded him to butcher like a common hog! For a few moments Lee watches as David naked frame struggles when sawing through bone, tendons and muscle so the problem would disappear.

Before Jefferson Bullraguard Lee took the time to slick back his thinning hair, he chose to leave his quarters dressed in his Navy white uniform, not his BDU's. Along with his usual trade of mark mirrored sunglasses, the Admiral resembled a too bit South American dictator! More than one of the last remaining Naval Officer in the United States Navy.

As he reached for the door handle, Lee glanced over his shoulder to see the crack of Dunston's hairless bottom staring at him in the face. Jefferson was tempted to walk over, slam David's head into the pile of puss, blood and his own vomit before forcing his awaking cock into that of David's always open asshole! Nonetheless, the Rear Admiral knew there would be time for such things later.

For now, he must deal with the beehive his actions will stir up. Admiral Lee strolls down towards the seldom used underground parking, where he ordered all non-Navy personnel taken. First, Lee understood something had to be done with the Army pukes. Fucking Special Forces Operators, fuck them, fuck'em all! When they are taken care of, he would cherry pick among his base, seeing which would be fit to serve among them as equals or be shown the door to forge a world in which they can live.

Still, Rear Admiral Lee knew that Colonel Lafayette would be a big goddam problem upon her return. So, taking her prized Special Forces Operators as hostages was key to having this matter wrapped up by chow time! As he descended the stairs from his area Lee was greeted by two Hispanic Navy enlisted personnel using the standard respect of the day.

"Admiral on deck."

None of his security detail knew the anger Lee held, for all he considered their heritage inferior.

If they had, they might have treated him like Caesar visiting the motherfucking Senate! As he moved among his command, Jefferson could only wonder if he killed Colonel McKinney for sport. Or practice for the bloodletting to come?

Meanwhile, Captain Brown's SF team was done hiding among the rafters. They moved like squirrels leaping from one set of walkways to another until they could descend to the labs. Using the seldom used east stairwell the three person teams moved swiftly, yet covertly. Silencers have been equipped, even so Captain Brown has come to know some of these recruits, and he doesn't really want to kill any of them. If he didn't have to.

In his mind, all this crazy began with Colonel McKinney having to turn over base command to Admiral Lee. Now, all he can do is secure the lab and sit tight until Windu makes it back, she'll know what to do, thought the young Captain.

Little does he know Colonel Lafayette is having her own set of problems. One thing the Apocalypse is famous for, fucking up your day, where you can stand it or not!

Chapter III:

IT'S STILL CHICAGO, THIS CITY CAN KILL ANYBODY!

The moment the rear rotary blade of Colonel Lafayette's Black Hawk was impacted by a slack jawed RAGER weighing no less than a biscuit short of 290 pounds. It was pretty much like being on a roller coaster heading straight down! Just as your seat restraints suddenly switched to EPIC fucking fail. The wind's whipping through the cockpit as the spinning blade chews through the blubber, bone and grime of the infected spewing diseased blood among the warm summer wind.

The pilot, Chief Warrant Officer Larry Price- a fifty-year-old career Army man, twice divorced, an Oakland Raider Fan, who is always happy to be flying- did his best to right their aircraft out of its temperamental death spiral. Mind you this was amongst a tight grouping of commercial real estate presenting a staunch Chicago Bears Defensive line; looking to employ a violent quarterback sack!

His copilot, Warrant Officer Chloe LaVega- a forty-year-old Illinois National Guard pickup, and a firm supporter of LGBTQ rights- wasn't so lucky as she's helplessly propelled out of the spinning helicopter! And just like that an original abstract painting of blood, flesh, bone and unfilled dreams; was all that's left of Chole's helpless body as it impacts a burnt concrete column with the force of traveling nearly 75 miles per hour!

Monique firmly holds on to one of their cargo as the other clutches with all her tiny might to Wynolla's torso. Everyone is suspended in midair as time halts for a mere fraction of a second. All the free-falling Black Hawk's capable of doing was smashing into the eleventh floor of a forty-four story, one time residential, hi rise apartment building. The aircraft fell thirty floors, in less than the time it took to foster a scream!

The smell of charred metal was followed by the sounds of crunching steel, splintering wood, breaking of windows and the constant moaning of the goddam dead. The impact of the crash should have fractured every bone in any of the survivors' bodies, if they had not been trapped into their seats. However, their whiplash and near concussions like synthons will have to be put on a back burner for the time bein!.

Windu strains to look towards her right at Army SPEC-4 Ray Oliva a 21-year-old of Mexican descent from Fresno. Yet the pain that's shooting through Wynolla' s neck, further instructs her to take it slow. She can see the young Army Ranger moving his hands and trying to speak, that's when Colonel Lafayette notices the charred steel rod jammed up through the seat into Ray Oliva's slender thigh.

Monique titles her head to see if the other Army Ranger's still alive and she is. Army SPEC-4 Melody Belladonna; another 21-year-old, the product of an Italian father with one quarter Lakota Sioux heritage and American woman of Korean descent.

One of the first of the "new" Army, Specialist Belladonna was as professional as she's deadly with small arms! Known as Mel to her friends, Donna to her close friends and BELL to the rest of her squad.

She flashed a quick thumbs up signaling, ready to rock! That's when Specialist Oliva lets out a muffled yelp of pain, Wynolla clears her head and moves into action. She whispers her next command. "BELL, get yourself free and watch out for dead fuckers. "

The Army Ranger nods her head signaling, affirmative. Next Wynolla looks down at the child clutching her and then across the smoldering cockpit to Monique and said in a warm tone.

"Sweetheart, I really need you to go across to the pretty Doctor Littlefield so I can help my Soldier."

Monique's eyes are wide open not as much in fear, but as in complete absorption in the moment. Simply her mind's racing with thoughts of survival! She quickly nods her head and reaches across the aisle for the sibling of child clutching the life out of her rib cage.

Colonel Lafayette gently scoots the terrified package off towards her sibling, before attending to her wounded soldier. Ray Oliva must have a high stress hold when it comes to pain. Because was holding it together, still his yelping and breathing was getting louder and louder!

Windu does her best to offer some sort of humor when she said. "Dam Oliva, looks like you won't be dancing in the Christmas play."

SPEC-4 Ray Oliva did his best to maintain as he replied. "Sorry for letting you down ma'am, I know how much you are into West Side Story."

Both share a soft chuckle as Colonel Lafayette whispers. "I'm going to lift your thigh off this metal. Just don't scream..."

Ray shakes his head repeatedly signaling yes, as Wynolla moves to position his hands under both sides of Ray Oliva's thighs.

"Ok on three.. One, two.."

And with all her might, Wynolla snatched the nimble thigh of the young Ranger up, clearing the intended target. The wet squishy sound was vivid enough to nearly make Monique cry in frustration as she leads the two twins out of the smoldering wreckage.

The searing pain was past intense! SPEC- 4 Ray Oliva passed out from shock, allowing Colonel Lafayette the time to place twin compresses on to the young Rangers wound. Before breaking a vial of smelling salt compound under his resting right nostril.

All the while the sound of the dead and the not so dead, could be heard stirring among them. SPEC-4 Belladonna's silenced AR-15 with bump stock was making short, muffled burst at figures looming around the broken section of wall.

Monique found it difficult to move with twin 55 pounds of terrified younglings attached to your hip, yet she manages. Doctor Littlefield knew it's better to hold off from firing her unsilenced sidearm, until she has no other fucking choice! She could feel the twins shaking so hard, it made her shake in turn.

BELL whispered in a hushed yet noticeable stressful tone. "WE need to move!"

Ray Olivia awoke with a start mumbling, "Put me back in the game coach, I, I can take it."

Colonel Lafayette whispers, "I know you can, come on Specialist, it's time to be ARMY strong."

The young Airborne Ranger fights through his pain to mumble, "Roger that Colonel."

Windu lifts Ray as best she can in order to maneuver around the piece of wreckage that cost him the use of his leg. Each bump and twist caused Ray to groan louder, which causes their ever-present enemies to ramp up their unwanted attention.

The smell of death fills everyone's nostrils driving the urge of their untampered will to live into critical motherfucking overdrive! SPEC-4 Belladonna does her best to make out the shadows dancing at the edge of the room. Each well place shot from her M-17 does its job with a seasoned executioner's sense of utter calm and purpose!

Wynolla helps the injured Ranger out of the dangling helio and on to the relative safety of a solid floor. She scanned the room for anything Oliva could use as a makeshift crutch, sadly nothing was of use. Furthermore, the young Ranger knew the deal. Specialist Olivia understood they need to move, and you can only move as fast as your slowest man is able to move.

He mutters, "Just leave me ma'am, all I can do is slow you down."

Colonel Lafayette scoffs, "We have a long way to go before I even consider that course of action Specialist. Lock and load, I'll help you down these stairs, but I need you to cover our six. Are you locked and ready?"

The twenty-one-year-old Northern California native forces a brave smile to cover up his mounting pain as he mutters.

"Airborne leads the way Colonel."

Colonel Lafayette whispers to the young Solider.

"Ranger, you know that's only because we are crazy enough to walk out of a moving aircraft. Stay with me troop and I promise to get you home!"

Oliva replies, "Roger that Colonel.

Windu signals to BELL to start the descent, even though she can see Monique struggling to move with the twins hanging on to her hip.

Her only concern was that Doctor Littlefield didn't accidentally shoot SPEC- 4 Belladonna as they make their way down the dark and uninviting stairwell. Wynolla wanted to get everyone home. Not just for their sake, but for the mission. She knew Lee would view the loss as a stamp of how they should move forward.

SPEC-4 Belladonna's night vison glasses came in handy allowing her to place- *even though others of her team laughed when she packed her gear, saying it was dawn, not dusk*. - short, muffled three round bursts, barely audible to the naked ear, wherever needed. Suddenly those sounds were compounded for the next two flights of stairs for it seemed like every survivor except SPEC-4 Oliva are holding their collective breaths!

The young Airborne Ranger from Fresno was doing his best to pull his weight as Colonel Lafayette hauled him down the stairwell. The wounded warrior wasn't sure whether his eyes were playing tricks on him or not. Were those shadows indeed moving towards their direction? Instead, Ray Oliva relied on his training of short three round bursts. And instead of aiming for center mass, SPEC-4 Oliva aims face high and hoped for the best

By the time Belladonna reaches the top of the next floor stairwell, she can see its partial block off by numerous sofas, desk, coffee tables and big screen televisions. Their escape route was blocked, leaving the other doorway, at the end of the hall. As the only access leading down, the Survivor's gathered at the door. As their young cargo muttered in unison.

"They, they mostly gathered downstairs, mostly."

Colonel Lafayette understood every second they were cut off from air transport, means their chances for survival drop considerably! She risks attracting unwanted attention by talking into her headset, to contact any of the other two Helios.

"This is Windu, I have one wounded, two KIA and we are moving towards the street. I need a SIT-REP, ASAP!"

There's a momentary pause and crackle, heard on all the survivors' headsets, before the voice of Army Chief Warrant Officer Warren Phillips- a lean silver haired man with blue eyes, 48-year-old from native from Tyler Texas- can be heard saying.

"Good got dammit Colonel, it's great to hear your voice! We were circling the building, and I was hoping someone was still alive in there. Base has ordered us to return, however we are disregarding their advice, sir. Awaiting your orders, Colonel!"

Colonel Lafayette pauses for a brief second before saying.

"How's traffic by the front door?"

It takes the Army Pilot a few seconds before saying.

"Heavy as a fat cow's daily dump. I think our presence is drawing them out by the thousands."

Wynolla quickly replies.

"Lead them away, get low enough to attract their attention, I don't care if you got to fly 8-18 blocks away. Just get that herd moving away from the exit. Hail us when you are heading back Chief."

The native from Tyler Texas lets the group know that they aren't alone.

"You got it Colonel; it'll be just like herding cattle on my granddaddy's ranch! You hang in there; we'll be back to swoop you up in under five minutes. Stay alive!"

Monique mutters," you don't have to tell me twice."

Outside the shell of the CNA office, the herd has been building like it was free donut day at Dunkins! What started in the hundreds was quickly ushering into upper thousands. RAGERS threw anything and everything at the whirling birds hovering just out of their throwing range. While the moans of the dead, more than equaled the sound of two of McDonald Douglas finest aircraft engines.

Just as Chief Warrant Officer Phillips envisioned, dead and dying hands reached for the sky. The two Army Helios and their Operators made sure the bulk of the herd begun moving away from the CNA building before leading the herd through the obstacle course of the burnt-out husk of stalled motor vehicles and bloody piles of human remains!

Inside the CNA building some emergency lights still flicker as SPEC-4 Belladonna slowly works her way down the eighth floor. From her P.O.V. the night vison goggles –NVG- reveal more than a few apartment doors are wide open. It is certainly an invitation of unseen danger and certain murder, deaths and kills!

Monique does her best to move with the twin attachments she picked up after their crash. The frightened little girls were either 7 or 9 years old, of mixed heritage and one hundred percent scared as shit!

However, neither of the children were sobbing or even crying. Shaking, well hell yeah. Much like it was thirty below zero! Then seemed numb and Doctor Littlefield could recognize shock and PTSA when she saw it. Feeling both trembling little girls desperately holding on to her legs as if Monique could protect them. When their parents could not, that nearly broke her heart!

Nonetheless, Monique Littlefield wasn't one to fold under pressure and now she feels personally responsible for her cargo. Monique trained her weapon on every doorway that Bell approached, knowing she might have to fire her 9mm Glock in self-defense! It's dark, just like in Somalia when she had to fire a Chinese made AK47 at kidnappers whose business it was to steal children. In this darkness one of Doctor Littlefield many concerns not shooting Belladonna in the back of her head. Dam she wishes she bought Wynolla's extra pair of NVGs!

SPEC-4 Belladonna slowly approached the first open door, from her crouching position she can't see anything by the door or in the adjacent room. Bell slowly reaches her hand up and pulls the door close, making only a small clicking noise.

Everyone collectively lets out a sigh, as the young Ranger leads her team to the next open door. As they approach, they can hear it, the bumping and smashing of items. Signal RAGERS.

Bell whispers, "Wait."

As she slowly peeks her head into the open apartment, from her P.O.V, Bell witnesses in horror as three RAGERS- *who should have been attending middle school-* play what looks like the game hot potato with an infants' severed head. SPEC-4 Belladonna must fight the urge to vomit, as well as shoot the three psychos in front of her!

Nevertheless, she did neither, getting out of the building was her mission. Secretly, Bell liked Ray Oliva, because he never gave her any sexist bullshit and plus, he's cute. Bonus, he was also interested in books that weren't Army manuals, Wrestling magazines or gun magazines.

Tragically fate generally has other plans that may not always adhere to what we may desire! SPEC-4 Oliva let out a gasp of pain. Not a cry, more, more like a loud sigh. Still, it's enough to get the attention of the trio of 13-year-old RAGERS.

They turn, with red eyes bleeding, towards the sound and SPEC-4 Belladonna doesn't know if the murderous trio can see her or not. She fires a quick three round burst and a tight shot grouping of three head shoots, putting the middle school RAGERS out of their misery. Belladonna quickly shuts the door only to see others emerging from various open doorways along their path.

She mutters, "SHIT."

Three, six, nine, twelve, fifteen, eighteen muffled shoots it takes to clear the path!

Bell mutters, "Changing mags."

Ray mutters to Colonel Lafayette.

"Colonel, let me go. The pain, I can't stop for passing out and you can't expect to firemen carry me and make it out of here."

Windu sternly looks at the brave young soldier and shakes her head no!

"I'll drag your sorry ass out of here by your got dam ear if I must. You got me?"

Ray smiled and nodded his head yes before saying.

"Thank you, ma'am, thank you for giving a dam, about all of us."

Colonel Lafayette smiles and nods back, yet she wasn't prepared for SPEC-4 Ray Oliva placing the barrel of his Assault Rifle with silencer attachment under his chin and pulling the trigger. Windu was indeed lucky once more for the bullet exploded out of the left side of young solder's cranium, not the right which faced her.

Blood and brain matter still find its way onto the Colonel's clothing and face. She can't help but mutter.

"No,no,no, Ray. Why? Fuck Man, we could have gotten you home!"

As she laid the body down, SPEC-4 Belladonna fights back her own tears, feeling somehow, she let them all down.

Colonel Lafayette takes Ray Ollvia dog tags his weapons and ammo before taking point, she tells Bell.

"Cover our six, it's time to take our cargo home."

Just then Chief Warrant Officer Phillip's voice was heard over the headset.

"Anyone ever see that classic Vietnam War movie, Apocalypse Now? Man, I feel like we're rolling down on some VC! Shit, all we need is speaking playing some slasher rock and we would have every Dead Head and RAGER would be following us like we were pied fucking pipers. We led the main group away, holding at one city mile away from your location, awaiting orders, Colonel."

Windu replies. "Give us three minutes and Chief those mini cannons better be empty by the time you park at the front door."

Phillips replies, "VIP treatment coming up!"

These Army Pilots are probably some of the few remaining people on Earth capable of achieving flight. The joy they must feel, in their aircraft which resemble birds of prey swooping down and capturing helpless field mice! Instead of capturing, the 50mm cannons effortlessly shred infected flesh, bone and brain matter. 50 mm rounds impacting with gas tanks on stalled cars, city buses and delivery trucks was just icing on the cake! BOOM goes the already wrecked property value.

Giant fire balls erupted alongside vivid colors of crimson and mustard incinerate anything in its path! As multiple explosions rocked all the way to what was once 333 South Wabash Avenue, in what was Chicago Illinois. The thousands of military rounds add to the already heavily saturated air with another lingering smell, sulfur! Nevertheless, unless bullets impacted heads, or explosions destroy brain matter. A Zombie will keep moving towards the next infection waiting to happen!

Colonel Lafayette had been busy leading her group to the first floor, between Belladonna and herself they have gone through a hundred ninety rounds a piece- three clips- and now ammo was getting sparse.

Each soldier was down to their last two clips for their primary weapon. While Monique has yet to fire a shot, only because Wynolla and Bell happen to be about their business! Right before they reach the lobby, Monique noticed a pair of bite marks on both the young girls' inner arms, however, they seem to be scared over.

Even under the stress of certain death, it's hard for Doctor Littlefield to conceal her excitement as she communicates her find through her headset.

"We need to get these children back to the lab! I don't believe my eyes, they, they have been bitten. It seems some time ago and neither has been infected!"

By the time Colonel Lafayette's group reaches the lobby, there are eleven Dead Heads and five RAGERS mingling by the front door. Windu nods to Bell and they dispatch the infected with a cold dispassion for their work. When one of the RAGERS turns towards Bell holding a bloody bent tennis racket. She lets out a primal scream and bashes the lanky, bleeding eye RAGERs with the butt of her M-17 until its head bursts open like a ripe melon!

Bell was panting hard, in an attempt to regain her composure. Colonel Lafayette whispers to her fellow soldier.

"Deep breathing is good for the soul. Frankly right now, I need you to get back in the game Bell. We still need to make it to the Helios."

She nods, then replies. "I'm locked on, Airborne gets it done."

While Colonel Lafayette and SPEC- 4 Belladonna step over the bodies to look out of the front set of windows. Monique bends down, to talk to the two little girls.

"Hi, my name is Monique and I, I know you both have been through so much. I, I can't even begin to... I'm sorry all this has happened to you and your family. But do, you know when you were bitten?"

Neither child utters a reply or even a dry sob. Instead, each child scans their environment looking for danger like mice looking for cats or maybe even an exit! From Monique's P.O.V she noticed each twin sported one semi red eye. As one could only imagine their nerves are more than on edge. That's when she saw each little girl sporting a small camo backpack sporting the logo of the local baseball team, the *Chicago WhiteSox's*.

Monique's voice is kind and tender as she asks one of the twins.

"Huh, may, may I see what's in your backpack?"

The little brown skinned girl poked out her bottom lip yet doesn't resist when Doctor Littlefield reaches around unhooks the cover, reaches her hand in and finds something she isn't prepared for.

At the window, Windu and Bell noticed the traffic outside consists of maybe fifty infected, still mingling by the intended LZ. Chief Warrant Officer Phillip's voice blares through each of the remaining teams' headsets.

"We are 45 seconds out Colonel and we kept enough ammo to clear any stragglers in the LZ. However, what's left of the herd is still trailing our sorry ass!"

Colonel Lafayette replies. "Roger that."

She looked at Bell and nodded giving the young Ranger a look of confidence, signaling I believe in you. Before heading to check on Doctor Littlefield and their cargo, who could hardly contain herself.

"Wynolla, oh my, there are handwritten journals, on the infection... It seems their parents or guardians were ER doctors. Oh, my, oh my, y, my God. This is incredible!"

Windu could see the excitement of Monique as well as the shock and horror of the young shivering little girls.

Colonel Lafayette whispers to Doctor Littlefield. "Hey once we exit those doors, you are going run towards the first Helio with our cargo. Bell and I will hop in the other."

She smiles and nods ok. They share their last tender moment, by touching foreheads.

That's when the force of 50 mm cannons signaled that their heavily armed air Uber had finally arrived! Blowing up the street and all on it, as bits of spraying concrete crack the so-called shatterproof front windows, causing a momentary shock to everything living!

From the twins P.O.V, they see SPEC-4 Belladonna following Colonel Lafayette out the front door. The monstrous noise of the Helicopters forced each of the little girls to use one hand to cover an ear as their other hand to latch on to Doctor Littlefield's pants leg. From the eyes of a middle schooler the sight of two Helio descending like ancient dragons in the morning mist. Full of fire and smoke, must have been cool!

Even so, for the first time Monique had to raise her 9mm Glock and fire at the mangled yet shambling Zombie baring down on her. She fires, barely missing the head as the Zombie moved closer, nevertheless Doctor Littlefield made the next three bullets count! By the time she reached the first Helio, the horde was back in pursuit and pouring out of dank alleyways and down no longer vacant streets.

Colonel Lafayette and SPEC-4 Belladonna must continue to provide cover fire as RAGERS and the Dead run, shamble and crawl towards whatever is still living! Time seemed to slow down, as Windu could only watch the horde grows closer as she and Bell successfully jump into their transport.

However, for Doctor Littlefield the cargo will not let go of her leg. It takes some doing to peel the hands of the twins off her thighs. With all her might she rips pairs of hands off her long enough to toss each shell-shocked survivor into the waiting hands of two Air Force Black Berets. With all her might Monique screams out in frustration as fires her Glock again and again, emptying fourteen rounds into anything coming her way. Nonetheless, RAGERS can take some rounds and keep on coming to stab, slash and bash your goddam head in!

The Army Pilots have nerves of steel, for they saw the tens of thousands of infected baring down on their position and they didn't lose their shit!

Yet, by the time Doctor Littlefield loads the last of her cargo, nearly three dozen are close enough to touch Chief Warrant Officer Phillip's door.

Colonel Lafayette's Helio is first to rise about the fray and they can only watch as the other chopper is completely engulfed! As it tries to get airborne hundreds of hands reach out grabbing at anything they can get their hands on. The next events seem to happen in slow motion as Doctor Littlefield attempts in vain to climb on to the rising aircraft, even so, Monique couldn't cleanly make to safety.

For countless dead and undead hands latch on to Monique's arms, shoulders, legs and finally her neck! Pulling her down into the mist of their fucking chaos.

She helplessly reaches up towards the ascending helicopter and the lost look from the twins may be the last thing the good Doctor probably saw. Nonetheless, Doctor Monique Littlefield was the reason Chief Warrant Officer Phillips helicopter was able to rise away from the impending slaughter!

The Undead stopped latching on to the aircraft and began their feast, ripping and tearing her flesh off bone. Just like that, the beautiful, intelligent worldly woman that was Monique Littlefield was gone! All Colonel Wynolla Lafayette could do was fall back into her seat! For the moment numb to the rest of the world.

Chapter IV:

THE FALL AND TRAIL OF JEFFERSON BULLRAGUARD LEE.

Five Weeks into infection, time 0930- date 07-04-2021

The ride back to base was needless to say, somber. No one knows what to say, even if it was the words would have mattered. The facts are present, Operation Goose Chase had lost a lot in an effort to obtain their precious cargo. Even so, when Chief Warrant Officer Phillips relayed the information provided by Captain Brown to Wynolla her mood turned from despondent to cold unbridled anger!

The Special Forces Operators under Captain Brown had secured the roof and landing pad without a struggle as well as secured the lab with most of the scientists involved in the project. He has requested to see Colonel McKinney several times and so far, the only response was from the XO saying surrender of face a firing squad!

When Colonel Lafayette's helio touched down, she assigned the two survivors to Bell. Then double timed it straight to the forward area held by a trio of SF Operators. Captain Brown can be heard over their headset.

"Good to have you back Windu, I'm currently in the main lab with nine of the egg heads. We are facing a dozen or so nervous Seabees and a few Jarheads! At this point, no shots have been fired. However, Marine Guards have marched out of a few of our people and they have them kneeling in front of our position."

Colonel Lafayette calmly orders the soldier to patch their conversation into the lab's external speakers. It takes a few moments for Captain Brown to do as ordered, once he's done Wynolla' s words speak volumes.

"This is Colonel Lafayette; I have no idea what has transpired since we left these walls. Nonetheless, listen up! We lost four of the living, including the chief doctor in her field and we have little time to mourn. For the Dead won't rest! Our mission retrieved two survivors, who even though bitten have not succumb to the infection."

She lets the last portion savor in the air for a few moments, before continuing.

"My charge as is yours is to protect the scientist working on a cure that might just save the rest of humanity! Where is Colonel McKinney? Admiral Lee and Colonel Dunson bring Colonel McKinney to the South roof ASAP! Do not place these young recruits' lives in danger Lee. We are Special Forces! While you, hospital jag-offs, rear support staff fuck ups, and bullshit Navy Seal washouts had easy duty. We are SF, we get shit done! Get your sorry ass up here now, SIR!"

A hush of silence washed over the base like a tsunami of fear. One that gestates the foul taste of civil war or at least an attempted coup has struck Base McCormick. From the young Marines and Navy recruits aiming weapons at kneeling Army Rangers in front of the main lab.

To the roof where battle harden Green Berets aim their weapons at trembling Navy recruits, who must be wondering what suddenly happened to the command structure and code of the military they had bought into!

The atmosphere was like being held hostage by suicide bombers and with each passing second getting you either closer to freedom or a goddam body bag. Windu knew she had to remain calm, she doesn't want a blood bath, even if Lee might! Wynolla knew the people inside their base might as well be the last living people for hundreds, maybe even thousands of miles! Death wasn't what anyone needed, there had been too much already.

All while inside Admiral Jefferson Bullraguard Lee's quarters, he sat in his makeshift office. Still dressed in his full Navy dress white uniform, while quietly staring at a photo of himself at the beach. Outside his door and along the hallway and stairwell leading up to his den. Lt. Colonel Dunson handpicked eight Marines and ten Sailors to stand watch and die if need be!

For he knows why Colonel McKinney is nowhere to be found. He knew there was no coming back from this. Even now Dunson wasn't sure what the fuck Lee's thinking! Why he hadn't seen that the Admiral had lost his grip, was easy. Lee had him in his twisted grasp of sexual deviancy! It was the thought of Lee telling what's left of their world how Dunson's enjoys male bondage and rape fantasies. Well, that kept David from being forward thinking about something other than his fucking career. Hell, the Marine had never even considered himself gay or racist, until he let Lee cum inside him! Then his world, needless to say became upheaved.

Now that goddam Army Colonel Lafayette was back and she's right about one thing. Her group has been bloodied in combat! Frankly without the Admiral at least giving the troops a reason why they should risk their lives against fellow Americans. This thing is over before it starts! Then what happens, thought the Marine Colonel.

No one will ever find the body of Colonel McKinney, thought David. He knew he had cut him up into very small pieces. The sickening sound of saw cutting though bone and the smell of warm blood and shit crossed his mind and nearly made Dunson crap his BDU's.

It's nearly eight minutes later when Colonel Lafayette's voice crackles over the entire base.

"This's Colonel Lafayette, I've confirmed with the Sailor previously assigned to protecting Admiral Lee's corridor that Colonel McKinney entered the Admirals' quarters two hours ago and never was seen exiting by anyone. Are you holding Colonel McKinney hostage? Just like you are holding these other base personal hostage, Admiral Lee?"

Wynolla lets her words sink in for a few beats, before continuing.

"I think Colonel McKinney is either dead or dying in your quarters Admiral. You have left me no choice, I am temporally relieving you and your XO Colonel Dunson of command, until Colonel McKinney is located. I'm ordering none combat base personnel to place their weapons on the ground and head towards the main auditorium.

Anyone holding or pointing a weapon at a Special Forces Operator from here on out, will be treated as an enemy combatant. I will repeat, you will be treated as an enemy combatant..."

Those final words slam the door on the few Navy or Marine personnel looking to stick their necks out for Admiral Lee. Even the few Air Force personnel assigned to this project wouldn't budge until they knew what happened to their fellow officer McKinney!

Lee and Dunson are screwed, and they moved too late to commit suicide. For Windu selected three Air Force Black Berets, two Army Green Berets and One Marine then marched right up to Lee's front door without so much as a whistle, shot or sound of alarm. No one was looking to die that day, for so many already had given their lives!

When the Operators breached the room, they found Dunson pleading with Lee to get up and address the troops. Yet, it was the entire scene of several candles, plastic flooring and the strong smell of bleach that caught most of their attention! Nevertheless, the Admirals quarters somehow managed to combine the unique smells of death, sweat, baby oil, sodomy and sandalwood scented candles. Lee looks up with a starry-eyed gaze, much the malaise of the criminally insane and an opium addict then replies.

"I thought I killed your Nigger ass already. I saw it, saw it in a dream. Just like that shit stain McKinney! From here to eternity, we the true white race won't tolerate your kind and more! You goddam fucking monkeys or all you weak liberals shit stains! I say fuck the media running Jews until they beg for mercy then shot them in the back of their heads! How about we sodomize the lice carrying WELCH bloody before any more of their unwashed masses turn up on our goddammed shores!"

Colonel Lafayette was doing all she could not to break his soon to be former base commander's jaw before he answered on the where about of the Air Force Colonel McKinney. Instead, she lowers her tone and made her words precise.

"Admiral Lee, what did you do to Colonel Kevin McKinney?"

Lee looks up and smiles before replying.

"Why I beat him to death and stabbed him until that pansy shit his uniform. Just like I'm going to do to you Army bitch!"

With that Lee leaps to his feet in a haste like he's ready to do something. However, Wynolla been ready to hit somebody for the last hour and Lee makes an excellent fucking target! Her first three punches caught Lee as he was starting to rise. Colonel Lafayette's first punch hit Jefferson in the middle of his chest bone, the crack sounded much like a 95 mile an hour fastball slamming into a wooden bat!

Windu's second punch lands directly in Bullraguard stomach and the wind rushed out of him as fast as his feet began to wobble. That's when Wynolla's' last punch impacted Lee in his jaw and by then Bullraguard went for a quick nap, nap. A new base commander has risen and she's Special Forces!

Colonel Dunson meekly dropped his weapon. Even so the fool rushes forward to restraint Wynolla. Frankly, that didn't work out as David Dunson thought it would. First Windu spun away from

Dunson's clumsy reach, by shifting her weight to a 70/20 balance between her front and back feet. Without much effort Colonel Lafayette places an outside crescent kick along the right side of Dunson's face, knocking his two rear right molars out before the ground rushed up to meet David Dunson's unconscious face!

It doesn't take long before Camp McCormick returns to a bit of the usual normalcies that surround military life. Chow was still 0600--0830, showers still go off at 2300 and the dead still surround their position! However, for now the moaning and wailing of the dead don't seem to notice that the living happens to be still living among them.

It's been two days since Colonel Lafayette returned with the most precious cargo to date! Even though Wynolla wanted to sulk, she was now the ranking military person on site. She couldn't even pass on the trial of that sick son of a bitch Lee! He murdered another Officer, so it was a military tribunal all the way.

The next ranking medical doctors were civilian Doctor Janice Seresh-*a 47-year-old Minnesota Native- and Doctor Robert List- a 35-year-old suffer dude formerly of Portland Oregon!* They quickly dove into the manuscripts that came with the twins' girls, leaving Wynolla to fulfill other duties. The information included their names, the first sight of infection, their medical history and the treatment used to fight their plight in its first few hours.

Apparently, the middle schoolers were bitten in the first few hours of infection while attending a school outing at the museum of Science and Industry. The bites were so bad and their fever so quick in setting in the two quick thinking ER doctors, placed their young patients into ice baths of pure saline solutions. It took nearly two days before their fever broke and the patients began to feel better.

However, by then, in horrific fashion, the shit had hit the fan! After further reading, it seems the two protectors that tragically died in the CNA building in an effort to get their previous cargo to some sort of safe harbor. Were the two ER doctors assigned to the only people known so far, to survive infection!

Sadly, the dead and not so dead make the hospital unsafe for the living and no one ever showed to speak or care for the two hazel eyed middle school girls. Leaving Izsak Levin- 31 years old and 28 years old Karen Kampler to take it upon themselves to take them from their hospital room and to their apartment in the CNA building- where they had been living together for only four months.

Frankly, history will barely mention that Izsak and Karen might have saved humanity! Still the pressing business of the day swirled around the court martial of the Lee and Dunson! Even so on that first day when Wynolla finally was able to return to her quarters after setting the base back on its path.

Sadly, she was quickly greeted by the sight of Monique's belongings, the soiled sheets in which they previously made love, her half-filled glass of water and Doctor Littlefield's phone still docked in the speaker!

She cried for nearly an hour and slept for an entire fifteen hours. It was two days later and the court martial and trial of fellow officers fell on of all dates, July 4th[th]. It doesn't take long before the weak link spilled the beans. Dunston was attempting to jump in front of what was coming! The Marine Colonel David Dunson recounts a tale of how Admiral Lee and Colonel Kevin McKinney had gotten into a shouting match. David attempts to spin a tale on how Jefferson hit Kevin with one punch, killing the man, when he fell and hit his head.

Dunson even cops to disposing of Colonel McKinney's body, one a piece at a time! Frankly even if the jury of his- *Two Air Force Officers, Two Army Officers and Two Navy Commander-* peers had believed that the Marine was just being a loyal officer. You know, just one Jar Head doing his best to protect his commanding officer, even from himself.

Even so, Jefferson Bullraguard Lee was their own worst enemy! For he denied his XO's account and shares his vision of a new society, as well as his views on Satanism & the Catholic church. The so-called Ancient Aliens theory, the divine destiny of the white Alpha male, the science behind ethnic cleansing, his theory on Flat Earth and how strawberry Mountain Dew turned the country into a nation of gluten free pussies, transgender faggots and liberal crybabies!

To Colonel Lafayette and the rest of the base it was clear that Admiral Lee was never fit to command. Nonetheless, there was a question of what to do with Dunson, Lee. While the entire base lingered in the air for a few days Wynolla was at a major crossroads. Even though it is in the hands of the military, the civilian doctors needed to see justice not mere vengeance! If they are the last bastion of humanity, everyone needs to understand the rules and standard of law.

Captain Brown was on the board of six officers that were selected to render judgement of both detainees.

Captain Brown grew up in this area and he remembers a mental hospital located about a hundred and ninety miles away from what was Chicago.

"Colonel, we can't hang them! That will be bad for morale, and we can't just push them out the door either."

Colonel Lafayette stated. "Captain, base Morale can't get any shittier than it already is, besides Lee and Dunson are murders and maybe even cannibals. By the way, it's not like Lee and Dunson will get needed mental health treatment today, tomorrow or in the near future."

Captain Brown is upbeat yet respectful of the situation.

"Yes, ma'am I understand that. We could hang them or shoot them in the back or the head. Still if we want to keep the mission alive, I suggest we relocate those evil sonofabitches, Windu."

Other than Captain Brown, in under 72 hours Colonel Lafayette had lost her closest two allies, sounding boards and of course lover. As much as she may have not felt like talking to the young Captain on the subject of hanging or shooting Lee and Dunson down like rapid dogs! Wynolla knew the advice was sound and at least she gets to punch Lee in the stomach for the last time before they cut the demented shit head loose, far, far, far away.

Book Four

Chapter I:

BOOK IV: HEAVEN MUST BE LIKE THIS!

Five and a half weeks since infection 07-07-21

One thing about being on Death Row your selection of music was limited! Nevertheless, John loves to plan ahead. Hammond didn't know how or why, yet he yielded a strong sense he would not die behind drab gray prison walls. John loves his music and since arriving at Shangri-La he started each morning out with an inspiration song of love, peace and soul. On this day he chooses the **1974 LP from the Ohio Players and the track, Heaven Must be Like This**.

"You know what I think HEAVEN is, heaven is YOU, did you know that? A place where I can find happiness, I place where our love can rest, it's a place to rest my aching, mind. Even the love we just made, oh heaven, you're divine. Heaven must be like this, it must be like this, oh heaven must be like this..."

John Hammond pumps the easy listening music through their compound speaker system as he continues humming the rest of the song. John checks the video monitors, ensuring all systems are up and running as designed.

Hammond's survivors- *as they will be known generations from now-* celebrated the Fourth of July last week and everyone enjoyed a normal day, even though it ended with several Dead Heads crashing their outdoor picnic and ruining their mood! Later that day,

John could see the gym was filled with survivors, working off love handles and toning up unused muscle groups.

Even Calamity has scaled back her use of non-prescribed pharmaceuticals! Enestro said she does up to two hundred sit-ups a day and that type of dedication pays off. Thankfully, after his unsuspecting acid trip. Earl was on his best behavior and John didn't feel it was an act. Earl Grimes- *serial killer renowned* -seemed to be living the life, he never thought he would have.

Pardon the expression, yes Earl was in hog heaven! With Paradise Hunter and Semaj Johansson, two attractive pre–Op Trans women, he had planned to spend the rest of the Apocalypse getting to know on many levels. Hopefully, will never include their brutal murder and dismemberment! Let's just say sometimes a couple performs wonderfully as a trio.

In the last few weeks even Hammond and his estranged daughter Robin have made some headway to a stable relationship. John the father observes that his daughter and Sky have something going on! If it helps her smile, John was more than happy not to ask, so she won't have to tell.

Indigo Roberson the ex-prison shrink has been working overtime, dealing with everyone else's anxiety, PTSD or depression. Still, John Hammond wonders how she is dealing with her own.

Indigo well, seems to be put together a bit tight, some moments she seems to be warming up to Hammond.

While other times the middle-aged woman was a cold as three-month-old frozen pizza. He couldn't figure it out, yet that doesn't mean he doesn't greet her with a cheerful smile, the moment Indigo walks into the main control both.

John said, "Well hello and good morning to you Ms. Roberson. How did you sleep?"

Indigo could smell the coffee two flights down and she knew she could have gone to the cafeteria to grab a cup. Furthermore, she also understood that the control room's closer to the living quarters and there's coffee in there as well. She flashed a warm, yet clearly distant smile to John as she replied.

"Like a rock, it's so quite down here and the rooms are nearly soundproof."

John informs her, "Twelve-foot-thick concrete, limits the rate of sound."

Indigo smiles again, this this a bit warmer, as she fishes for answers.

"It's amazing you got all this done from the confines of a prison cell. "

John flashes a warm smiles and said, "old people used to say where there's a will, there's a way.."

Indigo continues by asking, "how did you know? I mean, how did you know all this?"

She motions towards their surroundings.

John sighs as he said, "besides the fact I'm INNOCENT! It seems the people that put me behind bars wanted me to live. Yet, I lived with the threat of destruction every single minute I was imprisoned. So, I began to realize, however THEY are. Wanted me where they could find me, if they ever needed ME."

Indigo took a few moments to take all that in before asking, "Riiigght. Now WHO are THEY?"

Down in the exercise room with the help of Sky Harrison, Robin Aquila has put down the bottle and re dedicated herself to her martial arts practice; she's in a room lined with Wing Chun dummies, swords, wooden staffs and punching bags. While Enestro and his darling Celeste pump iron and work the heavy bag. In a mirror lined room adjacent to the weights, Cherish leads fellow ex erotic dancers Destiny and Dawn in waist trimming and booty building exercises! After their five-mile simulated bike ride of course. Everyone has some sort of routine.

One flight up down, in the east corridor was Earl's living quarters. And in the past few weeks, the deep dark chocolate transgender, Samej has begun to bloom, losing nearly 21 pounds- mostly tummy fat- has brought him/her out of their combined shell!

While Paradise had gain 10 pounds- mostly in his/her rear end and thighs- both are engaged in what is best describe as a total makeover of the serial killer formerly known as Chicken Head.

Each Transgender took turns dressing up then dressing down Earl Grimes, attempting to see which outfits brings out the mellow in his extremely complicated harsh aurora!

As for Earl, he is having the time of his life! For the first time he's the center of positive attention. Which should bring to the surface the best in anyone. Really, who doesn't desire to be the center of attention, among family, friends, peers and lovers?

Rarely in his life had Earl been the type of person others wanted to celebrate. If his newfound allies suggested having a tea party, Earl will be head over heels- *and I do mean heels*- in love!

Everyone inside Shangri-La was fitting into their little groove, inside the bigger fabric of their fledging society. Even the few survivors that they were able to recuse from the catholic school adventure seem to have adjusted to their new reality. Working to put their grief behind them, while embarking on their personal journey through this new frontier of the walking dead and the criminally insane!

The cares of whatever that was left of the outside world no longer hold any traction with the survivors inside Shangri-La. Each has gone through their own private hell just to get to this point in time!

Cities, governments and the entire planet have fallen to the COVID-MOMREL-6 virus. Whatever each survivor decides they want do from this point was their goddam choice! No longer will most of them have to worry about losing their job, flunking algebra, sucking up to arrogant bosses, playing the game or going to prison for life!

While John was sitting in his prison cell, he envisioned Shangri-La as the place civilization would have a chance to begin again. Equipped with one of the finest libraries left anywhere on the planet. John Hammond knew that without good people, their sanctuary could quickly become a pool of ignorance and indifference! Now they have a chance for not only redemption, but for the survival of humanity itself!

Lunch time and dinner are the two meals it's pretty much mandatory everyone attends. On Friday and Saturday nighties, the dress code was, you better dress to impress! All their clothing came from every Good Will Store in thirty-mile ratios – *and the jewelry*. Let's just say all pawn shops in the area loved when the former Mr. Hunnfield came shopping.

The styles in clothing in some cases went back as far as fifty years. Funky thick gold chains and pinky rings made the men feel young again! Plus, it's fun to play dress up and most of the adults loved the idea of long dresses and movie star inspired high heels. Nonetheless on the real, John knew gold and diamonds are generally great bartering tools! This Friday night is no different. Hammond always had the right song for the right moment and this time was no different.

Dean Martin's Ain't Love A Kick In the Head was playing as Earl arrives with his dates on either arm.

"How lucky can one guy be, I kissed her, and she kissed me. Like a fella once said, ain't that a kick in the head. The room wasn't completely black, I hugged her, and she hugged me back. Like a sailor once quote, doesn't that float your boat..."

Earl Grimes was smiling from ear to ear as he stepped in wearing a vintage white Tux right down to the polished Patten black leather shoes. On his right arm Paradise was decked out in a pink and white poke a dot dress, with three-inch white alligator pumps.

With her pink lipstick she resembles a 50s pin up girl, with a little something extra in her G string, of course. On his left arm Samej was wearing a skintight long yellow evening gown with a slit up her oiled down chocolate right thigh.

A view which reveals just the right amount of brownie completion on a hairless thigh for all to behold. Her purple lipstick signaled, this girl enjoys mouthwatering morning wood! The music continues as others filter into the cafeteria.

"My head was spinning and I can't help from grinning, if this is just the beginning! Oh, I'm finally winning and my life is gonna be beautiful. I finally have sunshine to spread and like that fella once said. Ain't Love, I mean ain't Love, a kick in the head..."

Next up Enestro and Celeste accompanied by the Hispanic ex stripper Destiny are dressed straight out that **1980s Miami themed Grand Theft Auto game**. Nonetheless, the trio oozed Latin sex appeal! Enestro has his white suit with black shirt open to his toned belly with a heavy gold chain that hangs with a tiny coke spoon on the end.

His lovely wife Celeste wore a red dress right out of 1950s Latin Quarters, it's sleek and accents all her curves! Her black high heels made Mrs. Valdez at least 2 inches taller. Interestingly her ruby red lipstick covered mouth made an inviting target for her husband's exploration. The ex-dancer Destiny was clearly Celeste to mold and control, for she's dressed in a similar dress only in midnight black!

Cherish, Sky, Robin and Dawn arrived together, and each was equally as beautiful as the next! The quads landed on sexy business causal. Right out of vintage 1990 style porn. White tight blouses that show much cleavage and ultra tight skirts – *Cherish wore the color beige, Sky chose black, Renee chose navy blue, and Dawn chose purple-* matching high heel pumps, stockings and of course thongs!

Even the few children the adults inherited were dressed in nice suits and pretty dresses. John Hammond knew that civilization begun with people being civil and communal with each other. Even the hot and cold running Indigo Roberson was dressed in her best Sunday dress and having a great time.

This was their third weekend together and the meal wasn't as important as their company. For Robin the more she looked at her father, the more she saw the man, not a monster!

The same could be said for everyone seated around the two long tables placed end to end. Even so, John and Enestro choose to conceal how the young Hunnfield boy needlessly and tragically died! It would have done none of them any good, including Earl, who is all smiles when he offers a toast.

"I would like to thank my friend. No, my brother John Hammond! Formerly inmate 997421 for without him and his lovely daughter. I, we would all be, well not here enjoying each other's company. Once again I say thank you.."

Everyone claps and whistles in their appreciation. Celeste raised her cup and spoke for both her man and their new girlfriend when she said.

"Yes, here's to Hammond. He brought me back my Enestro. And to the former Marshal Robin Aquila for introducing us to our new friends."

Celeste gave Enestro a deep soul kiss and followed it up with another to Destiny's oval shaped face. Once again claps and signs of appreciation from the small crowd. John signaled for everyone to calm down so he may speak.

"We may not be the last of humanity. However, I am assured we are... yes, we are the best dressed!"

Everyone chuckled and John continued.

"Some of you may or may not want answers on how the world died. If you would like to stay in the dark. The video arcade, movie theater and television room are open..."

All the adults stay, as the younger children are escorted out to engage in kid-friendly activities. As soon as the children are gone, Enestro pulls a bag of blunts out of his inner coat pocket, takes out two and passes the bag to his left.

Earl accepts it, takes out three, then passes the bag to Sky. She removes three passes once each to her girls and hands the bag to Indigo she declines and passes the bag to John who accepts one.

Enestro comments on the strain he selected.

"Thanks to the growers, we have a strain called LOVE CHILD, it's sixty percent Sativa and forty percent Indica, It encourages feeling of creatively, relaxation and arousal! And to think I grew up smoking what is considered shit, by today's standards at least. Sorry, sorry carry on mi amlgo..."

John smelled his hand rolled cigar and smiles before saying.

"I was in the Air Force for nearly nineteen years. I'm a trained infectious disease warfare specialist! With degrees in Biology and neuro genetic mapping."

John allows his words to sit in before continuing.

"After I left the Air Force, my work was more free-lance. I worked for different health agencies, right alongside BIG PHARMA. As well as with different branches of our intelligence agencies."

He finally fires up his thumb sized cigar leaf filled with medical grade marijuana and states as sure as the sun rises in the east.

"I know now, I worked on an earlier version of the COVID-MOMREL-6 virus."

Everyone sat up in the chair, not sure what was going to be said next. It was Indigo who asked the following question.

"Like I asked you earlier, who are THEY?"

John lets out a sly smile as he allows a bit of smoke to escape the corner of his mouth. He exhales fully, coughs a bit before continuing.

"My illegal clients generally paid in cash; my legal clients paid in stock options. Both were funded through dummy corporations based outside the prying eyes of Uncle Sam. It was the last project I worked on; it had two of the four compounds of COVID-MOMREL-6. Which included Ebola and Rabies. Someone employed me to combine the two and create a vaccine for my work.."

He takes another pull of his cigar, exhales and continues.

"The job was only to take two weeks. The employer requested two more compounds added and that's when the compounds *Ophiocordyeeps* or secretion of the so-called Brazilian Zombie Ant. As well as the Taiwanese Zombie parasite *Leucohloridium* had been added to my list of compounds to integrate and produce a vaccine for."

He let the words linger, and it's his daughter that asked the next question.

"So, you made this nightmare?!"

You could hear the air slowly being let out of the room as John took time before answering his daughter.

"I didn't consider it that at the time. But when I saw the potential of the work. I made sure my portion could be contained with the correct earlier application of anti-virials and early vaccines. By me asking one too many questions about who was paying the tab. Well, that question killed my wife, led me to death row, destroyed my family and got us where we are now."

John let his words drift off like the rings of marijuana smoke through the open bay door.

Enestro shook his head and stated.

"That's a tough cross to have to bear my friend. Don't carry it, plant it and move the fuck on. "

Celeste adds, "you caused this like McDonald's fries didn't go straight to my belly."

Sky asked in between puffs, "So, could you make the vaccine now? I mean I don't want to get bitten and then one of you have to kill me."

Paradise perks up and asks, "Will this vaccine cause me to experience any erectile dysfunction?"

Earl chuckles, "Don't want any of that Big John."

Robin was still trying to wrap her head around the fact her dad's the man that unleashed hell up Earth. She grabs the canter of wine and pours herself a decent glass, took a gulp and exhaled deeply before saying.

"That's why they killed MY mom? You know how to make a vaccine and even if they killed you, there's no way for them to ensure that you didn't make a vat and stash it somewhere. So, they murdered my mom and threatened to do the same to me! Am I right DAD?"

Sky and Cherish each rubbed a section of Robins back in an effort to pull her back from the brink of a total meltdown. They could feel her anger. Her father was mellowed by his blunt. He had not smoked in decades, so his head wasn't where Robins was. He was being to mellow for her, and the death of her mom still held meaning to Robin. Plus, she had not hit the mellow stick yet!

"Yes and no honey. The vaccine I made, didn't work. I made sure of that, if I didn't you and I will have been murdered as well. And yes, I hid the real vaccine or sorts in a place they never thought to look."

Indigo's interest is peeked, "you are saying there is a vaccine?"

Hammond stared into Indigo's brown eyes, and she didn't look away. John was doing his best to read this woman. All the same either he's out of touch or there's nothing to read! From his impression Indigo was just doing a job and the few times she lets the mask slip are far and in between a few bottles of expensive wine. John sighs as he replies.

"Truthfully what differences does it make at this point? The people responsible for all of this are both dead. Or circling the earth in their own private spaceships."

Cherish wonders out loud, "rich people with their own spaceships? Dude that's fucked up on so many levels."

The thick white ex dancer Dawn states, "When I danced in New York, Wall Street types would talk about buying doom day shelters in Norway."

Celeste injects, "but that's not a spaceship Blanca. Besides. I don't even think the cartels built those.."

Robin was bitter and she fought back the urge to hurl the decanter of wine at her dad. So, she excused herself, and was followed by Sky.

While Dawn and Cherish stay seated. Sky and Robin had forged a bond over the last few weeks and it's a indeed a truly romantic one. The clatter of twin sets of high heels striking concrete floors extends some fifty feet outside the party. Sky had to half jog to catch up to Robin near the southeast stairwell.

That's where she found Robin leaning against the wall, fighting back her tears of frustration, anger and overall fucking sadness! Sky thought about all the things she could say, instead she just gently rubbed Robin's shoulder and allowed herself to be a sounding board.

Robin no longer fought back her tears as she muttered.

"My dad is a great guy huh? He didn't actually kill my mother! No, no, no. However, he did actually assist in destroying our planet. A major, what the fuck type of day, huh!"

Sky attempted to lighten the mood by whispering.

"Welcome to the apocalypse and for the record. I'm glad I ended up here, alongside you..."

It takes a moment for the laughter to start, nevertheless once it does, the two women share a tender moment. Sky didn't want to see Robin feeling what she was feeling. So, she kisses Robin softly on her right cheek, as Robin allowed her mouth to search for Sky's, the tip of their tongues meet in delight. The dual organs perform a ritual matching dance around each other, until Robin reaches out to secure Sky by pulling her into a mutual embrace.

Sky's hands palmed her lover's scented back, while Robin's eager hands had a firm grasp on Sky's toned buttock. Robin hadn't been thought about falling in love with another woman in five years! Nonetheless she's lonely, fighting to stay sober, angry and more than slightly fucking aroused! Sky threw her head back, so Robin's long tongue may start its trek down the slope of her inviting neck. Her fingernails soft dig into Robin's shoulder, as Sky moans one word. "Yessssssss."

Like alley cats in heat, both women grope and paw at the other like clothes should be illegal! With her back braced by the gray concert wall, Sky leans further back, allowing her right leg to wrap around her lover's thigh, pulling her even closer still. Their embrace was followed by long deep kissing and deep labored breathing, pulling of hair and the unbuttoning of blouses. Breasts Be Free, will slowly become their mantra!

Robin could not help but enjoy the aroma of coconut scented body wash that the nape of Sky's breast presented to her senses. It goes to say that both women need some sort of release and if this is wrong, neither woman had any plans of being right!

Meanwhile the party in the cafeteria was starting to show signs of ending as the rest of the survivors have their fill of dancing and one by one and two by threes, leave only John and Indigo seated at the long metal table.

Enestro left with a woman on both arms, Cherish and Dawn leave holding hands and their high heels. While Earl left like a king, both his ladies catered to him like it's his birthday! Maybe, well yeah probably he will get to have his cake and eat it too.

The first to reach their quarters were, the Valdez's.

Enestro uncorked a bottle of Tequila and Celeste pulls out her secret, secret stash of cocaine- *there was no way Calamity was going to give up three kilos of pure Columbian GO-GO power without taking at least a few ounces*!- the couple took a few bumps as Celeste shuffles the songs download to her IPHONE and sat back as Destiny provides them with a special strip show! One that will leave nothing to be their imagination.

Slowly Destiny mouths the words as she seductively started unbuttoning her dress to the song, ***A Party Ain't A party* by 2Chains & Jamie Fox**.

"Wait a minute, wait a minute...Fresh kicks, fresh whips, baby can you feel that? Shorty with the booty sportin the nipple print shirt

must be here to see me off.. Turn around and let me see you do it, let me see you work it, come on twerk it... Go ahead girl work out your daddy issues on me, shorty with the booty dancing like she want do me. Turn around let me see you do it, turn around if you bad and let me see you work it! Shorty we ain't stopping until the sun comes up, because a party ain't a party, until I get up in the party.."

The part Navajo, Mexican and Cuban dancer enjoys applying her craft with a couple that knew how to appreciate her many hidden and not so hidden assets! Destiny Christina Mordovia has been on her own since fifteen, now at twenty-seven she has finally found if not love, at least, mutual lust!

She slowly straddled Celeste first, allowing the rose and vanilla bean scent of her body wash to capture Calamity's interest. As Destiny rubs her 34 C cups across Celeste waiting tongue. Enestro enjoy watching the scene upfold, for he knew when the women finished introducing their desire to each other, both would take the time to seduce and cater to his desire!

It will start with both their talented tongues tracking *I Love You* down his neck and chest, while each of his women will take turns stroking his thick cock and heavy balls. And as Mr. Valdez had come to find out, it's better forgo the GO-GO powder and slip himself the little blue pill, EARLY. Needless to say having performance issues with these two vision of modern art would be more problems than any one man needs to endure!

Meanwhile Earl, Paradise and Semaj strolled down the hallway that led to their quarters. Paradise was smiling as she still was toking on one of their blunt. Even though she and Sky had drifted a apart, Sky felt she had finally found a home. Crazy it took to the end of the world for her to feel somewhat whole. Paradise held hands with Earl as he held hands with Semaj. Who was just happy to be alive and allowed to live as she saw fit, without side eyed judgment from society! Plus, she was looking hotter and hotter each week, so the Apocalypse at least cured her of a negative self-image.

Bonus for the east of the world was no one would have guessed that Earl Grimes was one of the fiercest serial killers ever to make it off death row!

Nonetheless at the moment, Earl was as happy as a one-eyed pedophile Priest at a Blind Boy Scout Jamboree!

Semaj enjoyed being a bottom, for either Earl or Paradise, she/he can't get enough of the way Earl's long thick tongue was fond of exploring her hairless Bootylicious ass cheeks before parting her chocolate cakes with his uncircumcised cucumber shaped penis. Or the way Paradise slender hairless nearly a footlong penis felt sliding towards the depths of her more than accepting throat!

Just as much as the other enjoy Transwoman in the room enjoyed being the den "mother" for their pod. Mz. Paradise Hunter really loved getting head, much like a duck enjoys the feeling of water!

However, Paradise hasn't always been into giving oral favors and when she did, it's never the best she could do. Plus, she never let anyone cum in her mouth, ever! Paradise was more of a would-be Vers/Top than passive bottom. One could say in the past world, Paradise would be considered a selfish lover!

Sadly, it took the Apocalypse for the young Taiwanese, Mexican and Korean Transwoman to grow as a person and a human fucking being! At least now she shows genuine concern about her lovers' pleasure and overall mental and emotional health. Paradise will never be accused of giving a toe-curling blowjob, now she made sure to lick and hum on some man size balls!

Which was more than fine with Semaj for she was a pure fem bottom, one who always dreamed of being the happy upbeat wife in a relationship! The Apocalypse has given each an opportunity to grow as people and not be whatever society claims they must.

Earl Grimes was a top that enjoyed giving head and will on occasion bottom! **Fact,** in the past if Earl bottomed for any man or

Trans-person, he probably would murder them shortly after! Not out of anger, more out of shame, even so that was the old Earl Grimes.

It took the end of civilization for Earl, not to feel the need to be Chicken Head! He had never felt as secure in any relationship as he feels with these two. For they will never leave him, and Earl had no plans of returning to his old ways. The death of the Hunnfield lad at his hands taught Earl a valued less**, Human Lives Matter**. Even if the world around him will dictate, something completely different.

The demented serial killer that was Chicken Head had been put in box and Earl planned to never let him out! Well, maybe if the lives of the people he now holds dear are in jeopardy. Him seamlessly murdering the Hunnfield lad really shook Earl, he knew it's now the time for him to be a much better man!

Down near the Hydro gardens, Nefertiti "Cherish" McGill and Dawn Strubski's- *Polish, Jewish and Scottish decent*- took a stroll took down the three flights of stairs to the hydro gardens that they planted a few weeks ago. Each were finishing the last of their glasses of red wine and a blunt. Both ladies are full of wonder and female banter.

Every move from Dawn's- *34B 34-36—* frame took was being expressed by the tightness of the fabric she adorned. She stopped by a metal bench, took a seat, puts down her high heels and said.

"This place is amazing! Who would have thought stripping would save my life?"

Cherish sits next to her ex-coworker, and without warning, now a close friend. As Dawn continued by saying.

"I know we never talked much, well before the world went CRAZY... Be that as it may I've seen you dance before and you're fucking awesome!"

If Nefertiti "Cherish" McGill had not been the color of expensive coco, Dawn might have seen her blush.

She replied. "I never thought you even knew I worked there! You used to see me and just turn your head."

Dawn sighed and sort of chuckled.

"I am so sorry; I was living with a shithead would-be biker/meth dealer and professional bowler. Just to let you know I never used the stuff, and I know, I know I could have done a lot better! But we were high school sweethearts and he found me on Facebook. Then asked could he visit for a week, and that week was two years! Plus, the asshole took my virginity, so...."

Cherish just nods ok, while taking it all in, allowing Dawn to see she wasn't there to judge her.

Dawn continued in a meek voice. "I've never been one that has ever been charged with making great life decisions I, I don't know, I guess I'm easy to brain wash! Look I, I've freaked off with other girls for money, yet never for pleasure and I, I guess... Well, goddamit, how do YOU always smell like cupcakes? Anyone ever ask you that?"

Nefertiti's pea shaped breasts giggled as she replied. "Yes, I've been asked that time from time. Look, I'm not here to judge anyone, I've had my share of mistakes when it comes to love and lust. Great Dick! Well at times in my life have driven this bitch to do some real fucked up and crazy shit!"

Dawn threw her leg over Nefertiti Cherish McGill, while using her left hand to stroke the material that covers Cherish' s chocolate chip size nipples and sexy whispered.

"We have more than enough time, if you desire to tell me about your best, one love affair..."

Cherish seductively licks her lips and replies. "I'm into girls and guys. Sadly, most guys either get jealous of the other woman or develop feelings for the other woman he never had for me."

Dawn pokes out her bottom lip and replied in a child-like voice.

"Those bastards. Which one happen to you?"

Cherish ran her finger nails up Dawn's sheer stocking covered left leg, sending shivers of pleasure up her target's scent spine.

"I shot an ex-boyfriend in the foot, when I found him fucking my best friend! A friend I turned him on to with a threesome on his goddam birthday. It took that day for me to realize he was just a fucking asshole Puerto Rican with a huge dick! Not my boo."

Dawn leaned forward and blew a stream of hot air across the base of Nefertiti's neck. She felt Cherish's body slightly tremble in delight as Dawn replied in a husky voice. When her nimble fingers find a wet and inviting thong.

"Serves him right, you should have shoot him in his dick!"

Nefertiti's fingers move under the tiny fabric, housing Dawn's treasure. For her sweet nectar's ready to glisten on the slender extremity being introduced its way. That's when Cherish lustfully states.

"Oh NO, a Bitch's not crazy, I love diiicck! And that fool and a horse cock. His dick was so big, I guess that's what made that fool retarded! Plus, I knew he wouldn't tell the Police I shot him in the pinky toe, but if I shot him in his dick he probably would have paid one of his boys to kill me."

Cherishes' fingers quickly find the sweet spot and Dawn's head leans back and her moans are very soft and shallow! Dawn's body shakes a few times as Nefertiti withdrew her two fingers and inserts them into first her own mouth, then Dawns.

It doesn't take much for Dawn to lean forward and give Cherish a deep, long passionate kiss that leaves both women yearning for more! The ivory Dawn Strubski pulls her mouth away from ebony Nefertiti Cherish McGill and then said.

"If you find a guy you want to bang, I promise to only fuck his brains out if you say it's cool and you got to be there to join in on the fun! But if you find true love, I will gladly be your maid of honor. It's the Apocalypse Cherish, we should at least keep our options open. Right?"

Meanwhile back in the Cafeteria John and Indigo have performed the last of the cleanup of empty plastic cups and disposable plates.

Now they sit next to each other at one of the metal tables sharing what's left of a bottle of rather nice white wine. John had been in prison for nearly fifteen years and this as close as he has been to a woman who didn't have a can of mace or an armed guard escort in a very long time!

It's hard for him to judge Indigo Roberson mood, she's clearly a bit buzzed. However, that doesn't mean she into helping him ease back into society the ole fashion way! So,

John asked, "Tell me about you, I mean we are sharing this habitat and all I know about you is you were a prison psychiatrist. May I ask, was that your dream job?"

Indigo scoffs then chuckled, "Nope, I thought I would be counseling housewives in Colorado."

John took a sip of wine and said, "That's a long way from Indiana. What went wrong?"

Indigo's demeanor stiffs a bit and John can sense he might have trended in troubled waters, still she replies.

"You know, this wasn't my first stop, and I made my share of mis-takes, let's just leave it at that."

John nodded ok and asked, "When you got inside the Indiana Penal System did you think you were going to be like Billy Crystal in the movie Analyze This?"

Indigo scoffs, then laughed once more, "YES, I did! I really did, I mean don't get me wrong I've met some really interesting characters, you included, in my three-week crash course of inmate behavior, but still I thought I was going to be more effective. Then the world turned to, shit."

John had been out the game for a long time, nonetheless he felt it's now or never!

"Well then Ms. Roberson, are you interested in assisting an organic filled reformed former inmate, reintegrate himself from the betterment of his humanity? I hope so. And if so, the only question should be your quarters or mine? I'm sure I have a better collection of music than anyone here..."

A twinkle flashed across Indigo's eyes as her middle-aged fingers played with the pearl necklace adoring her neck. This time her smile was genuine, and she replied.

"Do you now? Ok, but I hope you have baby oil, I need a shower and I feel sexy when I'm all oiled up..."

John flashes his signature smiles and stated. "I think I have a gallon of it in my room. However, have you ever tried using olive oil?"

Several days later, the weather outside was humid and sunny, with a southerly breeze pumping in huge amounts of moisture, the dew point hung around 70. That meant the wardrobe of the day consists of shorts and nipple tight t-shirts for sun and bathing suits and skirts for others!

All adults agreed that the children needed to be outside, too much time away from anything seemingly normal only added to their PTSD. The adults can easily pass their time exploring sexual fantasies and or liaisons. However, not so much for the nine–*ages 7-14-* youngling in their care.

John recommended starting a reading, math, science curriculum and everyone agreed upon the rescued St. Mary's, former Math teacher Nabila Hussien was the woman to guide the youth forward. The day started like most, Cherish and Dawn liked working up in the grow house. It gives them the opportunity to wear bikini tops with skirts- *panties optional-* For them the smell of nature could be a real turn on to some and by far it beats the reek of the dead.

While outside Enestro, Celeste and their wing-woman Destiny stand watch over the young people thrusted upon their care. Enestro found a soccer ball in the storage area of their doom's day silo. He had never fancied himself the father type. It's not like the lifestyle that he had chosen to live would even condone it.

Unbeknown to him his darling Celeste has been thinking about the same thing. What else could she leave in this miserable world to remember her by? Now in the middle of the Apocalypse, watching her Enestro attempt to foster hope and joy by something simple as having fun was uplifting, for he got the kids and teenagers out of their shell!

The fragrance of the nearby river signals the water was still running but can do nothing to cover up the ever-present stench of impending doom! Earl's out and about sporting tan cargo shorts and a Hawaiian style shirt, Paradise on the other hand was wearing a powder blue sun dress and movie star sunglass. While Semaj happened to be wearing tight purple shorts and a carney yellow tank top that hugged her puffy nipples. The trio pick apples from the orchard, while talking about the future of the world.

Semaj stood on her toes to reach a red apple on a branch just out of her reach and then said.

"I don't know, when I think about all the dead people walking around, all the dead children and mothers… I get sad and I think why, me. Why am I here and others, so many others died without even knowing why or how they got sick."

Earl reached up and easily picked the red apple and handed it to Semaj, he looked deep in the face of the young Transwoman, smiled and then said.

"My dove, you are here and if my friends and I had not found you, you would not be."

Semaj smiled back and Paradise not to be left out of the conversation, adds.

"Karma might be a bitch, but in this case, she is definitely friendly towards our motley crew of misfits and former delinquents."

Earl leaned his massive frame down to kiss Paradise first, Semaj second and each continued their task of picking apples.

Back near the area with Enestro playing soccer, Destiny takes the time to further bond with Celeste.

"I grew up in Las Cruz New Mexico and I've been on my own since fifteen, also I tricked a bit when I was younger! Even so, I found stripping was safer than walking the streets."

Celeste smiles and replies, "I understand that shit, I was on my own until Enestro, well until we met. My parents went North when I was only ten years. Then died when a Coyote left his load in the back of a Semi somewhere in shithole Texas without water or a bit of fucking hope!"

Both women allow silence to offer comfort to those not so long forgotten bitter memories.

Celeste goes on to say, "the life of a drug smuggling, contract killer left me with no time or thought of kids... Now, here at the end of everything, I finally understand why people have them! I see how Ernesto would make a good father..."

Destiny rested her head on Celeste shoulder and states, "Don't hate me but I, I had a little Nino, three years ago. I,I, I knew I could not raise him right! So, I gave him up at the fire station in Des Moines Iowa three days after he was born. Then, I, I moved to fucking Gary Indiana!"

Meanwhile back in the control center Sky was busy discussing with John the daily readings of generators and the efforts of water distilling. John was an easy teacher to follow and Sky was a fast leaner.

"I want to thank you for helping my daughter out of her funk."

Sky sort of blushes as she replies, "It's no problem, trust me it's my pleasure! Robin just needed someone to show her it's alright to be happy."

John nods yes then asked, "Where is she?"

Sky adjusts a monitor near their lobby that leads to personal quarters as she replies.

"Down in the gym. She said something about needing to put in some extra work to rid her muscles of stagnation."

John nodded, smiled and mumbled. "I thought that's what you two were working out last night?"

Down in the gym, Robin was working up a monster of a sweat! She started with 45 front kicks, followed by 45 outside crescent kicks, then 45 inside crescent kicks and 25 spinning back kicks. That took twenty minutes! After that Robin moved on to punches.

John made sure her grandmother kept her in Hapkido from age five until her senior year of high school. Furthermore, for their effort Robin took to martial arts like a bird to flight. For the first time in a very long time, Robin Aquila can legitimately say that she was happy! As she performs her martial arts practice, Robin's mind focused on the task of striking, blocking and subduing multiple opponents.

As she practiced Robin performed these tasks as if her life or the lives of those, she has come to care about hanging in the balance of her performance.

She realized the craving to drink too much had left her with the need to inflict her pain on to others! It was one of the addictions, in a way the Apocalypse helped cure.

Even so she didn't think she could ever fall in love with another woman. Lust, yes! Robin has had affairs and one-night stands with as many women as she has men. Some she wished would have lasted longer, while most she wished hadn't lasted as long. Nonetheless Sky's delightful approach to life, even in the middle of the apocalypse, made Robin at least want to see where this happiness thing leads!

Yes, she has had one, two, even four one-night stand with various women she has left bars with. Nonetheless, it never led to a full-fledged ole school long-term love affair! Sky made her life fun again and that's enough for Robin. Even with this odd assortment of ex assassins, a notorious serial killer, former strippers and a prison psychiatrist, love may bloom large as you dare!

Meanwhile, Indigo Roberson did her best to avoid the cameras that monitor all hallways. She must be quick to make it to John's quarters. Indigo wasn't even sure she would even find anything in his quarters, still she had to find answers! The clock's ticking and even though Indigo had no idea even if her handlers were still alive. She continued the mission.

A single bead of sweat trickles down her Carmel forehead as Indigo palmed the Sat phone in her right hand. Her handlers made it clear, the fate of her sister rests in getting John to tell her where he hid the cure! Dammit she thought, she knew her sister Diana went to work for the Defense Intelligence Agency in 2008 during the early years of the "*war on terror*."

By 2015 Diana Roberson like most in her field moved on to

Government Contractor work. The stepsisters rarely spoke so when Diana approached Indigo with a new job opportunity it was after Indigo's divorce to a guy she never should have married- *a psychiatrist should never marry another psychiatrist.* - case closed!

In turn the last few months working for what Indigo could only describe as a Black Op on steroids had been extremely challenging for her own sanity. The company that employees her went by the title GSAL- Global Security & Logistics. They had offices in several Middle East countries including Saudi Arabia, as well in South Korea, Taiwan Panama, Mexico, Brazil and Antarctica.

GSAL pulled some strings and placed Indigo in the Indiana Prison System to get next to her target prisoner 997421/John Hammond. Only for their best laid plan to go out the window when the Warden stuck her in the women's prison instead of the men.

It was a matter that even the long sinister hands of GSAL could not quickly remedy! The prior women's psychiatrist took an early retirement and the slot needed filling quickly.

When she could not make progress, Indigo's sister Diana began making statements concerning her own safety! With no way to recharge her SAT phone without drawing attention, Indigo's only access to her sister and her clandestine employer was nearly out of power.

The fact was Indigo has not talked to Diana in over eighteen days, that was the last time Indigo was able to sneak away and make contact and her sister sounded worried! People were getting sick inside GSAL's secure bunker. If John has a cure or a vaccine the shadowy a-holes that run Global Security & Logistics wanted it ASAP.

In the back of her mind, Indigo hates doing anything that would set this lot off! Earl Grimes terrifies the living shit out of her. Not to mention Celeste by clinical definition was as violent as any man! Bile collected at the back of her throat, for Indigo has an uncontrollable the fear of getting fucking caught.

She figured John would be out for at least another thirty minutes, more than enough time to secretly inspect his room for anything that even resembles information on a cure. She peaked her head into John Hammond's quarters and the first thing that struck her last night when they engaged in a bit of physical release. The number of books he had stacked from floor to ceiling.

Last night as much as she wanted just to rest her head on John's broad chest and forget about GSAL, her sister Diana and even the thought of a cure or vaccine! Indigo feared the chip they implanted in the base of her spinal cord, probably, more than certainly was transmitting her position!

Indigo's eyes scanned the titles of various books, and she could see John's interested varied. There are practical texts of mechanical engineering, structural engineering, volumes of material from General Medicine, agriculture, agronomy, geometry, microbiology, Astro biology, the history of planetary alinements, virulent viruses, Secrets of a Assyrian Necromancer, Remote Viewing techniques of the KGB, Ancient Alien Theory and the history of stand-up comedy!

Indigo didn't want to disturb anything in John's lair. She saw first hand how prisoners could recall the exact position of a personal effects tossed by guards. It took great care to replace said item or the inmate would know their pod had been tossed. Indigo had no way of knowing if John possessed this skill. Yet she wasn't willing to disturb his effects, this time!

As she tiptoes deeper into John's quarters, she found nothing that screams out, CURE. That's when she heard the approach of someone, nonetheless it's too late to run or even hide!

Unknowingly John steps into his quarters only to be greeted with the glorious sight of Indigo stripping out of her halter top, jean shorts, her purple laced underwear smiling. As she slowly climbs into his bed.

What does one do when they find a beautiful lover climbing into their warm bed? Well John, couldn't help but smile as he said.

"Why thank, I didn't order breakfast in bed, however I will gladly accept the reservation."

Robin had finished her two-hour workout, and she feels GREAT. In the last three and a half weeks, she had even noticed how belly fat and smelly bowels movements have both gone away. The steady workout, regular diet and fantastic orgasms curtesy of Sky have softened her mood!

Whether she likes it, loves it or not, their tiny group is growing closer, and the bounds of survival and friendship are blooming. Robin chuckled to herself as the semi warm water from the shower, runs down the nap of her back, towards her toned twin booty cheeks and finally mingles with her freshly painted toes- *courtesy of Paradise*.

She never in a million years would have thought of being on friendly terms with a pair of Cartel Hire Killer and a notorious Serial Killer to boot! Furthermore, it surprise Robin how quickly she was able to put any of their past behind her.

Not to mention the former strippers, a really high-strung Transgender YouTube star and her DAD! Wow thought Robin, I have come a long way. As she washed the sweat from under her mango shaped breast, all she could think of is how the Apocalypse actually helped her get her shit together!

Robin quickly toweled off and puts on a black thong, under her camo cargo shorts, tan bra and loose-fitting white T shirt. Being in Shangri-La helped one push the utter horror and mass annihilation that's circling the planet, out of their sight. And for the briefest time out of mind!

Even though Robin was somewhat under dressed, she still carried her 9MM Beretta strapped to her hip and a boot knife in strapped to her left calf.

As dusk approaches, the survivors must contain their movements to the interior of Shangri-La! Outside, the Hunnfield mansion metal shutters are down and secure. With no lights the entire farm was hard to make out in the dark. Unless you already knew it's there you would never know it's there. The hordes of dead have not made it out here. Even so the ones that do, meet volumes of full metal jacket, sharpen swords, handy hatchets and chatty chainsaws!

Nevertheless, Indigo's fear of GSAL tracking her nearly a half a mile under the earth was driving her to make dangerous decisions with her life. After another passionate love making session with John Hammond. Indigo claimed to what to go shower and get some much-needed sleep. Honestly, she does the first thing she mentioned, yet has no intention to do the latter.

After her shower, Indigo waited until others are gathering to make dinner, to sneak into the empty Hunnfield house. She needed to access the interior hatch, so she may charge her SAT phone. Then attempt to check on her sister Diana's well-being. The entrance to the interior hatch rests on the middle level, past environmental engineering. All she needed to do is get there unnoticed!

Strange as it sounds, Indigo felt like she was not in control of her actions.

The need to know of the health of her bitch of a sister was only part of it. Indigo didn't know if black helicopters would be descending like angels of death to murder all these people! Some, some of them she was starting to care for.

Indigo had sat through one of John's morning briefings, where he explained that due to its own backup generators, electricity still runs through the semi abandoned mansion. That's where she desperately needed to get to, Indigo knew she must charge her SAT phone for at least seven minutes. eight minutes in, Indigo attempted to reach her sister. She didn't even know how long the satellites would be operational, every day she didn't take action, maybe Diana's last!

Indigo hesitated for a bit before dialing the six-digit code, she could easily smash the phone to bits and pray that everyone inside GSAL was fucking dead!

Nevertheless, Indigo hoeld her breath as it took several moments for the connection to be made. The guilt of her action nearly forces Indigo to hang up before the connection is complete!

Nervously her tongue licks her lips in anticipation as the phone on the other end of the connection begins to ring. Sweat beads down her mahogany face as the air around her seems to become thick with her own fear! The sad, bewildered voice of her once bitchy younger sister is hard for Indigo to hear.

"Indi, Indi is that... cough, cough, cough- you?"

Indigo swallows hard before saying, "Diana. Diana are, are you alright?"

Her younger sister lets out a bitter sounding laugh one that signals, FUCK NO!

"NO. Indigo, I'm, I'm locked in the communication room. Most of the base has been overrun by those goddam, THINGS. Other that, I'm just fucking peachy!"

The tone of her older sister's voice goes up several notches with concern.

"How, how did they get in?"

Her younger sister coughs several times before replying.

"I, I don't know. Some guard died of a heart attack and while attempting to relive him, he turned! Killing or injuring the trio of paramedics working on him. When the medical cart arrived, those that turned got them! I don't know from there."

She coughs, coughs again and coughs once more.

There's silence between the sisters for several beats before Indigo ask a sensitive question.

"Diana are you; I mean have you been infected?"

Diana coughs several times before replying.

"No, the air cleaners need to be switched back on line. Eight of the remaining twelve Security Personnel drew straws to see who would escort one of the remaining Techs to restart and man the main computer.... That was twenty minutes ago...."

More silence between the two sisters, followed by Diana saying.

"Enough about me, did you find Hammond's cure?

Indigo was at a loss of words, before attempting to offer her younger sister a bit of, hope.

"I think I am close; John doesn't discuss that part of his life. However, he has a lab here and sometimes late at night he's down there working on something. I just need more..."

Diana injects, "Time? Indigo, I don't know how much time I have left! We've been 36 hours without clean air and I'm starting to feel the need to sleep. I, I'm sorry for being such a total bitch! I guess I got that from mom, you, you got all dad's patience."

Indigo offers, "Well you got Mom's great looks, and I got Dad's lard ass."

For the first time in a long while the two siblings share a rare moment of joyful bliss! Before Diana replies, "I have a small office plant I keep breathing into, hoping it makes enough oxygen for me. Still, I have no water, no food and about fifty of the infected roam outside my door. It's just a matter of time before...."

Indigo's voice fights the urge to scream as she does her best to encourage her sibling.

"Listen Diana you have always been the stronger one, so stay strong, stay bitchy! I will get that cure and I will have John fly me to your location. All you must do is stay alive. Do you hear me?"

With that all the pain and suffering seem to fade out of Diana's voice making Indigo wonder was she being played. Diana was time type of bitch!

"NO, Indigo just tell me where you are, and I will come to you..."

It takes nearly three minutes for Indigo to sneak back into the main complex nearly unnoticed. However, as she's coming in, Sky catches the image on the monitor and logs the observation into the nightly duty log. Just as John Hammond taught them.

The clock on the wall reads 1835 or 6:35pm and it was Robin's turn to run the COMM. Dinner would be happening in 20 minutes and Sky had sat with her love for an hour past her own shift.

Before heading to shower and do some laundry just in time to meet everyone for dinner. Robin put the novel down she was reading by probably dead author **Joe McKinney**- *adequately named Plaque of the Undead*- as she noticed her father entering his lad- *located several doors from the laundry room.*

Robin picked up the log and wrote in the time her dad entered his lab as she downs the rest of her well-deserved Vanilla Coke a Cola. The strong scent of lavender, vanilla and strawberries pumps through the central air conditioners giving a calmer effect to a reforming serial killer, former assassins and stressed-out Marshals alike!

Robin wiped her hair out of her eyes as she noticed Indigo doing her best to not be seen by the security cameras and that caught Robins' attention as she chuckled.

"Honey, you are too old to try to act like you are not going on a booty call!"

John was sitting on the metal bench taking off the layers of protective clothing, when Indigo popped her head into the lab's dressing area. John's first reaction was surprise, then joy when he asked.

"Hey you, I thought I would see you in the food court in twenty or nineteen minutes from now..."

Before John could finish his sentence, he could tell by the look on Indigo's face that she's struggling with a problem!

Instead, John said, "You look like you have something bothering you? How can I help?"

Indigo exhaled a deep breath before saying. "Please tell me you have a cure or a vaccine..."

John looked deeply into the woman's eyes and asked with concern. "Have you been bitten or scratched by any infected in the last hour? How, there are no infected here?"

Indigo's big brown eyes attempted to hold back her tears as she shook her head no and John feels the pressing need to get to the truth!

One hundred and forty feet from John Hammond's lab is the laundry room. Sky had just finished washing out her and Robin's laundry for the week. She doesn't mind, seeing that Robin is comfortable wearing jeans all day. While Sky still likes to put on a dress as much as any other woman!

While inside Shangri-La you were free to dress as you wanted with some exception of course- *children are present*. Consider the modern tech a person cannot do without is still somewhat functional. Cell phones could no longer pull up the internet or even make phone calls. However, they could be loaded with songs and movies, you didn't need a network for that. Just a computer with a hard drive filled with over ten thousand songs and filled with other platforms of cinema.

John Hammond made sure of that even from a cell on death row, his computer room at Shangri-La consist of fifteen DELL PCs and thirteen APPLE Mac's. Each machine was crammed with crammed with as much information as it could hold. The desire to help human civilization rebuild provides some insight into John Hammond's true character!

Thumb drives filled with instructional videos on subjects ranging from Astrobiology, how to train puppies and even to how to grow corn!

So, with all this preparation, Indigo cannot fathom that John doesn't have some sort or cure or even a vaccine hidden away.

She doesn't want those murderous bastards from GL&S arriving here and killing them all. In desperation Indigo picked up a scalpel as her voice trembled.

"John, I. I need to know is there a cure or a vaccine here?"

At first John thought the constant inquiring on a cure or vaccine by Indigo over the past few days was just her fear of being bit. However, when Indigo brandished one of his lab weapons, for the first time John Hammond understood that this fear was from more than the undead!

"Indigo, what do you plan to do with that?"

Indigo Roberson wasn't a violent woman; she knew she had no chance in hurting him and she knew it as well. Instead, she places the scalpel against her own throat as tears run freely down her face.

Between sobs she whispers, "Is there a cure John, please, please tell me. I'm trying to save our lives!"

While leaving the laundry room, Sky was listening to one of the fifty songs downloaded to her cell phone. She was carrying a basket of clean laundry, and her ear buds were in. As if she had not problem in the world- *at time she had not-*, Sky twirled around, dancing and singing along with **TLC's No Scrubs.**

"A scrub is a person that thinks they're fly, but really, they are a buster! Always sitting on their broke ass. No, I don't want your number, no I don't want none of your time. I don't want no scrubs, a scrub is person that can't get any time from me hanging out the passenger side of their best friend's ride trying to holler at me, no I don't want no scrubs a scrub can't get no time from me..."

Robin's keen eye catches the monitor as the woman she has comes to admire as a lover and a friend was happily moving down the wide hallway seemingly in a world of her own. Sky was a dancer, through and through. The woman found music to be settling and it influences her to move her body!

Consequently, Sky Harrison was a buoyant, lively force that beckoned to be loved! Sky's back was turned as she continued to mimic's the **90s group TLC's dance** moves.

Only Robin can see her father slowly backing out of his lab with his hands held high! The former US. Marshal sat up in her chair as what she witnesses next will shock and toss her towards further acts of anger and bouts of unwanted depression!

The air between them was tense and charged with fear, John slowly backed out of his lab, with his hands raised high in effort to talk Indigo out of her actions.

"Indigo please calm down, we can talk this out. Just, just tell me what's going on!"

The tears that streamed down her cheeks were indeed real, Indigo moved the scalpel a few inches from her throat as she tries to explain the shit she had gotten herself into.

"They placed me in the prison John! My, my sister works for this sketchy company calling themselves Global Security and Logistics. They think you have a cure or vaccine. DO YOU? Please, please John if you have it..."

Sadly, fate has its way of inserting its unmitigated tentacles directly into a person's goddam heart!

As Sky twirled around, her ear buds pumping music to her senses, unfortunately must have blanked out any hints of dange!. At this point the vibrant soul felt like she had finally earned the right to be happy. Robin made her happy! Dancing made Sky happy!

Nonetheless, while pleading with John, Indigo unwittingly lashed the scalpel out into what she thought was vacant air, totally unaware of Sky's upcoming presence. Woefully as Sky was to theirs. Only father and daughter bare witness in horror as the sharp blade made a 1/1,000,000 strike across Sky's exposed jugular vein!

Sky must have felt the warm wet substance flowing done her tank top as the salty spray captures her lips. They say before one die, their entire life flashes in the crevice of their mind's eye.

All your dreams. All your failures. As well as your triumphs! It's a distressing display of theater, laid out only for the dying. The love's you have lost and the love that you have gained! Let's hope for Sky's sake, hers were of the love she found with Robin.

Indigo never meant to hurt anyone, including herself! Heartbreaking was the feeling of Sky's warm blood splattering across her face she backs up dropping her bloody weapon muttering.

"What? No,no,no,no.no...."

Sky dropped the plastic crate and shook as her blood pulsed out in a life ending rate! A stunned Hammond still rushed to render aid and he thought he even heard Robin's scream coming from three levels up. Blood gurgled up and out of Sky Harrison's mouth, as

John offers calming words as he does his best to place a tourniquet on her mortal wound.

“There, there just stay calm, I will get you too medical. INDIGO, don’t just stand there! Go get a crash cart, NOW!”

Even so, Sky’s eyes told the story as her life drained out of them and the cold stare of death begun to embrace its undeserved new home.

Chapter II:

THE BANISHMENT OF THE INSANE & THE UNWORTHY

Two months into infection

Before all of this, people would ponder how fast it would take for civilization to come to a grinding halt. How long before internet servers will go dead? How long before satellites plunge from their orbits? When will the nuclear plants begin their melt down? And finally, when will nature's green thumb begin its quest to reclaim its lost glory? The answer to that riddle turned out to be five weeks, fourteen hours, twenty- one minutes and 2.5 seconds!

Even armed with that information nothing will ever halt the hot lingering days of summer from beaming its cosmic rays on the living or the dead. It has been one week since Rear Admiral Jefferson Bullraguard Lee had been found guilty of murder and the mood of the base was certainly mixed. Even so, Lee sat alone in his makeshift cell, neither cursing his captors nor even accepting his fate.

Jefferson Bullraguard Lee showed no remorse for his actions. The two Navy psychiatrist who examined the former Admiral both came to similar conclusions. Lee may have always been a Sociopath! Military life just refined his delusions, so he was able to hide them so much better.

Even so, the apocalypse has propelled Lee' sycosis to help him be reborn as a full blow Psychopathic! One of the Navy psychiatrist- *along time golfing buddy of Lee*- even attempted to argue now that the rules or social NORMS that once governed us no longer apply! He argued in this extreme setting certain people will have a harder time not sampling their darkest impulses and if they do, that will quickly become the new NORM! With or without a strong authority figure in charge, the sick will only get sicker and bolder in their delusions, the Navy Psychiatrist sternly proclaimed.

By the look on Jefferson's face, he cared little for these insects that have come to be in his presence! The very thought they could set and judge a man such as himself mystified Lee to his lanky bones. The Angelic sounds of heavenly glory still await Jefferson, for he knew his story wasn't going to end because some mongrel Army puke blames him for her half breed dyke bitch's death! Or that of that Air Force jagoff McKinney. He was a mere sacrifice to the god of chaos!

Jefferson knew that the pathway to glory was steep with the inconsequential, the frail and the goddam unlucky! From Lee's viewpoint, he was none of the above. His great, great grandfather might have lost the war of Northern aggression! Nevertheless, Jefferson Bullraguard Lee has no intention of losing this war to the wicked, the dead or the RACIALLY fucking inferior!

His so-called cell at least allows Lee to keep up with his regiment of 400 push-ups in under seven minutes and 300 sit ups in under six minutes. Few saw his vision of what this new world could flourish into, not even that idiot Dunson! The very thought of his one-time slave causes Lee to mutter as he's doing his sit ups, he said.

"He folded like a cheap seat under a lard ass in a pie eating contest! Crying while doing his best to spend a tale of him being a halfwit with no knowledge of my affairs. That sorry cocksucker's the poorest excuse for an Officer I have ever seen. A true fucking faggot ass Marine!"

Down the hall some fifty feet removed from his onetime commander, the former Marine Colonel Dunson was still attempting to spin a tale that his mind will contain for others to hear.

"How could I be so fucking stupid?"

Mutters David Dunson to himself as he sat on the end of his Navy issued cot. Dressed in a dark blue one-piece utility jumpsuit and stripped of all rank. Naked as the day he entered the Marine Corps, he thought. David pondered long and hard on how his former commander got his hooks in him so completely.

Their off-duty relationship didn't start out homosexual in nature! It was Lee who exposed Dunson to North Side of Chicago dungeons and North Shore sex parties. Fueled with drugs, deviate sex acts and all the liquor one could consumer. Complied with no worry of failing any urine test, the two felt free to explore many illicit substances while exploring their Sadomasochistic tendencies! He had never hit a woman in his life, until Lee introduced him into the life of Master and Slave!

No Seabee, Shore Party or MP would dare question their base Commander and their Provo Marshal leaving or entering base no matter the hour. Once again David mutters to himself.

"I, I , I should have known when he nearly beat that spic Tranny hooker to death..that Lee was more than just a bit off! All she asked for was an additional fifty dollars if he planned to pee on her. Shit, that nearly cost that Mexican whore his goddam life!"

Dunson stood up and paced the small janitor closet/cell room wondering why none of the Navy Officers on his court martial at least gave him the benefit of the doubt.

"I've served with at least three of those cunts for over seven years. SHIT, FUCK, FUCK GODDAMMIT! I'm not supposed to be here. I'm not..."

The last card Dunson could play might be embarrassing, still it might save his life! He did his best to blur it out, nevertheless the truth's clear to only him. Jefferson Bullraguard Lee raped him, then blackmailed Dunson into helping him commit his heinous acts of violence!

Well at least, that's what David keeps telling himself.

Down inside the labs, the tragic death of Doctor Monique Littlefield has left some of the remaining doctors to wonder if it's best for humanity to bow out and allow the next superior species to take hold of the mantle! Even with the revelation that the two rescued survivors have each been bitten over two hundred and fifty hours ago.

Even though, neither have succumbed to the virus, the scientists behave like they have been drinking a large helping of salt water! Sick and totally numb from the events that rocked Camp McCormik. However, the news of survivors of this plague should have been a reason to rejoice!

Nonetheless, the feeling of impending dooming was slowly pressing its dank forearm across the exposed throat of the base's psyche.

Lt. Colonel Lafayette has many hats to juggle this day. First, the two twin survivors have been bitten, yet never turned. That miracle at least keeps their mission, alive. However, what to do with the disgraced Rear Admiral Lee still lingers over the command. It's 0930 and the lab's electrified with movement!

Windu can see hope in the frighten children who have been thrusted into her care. No one to Wynolla's knowledge has ever survived the COVID-MOMREL-6 Virus, now they have two!

Though a coaxing of ice cream and Coke-Cola, Colonel Lafayette finds out their names Chloe- sandy brown hair with one hazel eye and the other blood red- and her identical sister Faith. Each weigh around fifty-five pounds and both have a fear on needles.

Wynolla's first conversation with the survivors is for the most exploratory yet motherly, when she said.

"I understand me saying I'm sorry for the loss of your parents doesn't bring them back. Or anyway ease your pain, but I really mean it."

It took a minute for the slightly bigger Chloe to mutter. "They, they weren't our parents."

All the doctors listening to the trio had to take notice of the blank expression both young girls display. Each painted a vivid picture for what they have seen, has been the last days of civilization! Up close and personal like.

Faith stares into the abyss as she flatly explains. "On the first day our mommy and daddy turned bad, they bit us. At, at the hospital Jim and Donna, they kept us safe."

Chloe's voice trembles a bit as she said. "Now they are dead."

Even if Lt. Colonel Lafayette had many hats in the ring, for whatever reason her heart added another.

"Well, the best I can offer is my services. My name is Wynolla Lafayette, but my friends call me Windu. Just like the Stars Wars character, cool right?"

Faith replies flatly, "Never heard of it."

Chloe adds, "Can we have any more ice cream?"

A few hours later, inside a fully liberated Base HQ, Colonel Lafayette and Captain Brown are discussing what to do with their former commanders.

Captain Brown offers, "Ma'am. may I suggest we deal with the first matter at hand. What do with do with Lee and Dunson? We can't just push them out the door and we can't keep them locked up forever."

The thought of Lee and Dunston being pushed out and somehow surviving more than five seconds sent pangs of frustration through Wynolla as she sighed.

"Yes, it would be easier to take them out a mile into the lake and say jump. Honestly, I can't figure which would set a worse example hanging them or putting a bullet to the back of their twisted skulls."

Captain Brown looks up to the Colonel, for she has never put her pride or even the mission before her troops. He could only imagine the pain of having to watch someone you loved get eaten alive! Captain Brown floats an idea that might service the purpose.

"Windu, as you know I grew up in Illinois and there's a state mental hospital about one hundred and fifty miles or so away from here."

Wynolla chuckled and said, "ahh, my young padawan I don't think they receive the psychiatric counseling they each so deservedly need. "

Lance Brown possesses a rich endearing laugh, the kind that draws a person in signaling his true warmth as a human being.

"No ma'am, I'm envisioning your morale boosting speech intended on lifting the spirits of our base, in which you say how Lee and Dunston wlll be transferred to the crazy farm."

Wynolla sat back in her average executive chair and threw her shinny combat boots on the table and then said. "What good will that last part do Major?"

Captain Lance Brown beams as he replies, "They'll be many miles away on their own, forced to survive only by their wits! When was the last time you think those been in the field? I give them less than one hour and they will be Zombie chow, sir. That means the problem will get solved in the most horrific way possible!"

Colonel Layette nods her head in appreciation of the merits of Lance's plan before saying. "I wonder how many carriers and submarines are still under the control of the living?"

Captain Brown nodded his head I don't even know and replied,

"When it comes to those manmade floating islands and underwater dildos, frankly I prefer to keep land or sky under these feet."

Windu somberly replies, "Think of all the Navies around the world housing nuclear weapons being manned by RAGERS or got dam Dead Heads? Frightening, right?"

Lance sighs, "Yeah, it's a horrible fate either on land or sea."

Wynolla ponders long and hard as her thoughts of being trapped here alone! Maybe one of last citadels of humanity, how long could they hold this position?

"Major, we need to locate a fallback location, we don't know how much longer we may be able to deceive death the ocean of death around us. One careless action brings hundreds of thousands of Death Heads or RAGERS right into our lap. The it's game over!"

The young Army Ranger tilted his head at being called out his rank before once again, offering his knowledge of their area.

"Ah ma'am, my uncle Resse, who's probably dead now... Use to work at a US Treasury Depository. The facility has huge vaults containing pallets of vacuumed sealed money. He always bragged that it would make doomsday bunker when the terrorist let off the big one!"

Wynolla swung her legs down, leaned forward with interest and said, "Major it sounds like a very quiet place to, die."

Lance was excited and a bit confused when he replies, "No, no you don't understand it sits on thirty acres of razor wire fence lined property. My uncle uses to brag about how the faculty consist of seven floors, five underground and it has its own backup generator and an onsite underground fuel tank of no less than three thousand gallons of fuel."

Windu proudly looks at the young Solider she has known since the man was fresh out of Ranger School as a BUTTERBAR or 2nd

Lieutenant. She was so proud to see the young Officer was coming into his own and she shared that pride.

"Captain Lance Brown you have always shown bravery under fire and continue to provide tactical leadership in the face of overwhelming odds. As base commander I hereby issue you a battlefield commission to the rank of Major; in whatever is left of the United States Army!"

Lance's face ushers from shock to glee before finally settling on humility as he salutes his commander.

"Why I never, thank you ma'am. I, I was wondering why you kept calling me out my rank. Windu I won't let you down."

Windu returns the salute and offers Major Brown a heartfelt handshake before replying.

"I never considered you would. Head down to supply and see if there are any chevrons more fitting of your new rank. In the meantime, I will start on my heart and minds winning speech. Oh, have Chloe and Faith escorted to my new quarters, make sure to have three cots set up, they'll be rooming with me for a while."

Meanwhile, back inside Shangri-La the mood's a mirror of Base McCormick. It has been three days since the death of Sky and her death has been taken hard by all!

Flashback: Especially by Paradise, the sight of Sky's twitching body bleeding out under John's fingers desperately attempting to contain it, broke Paradise. The young Transwoman's screams were as piercing as her sobs were deep and loud!

"AHHHHH, NO, NO, NO Sky, noooooooooooooooooo.."

By the time Robin made it down to the lower level, Sky had quietly passed away. Her father saw the look of surprise on his daughters' face turn to murderous rage! Before he could shield Indigo, his daughter launched herself, connecting her right fist to the murderer's exposed jaw!

When Indigo awoke, she found herself in the machine shop, in a bit of pain and bound to a plastic lawn chair with gray duct tape. Nevertheless, fear crept up her spine and fixated behind her pupils when she noticed she was alone in a room with Earl Grimes! It doesn't take long before he could smell the scent of fear through Indigo's sweat. His soft Southern cadence hides the evil that dwells just below the surface of his skin.

"You might not find this hard to believe, but Big John and Enestro are the only two friends I have ever had. Just as this little community happens to be the closest thing, I have ever resembled a loving family."

Earl's slow southern drawn was unnerving to Indigo, she so wants to scream! Even so after what happened to Sky, Indigo understood If John left her alone with Earl Grimes, no help will be offered! She tried to explain herself.

"Please, PLEASE don't do whatever you plan to do. I'll talk, I swear I will tell you everything! I, I didn't mean to hurt anyone but myself..."

Sweat beaded down Earl's shinny bald head as he turns holding a bottle of bleach, his tone was soft yet menacing.

"Oh, I know you will Ms. Roberson, for if I suspect you are lying, I'm going to pour bleach in your eyes, and you will see no evil! Then I will pour it in your left ear, so you hear no evil. I think you get my point... Now go on, for as you can see, you have my undivided attention."

It doesn't take long before Earl has all there was to know, and he didn't have to harm one hair on Indigo's head! Three floors up everyone's gathered in the cafeteria, some drinking coffee, others hard liquor. Earl begins with.

"She didn't mean to harm anyone but herself, still as we known, Indigo's actions held consequences for the departed Ms. Sky Harrison. Ms. Roberson claims her sister works for a shady organization called Global Security & Logistics LLC. Well, they want what they think you have Big John... A cure for all this death! Is it true, do you have a cure?"

If the room wasn't quiet before, all the air was sucked out the area with that last statement! All eyes lock on to John Hammond for answers, however it's Calamity who said.

"Did this Global whatever assholes plain to barter for this cure or just kill us all and take it?"

Big John Hammond shook his head with disgust and replies with a bit of anguish.

"There is no cure!"

He let that linger before saying. "I, I might had been on to a vaccine that could have halted the infection. However, that was so, so very long ago. Either way, once you have been infected, there's nothing, nothing! I have nothing that will stop an infected corpse from being reanimated. No sadly, there is no cure."

Robin slammed her empty shot glass into the metal table, shattering it into tiny pieces, slicing up her hand in the process. The quivering of her voice made no attempt to conceal her pain, anger or frustration when she said.

"Then she dies, just like Sky!"

Big John didn't understand why he said what he did, yet he said it anyway.

"She doesn't deserve to die..."

Robin's fiery tone spoke volumes about her notions about right or wrong.

"Really that's rich coming for you!"

Paradise chimes in as well.

"Yes, accident or not she has to PAY. Sky was my only real friend, until now and she's gone!"

Cherish joins Semaj in offering Paradise four supportive arms to help ease her pain. Nonetheless, thank team Valdez for thinking with more than their hearts, when Enestro asks.

"Do you think Indigo has told these Global cocksuckers our location?"

Earl softly replies, "No, she protected us by not sharing our location. Yet, she does have a fear of some chip them may have placed near her spine."

Dawn mutters, "Near her spine? Shit that's sinister as all fuck!"

Robin looked down at her bleeding hand as her father picked up a cloth dinner napkin and binds her wound, he said.

"Like Mr. Grimes said, he's been doing this a long time, he fully knows when a person is lying or not."

Celeste goes on to say, "Well the way I see it if these Global fuck boys don't have a clue where we are. Let's invite them to a secure location, for what I think everyone should be in agreement in what we have to do...Right?"

Robin looked into her father's eyes as he cleans her wounded hand and calmly said.

"Kill them, we'll kill them all!"

It takes another few hours or so, before Big John went to check on Indigo. Part of him, feels foolish to think she was ever interested in him on a romantic level. Just the thought of how she made him feel was partly built on Indigo Roberson knowing her target. That part of John needed to believe that she is just an unwilling pawn, still he wanted some goddam answers!

When he stepped into machine room, the sight of the bound woman, sitting in a puddle of her own waste ushers' waves of pity all over his psyche. However, he wouldn't break, for John understood the stakes of this conversation! Still, he did the first kind thing for Indigo Roberson anyone has done for her in the last 72 hours.

John Hammond releases her from her bounds. The muscles in Indigo's legs were like jelly and she couldn't support her own weight. Lovingly as possible he picked up the soiled and frightened, dehydrated, sobbing woman up and carried her to the mud room. Gently placing her on the toilet seat, next to the bathroom sink.

Indigo's soft cries of shame and or pain were attempting to creep their way directly towards Big John's exposed heart strings! Nevertheless, it took several minutes for him to get her undressed, as the warm sensation of running water helps quell Indigo's tiny sobs. Only she may see the bubbles of snot appearing and disappearing out of her nostrils.

"John, you, you must believe me. I didn't know Sky was behind me! I, I'm so sorry..."

Hammond's smile was genuine as he handed Indigo the moist face towel as he said.

"Take a warm shower, then we'll talk. Ok?"

Indigo slowly shakes her head as she replies. "Just, just you? I, I don't ever want to be left in room with Mr. Grimes again... He's frightening..."

Back in her room it takes forty minutes before Indigo peeked her head out of her bathroom. Limping as she exited wearing her Shangri-La issued white cotton robe, Indigo right eye was sort of swollen and her hair was wet for dunking her face in the bathroom sink. John Hammond must fight the urge to rush to Indigo Roberson's side, offer her his broad shoulders for comfort! Even so, he did none of that as John sat on the push tan sofa waiting for Indigo to join him.

She whines in pain as she slowly sat down and then said.

"I, I think your daughter may have broken my ribs."

John forced a smile as he assures Indigo that her concerns are directed towards the wrong set of hazards.

"No, no, no your ribs are more than likely bruised. If they were broken, you would be spiting up blood. Listen, there's no way out of this without you helping draw these operates out of their hole."

Indigo chewed on her bottom lip as she looks up into John's brown eyes for some sort of clue if their brief connection still held any weight.

"I don't know where they are or even how far they are from us. I, I just use my satellite phone. We have prescribed times to try the call, generally 6am or 9pm."

John nodded his head slowly, then said. "That might put them somewhere West of us. What about the chip you think they placed by your spine? Plus, where's the phone? I need to talk to your contact at GS&L."

Indigo didn't hesitate to rise off the sofa and limped over to metal dresser. She moved her old clothes to the side and pulled the black phone from out of a pair of heavy socks. John accepted the device and then said.

"I suggest you stay put. Do you have an established code you use in dealing with these people?"

Indigo shakes her head no and replies, "It's my older sister, and her name is Diana. She might ask you something personal, just tell her I'm...?

John holds up his hand to silence her worries by saying. "I'll tell her you are alive and well."

Indigo mutters, "Ok, for how long?"

24 hours prior Colonel Lafayette had prepared what she thought was a memorable speech to be delivered to the entire base. However, as he stood up at the front of the giant bay, looking at the faces of young Sailors, Seasoned Rangers, Marines and qualified Air Forces Berets eagerly standing at attention. Right alongside the Civilian Doctors, she could see in their eyes everyone's looking for some direction! Be thee young, middle aged or old; in the face of certain death everyone needs to know where they stand. Wynolla tossed out her prepared script and went with what is in her heart.

"Parade Rest!"

The military personnel go from standing at rigid attention to a relaxed posture. Their base Commander goes on to say.

"I've always felt a good base commander puts the needs of his command alongside the mission. The rumors of this being a coup against Admiral Lee and Colonel Dunson are as unfounded as the lunacy of thinking eating another human being is rather sane!"

Colonel Lafayette pauses for a few moments to gather her thoughts. She sighs before issuing her final set of mission statements.

"Each of us who volunteered to put on our various uniforms did so to proudly service our country. For everyone one of us that raised their right hand and honestly said. This I Will Defend...Frankly, I am here to tell you as of today your job is done!"

Wynolla's words shocked and floored everyone, not even Major Brown could suspect what came next.

"This command was set up to find a cure for the death outside our doors. However, we have not heard from anyone else in over forty-one days. I am continuing my mission, but that doesn't mean that you must. Americans have always prided ourselves in seeing the job through, still today everyone of you will have to make a choice!"

There's a murmuring through the crowd as Wynolla pauses for a bit then continues.

"What former Admiral Lee represents isn't the America many of our ancestors fought, died and were killed defending! I'm the descendant of former slaves, this is my land, as it is yours. From here on out, I'm only seeking volunteers to see this mission through! Anyone currently in uniform gets the chance to walk away, without penalty."

The murmuring in the crowd grows louder one of the Navy Petty Officers asked over the rabble.

"Excuse me Colonel. What happens then, we are given all the supplies we can handle and shown the door?"

More murmuring before Windu replies easing the worries of the survivors on the fence.

"No Petty Officer, only the former command is being shown the door because Lee and Dunson are being transferred to a Psychotropic Hospital over a hundred miles from this base."

Another Sailor asks, "I thought you said the base isn't in contact with anyone sir?"

Colonel Lafayette did her best not to be one of those screaming jerkoff officers from the movies, so she continues to win either heart or minds.

"Correct I did say that, whether anyone is still alive or not; or whether Lee and Dunson receive help or receive some sort of cosmic justice that is beyond mercifully should be ok by us! Let's not forget both have been found guilty by court martial by a jury of their peers of murdering and dismembering Colonel Kevin McKinney."

Wynolla paused to see if there were any more questions before continuing.

"Now to answer the first question, anyone wishing to continue to serve and protect what's left of our democracy will accompany base command and half the civilian personal to our purposed backup site."

More muttering, but this time Colonel Lafayette deepens her voice and shouts.

"AT EASE! We can't keep all our eggs in one basket. This base is stock to feed and house nine hundred people for two years. The late Colonel McKinney, god rest his soul. Made goddam sure we would have no logistical concerns in fulfilling our mission."

Wynolla paused to give the late Air Force Colonel his proper respect before saying.

"I'm asking the civilian doctors to draw lots among themselves to see who goes and who stays. Anyone taking off their uniform must write their resignation letter and present it to Staff Sergeant Belladonna! In turn she will present them to my EXO- Major Brown. Anyone still here will be left to organize a civilian council before we transfer this command to Site B. This move will be on coming and I remind everyone present, Camp McCormick is still under martial law!"

The following day, back at Shangri-La, John's having the conversation that will paint life and its six degrees of separation. He and Indigo used the secret escape hatch to leave their secure bunker nestled in what was the Illinois countryside. For mid-August the air's its normal humid and the smell of rain proceeds the hint or thunder in the Northern sky.

With a strict light out policy, the Hunnfield property doesn't stick out in the darkness. Few if any aircraft still traverse the sky. Nevertheless, RAGERS do see light as would any survivor looking for lodging away for the dead! Indigo held John's hand as tight as she could, as they made their way to the rear door of the mansion.

Indigo held a low beam flashlight allowing John to use the master key, for them to enter the dwelling. The humid state of the room causes Indigo's sinus pressure to build as John locks the door behind them. He followed Indigo's led to her hidden phone charger was located. The steady creaking of stairs signaled the decay of materials in what was once a pristine environment! Indigo opens a dresser draw and pulled the charger out from under some molding moth ridden men's underwear. It takes more than 25 seconds to get power and any sort of dial tone. Once she does Indigo solemnly punches in her code before handing the phone over to John.

There's heavy static on the phone for a few moments before the metallic ringing begins. It takes fifteen rings before a woman picks and said.

"Password?"

John looked at Indigo, for she had given no password, so he handed the phone back to her. With a confused look she speaks into the receiver.

"Hello, Bitch?"

There's no answer for several moments before the voice on the other ends replies.

"Your sister is under quarantine. She, may have been infected..."

Indigo blankly hands the phone back to John and she lowers her head into her arms being propped up by her knees. John took the receiver then said.

“This is John Hammond, who am I speaking to?”

Silence for several moments before John said.

“Do you want the cure or not?”

The raspy female voice on the other side replies, “YES.”

Indigo can feel John smile for the first time since she pulled a razor on him as he states the terms.

“Good, first I need whole blood, O- and O+.”

The voice replies, “How do I know this cure works?”

John’s tone turns from cold and unemotional, more like Earl Grimes downright menacing.

“You don’t!”

The voice ponders the situation before answering. “Then we have nothing further to discuss.”

John ups the stakes. “Let’s be clear, nothing can cure you once you’ve been bitten. I have a vaccine that if you’re bitten, you won’t turn RAGER. However, once you die you will still turn flesh eating dead head. That’s the best you can hope for, take it or fucking leave it!”

The silence coming from the other end of the phone was deafening, yet a deal needs to be struck.

“We have type O+ and O- blood in stock. How much are you talking about?”

The walk back to Shagari-Li in the dark and in total silence. John escorted Indigo back to her quarters and did his best to contain her fears the best he can.

Next John gathers up the four people he knew he could not do this without. Earl, the Valdez's and his daughter Rene. John explained the conversation all the way down to what he used as bait to lure the GL&S people out of their equally dark hole. The only thing that was left for some was the location he picked.

Enestro was a bit concerned with the vastness of the property John intends to use when he said.

"Only if you would have told me I would be going to a Federal Reserve twenty years ago! Hombre, I swear I would have cum in pants with thoughts of millions upon millions of dollars waiting to be liberated! Instead of me worrying about how many FEDS could be hiding waiting for a fool like me."

Celeste hushes her lover and best friend by saying. "Well, now money is worth nothing but toilet paper now my love. So, anyone hiding out there, won't be our concern, unless they fire upon us of course."

Earl chimes in with "You said this place is over thirty acres Big John, that could hold a number of those dead fuckers or a shit ton of RAGERS."

Robin thinks tactically, "We need to scope this place out first thing tomorrow, and I do mean sunup! When did you set the meet for, Dad?"

John's smile was real as he replied, "I told them it would take me 48 hours to reach the coordinates I provided. Honestly, it's only going to take us thirty minutes by air. Just before sunrise we fly to the location so we may scope it out. Then we'll plan an ambush that won't get any of our people KIA."

Two days later the sun rose across Lake Michigan casting warmth across the rooftop of Camp McCormick. As the disgraced captives Lee and Dunson were being led to waiting Helios. Lee was escorted aboard Colonel Lafayette's bird and Dunson to Major Brown's. It doesn't take long before both copters take off towards the sun, directly over the lake for a quarter of a mile as the late Colonel McKinney had laid out.

Once secure that no hostile could be tracing their moments, Army Pilots exit the lake near the Indiana side and plot their course to the Illinois State Psychiatric Hospital in Waterman Illinois nearly one hundred and thirty miles away from Camp McCormick and eighty miles from Saint. Charles.

Inside Windu' s aircraft, Jefferson Bullraguard Lee's feet were chained to the bottom of the seat and his hands zip tied to his belt. Yet he still displays a more than superior attitude to his captors!

"You think you will be able to find a cure for all this? God's wrath will not be stopped by the likes of you! His cleansing touch will rid our planet of degenerates like all your dyke friends. Not to mention all the Christ killing Jews, your mentally inferior Blacks, those breeding like roaches Mexicans and the intellectual property thieving Chinese. Oh, not to forget the mongrel Russians, even the tedious hairy goddam Italians and of course the fucking drunken Irish! Each and every fucking one of you will die screaming and my Lord God will never hear your pleas for his divine mercy."

Colonel Lafayette nods her head in awe, chuckled and then said.

"Wow, you are telling me the French didn't make your list or most hated?"

Lee replies with pride.

"Certainly not most of my mother's people are of French descant! Much like yours I suppose. My ancestors maybe even noticed yours on the trading block! I didn't mention the Muslim either for I respect their single mindedness when it comes too committed to their cause. As well as their blind hatred towards Jews and their subjugation of their own women!"

Wynolla leaned forward so Jefferson could hear him over the roar of the helicopter's engines.

"Well, well, well look, at you now Lee. A prisoner of someone you consider inferior! You should get some rest, because where you're going, you are going to need, dare I say; your WHITS about you. Which by this point, you've clearly fucking lost, long, long, long ago!"

The landscape underneath their aerial transport resembles various Sci-Fi and horror movies that have attempted to broach the subject. In less than ninety days, the world stands still! No blaring music from passing vehicles. No impatient idiots laying on their car horn. No Semi trucks brakes screeching to a sudden halt!

The world had been laid barren except for the sound of moaning from countless Zombies and the destructive behavior of the RAGERS!

Even now some buildings still smolder under the weight of unchecked fires. Only the downpour of summer rains will fully extinguish what humans can longer deal with! Herds of Dead Heads wander aimlessly down county roads, up city streets and anywhere In-between. The overwhelming stench of uncollected garbage, festering sewage, ruptured gas lines and an assortment of decaying corpses makes breathing nearly hazardous to the living.

Ever shrinking pockets of the living still exist, making hostilities among those drawing breath somewhat unwise. Even so that won't stop the vengeful or cruel heart! Two days later at 0645, John and Indigo sat among paint cans on a soiled painter's tarp on the roof of a Federal Reserve building- *about the size of a professional sports arena*. The morning sky is slightly overcast due to the high humidity, which signaled storms clouds are on the horizon.

Indigo did her best to look calm, sweat from the oppressive humidity forced her to drink from her water bottle. John looked at his watch and went over what's going to happen next.

"When they get here, I assure you these people will extend a display of force in a vain attempt to show that they are in control! All you have to do is to remember to remain calm."

Indigo nods her head okay before saying. "They are thirty minutes late. Do, do you, think they're still coming?"

John shrugs his shoulders as he replies, "Depends how far their evil lairs locate from this spot. Whatever happens, I will do what I can to keep your best interest in mind."

Indigo's eyes wanted to tear up, instead she flashed a genuine smile. However, before she could utter any words, the sound of helicopters caused both to cast their eyes to the sky in search of the source. It took a while for first they appeared like black dots heading out of the Northwest. Nevertheless, as the trio got closer, John recognizes the brand- **AgustaWestland** and the make **AW 149**-, of the helicopters heading their way.

John and Indigo stood up and walked towards another set of paint cans and soiled tarps nailed to crates and assorted tools. The trio of circling black corporate helicopters caused the secure tarp to struggle with their bounds. John moved a bit to shield Indigo from the intense down draft as the trio of helicopters were forced to land of the opposite end of the large roof.

John whispers to Indigo, "Just remember what I said, no matter what's said. Stay calm!"

A thin snobby looking woman of mixed heritage was dressed in black cargo pants and royal blue T-shirt was being escorted by half a dozen similar dressed Mercenaries brandishing fully automatic Israeli hardware! John waited for them to walk the hundred and twenty-nine feet to his position. The lead Merc was bald and had the traditional bad guy scar running across his cheek and an cheeky English accent, he barks.

“GET YOUR BLOODY HANDS UP!”

John and Indigo slowly compile as the menacing opposing force arrives directly as planned. Square in the middle of four separate areas of covered paint cans and tarped tools.

The woman was a few years younger, obviously different fathers since she was as beige as Indigo was dark and sported freshly washed auburn hair. Still, the family resemblance around the eyes was hard to conceal. She introduced herself with all the arrogance of the fly saying fuck you to the spider!

“Hello Indi, I see you are fine. Hello Mr. Hammond, I’m Diana Roberson and I represent what’s let of Global Security and Logistics. As you requested thirty pints of O and O- blood. Now, where’s my cure?”

John smiles as he replies, “You sister has told me so much about you.”

Diana looks miffed, then slightly annoyed.

“Peaches, great my big sister spoke very highly of me! Now where’s the goddam cure Hammond?”

John continued, “How long have you worked for GS&L Ms. Roberson?”

Diana breathes in deeply as her annoyance of this bothering frustration wasn’t the answer she sought.

“That is not important Doctor. Hammond. What’s important is whether you and my talkative big stepsister will make it off this roof alive. If she really told you what type of cunt I am able to muster up, then you should turn over that cure!"

John sighed as the tension is building to a head, he states.

"Like I told whoever earlier, when someone said you may be dead. There is no cure, just a vaccine, in theory. The O plasma will make it easier to genetically modify for the purpose of delivering said vaccine."

Diana took a few moments to take in the information before saying.

"Ok, I don't have time for shit. Put my sister on my transport, take Hammond to yours..."

John and Indigo take three steps back, drawing the GS&L force even closer still. However, before the hit squad of Enestro, Robin, Calamity, Destiny and Paradise can spring their well-planned trap! The sound of more helicopters came into ear range. Forcing everyone to look to the sky for the source. As the clouds break, the sight of three Army Black Hawks heading their way forces the action.

Seconds after that sound Enestro, Calamity, Destiny, Paradise and Robin silently squeezed out from under slits from the back of the tarp. None of the Mercs were as keen as they portrayed, unknowingly they walked into a lane of fire of professional assassins!

It was only the slight and sound of three Army Helicopters swooping down over the intended killing fields that caused hardened killers and vengeful friends and lovers to pause alike.

Colonel Lafayette's copter lands directly behind the confused Mercs, cutting them off from their own transport. Windu exits her Black hawk followed by Sergeant Belladonna and two more Army Rangers. When the Mercs turn to face the approaching military personnel, they find themselves surrounded by another opposing force, Hammond's! Confused about how they lost their seemingly upper hand, Diana's Mercs are unsure on who to aim their weapons at.

Nonetheless, Colonel Lafayette and the RANGERS don't flinch as they walk into the lion's mouth. While their patrolling Black Hawks as their over watch. Windu takes a few moments to scan the faces of the crowd. Yet for whatever reason she and Robin locked eyes and she sort of smiled as said.

"Seems like everyone should just take a breath before your standoff turns deadly. Think about it, the last thing we need are more dead people, right?"

Diana puts her hands on her hips and replies with scorn.

"There is no more America! You have no authority over us!"

Colonel Lafayette replies with the authority of having to deal with people like Diana Roberson before.

"As long as I have this uniform, I have those Black Hawks and loyal people depending on whether I make the proper decision, I would agree to disagree with that utter bullshit! This installation belongs to the United States Government. That means it belongs to me!"

There's silence for several moments before John Hammond asks.

"Any word of putting all this back together."

Wynolla tries not to laugh or cry, instead she maintains the steadiness those that came to follow this Colonel look to when times are hard.

"We're doing our best sir; this plague is worldwide. Its effects as you can see devastating, but I feel there's still hope."

Diana replies in a huff. "Well then, it's time to leave, men collect the coolers."

Wynolla shouted, "FREEZE, what's in the coolers?"

Diana didn't try to soften her tone, but she did answer by saying.

"I don't think this facility stocks O plasma, which is what's in the coolers. Now, I think you should get out of our way!"

Belladonna raises her silenced COLT Made 7.62mm semi-automatic rifle and aimed it directly at Diana face. That action causes a chain reaction of events, but no more amazing as when Wynolla calls out.

"Is that you Marshal Aquila? It's been five years since CONACO."

Robin kind of grunts something, before replying.

"Yeah, I, I, look this isn't the time..."

Colonel Lafayette nods her head and told Diana with all certainty.

"Leave the plasma, in exchange for your lives! You came here to make some sort of deal, so make it. If we had not shown up, you would be dead now! Maybe, some of them as well. Is all that worth it? How many humans do you think are left? We've lost this WAR, the dead won! How you plan to live your lives after that is up to you. I would hope no one needs to die. However, if that's your choice, I will step aside and let the Marshal's people finish what they seem to have plan to start."

The Mercs backed away from the coolers and lower their weapons in the process. Still Diana acts like she's up for a fight.

"We can't go back empty handed, we can't! People are dying if we lose our base..."

John speaks with the calm of a wise man.

"Colonel, before all of this I was a Major in the Air Force and Infectious warfare was my specialty. May I suggest to you Ms.

Roberson continue to quarantine the sick and burn the bodies after driving any hard object though their brain."

Diana huffs, "what do you think we have been doing Doctor Hammond? Using harsh language and taking away their IPADS."

Wynolla's face lite up to John's as she knew scientists in their field were hard to come by.

"Really former Air Force doctor, is it? Then it's still a small world. Sorry, but I have a previous matter to take care of. From here on out humanity needs to learn to work together. Find some other way to settle this without slaughtering each other would be a good start! Marshal Aquila, may we speak?"

Robin hesitates for a bit before walking out from behind her make-shift hiding space/barricade. The former Marshal came loaded for bear, body armor, her customary three handguns and AR 15 with sports stock.

For whatever reason everyone kind of tried not to stare, but ended up staring at the two, who are engaged in an awkward conversation.

Big John broke the moment by saying.

"I will work on the vaccine and let you know if I can get a working version ASAP. The only other thing I request, Indigo must go with you."

For the first time she spoke," No John, I, I don't want to. I thought, you, WE could.."

John moved closer, giving Indigo a tender hug as he whispered.

"You can't stay with us anymore. Your safety is not a given. Go, make up with your family. It's now or never.."

Diana huffed and replied. "How do I know you'll keep your word?"

John smiled, "I can't tell you if I'm a day or a week or a decade away. What matters you'll given me the reason to keep searching? I will do my best Ms. Roberson."

Shortly after, Robin and Wynolla walked back to the crowd and she said.

"I am going to go with Colonel Lafayette, and they'll drop me off on the way back."

John like any protective father replied, "what?"

Calamity muttered to her husband, "Don't you hate when we get all dressed up to kill people and something comes up from the to do list?"

There was much discussion about who would be on this mission and Paradise argued why she should stand for Sky and since Earl's too large to conceal, she got the job!

So it was Paradise who bitterly muttered, "This is bullshit! She's not going to pay for Sky?"

She slowly raises her weapon, yet it was Enestro forcing it down and softly said.

"Some day's personal revenge must take a back seat to your own survival."

Chapter III:

BE YE FRIENDS, FOES AND COUNTRYMEN.

With Robin on board Wynolla sort of ignored the prisoner. Even so, Lee looked down his nose at both, before asking her about the Marshal's star on her body armor.

"Where did you get that badge? Steal it off a dead white man?"

For the first time in a long time Robin laughed and the tension of nearly killing several people drained away. She chuckled as she said.

"NOPE! This is real piece of shit you have on your hands Colonel."

Colonel Lafayette informed her captive.

"Listen up shithead. Let me introduce you, to Marshal Aquila. Oh yeah, she a the real deal, pistol packin, ass kicking, shot drinking United States Federal Marshal! We met at CONACO nearly five years ago and yes, Marshal this piece of shit is also the real deal."

Lee frowned at the insult, yet does not bother to engage the two anymore. As Robin and Wynolla, they kept the conversation for the most part semiprofessional.

"Marshal it's good to see you survived the apocalypse! Would you mind filling me in on what was going on back there?"

Robin fought back the bile and anger attempting to creep its way back into her being. She looked at Lee with violence and her words deflected Wynolla's.

"What did he do? This is the apocalypse, so what could he have done for you to be taking him Gods knows where?"

Wynolla replied with a stone face. "Here sits the former base commander of Camp McCormick, charged with protecting the scientist working on mapping out and hopefully finding a cure for all this death!"

Colonel Lafayette paused for a moment before saying, "Nevertheless, here sits a man found guilty of murdering a good man! One, Colonel McKinney of the United States Air Force. We're not sure, but Lee there probably ate parts of his internal organs or penis as well."

Robin sits back and mutters, "Oh snap! He's bat shit crazy!"

Lee responded with a bit of passion. "That's a bold face lie told by a traitor! How do your people say it, I beat that pussy up! but I never ate it.

Wynolla replied with a bit more joy. "I rest my case Marshal, so we are on the way to drop him at what used to be state run Mental Hospital for the goddam criminally insane!"

Marshal Aquila snapped her fingers and said.

"You mean the one about eighty miles west of here?"

Wynolla smiles and said, "That's the one."

Robin continued with, "What's your plan go looking for a shrink to take his oval sided head out his narrow white ass?"

Colonel Lafayette chuckled before saying, "No, nothing that wildly insane! We're just going to drop him off and from there FATE will be Jefferson Bullgruard Lee's compass! He will no longer be able to hide behind rank, privilege or inner circle connections."

Jefferson turned to face Wynolla and stated with cold venom. "You think you hold the upper hand, that you are somehow superior to ME? You are nothing but decay, while I've seen the future!"

Robin interrupted his speech with, "And BOOM, you have not been invited! Shut the fuck up, you weirdo. I would so love to drop kick your sorry ass out of this moving helicopter! How about it Colonel?"

Lee snarled at Marshal Aquila, "If we ever meet again, I will feast of your still beating heart. These are the END TIMES and we are the unclean and unworthy! Properly left to perish under the weight of those anointed to do God's bidding. Even so, I will fucking survive to piss down both of your cock-sucking, goddam dirty dyke throats!"

After that, the last twenty-eight minutes were done in utter silence. Colonel Lafayette smiled and looked at Robin, remembering back when they shared thirty-eight interesting hours stranded by a blizzard in Washington DC! All Wynolla could think about was their teaming up on karaoke night the before a freak storm dumped nearly 2 ½ feet of snow up and down the Eastern seaboard. Nonetheless, the night led to some serious drinking in semi deserted bars, dancing in dark lounges, drunken snow walks and very sensuous love making!

One the other hand Marshal Aquila remembered finally waking up to a cup of still warm Starbucks coffee. As well as a thoughtful note on how Wynolla didn't want to wake her and of course duty had called her away. Oh, sure the wonderful Solider left all her need-to-know information. Nevertheless, Robin didn't bother kidding herself with thoughts of a long-distance relationship, so she never bothered perusing anything other than the booty call they shared. Still, that night they had chemistry and right now both women needed some sort of an emotional floatation device.

Furthermore, when their eyes met once more, Robin felt nervous knots in her now toned belly! So, when Wynolla smiled at her, not even saying a word, just armed with just her pleasant smile. It melted Robin's anger like a snowball in fucking July! Marshal Aquila couldn't understand why, maybe it's just seeing someone she knew before all this shit started. That simple smile helped jumpstart her depleted heart with a heavy dose of HOPE! Robin found in their short time she spent Wynolla; their chemistry easily returned to co-mingle!

It's the Army Pilot's voice that breaks over the roar of rotors.

"Colonel we're approaching Hotel Psycho and by the looks of it, business has been pretty fucking awesome!"

Flashback to the first day of infection at the Illinois State Psychiatric Hospital, honestly at first the staff reported for work and did their best to be professional.

It took a few days before the first signs of the infection began creeping into view, as long-term Patients start becoming violently ill with some sort of upper respiratory illness! Moving on to day five, most if not all of the staff either simply didn't report to work. Or walked off the job in the middle of their shifts!

Even before that, the medical ward filled up with sick patients at such an alarming rate; patients had to be transferred to two local hospitals! Even so, the State's more dangerous patients were left to languish, locked and secured in their soiled beds. As well as being locked in their padded rooms. By day two, the morgue began stacking bodies as the Hospital burnt all cadavers who have no next of kin. Sadly a few attendants are bitten by patients thought to be dead, but to everyone's chagrin, they were somehow still alive and ultra-violent!

Nonetheless on day five, one of the Guards didn't feel right about locking non-sick patients up in their rooms. So, Mama Pat, as she was called, went around and unlocked the doors of five patients she had developed at least some sort of bond with! Then placed the keys in the officer's lounge knowing they would be found soon enough.

After that inside the Illinois State Psychiatric Hospital in what was once Alton Illinois, the residents were left to fair for themselves!

Flash forward twelve weeks later, and the grounds resembled the aftermath of a rock concert! Thousands of Zombies roamed aimlessly without a direction until the sound of approaching helicopters broke the stillness of their morning! Rotten flesh of boney fingers reached towards the heavenly sound, which to them was seemingly just out of their reach. The dead were so thick they bump into each other, toppling over and rolling down delivery ramps and embankments alike!

The three helicopters swoop in like birds of prey selecting the East Wing of the Hospital for a landing Zone. Major Brown's touched down first and Colonel Lafayette's followed, leaving the third bird patrolling in an over watch position. Before the outbreak, the East Wing of the Illinois State Psychiatric at Alton Illinois, housed the less violent short-term patients, generally court ordered and more of a danger to themselves than others.

However, the RAGER portion of the virus hit that section of the hospital hard! Yet, not as hard as the West section that housed the more dangerous patients, those deemed harmful to society.

Major Brown and two Air Force Black Berets escort the disgraced Marine Dunson to the center of the roof. Joining Colonel Lafayette, Marshal Aquila and Jefferson Bullraguard Lee standing on the LZ. Major Brown salutes his commander and Wynolla gave the introductions.

"This is Marshal Rene Aquila, Marshal meet, Major Lance Brown."

Both nod hello, as Windu cuts the zip ties from Lee's wrist. They stare at each other with distain and contemp.

Wynolla asks, "any famous last words?"

Lee's top lip curls as he states with his usual southern drawl.

“Believe me, the gods of chaos, mayhem and destruction reside in my every fiber! I will live long enough to shit on your grave.”

As Major Brown cuts Dunson’s zip ties, he muttered.

“You guys leaving us with some sort of weapons, right? I mean how about some MRE’s and water?”

Major Brown chuckles,

“I guess you never went to Survival School? Let every Marine tell it, they aced it without getting water boarded or cattle prodded once! Well bub, here’s your chance to play the game SUVIVOR. Today its contestants are the few, the not so proud and clearly the morally bankrupt.”

Robin’s gaze looked at the security enforced windows, only to see faces popping up to stare back. She upholstered her shorty .40 caliber Smith & Wesson and then said.

“Hello there, huh, you might wanna cut your goodbye speech’s short, company’s about to come to looking for their dinner.”

Wynolla exhaled, does a quick an crisp about face, followed by Robin they walk briskly back to the awaiting chopper. Major Brown slapped his former base XO on his back very hard as he told Dunson.

“May the Force be with you.”

Ten seconds later the two men are standing on the roof alone, nevertheless not for long... Dunson’s frantically searches the roof for anything that could be used as a weapon. Muttering to himself.

“Oh shit, oh shit, oh shit...”

The sound of impeding footsteps finally forced the Marine in Dunson to finally present itself! David notices a bundle of steel pipes nestled not far from the rooftop door. The former Colonel in the United States Marine Corps snatches at the taunt plastic, attempting to twist and tear enough of the restraining material to finally free one of the three-foot-long lead pipes.

He curses at his former commander. “Lee get your ass over here and arm yourself dam it! Don’t you hear them coming?”

Only for Dunson to turn to find Jefferson Bullraguard Lee, stripping off his clothes and placing them in a neat pile by the edge of the roof. The former Admiral cracked his neck and told David in a calm, emotionless voice.

“You are not worthy to be part of this new world. You are part of the weak and the weak shall perish. Now bitch, watch as I am reborn! For I worship at the gods of Chaos and serve for their pleasure”

By the time Dunson’s able to free one of the lead pipes, the rooftop door burst opens!

A horde of RAGERS rush out brandishing a variety of homemade blunt and cutting weapons. David catches his first attacker across the face while parrying out of the deranged man’s makeshift machete made of bloody needles. Only to back pedal into Lee standing like the Brazilian statue of Christ on the cross!

Jefferson pushed David off him and back towards the crowd of murderous attackers. The Marine feebly swings his merger weapon at the crowd of puss bearing crazies, until makeshift knives viciously impact his exposed stomach, face, chest and groin.

The crowd of a dozen or slightly a bit more, partake in stabbing and clubbing the disgraced Marine Colonel until they are covered in his warm blood. Even so, without hesitation, the RAGERS toss David Dunson’s still twitching corpse off the roof. Right down into the crowd of festering Zombies!

The lead RAGER turns his bloody face, to reveal his right eye was missing and his nose was smashed like an old sofa can. Slowly the rest turned their attention to the stark-naked Lee. Who patiently awaited their greeting as he sung with all his might in the melody of Glory Glory Halieijah

"My eyes have finally come to see the coming of my Lord. He strikes down the Muslims, Buddhists, Jews, Catholic's and all the goddam holy frauds with his flaming vibrant sword! I'm your humble servant use me oh Lord of Death and I will see your plan through, marching wretched souls towards the breach two, by, two, by two! Allow your power to flow through, MEEEEE.."

It doesn't take long for Colonel Lafayette's small task force of three Black Hawk Helicopters to be more than eighty miles in the opposite direction, flying over what's now a planet of Zombie herds or pockets of RAGERS. Little does anyone presently understand, their action will spawn an anomaly. It's festering and still beyond their horizon!

Inside Windu's helicopter, she and Robin kept it causal and friendly as they head back towards the Federal Reserve building. Wynolla finds their Q & A session a bit flirty.

" Marshal Aquila, you and your people have managed to do what few other humans have..."

Robin interjects, "You mean survive? Yeah, staying away from the major cities was the first part. Still, even that was tricky! Then we found an old Soviet Transport at what was left at the Gary staging area of the Air & Water show..."

Wynolla clapped her hands, and her laugh was sincere as she replied.

"Several weeks back, Major Brown saw that aircraft, but we were busy with other stuff and couldn't investigate the sighting. I didn't know you were a pilot?

Robin leans forward so she doesn't have to shout over the engine.

"You forgot I could work a joystick?"

Windu always the one that's cool under pressure replies, "Not at all. However, I could stand another block of instructions..."

It took another nineteen nine minutes for the Helicopters to travel the last fifty miles back to the Federal Reserve. Much to Robin's surprise her father was still on the roof, with Enestro.

Colonel Lafayette's task force landed on the roof, she directed Major Brown to establish a security perimeter with eight of their eighteen Operators. The remaining ten Special Forces & Ranger task force followed Colonel Lafayette and Marshal Aquila back to the spot in which they met.

Robin took off her sunglass smiling. "I thought you would have left. I had planned to radio you for pickup once we got back here?"

Enestro huffs, "Please! You actually thought your father would leave you? Celeste couldn't wait to put want she learned in piloting the old war hog. My love took the others back and here we wait?"

Windu steps forward to formally introduce himself. "My name is Lt. Colonel Wynolla Lafayette U.S. Army Special Forces Command. Infectious Warfare is my forte. Your daughter has been giving me a little information about you as well Major Hammond."

John forced a faint smile as he looked his daughter, the dark mood that washed on to her at Sky's death, was seemingly lifted by this charismatic Officer. The father in John cannot help but say.

"For your presence to place a smile on my daughter's face, means you two must have some history. Whatever it is, I thank you from the bottom of my heart."

After a few uncomfortable seconds Robin goes on to say.

"Thanks dad...Huh, the military is looking to expand to this here property, I've never been inside a Federal Reserve before or know what's it's like to sleep on a big bed of money, but now's the chance."

Wynolla attempts to clear a few things up by saying, "Mr. Hammond at the time of infection my command had been charged with attempting to find a cure for this virus. We were set up at the McCormick Place in Chicago, yet that's not going to cut it anymore. I have a dozen civilian scientist under our wing and some pretty interesting factors that another set of eyes might find interesting..."

Wynolla lets her words linger, before Enestro asks.

"May we go inside with you while we wait on our ride to return? I really need to take a wicked dump."

Colonel Lafayette asked in general, "Did any of your people breach the building yet?"

Enestro turns his bottom lip into a frown and said. "No, Big John would not allow it. For there might be someone or no one alive. By the way, that thing is not on a motion sensor..."

Enestro pointed to the security camera high on the west corner wall. All the seasoned Military personnel figured the camera was too far away to be motioned sensor as well.

The wind whipped the numerous tarps around as Windu looked at the camera before scanning the roof for anything to make a sign out of. The blue tarp and yellow paint did the trick. Two of his Operators held the sign up towards the camera, and it read.

"Open the door or we will blow it off its hinges, sincerely Colonel Lafayette, U.S Army Special Forces Command."

Nothing happened for several seconds, nor did the camera move from the sign. Nor did the door open. Colonel Lafayette signaled two of her Operators to place C-4 on the door's hinges as John Hammond attempts to offer a bit of wisdom.

"Excuse me, Colonel I don't mean to tell you're your business. Nonetheless it may not be wise to breach this facility. What if it's full of survivors or worse?"

Wynolla nodded her head that she understood the risk as she said. "Yes, Mr. Hammond there are numerous possibilities. There's only one fact, we need to gain access to this building. Besides, your friend said he needs to use the restroom! We're the United States Army sir, every now and then, we aim to please."

Windu winked as she gave the signal to blow the door of its frame. Nonetheless, before the Air Men can complete the order, the security door unlocks with a loud CLICK. Colonel Lafayette's Operators remove the explosive devices from the door frame as they hold the entrance open for the rest of their team. Colonel Lafayette instructed one of his Operators to stand at the door and keep it open.

Emergency lights provide the only light in dark stairwell. Sergeant Belladonna and Specialist William Crow- a skinny brown eyed twenty-year-old of Hopi, Mexican and Belizean descent from New Mexico- take the lead. Both slowly descending down the metal and concrete stairs with their weapons leading the way.

As they approach the door at the bottom of the stairwell, it buzzed open as well. Like the door above them, another Solider is instructed to keep the door open, as the rest of the squad presses forward.

The smell of plastic and recycled air nearly overwhelms the thoughts of how many millions of dollars sat sealed, packed and never probably will never have any meaning to future generations other than toilet paper! The echoing sound of over a dozen footsteps gave the tomb of soon to be forgotten trinkets of human endeavor one last gleam of attention.

As Colonel Lafayette and Marshal Aquila's walk, lock step into a larger room of cached stacks of freshly minted twenty-dollar bills.

Both noticed the security camera's following their every move. Enestro can't help but express to John his thoughts about walking through maybe a billion dollars.

"Mi Amigo, all this chedda and its worthless homes. This so fucking depressing!"

John can't help but huff as he replies. "Yes, a sad reminder of what help drive humanity to the brink of extinction. GREED!"

The sound of military boots keeping time as they strike bare concrete in unison in music to anyone that's been in the military. And for that reason, John Hammond once more felt like he was in his element. He cannot help but see how his daughter had some sort of feelings for the brash Army Officer. Furthermore, John saw how Colonel Lafayette wears the crown of leadership with dignity, confidence and responsibly to those under her command! However, fatherly instinct still needed to know more about this woman. So, John walked a bit faster so he can sort of ease drop on their conversation.

As they approach the last of the dark steel doors, Robin mentioned to Wynolla.

"What are the chances you and I not only survive the apocalypse, but we meet on the roof top of a Federal Reserve?"

Wynolla never to be the one caught off balance, prided herself in generally having the right words for the proper situation.

Smiling she replies, "well I used the Force to swing a satellite overhead and I saw your pretty face..."

Robin chucklds, "Oh shit I forgot you are a Star Wars Nerd! I remember your call name, WINDU, right?"

Wynolla winked as she replied, "Like you could ever forget my FORCE."

Robin is just as mental and verbal quick as she slyly states.

"I can't say that I remember you might have to re-edify me. Besides, I'm a Star Trek kind of gal! I always had a thing for the Borg Queen and sometimes even a sweaty Klingon."

When the last door didn't open Colonel Lafayette looked at the camera, shrugged her shoulders signaling WHAT'S UP.

On the grey concrete walls there's an intercom and it crackled with static and finally a gravelly voice of weathered man said.

"Listen Colonel who ever you are, this facility is under the command of the United States Treasury Department and that means ME!"

Wynolla exhaled as she asked, "Who am I addressing?"

There are few moments of silence before the answer only adds to the tension.

"Lieutenant. Walter J. Portwell, Treasury Officer."

Wynolla once again probed for information for the mysterious voice.

"Lieutenant Portwell are there any other Treasury Officers under your command?"

He promptly replied, "That's need-to-know information and I don't think you need to know that."

Either of Robin's hands rest on her gun holster or on her hips as she answers in frustration.

"Look, guy before the world went bat shit crazy, I was a Federal Marshal and you were a Treasury Officer! However, that was then and now these Soldiers are still soldiering on! You don't want them to blow a hole in your pretty wall, do you?"

There's silence for several moments, before the sound of mechanical devices moving behind the grey walls. Everyone takes a few steps back, clutching their weapons, scanning for the sound. John Hammond notices slits opening in various spots in the wall.

Enestro noticed it too, for he stops dead in tracks, when a half a dozen 50. Caliber automated machine guns popped up out of their converted dens!

The voice of the intercom once again sounds deviant.

"Lady, I still am a fucking Treasury Agent. Now you and your skelly wag band of dip shit better unass my A.O. Or you better be prepared to rest in fucking pieces!"

Windu mutters, "Let me guess you were a Marine? If you go any further down this route. You'll doom humanity to be a foot note in the history of everything that has ever gone extinct."

Enestro could see that this hallow tomb was a lonely place to die. He cleared his throat, raised his hands and walked forward to the intercom so he could be heard.

"Hello in there, my name is Enestro and first let me tell you this tomb isn't worth killing for. You must know it's certainly not worth dying for! All this money is, well it makes me sad to say is worthless! You know that right?"

Once again there's silence for several moments before Officer Portwell replies.

"Well, it's fucking still real to me! I have food, water and enough fire power to turn all of you into hamburger meat. LAST WARNING, GET THE FUCK OUT!"

Enestro rubbed the stub on his chin, nodding his head towards the camera. He turns to walk away, gets two steps and turned back to ask.

"How would you like a quarter of a kilo of cocaine and two pounds of primo Marijuana?"

There're a few moments of silence before Walter Portwell mutters.

"Wha, wha, what, what did you say?"

Enestro smiles as he looks at the camera then said.

"Ok, ok you drive a hard bargain, one kilo of cocaine. We cool yet? I live on a marijuana farm and bonus for you because my wife has a shit load of cocaine! That let's say fell of a truck in Gary. Now if you want it, consider it payment to allow these Army people to save the world..."

John nodded his head to his friend signaling, NICE. Before looking and his daughter, everyone was thankful that no one had to die today!

Back in Alton Illinois, the sun had gone down over an hour ago and Jefferson Bullraguard Lee had been severely beaten. As well as sodomized several times and slashed with several bladed instruments. Nevertheless, where's there's a will there's a way for Lee was still alive! His mind revolved around the fact that he had been left to die by that rogue black bitch Colonel Lafayette! Jefferson's eyes were nearly swollen, still his bloody red pupils, signal the infection of the RAGER virus.

It took Lee a few minutes to gather the energy to stumble to his feet. The former Admiral does his best to stand, yet he can gather that his ankle is at least sprained, and he might have a few bruised ribs. Lee limped over to an air conditioner unit and propped himself up to do a self-check as other RAGERS filter back upon the rooftop. Jefferson noticed how RAGERS stumble and bang into each other, then either scream, shout or punch each whatever was in their way! They don't seem to have the ability to utter verbal communications, even so when Lee shouted out.

"Hey, anyone of you assholes have an aspirin?"

The RAGERS stopped and looked at Bullraguard like he was the goddam freak! As he staggers into what was once the Nurses station on Ward B. Six blood stained RAGERS mingle about, piles of broken glass, scattered patient flies, dried blood and smashed up hospital equipment.

Whether it's the crunch of broken glass under his bare heel or the words escaping from his mouth, either way Jefferson received their undivided attention. He asked once more, but with a bit of sarcasm.

"I asked if any of you chattering rectal worms have any fucking aspirin? Who do I have to kill to gets some goddam cooperation around here!"

FYI, WARD B use to hold some of the state of Illinois most dangerous felons. Felons who have been found guilty of their crimes, however by the letter of the law they considered insane.

Exhibit A, a rather pudgy RAGER who once went by the name Mike Burcolski! A patient who one day snapped and beat this verbally abusive boss to death with the office telephone. In front of the rest of the sales staff no less! Growled a set of deep primal noises that seem to develop in his belly and rush out Mike's mouth like it was alive.

The RAGER rushed Jefferson Bullgruard Lee as the former Navy man picks up a thick metal medical bind and defended himself. What was once Mike Burcoski was now just a skin suit of anger and unrighteous fury! Nonetheless, no RAGER could talk, think rationally as well as tactically, until now!

The RAGER rushes forward all fist, and teeth fully prepare to plummet Lee once more. However, the former Admiral blocks the first punch, before jamming the metal folder into his attackers exposed throat. The sharp end of the metal folder slices deep into the RAGERS neck forcing Mike to halt his attack!

Jefferson follows up by using the folder to bask his attacker in the throat three more times, forcing Mike Burcolski to his grimy knees. Lee quickly followed up by kicking the RAGER in his stomach, flatting his attacker on his back. Bullraguard leaps high into the air coming down feet first in Mike Burcolski's undeveloped blood-stained chest!

The snap of a chest bone reverberates like the sound of two vehicles traveling 40mph slamming into each other, because one of the assholes failed to YIELD. Lee snarls as he grinds his 195-pound frame down, crunching the broken bones that just punctured the heart of the former Precious Metal's Salesman; that was known as Mike Burcoiski!

For Lee's effort a mixture of deep dark red and black blood spews out of the RAGERs mouth. Jefferson didn't stop there he straddled the bloody body so he could be face to face his soon to be dead attacker. As the light slowly fades out of Mike Burcolski's right eye, Jefferson uses his long finger to press into the pupil with enough pressure until the eyeball goes POP! His slow Southern draw was still intact, it's just deeper and more aggressive.

"I ask once more, who do I have to kill to get a fucking aspirin around here? Oh, no one better every put a hand or hard penis on me ever again, or I swear I will cut out your liver and make you watch me eat it! Yeah, that right. I'm still a fucking Surgeon!"

Book Five

Chapter I:

TELL ME IS OUR FIGHT AGAINST THE LIVING OR THE DEAD?

Summer entered the Midwest with a roar, storms rumbled through as usual. Apples, Pears, corn and wheat will grow untamed for generations to come. Deer will populate if they stay in front of herds of Zombies and RAGERs long enough to mate. The world had been sent back to the technological Stone Age and few humans outside of Shangri-La had power! Not alone AC or a working furnace. By the time fall creeped in, Colonel Lafayette has finally transferred all of the Survivors who were still looking to uphold their oath and safeguard their mission for the continued existence of humanity.

When the last of the equipment, JP5- aircraft fuel- and Civilian Medical personnel had been accounted for, Windu boards her Helio and nodded goodbye to the forty-seven former Naval recruits, mid shipmen, six Marines and one former Federal Reserve Officer named that would rather see where this world would take them, than the latter.

Wynolla understood their mission had no use for anyone not serious about the fate of us. It's sad but true, cutting the dead weight before it drags you towards a bottomless pit should be considered a surgical application of much needed logic! Colonel Lafayette nodded goodbye, yet never looked back. Leaving a copy of their research in what was once her desk just in case someone changed their mind.

Three weeks later the first hint of autumn shared its familiar myriad of brilliant colors meant to bestow the beauty of one phase moving into another. Unfortunately, if it wasn't for the dead, the overall stillness of a non-techno driven world was very, liberating! Colonel Lafayette's task force of one hundred and twenty survivors went about converting a 22,000 square foot facility into a dwelling for the living. As well as a lab for developing a vaccine!

With Shangri-La close enough to reach on HAM radio, conversing with John Hammond about the virus was easy to do. The military chatter alerted other bands of survivors much further down the Fox River; that there was still life outside their fortified hamlets or makeshift bunkers. Nonetheless, few if any want to join anything larger or one controlled by whatever was left of the government!

Most just want to know about this "so-called" vaccine, that's when Colonel Lafayette sent Major Brown in a Helio to Shangri-La to personally deliver to John Hammond their new radio frequency and times they should get on the airwaves. It was the first time he had been to Shangri-La, furthermore as soon as Major Brown's Helio touched down he was met by a sight that has him in awe!

Cherish was wearing a tight blue button-down shirt, tied to expose toned belly muscles and wearing equally snug tan jean cargo shorts. She's carrying a bushel of corn with her BFF, Dawn- who's dressed in a tight white T-shirt and firm fitting faded jeans shorts- *they are talking and laughing like giddy teenagers*. That's when the helicopter landed and the equally dashing 6'2 Army officer exited and walked directly towards them.

Lance tired not to notice the two pairs of nipples perturbing through their thin material. However, it is nature's way of saying HELLO! He smiled, nodded his head in respect and asked in a calm as tone as he could muster.

"Hello, I'm Major Brown, I, I, well is Mr. Hammond around?"

Nefertiti "Cherish" McGill hazel eyes locked in with that of the brown in Lance's and the flirting didn't need to happen. Yet, it did anyway, when Cherish asked in a baby doll voice.

"Are you the big, brave Army Officer that has Robin in a not so bitchy anymore?"

If Major Brown had not been the color of a famous candy, the women might have seen him blush when Dawn said.

"Oh my god! Doesn't he look like a Hershey's KISS? He's simply, delicious."

Cherish put down her bushel of corn so she can take all of the man that is standing in front her into her mental gaze. She can feel him grow sort of uncomfortable from her stare as he stammers.

"Ah, I, well I am at a loss for words right now. Could we pick whatever's happening between us up after I deliver this important message from my C.O."

Dawn snapped her nibble fingers and said. "Oh, I remember C.O. means commander. Whoever that person is, has Marshal Aquila in a rather friendly mood. Thank goodness! Maybe, this one is a mood changer as well?"

Nefertiti replied in a semi whisper, "He already has..."

Lance Brown couldn't help but smile like a grateful boy who was just chosen to be the class president! Cherish went on to say. "If you carry my bush-al, we'll lead you to where you need to go."

The two women walk in front of Lance, holding hands and giggling as they lead the grinning young soldier into the world of Shangri-La.

Inside, Paradise has done her best in the weeks since Sky's death to get her life back on track. She started joining Semaj in the computer lab to learn how to build servers and learn Spanish. She even allowed Earl to teach her how to cook by volunteering more in the kitchen.

Even the anger from not being able to repay Sky's death and

somewhat begun to subside. On this day as the two Transwomen made their way to the gym to work on booty building and tummy flattening. They noticed Cherish and Dawn leading a handsome Army Officer though Shangri-La. Paradise could not help but mention.

“Look at those thirsty Ho’s. Dammm, he’s cute!”

Semaj smiled and replied, “Yeah, he’s cute. Even so, we never ever should let Earl hear us talking like this.”

Paradise stopped in her tracks, looks Semaj in her brown eyes and said.

“Why? He doesn’t owe me! Don’t get me wrong, I like Earl a lot. He’s a big, bald cuddle bear. Still, he doesn’t owe me. Our relationship is based on the here and now! Not the future, what future do any of us have anyway?”

Semaj exhaled as she states. “You’re right he doesn’t owe us, and all this may just be temporary. But..”

She sits down and Paradise sits down on the metal bench right next to her and whispers.

“But, but what?”

Semaj licks her thick lips and utters in a hush.

“I. I remember something, well something I remember seeing. It was a Netflix documentary about people behind bars and there was this story about a trucker that had bodies in his freezer and his name if I remember right, was Earl.”

Paradise lets out a nervous laugh followed by silence for a few moments before saying.

“You’re fucking with me, right? I mean that doesn’t mean it’s this

Earl, right? Earl is a common name for fat, bald, white men born in the South, right? I mean, what's the chances of that Earl, being this Earl? Stop fuckin with me..."

Once again silence for a few moments before Semaj said.

"Girl, all I know is I've come too far to be murdered."

Which forces a reply from Paradise, "you mean like Sky?"

Semaj exhaled once more, shook her head, I'm sorry and then said.

"I'm sorry, I should have.....Well, I just don't want to do anything that destroys the only family I have left. And let's face it, we are family now! Even if he's that Earl."

The pretty brown Transwoman lai her head on Paradise shoulder signaling please forgive me.

Inside the command center there's a makeshift map of their present surroundings. It's accurate enough to make the survivors understand that for the time being death wasn't breathing down their collective necks. Shangri-La's ham radio stays tuned to the emergency frequency, listening for any signs of life from the outside world! John Hammond sat alone, battling an emotional funk that's attempting to sequester itself inside his soul. Their resident teacher and fellow survivor Ms. Nabila Hussien have begun sending John signals of attention, yet he's too wrapped up in his vaccine research to consider his own happiness!

When young Major Brown was led into the area by two giggling members of his community, John does his best to pep up. Cherish let's go of Dawn's hand and informs John Hammond.

"This cutie is here to see you Mr. John Hammond, sir. When you are finished kindly send him back outside to us, thank you."

Both women kiss Lance on opposite sides of his cheeks and walk out of the area. Lance takes a few moments, cleared his throat before saying.

"Good day Doctor Hammond, here are the blood, hair and spinal fluid from the Gavenson twins. They are the cutest little kids, dam that spinal tab hurts then like hell sir."

John could only nod his head; he understood the level of pain it produces for an adult. He can only imagine how middle school children would react.

"Thank you Major, hopefully we won't need any more. I have something you might want to discuss with your commander. It involves some very serious chatter I picked up on the ham!"

Lance's eyebrows go up in surprise as he asks.

"You mean there are other survivors out there? Do you have locations? Maybe we can scoop them up, there's safety in numbers."

John sighs as he replies, "I don't think it will be as simple as that. From the conversations I've had. Some of these survivors are the I hate the government type! While others are just to frighten to leave their bunker."

Major Brown's reply was filled with passion for what's becoming a lost cause.

"Here we are with the fate of humanity see-sawing on the brink of disappearing forever. And people are still hung on their miss guided motions and backwards prejudices? "

Big John stares at the young Officer and saw bits of his own youth, so his smiled and words are indeed genuine.

"This plague will wipe out most ISMs. Racism, classism, sexism even ageism. Nevertheless, what it won't wipe out as long as there are people is, stupid."

Both men share a warm heart filled laugh, before John went on to say.

"What I need you to tell your C.O was about chatter on the ham, turn to channels 74, 38 and 51. Survivors are talking about bands of RAGERS, organized! Using weapons and driving vehicles."

Big John's words do not take long to register an effect from Major Brown when he said, "SHIT!"

Hammond goes on to say, "Yeah, I know, a real buzz kill. I hope the channels your C.O. wants to use for our comms have been comprised, either way we should be careful. It's scary if RAGERS are somehow becoming aware, that could be an extremely unique problem.

Lance handed him a yellow piece of paper and replied.

"Here's our new radio channels from the Colonel. She felt too many people were hearing us talk as well."

Major Brown sighed and snapped his shoulders back and nodded goodbye, then John teases.

"Anyway, you have not one, but TWO lovely goddesses looking for your attention! Dam you are a lucky man Major Brown. You must have a four-leaf clover in your front pocket? Now go forth and be fruitful and multiply, young Ranger. Remember more now than ever, children are our future!"

Inside the Valdez's quarters Calamity and Destiny discuss current events as they fold their laundry. Destiny's a bit curious about what's next for them all.

"I don't know, it feels like we are hold up like rats. I mean this place is the bomb and everything. Even so, at times it feels so empty and goddam soulless."

Calamity sighs as she hands Dawn her white boxer brief underwear and said.

"It's the concrete. What I hated most about prison was the concrete. Surprisingly, I found the group showers very acceptable and somewhat liberating."

Destiny replied. "You know from the cocaine fuel parties I am used to going too, this took a major fucking adjustment! "

Celeste out of nowhere confirmed something she would have never said weeks ago. "Yet having you and my Ernesto and with those kids running around makes it easier for me to just, be at peace."

Destiny smiled, that little acknowledgment, goes a long way to bring her mood from despair to somewhat frisky! She blew an air kiss to Celeste as she replied in a bad English accent.

"Well thank you mi lady, will you be escorting me to the high school dance?"

Celeste replied in a lustful voice.

"Only if you go down on me in the parking you sexy slut."

Destiny smiles giggled and said.

"I was always told my tongue is a real people's pleaser..."

She leaned forward and gave Mrs. Valdez a romantic kiss, reserved for newlyweds and secret girlfriends. Celeste can't help but pull Destiny closer allowing her hands to roam all over her soft almond colored bottom! As their faces part and Destiny's slender tongue licks Celeste exposed neck, she moaned.

"See chica this place, not, not so bad. I have Enestro and you have us... Beside you enjoy anal and any man that's been in prison for a period of time. Very much needs a woman like you!"

The world outside was an ever-changing organism and without technology few if any survivors would see it coming, until this new world landed on your front door! Jefferson Bullraguard Lee was what Darwin referred to when he mentions an organism's evolution was tied to their environment.

Whether it was Lee's prior bouts with Malaria or his violent childhood incident with a neighborhood rabid dog! Something caused him to retain nearly all his mental functions after being infected by the RAGER virus. Furthermore, his introduction into their ego system helped RAGERS in direct contact with Lee to relearn basic mental and motor skills.

Lee quickly dubs his new legion as the **Army of BLOOD**! Among the first skill he began fostering in his troops was how to drive. With no fear of the mindless Zombie Horde, Jefferson walked out of the Mental Hospital with several dozen RAGERS behind him. Numerous abandon vehicles litter the roadway making traveling difficult at best.

In the weeks since teaching the smartest of his BLOODY ARMY how to drive, they had cleared three miles of roads! Thousands of vehicles are stripped of gas and parts, then either pushed to the side of the road or used to make corrals to contain the dead. All that in a little under twenty days and twenty nights. Left unchecked, Jefferson Bullraguard Lee's new sect, will become the dominate species!

That's when they began plundering tactical assets like gun stores, police stations, firework stands and big box stores. Weapons, gunpowder, batteries and drones are the objectives! Without much hassle Lee's BLOODY ARMY found plenty of all the above.

Sadly, any survivors of COVID-MOMREL-6 virus found hiding in those areas, where put to the sword, raped, beaten and either infected by the RAGERS virus or left to turn Zombie. Lee's Army was fair and simple in their approach. Everyone gets SOME!

Like any true tyrant or strong man type leader, Jefferson pointed to the obstruction in the road, signaling for the RAGERS to move them. With their anger now focused in a somewhat positive direction.

The murderous madmen move tons of Michigan's and Japan's finest hunks of overpriced metals with ease!

They had to clear nearly ten miles of road before Lee found what he was looking for. A National Guard Troop Armored Carrier with 50 caliber mount gun, two tanks and a duce and a half troop transport. As Lee climbed aboard his new command center, he saw the waves of dead have followed him this far so he proclaimed.

"My ARMY of BLOOD ,my Army of Chaos! We shall march forth as a cleansing wave of what was humanity. Those that are worthy shall join us. Those that are not shall join them!"

Lee pointed to the dead, as the RAGERS grunted their approval, Lee continued.

"I will teach you how to re capture some of what you have lost, and you will teach others to be like us. Then we will direct our RAGE towards the true enemy, a traitor! Colonel Wynolla Lafayette, bitch I'm coming for you."

Hours later, when Major Brown returned to the new U.S. Army infectious command center- formerly known as the U.S. Federal Reverse Midwestern branch 27. He found his C.O. playing with the twins! The trio were blowing bubbles out of a bubble wand-*courtesy of Shangri-La*. Each child helps Wynolla Lafayette to laugh and giggle harder than she has in several years!

Having to extract bone marrow from the two-doe eyed little girls nearly made her cry during the procedure. And silently she vowed not to let that happen again! What if there's not even a cure for this madness, Windu pondered to herself. Why should he torture, Deanaa and Hanna?

When she notices Lance smiling at her, Wynolla knew it is time to get back on the clock. After a snappy salute, the two Soldiers talk as they walk towards the command center. Leaving the twin girls with two of the CDC younger scientists who gladly accepted the task of teaching the girls how to read and do math.

Major Brown led with, "You look like a natural parent out there ma'am."

Colonel Lafayette flashed a quick smile and nods sure, as Major Brown goes on to say.

"Doctor Hammond wanted me to inform you that we should be monitoring ham stations 33, 56, 72 for survivors."

Wynolla's response is upbeat, "Glad to know there are still living out there. Anything else?"

Lance scratches the back of his neck as they reach the makeshift command center in what was once a money counting room. His voice hinted a worry.

"Well, he said survivors are chattering about RAGERS being organized."

As Wynolla heads over to the radio room, he replies. "Well, that's very goddam disconcerting! We'll have to investigate that after we solve todays set of problems."

Once at the radio room, Colonel Lafayette orders the PFC in charge of base communications to start monitoring ham radio stations that John Hammond told Major Brown about. With Major Brown in tow, their stroll took them towards the roof or base LZ. That's when Colonel Lafayette explained today's problem.

"We need JP5, Chief Gomez said without the additive needed to keep fuel from degrading our supply will be useless in three weeks."

Major Brown replies, "Well fuck me sideways."

Windu kids, "Spoken like a true prodigy! Well, we and by we, I mean you, will take Sergeant Belladonna with both an A and B team to the Gary Airport.

That's where John Hammond got their Soviet bird. There might be something there we can use. We don't want to try Midway Airport, because we know it's a death house. In this case little airports are better. Chief Gomez will provide you will the fancy name of the stuff you will be looking for once your boots hit the ground. Lance, get in, get out and bring our people home!"

Major Brown nodded his understanding then replies.

"Roger that Colonel, Airborne leads the way."

Robin wishes his sentence with, "Just like Cavalry saves our day!

Major Brown sheepish continues by saying, "huh, there is just one more thing ma'am and it's kind of personal I need to discuss. And it's either you, my aging mom or my gay brother."

Colonel Lafayette stopped halfway up the stairwell, turned to her young X.O and said.

"Wow, that's a list. Ok, tell me what's wrong my young padawon..."

Lance sheepishly smiles, then mutters. "I, I think I'm in love."

Wynolla looks surprised, forcing Lance to clear up what he means.

"NOOOO, not with you ma'am. I mean you are a hellva human being and all. Sadly, NO, no, no, no."

Lafayette jokes, "Hey I am standing right here, you don't have to keep rubbing it in. I get it okay! Spill it, what gives?"

Lance chuckled a bit, then replies with all honesty.

"I met someone, well two women. Well, they kind of met me and then I don't know what happened, but they had me promise to come back. These are their word's Colonel. So they could ROCK MY WORD and then some! Honestly, I don't think I have ever had my world rocked in that nature ma'am."

Wynolla' s at a loss for words, for she can see in his young officer face that the women had to be beauties to behold, and she replied.

"Well, if you ever have to think about if you have or haven't. You haven't Major! Two? WOW, must be all that good livin Lance."

Major Brown could barely contain himself as he said.

"YES, Nefertiti Cherish McGill beautiful brown skinned woman with a body out of this world! And I guess her girlfriend. Dawn, a wonderfully thick snow bunny and they said something about wanting to have my babies, Windu! I didn't know what to say."

Wynolla could not help but hold out her fist for a fist bump as she said.

"You should have screamed YES! Then let the force be with you and your Lightsaber never falter to hit its mark, over and over and over again my brother. Go make baby Rangers my padawan."

Robin was covered in sweat and her muscles ached, but that's what happens when you start your day with two hundred push-ups! Followed by a combination of four hundred sit ups, which include the dreaded butterfly sit ups. Which was chased by two hundred kicks, one hundred strikes and twenty minutes on the speed bag. Plus, if she still feels motivated, a hundred squats to enhance her booty muscles. She threw on a two-mile run to make sure she had stamina to flee, if need be.

That's one of the great things about the end of the technological age. Less time on social media and more time working on oneself! For in the apocalypse the slow and out of shape or young and very old are generally first on the Dead Head takeout menu.

Seeing Wynolla again may have also helped a bit. Damn, she still looks as GREAT as the morning she left Robin sleeping in an upscale DC Hotel! Just a bit more distinguished, Robin thought. Marshal Aquila may have been a hard ass enforcer of the law! Nevertheless,

Robin was still a human being, and she needed to feel beautiful in someone's eyes other than her Dad.

Deep down inside, she's so happy that he's still alive even after all of this madness! For now, Wynolla felt like she was stepping back into her life everything was beginning to feel somewhat normal. Strangely, that what's scaring Robin, for she doesn't really know if she could handle another death. Not after Sky, Robin just wanted to drink and forget!

Then she saw Wynolla's smiling face once more and all the hate and anger just melted away. Furthermore, when they kissed, it made Robin feel like tiny jolts of electric jump starting her heart once more! So, there's no way Wynolla was going to see Robin with an ounce of fat that didn't belong where it's supposed to be. Namely shapely thighs and delicious ass, thank you very much!

After her shower, Robin's headed towards the lab to check on her father. Along the way she found Paradise painting a life size mural of Sky on the wall leading towards the HYDRO unit.

Paradise was still a highly skilled artist and her devotion to her lost friend was as heartfelt as it can be. Her attention to detail, brought forth the kindness in Sky's eyes and the beauty or her departed love.

Robin could not help but say.

"That's beautiful.."

Paradise replies, "Oh hi Aquila, I,I didn't see you standing here. Yes, Sky was so inside as well as out. I wish I was more like her. Honestly, I am glad you two found some happiness."

Robin sighed, fighting back the feeling of gloom and anger by saying.

"Paradise what you're doing is good, it's your private therapy I mean.."

As she turns to leave, Paradise asks.

"Former Marshal Aquila, what can you tell me about Earl Grimes?"

Robin stopped in her tracks, turned to face Paradise with that, you don't know look plastered across her face.

"Besides the fact he was on Death Row with my Enestro and my father. Anything else you should get directly from Mr. Grimes. I caution you to beware, don't go looking for problems where problems don't need to exist. Whatever Earl was, he doesn't seem to be now, and I sure hope for our sake, he never will!"

Robin left Paradise alone with her thoughts as she headed to her father's lab. She found him sitting at his desk, staring at various formulas written out on an ole fashion chalk board. John was so deep in thought, he didn't even hear his daughter when she entered. It wasn't until Robin was a hair's breadth from his neck, did he turn around.

"There she is there's my pumpkin! How are you doing sweetheart?"

Robin smiled, as she blushed a bit then replied. "Dad, I'm not a little girl anymore, you can quit the pumpkin talk."

John smiles, "Well you're sweet like pumpkin pie, so it just stuck with me."

Robin tries not to blush, but she failed. Quickly changing the subject, she asks.

"Any closer on your miracle serum?"

John chuckles, "You mean my vaccine? Well yes and no. I need to test it and that's where the no lies. The bone marrow from little Deanaa and Hanna helped me recreate a portion of my work. Even so without a proper test, well you know....."

Robin understood as she replies, "Then we need to find a test dummy. I recommend we grab a few dead heads..."

John shook his head no, as he replies, "No, any test subject has to be alive."

Robin sighed as she said, "As well as any vaccine hds to contain the virus in which it's trying to fight, right?"

John reached into the tiny refrigerator and pulled out two beers and tried to hand one to Robin who said.

"Dad it's only eleven am."

Hammond smiled as he replied, "Well, I'm sure it's five pm in whatever's left of Paris, just drink a beer with your old man as he confesses something to you."

Robin nods ok and accepts the cold brew as her father said.

"I can't ask anyone to test this vaccine for It contains live COVID-MOMREL-6 virus. "

Robin slowly sipped her beer as she replied, "I understand, it could be a death sentence."

John took a few moments before saying, "Yeah it is and it's something, something...I need you to understand it's something dear I must do myself. So, I am glad I got to tell you first..."

Robin pretty much drowned out the rest of what her father was saying! His daughter slowly put down her beer, fully knowing that was not going to change what he just said. She replied with shock and a whole lot of repressed anger.

"NO! No, no, no you can't do that John! Fuck you! Fuck you, Dad! We, we just are getting to where things are sort of normal. Whatever that fucked up shit means in the apocalypse, and you want to leave me again? AGAIN!"

John sat back in his chair; his mouth hung up for he never saw the hurt his life had heaped upon his little girl, until now. She goes on to say in a commanding voice.

"I am getting on the horn with Colonel Lafayette and you better goddam not take that vaccine until I see if there's anyone or any other way. Dad, please, Wynolla may have a way to test this so-called wonder drug! I need you to promise me dad, promise me! You won't do anything to yourself before then. Promise me John! I, I can't lose anyone else not now."

Smiling, John reached out to offer his daughter a hug, and she gladly accepted, allowing him to whisper in her ear.

"Don't worry pumpkin, I plan to be around long enough to see you and that brash Army Ranger make the cutes couple this crazy world has ever seen!"

Meanwhile it took just under forty-three minutes for three Army helicopters to make the trek up from the Fox River basin. To just under to a hip, skip and rock throw from the shores of what was known to locals as Lake Michigan. The Army green birds of steel attract dead and RAGER alike for their presence could not be denied. For their comfort the air was blowing in off the lake and that made the day a bit cooler than a normal September.

The overhead sound caused a flood of Zombie's shamble out of every lodging, overturned vehicle or burned-out hamlet they use to call home! Same with RAGERS, the only real difference between them at this point was the speed at which they are able to move.

Major Brown's Helio contains SGT. Belladonna and three other operators of various ranks, ethnic backgrounds and religious beliefs. Each intent on fulling the only part of the mission that makes any sense at all. Making it back to base alive and not infected! Yes, each team member knew the importance of the additive needed to keep the Helicopters airborne.

Still how many wanted to die to preserve the right to remain vertically tactically superior? A ruse was needed and Major Brown being a student of cinema, remembered the scene from the Oscar winning Vietnam War drama, **Apocalypse Now**. The ionic scene of American Helicopters descending upon an enemy's village blaring Germanic opera music. Lance figured out, why not!

Using the Helio external speakers, Lance's choice of music was equally as loud.

Just a bit more modern when he chose, **It Takes Two To Make Things Go Right** from the probably deceased musical artist **Rob Base** and **DJ EZ Rock**. His Helio drive bombed the tarmac, several times getting the attention of every infected fucker in the area, and let's just say the music was booming!

Army pilots dropped it low, hovering their wide bodies over the opposite end of the tarmac, away from the only set of buildings on the airfield. Like any good artist, Major Brown's stationary helicopter didn't take long to gain a loyal following! RAGERS bashed Zombie's brains out just to be underneath the metal birds, like babies waiting to be fed.

I80-94 was a parking lot covering three nearby states and it seemed Major Brown's Helio seemed to be attracting company by the tens of thousands.

His airship was positioned just out of the reach of countless rotten, broken and decaying fingers. The moans of the dead nearly drown out the humming of rotors leading the stumbling Zombie horde as it marched the mass infection away from the target.

When RAGERS begin tossing rocks, computers and other various hazardous items at his aircraft.t Major Brown gave the order to climb fifty feet higher. The cool September winds had visibility across the lake, Lance could see a black smoldering fire on the horizon. A sharp pain hit him in his gut as Major Brown could sense where the smoke originated from! Using his headset, the Army

Ranger contacted his B Team scourging for the fuel additive at Gary International Airport.

"This is SHAFT, checking in with Chief GO-GO."

The other pilot nicknamed GO-GO- Otherwise known as Thomas Parsons- *originally from Hawaii-* chuckled as he replied.

"Ahhhhhh, no sir on the handle SHAFT. Straight from Windu, your call sign is NIGHTSABER."

Major Brown sighs, "Really?"

Chief GO-GO attempted to conceal his mirth but fails as he replied.

"Take it up with the boss, Major."

Lance replied with a bit concern. "Roger that. How's it coming on your end?"

The army pilot cheerfully replied. "So far so good, NIGTHSABER. Your rouse drew most of the Dead Heads away. The B Team encountered a bit of resistance, but everyone's safe. Even so, we found eight 55-gallon drums of the stuff. They are bundling them up, even so it might be a handful. We'll be right at our haul limit.

Major Brown weighed his decision before saying.

"Chief there's smoke coming from Camp McCormick. We are going to check it out."

There's silence for a few moments before Chief GO-GO replied.

"Roger that sir, we'll get the payload back home safely! Take care out there Major."

Major Brown replies, "Roger that Chief."

The mixed horde of RAGERS and Dead Heads follow the buzzing whirling bird of prey nearly four miles before it peeled off across the lake, dropping down low enough to barely not be touched by the waves lapping at its olive-green frame. Any of the Zombie horde that seem still keen on following found their decaying bodies disappearing under the hungry waves of Lake Michigan.

The city that once was **Gary Indiana** had been roughly thirty odd miles from what had been the city of **Chicago**. Even so by car on a good day would have taken up to thirty-five minutes. However, by air it took less than five.

By the time Major Brown's Helio got in range of what was once Camp McCormick, he could see the remains of what happens when large amounts of cocaine are introduced into an environment with no strong oversight!

Windows on just about every floor have been shot out of smashed into shinny jagged fragments. As Dead Heads roamed over barriers designed to keep them at bay! It appears a lower loading dock wall had been breached. RAGERS aimlessly mingled around the entrance, until they heard the sound of an approaching airship.

Most if not all infected ran into the street with eyes pressed to the sky searching for the maddening sound that helps fuel their rage. Major Brown's helicopter comes off the lake like a balk eagle about the snare a rabbit! Circling the once enact enclosure, Major Brown could see fires had burned on every floor and charred bodies still lay in crumbled heaps. He mutters.

"How could this happen? We just heard from Camp McCormick four days ago, Chief take us to the roof."

His pilot replies, "Roger that."

It doesn't take long before all eyes are peeled on what will be labelled as the *Massacre of Camp McCormick*. Nothing could stop hundreds of Dead Heads from picking over the bones on former residents. The pilot muttered.

"Oh, my, god!"

Major Brown sighed, before muttering more to himself.

"Looks like whoever was left tried to secure the rooftop doors but failed. Jesus! Why didn't someone use the Helio we left? It's right fucking there!"

As Lance expressed his frustration on the loss of precious human life, that's when he noticed someone attempting to get his attention from inside the Navy transport Helio parked unmolested on the bloody rooftop. Inside was the former Federal Reserve Officer and a middle age former doctor from the CDC named Joann Wang.

Eight RAGERS took eager notice of the approaching bird of prey and decided to start tossing various debris at the approaching foe! Mostly metal buckets of flaming books, papers and medical flies. Sergeant Belladonna muttered.

"Sir, isn't that the shithead that Cartel guy gave two kilos of booger sugar too?"

Major Brown acknowledged Bell by saying.

"Yeah, I guess we should recuse him and want looks like Doctor Wang."

Sergeant Belladonna replies with vigor.

"ROGER THAT!"

Lance directed his pilot by saying.

"We need to see if that Navy Huey can fly. Chief Warren, can you fly that old thing?"

Chief Warrant Officer Karen Warren, a fifty-five-year-old co-pilot- *of Italian and Hungarian and Iris descendant*- from the Illinois National Guard replied with bravo.

"NIGHTSABER compared to this, that'll be like riding a tricycle."

Major Brown would have rather chosen his own call sign. Nonetheless, his commanding officer had spoken, beside NIGHTSABER did sound kind of cool! So, he said.

"Ok fight fans, lets clean up all these sacks of shit and see if that transport has any life to give the cause. No one escape in it so maybe it's broken. Either way we need to find out!"

The Army Helicopter circles the rooftop once before taking position directly over the small group of RAGERS. Belladonna signaled for another member of their SF team to use the business end of their NATO inspired 5.56 automatic weapons. Quick three round burst impacted the top as well as the front of various infected skulls!

Promptly sending bits of diseased bone and deformed brain matter splattering against the underbelly of Major Browns transport. It took less than 45 seconds to clear the rooftop of current dangers. The Army Helio touched down on the remains of McCormick and the first pair of boots to hit the roof was Major Brown. Who was swiftly followed by Sergeant Belladonna and Chief Warren.

The air smelled like puke, dried blood, smoke and human waste! Nevertheless, the trio advance with weapons held high. Directly towards two sets of darting eyes. Before anyone could reach the door, Belladonna offered a bit of advice.

"We should make sure, they're still part of the human race, right?"

Chief Warren slowly walks around the aircraft with her weapon leading the way. Carefully the former grandmother of three did her best not to trip over charred body parts and spent ammo casing.

Lance nodded to Belladonna as she uses the barrel of her weapon to tap on the bloodstained windshield, before telling its inhabitants.

"Hello in there, anyone still human? Say, McDonald's I'm loving it!"

From their P.O.V. they can see the former Cash Cop, dead and secured firmly in the front seat by a seatbelt. He was snarling and clawing at the silhouette outside his bubble! While in the backseat a very frighten and dehydrated Doctor Wang stepped out the aircraft with her hands up, trembling and then said.

“I really wish I loved McDonalds. Please don’t shoot!”

Belladonna informed Major Brown.

“Sir this dead head is covered in several ounces of Columbia’s finest.”

Doctor Wang said, “Yes, this fucking asshole! He OD, two days ago! I have been stuck in here with, with him, since. FUCK! Thank, thank you for saving my life.”

It’s nighttime, back at Shangri-La friends, lovers and one-time foes go about their personal business as the smoothing sound of waterfalls, birds chirping, and wind chimes are being played over the intercom! However, inside the Earl, Paradise and Semaj quarters for one of them, shower time had just concluded. Semaj walked into her hatch unaware of events transpiring while wearing her favorite lavender bath robe equipped with pink bunny slippers! She’s toweling her coarse hair dry and singing.

“Baby, I love you, oh my, baby I need you. Oh, baby I love you, I do, even when I’m with my boo, I’m thinking of you...”

Only to find herself square in the middle of a heated conversation between her pod mates, Earl and Paradise. Semaj entered just in time to hear Paradise nearly scream.

“Just tell me Earl, just tell me!”

Her shrill voice sent shivers up Semaj’s ebony embraced spine, she attempted to avoid the drama by hurrying into their shared bedroom. Earl halted her with his massive frame by standing up, he said.

"Would you please wait from applying those wonderful oils that keep your skin baby soft for just a few moments Semaj? There's something Paradise needs cleared up."

Semaj tried to fight back the words, yet they kind of just slide out of her mouth anyway.

"If I have a choice I would prefer to wait and let you and Paradise handle whatever this is among yourselves..."

Both of her pod allowed their equally stern glares to force the twenty something Transwoman to swallow hard as she replies.

"Well, I guess I can sit here on this cold metal chair until I hear what needs to be said."

Earl paced a few steps rubbing his bald head, before saying.

"I didn't get to Indiana's State Penial Institution a lost soul. Nor did I arrive on Death Row because I was a saint! No, no, the Apocalypse has a way of forcing all of us face some troubling facts. I was, well in some ways am, still a very much a monster."

Semaj squirmed as Earl's even slower than normal delivery made her feel uneasy. On the other hand, Paradise didn't seem fazed as he continued.

"Do you still want to know who I am? For once I pull back that scab there's no turning back. So, I implore you to just let it rest! You will feel less of me and that will hurt me dearly. As much as I wish it wouldn't, it will to a level you may never understand."

Paradise replied with vigor and rage not aimed at anyone in general!

"Hell motherfuckin YEAH I want to know! Who you are Earl."

Semaj threw her hand over her hears, pleading, "No, no, no, NO!"

Earl looked down at the frightened Semaj and then down on the deviant Paradise and he wonders which road would he travel.

Murder these two, then go about killing everyone in Shangri-La? Murder and dismember the only people he has ever known as friends? Sure, Estero and Celeste may be handful, yet Earl knew if he chooses Door A, doom awaits them all! Before the Summer of Death, maybe. However, now we move into the autumn of discontent and the dead are only growing in numbers!

So, Earl said. "Whatever I was then, I am not now, and I owe it up to the people I currently live with and among. I'm a work in progress, that's for sure and I've never been happier."

Semaj stood up, takes her hand away from her ears, kisses them both on their cheeks and replied.

"That's good enough for this girl."

She turned and quickly entered their bedroom and shut the hatch, locking it from the inside. Paradise turned to Earl and goes on to say.

"WELL, that's that is not going to work for me!"

Earl headed over to their makeshift bar and poured himself and Paradise a mixed dink of two tablespoons of lemon juice, two packs of pink lemonade powder, two teaspoons dash of lime juice, four shots of pineapple juice and six shots of tequila into red plastic party cups. Add a few ice cubes and they create Mexican Pink Lady Lips- *taught to him by Calamity of course*- he handed Paradise a drink then said.

"I understand, you're upset because you didn't get revenge for your friend, Sky. Now that anger is festering in your gut like John's beef stew, and you need someone to take it out on! Once again, my dearest. I do understand how you feel."

The anger in Paradise's green eyes burnt with such a fierceness they could seem to invoke the sun! She took a sip of her drink before replying.

“Oh that’s so fucking good! Never mind that, this has nothing to do with Sky. Or that murderous bitch Indigo. It has to do with who I am living with.”

Earl took a sip of his drink, his voice steady and calm as he replies.

“I’m the person who found you before you knew the information you seek. As well as the person you won’t want, once you can access the information you want. All I can tell you is this is close as I have had as a family, ever! If you need your own hatch, I understand. I’ll even help you move, but my old life is just that. This is me, the new Earl Grimes!”

Paradise stared him down, her slender arms on her equally slender hips and nearly shouted.

“What do you want to know about me Earl? Did I trick off with old men for money? Yeah, I did! Did I fuck their faces or let them fuck me up my ass in their backseat of their family SUV; with my face pressed up against their kid’s child seat so less? Bingo! Was I abused as a child? You nailed it big guy! See, I don’t care if you know I tried to kill my stepfather for raping me!”

Silence blanketed the room, as Earl slowly exhaled deeply, before opening his massive arms and signaling his head come here.

Paradise was equally defiant for several moments, before just melting into Earl’s Mountain size pecks. Earl whispered, as she began to silently sob.

“I am, or was just as I said, someone not worthy to walk among the living. However now, the living no longer rule, fate! Now let me tell me what that means for reformed people like us. Honey child, we are the meek that inherited this land! I may not be perfect, nevertheless I will never be fake. I promise you as long as I draw breath, I will work harder than anyone to never let you down. That's who I am now!"

While back at what has been renamed. CAMP PAYDAY. The over hundred inhabitants gain another when Major Brown's chopper touched down, depositing Doctor Wong into the medical ward. It doesn't take long before he found Colonel Lafayette in the coms area listening to radio chatter. After a proper military salute, the two officers find themselves discussing current affairs.

"Yes ma'am, Task Force Alpha found Camp McCormick uninhabitable. Doctor Wong painted a picture of someone coming up with the brilliant idea to make moonshine!"

Colonel Lafayette asked in shock, "Why with all the liquor the departed Colonel McKinney supplied before his death?"

Lance rubbed the half a day-old stumble on his chin, shrugged his shoulders before saying.

"I guess it some good ole boys who got their granddaddy's method wrong. Dr. Wong said three days ago there was an explosion and wholesale slaughter therefore forwarded! It was so sudden that the area was overrun by RAGERs and the Dead before the base could mount a proper defense. After talking to Dr. Wong, I saw no reason to risk further lives searching for possible survivors."

Wynolla shook her head signaling her frustration for the loss of life. Even though most of those survivors opted out of the mission. They might have been some of the last people on the planet!

A young Private 1st Class monitoring the radio, heard something strange and he called his commanding officers over.

"We have something, I mean there's something you got to get ears on."

Major Brown followed his commander to the table housing the old-world HAM/CD radio as the young solider said.

"Colonel, Major, I was flickering through those new stations you provided looking for any signs of life when I came across this."

He pulled the headphone jack from its female coupling and the words blare into the room.

"Hello, hello, hello... Is anyone out there? He, he, he said someone would be out there.."

Sobbing was followed by the clear shuffling of feet, followed by a low humming that was hard to make out at first, as the woman continued to plead for help.

"Please, PLEASE, is someone out there. He, he, he keeps saying you are out there! If you aren't they, they. They've murdered my entire group! PLEASE is someone out there....."

As the pleading becomes less and less, the humming grows louder. That's when Major Brown reached for the handheld mic.

Windu was forced to stay his hand as she recognized the song being projected from the throat of another human being! As the shuffling of feet and trashing of the teeth grew louder. The helpless victim pleaded once more and her words were dripping with fear!

"PLEASE, please hel..."

The only sound left was that of a mad man signing a racist and demented version of Glory, Glory Hallelujah at the top of his lungs.

"Glory, Glory Hallelujah! Listen to what's coming to ya, wake up MY PEOPLE to the trampling of the inferior Jews. Gonna wash the land with Nigger blood, Asian mongrels and of course all you filthy rapist beaners too! Gonna find you traitors and we are coming two, by two by two. My RAGE is marching on! I died yet I have risen to be cast above your mortal prison! Only my God understand on how the might has grown. Glory, GLORY, I'll gut you, glory, GLORY I will gut you! Glory, GLORY I will gut you! Colonel Lafayette my Army will find you and then you will join the dead. I told you bitch, this white, man, marches on!"

Chapter II:

THOUGHTS OF A BETTER TOMORROW.

It's been two weeks since the fall of Camp McCormick and the approaching signs of autumn would no longer be denied! Leaves were turning brilliant colors of rust, orange, red and brown. All over the planet apples and pears trees were loaded down with nature's finest. As miles upon miles of corn, wheat and soybeans fields rot patiently in their beds of soil. Well, the ones that glutton size birds have not claimed as their own of course.

At Camp PAYDAY as well as in Shangri-La they noticed CB/HAM radio chatter had gone from regular conversations among the remaining survivor outposts in the area. To frantic calls for help! Survivors were reporting large groups of over one hundred RAGERS working like some sort of Army. There are even reports of RAGERS driving vehicles and using automatic weapons!

This had all the remaining scientist scratching their heads and wondering how did the virus morph into something this new. On that day Robin flew Big John along with Cherish and Dawn the twenty-seven miles to CAMP PAYDAY. John wanted to brief Colonel Lafayette firsthand, and the ladies just felt like saying hi!

Robin's attire doesn't actually scream fuck me now, fuck me hard and don't let go as much as Nefertiti - hip hugging blue jean skirt, tight white t shirt, white two-inch Bike- *knockoff*- hi top gym shoes, with no bra- *to complete her effect*.

Nonetheless, Robin's skintight faded Levi's jeans, with holes in the knees and tan executive style shirt tied to expose her toned ads doesn't suggest I am a boring underage Quaker bride either!

Dawn on the other hand went with a classic white cotton skirt, with slit from her ankles to her right thigh, beige desert Army boots and a tight beige T shirt, with no bra also for effect!

Major Brown was waiting on the tar mac to greet the aging Soviet Aircraft and he marveled as Robin touched the heavy bottom bitch down without so much as a bellow on its part. Lance smiled as the four inhabitants exited the aircraft and just like a 90s Rom-Com; Nefertiti Cherish McGill rushed and gave the shy Army officer a big passionate hug. Forcing her tender nipples to poke through her thin cotton shirt and they didn't have to fight hard to push themselves right into Lance's rapidly beating heart. When their embrace faded Nefertiti Cherish McGill whispered so only, he could hear.

"I've been thinking about you so much! I'm hoping you'll show me around. Thinking about it, if you don't mind could we, we start at your quarters?"

Dawn could plainly see the chemistry between the two and she suddenly felt like a third leg in a two-legged race! As Robin and John exit, they take in the scope of what is now Camp PAYDAY.

Pallets of shrink wrapped never used 20, 50 and 100 dollars bills now form makeshift barricades to halt an onslaught of undead attackers from reaching the main entrance of their building.

The mood inside leads Father and Daughter to believe that something big was up! When the young Major was able to pry Cherish off his chest.

John was quick to seek information.

"It's all this money out here a fire hazard?"

Lance replied with a bit of vigor.

"Oh, I never thought I would ever say that I have a lot of money. Still, there's just so much of the stuff Mr. Hammond. Even so, if it comes to that, yeah, we will burn it. Please, if you would follow me, Colonel Lafayette's in the coms room monitoring the current state of affairs."

The walk doesn't take long to go, down a few winding hallways and up a flight of stairs. Even more with each step, Dawn could see there's no future being a third wheel. Lucky for this wonderful white woman who hailed from nowhere special. Dawn came dressed for the position she wanted to have filled. Furthermore, she could feel eyes firmly locked on what she's promoting! Suddenly, Dawn didn't feel so awkward, like she did all through high school. Doing stupid stuff to fit in with an older crowd that just used her mind, body and soul to the point where she nearly committed suicide! No, the stripper in Dawn, knew how to get what she most desires, a genuine love.

Numerous men and a few women in their tan or olive-green camo go out of their way to catch a glimpse of Dawn's toned thigh or her bouncing slightly tanned restrained glorious flustered pink nipples. With each step through Camp PAYDAY her confidence returned! When the small group reached the COMM center the look on Wynolla's face goes from concern to one of joy. As she rose to greet their visitors the Colonel kept it loose but somewhat formal.

"Ahhh Marshal Aquila, Mr. Hammond and some rather lovely acquaintances, welcome! I'm sure Major Brown has been, hands on, when it comes to making everyone feel at home?"

Everyone kind of smiles, yet Lance caught the hidden jabs much like a shadow boxer. Colonel Lafayette ushered John and Robin over towards the CD/Ham radio. Leaving Lance, Dawn and Cherish deciding on whether to stay or step off on their own meeting of minds.

That's when Dawn takes a stand that will change her life forever when she said.

"You two should take off. I'll, I'll just mill around and see what this place has to offer."

Cherish gave the kind of half plead, half whisper of thank you as she gives Dawn a quick hug then follows Lance out of the room!

Leaving Dawn feeling under dressed to be in such company. Nevertheless, it wasn't long before a strapping Army Ranger of Afro Cuban American descent, offered Dawn the shirt off his back to cover her exposed nipples. And that's how friendships are made!

The last outpost to meet their fate by the hands of Lee's Marauders happened to be a point of interest for the living and the not so dead. A pervious Illinois Air National Guard barracks was just about sixty miles north of what was of Peoria Illinois. Jefferson knew what he sent his troops to find would be intact, for only the living could achieve fly.

Yes, the former Admiral did know how to fly and having his own heavily armed aircraft should come in handy. Mostly if he can tutor any of these violent monkeys, under his command to serve as his flight crew.

Each day Jefferson Bullraguard Lee's army pressed onward, clearing cluttered roads and spreading his reaction to the virus ruining through all their veins! RAGERs, whom his band encountered, begin having somewhat rational thoughts as well as a better command of their own motor skills.

Each mile of road clear of trucks, buses, cars, SUVs and motor homes allowed Lee's Army of Evolved RAGERs to grow! The Zombies being Dead Heads just aimlessly follow behind the RAGERs waiting for a hot meal. By the time Lee's Marauders made it to outside Peoria Illinois, the numbers of the dead alone were straddling near twelve thousand!

To the living inside the swarm of biting flies hit the Air National Guard Armory long before the smell of the dead arrived. Hundreds of thousands of disease carrying flies ascended upon the area like a buzzing shadow of death! The former Illinois Air National Guard Armory was a modest group of three simple barracks that was set on twenty acres of chain linked fenced land. Which included a Helio pad and mechanics shop to repair Helios inbound from whatever war America happens to be fighting at the moment! Lee's drove his red Range Rover right up to the closed front gate and announced to no one in particular.

"I am Rear Admiral Jefferson Bullraguard Lee, formerly of Great Lakes Naval Command. I would love to speak to your base commander, please."

Inside the first barracks, Air Force Reserve personnel and their families have bunkered down and are doing their best to keep their defenses unbroken. Nevertheless, there aren't enough willing warriors to repel the overwhelming horde outside their gates. The few pilots they had on the base, managed to escape with their families in the only working Helio that was on flight line. Furthermore, that was long before the reservist inside stepped upon the property. Nevertheless, those inside found themselves stuck between a jagged rock and a shit storm!

Lee wants his air chariot, yet not just any Helio. Jefferson wanted an attack Helicopter! There was a time when electrified gates with its dragon teeth of razor wire would have deterred the living or the sane.

Sadly, neither of those columns are present today! With a simple nod of his brow, a few of Lee's minion produce a thin shell-shocked man in tattered business suit and a long grey beard; from out of a steamer trunk in the rear of a school bus being driven by a one eyed Evolved RAGER.

The exhausted shadow of a man must have been someone with a bit of prestige before the war on the living. For his one battered black shoe hailed from a top tier line of smart business footwear! Blinded by the sun light the tattered man stumbled forward, with a well place kick across his unwashed narrow backside for good measure! This caught the attention of the forward section of the horde of Zombies that have been tagging along for these types of moments.

The first low moaning sound that began from what's left of some of their dead intestines magnifies as each Dead Head caught the meaning of the tune! Moaning, groaning, growling and more important moving forward towards the weary bearded man in the tattered business pants and one expensive black shoe.

As Commander of the Dead, Lee sternly informs the frighten man the depth of his plight. His Southern drawl was still present, nonetheless his breathing was much deeper and his mere presence might even have given Chicken Head a run for his money in the most interesting demented man of the era category!

"You may stand there and be devoured like a cheeseburger with feet, or you can run towards that gate. Climb it to for your freedom! What do you say brother? You ready to meet your maker or just be the maker of meat?"

The badly malnourished man with the one black shoe tried to stand up straight. Nonetheless one too many beatings and or rapes by his captors may have broken at least two disks in his back! However, that doesn't keep the bearded man in the tattered business pants and one expensive black shoe from limping towards what he can only consider his freedom over certain fucking death.

The beaten and abused man should have plainly scene the sign posted in English about the gate being electrified. Maybe he didn't read English or at that point didn't give a fuck! For the Zombies finally have warm flesh to pay attention to and that meant their portion of the virus was open for business. Their pursuit- *much like their stench-* was constant, never breaking off until you are found. Then they will you eat you alive! Maybe, if this survivor was lucky, he could cheat death once more by surviving this dead head onslaught.

When the weary man in the tattered business suit and one expensive black shoe's broken fingers finally touched the live wire. His frail body shook as the force of seven car batteries hooked up to the fence provided enough juice to power a small Ferris wheel. Happily, it fried the feeble survivor's internal organs! The weak man with the one black shoe cried out only once before his eyeballs exploded out of their sockets and brain matter boiled out of his broken nose!

That didn't stop the Zombie horde from having their prescribed snack. The dead crashed into the gate to claim their flaming A la carte! Some of their grimy and soiled clothing quickly caught fire adding to the simmering bonfire of walking corpses. Pressing their collective weight against the frame, close to eight hundred to nine hundred Zombies crashed through the survivor's first fortification.

There was enough electricity delivered from the car batteries to explode infected dead brain matter,*-much like living brain matter-* to whatever direction the wind's blowing! It clearly didn't matter for every one Zombie that fell, four more stumbled in to take its goddam place! The clawing and chomping on the charred corpse laying against the fence. Pretty much signaled to those inside the Air Force Reserve barracks who just witnessed the events via their base security Monitors. That the BARRBARIANS ARE NOT AT THE GATE, they are in the room!

Several minutes later, the car batteries charge faded, so that not even a dead head was affected by their presence. Lee signaled for his RAGERS to get to work tearing down the simple man-made structure. Working together they latched chains through the loops in the fence and on to the back of trucks. And it doesn't take long for the barriers meant to keep out the living safe, usher harbor to the diseased and the dead!

Jefferson Bullraguard Lee presence was much like a mutated Roman General in a campaign to destroy opposition to its core concept. The RAGER in Lee allowed those under his command free rain once they breached the grounds. Sure, the bullets didn't stop flying for five hours. The Air National Guard Members and their families fought valiantly in their own personal Alamo! Nevertheless, the gunfire did stop.

Furthermore, gunshots only attracted more of the dead from miles away, tens of thousands heard the call and searched for the direction to roam. When new RAGERS arrive attracted to the sounds of war, they either quickly succumbed to Lee's mutation or were savagely beaten to death by his new tribe. It's evolution of the species whether they like it or not!

Back at Camp PAYDAY, Big John was still looking to brief Colonel Lafayette on his experimental vaccine. John, Robin and Wynolla had been touring the Camps' makeshift bio labs contained of airtight vaults built to house a nation's wealth. Colonel Lafayette took the time to explain.

"We had little time making this area ready, but fortune smiles when you travel with your own Engineers."

Big John couldn't contain his smile, for he liked the young Army officer. Probably as much as his daughter. And it's John thinking of her, which will assist him in molding future events. But for now, John words caught both his daughter and Windu with surprise.

"I don't want to say this lightly, however, feel I have come up with a working vaccine."

Robin frowned a bit before saying.

"Dad, I thought we discussed this already?"

Windu glanced from daughter to father before she inquires.

"A vaccine you say. I must say, you got my attention are we dancing or not?"

John exhaled before replying.

"One that puts an end to this war."

Colonel Lafayette's right eyebrow etches up signaling, she's more than curious on the details.

"Doctor Hammond, do you mean Hana and Deana's one marrow helped in your research?"

John shook his head yes and stated. "Their ability to have the live virus and not turn was a fortunate mutation. When you found them, I remember you mentioning something about being trapped in some sort of office hi rise."

The brief expression that passes on Wynolla's face, subscribes to a flood gate of memories attempting to break free of their restraints! She offers a brief nod and does her best to keep the thoughts of Monique and everyone that has lost to this point, at bay.

John continues by saying, "By using their samples along with my original notes, I suspected the dead were never interested in the twins."

Wynolla fought back the anger in Dr. Hammond's assertions, still she knows it's best to focus on science not her emotion.

"We were surrounded in a high rise. I think those fleshing eating sons of bitches were after us all doctor."

Hammond doesn't understand why Wynolla's demeanor went from friendly and loose to stiff and unforgiving. Nonetheless Robin does, she sensed her back straighten, saw Wynolla's jaw line tighten. She lost someone close to her that day!

Someone who Wynolla didn't want anyone to disturb their memory. That doesn't stop Hammond from doing his best to hammer the point home.

"You don't seem to understand Colonel, they didn't see THEM. It's like a cloak! Anything dead or even near dead was chasing you. They're CHASING US."

When her dad raised his voice, Robin steps in by saying.

"Ok, ok let's take a few deep breaths and understand we're on the same team. GO LIVING, YAY!"

That brings the mood down to a semi normal level, Colonel Lafayette clears her throat and then said.

"Ok, Doctor Hammond, how do we see if your science meets the road?"

John rubbed his head and sighed before replying.

"The only way will have to be with live trails. That requires with volunteers. If this works, the vaccine makes us invisible in our enemies' eyes."

Wynolla was forced to ask, "To both the dead and the RAGERS?

John shrugged his broad shoulders signaling he had no idea. Before letting his words linger as he kind of tilted his bald head to the side, signaling he hopes so. Leaving Robin to counter with.

"Dam Dad, that's the worst if it doesn't kill you, it will only make your stronger speech I've ever heard!"

Meanwhile, Camp PAYDAY has plenty of unused space. Nearly everyone has their own lining quarters, even if those quarters consist of millions of dollars of shrink wrapped twenty-dollar bills serving as makeshift walls.

Major Lance Brown's quarters happen to be a converted office that used to belong to the head of base security. When he led Nefertiti though the door, she doesn't have to do much to get him feeling uncomfortably aroused.

Cherishes deep rich mocha skin brushes lightly against Lance's butterscotch complexion and a shiver of static electrify momentarily jolts their inner being!

He could swear Nefertiti Cherish McGill has an aroma of vanilla and honey. The moment their bodies press up against each other. Lance leaned forward to close his door with the bottom of his black jump boots. Cherish eyed the simple surroundings as she saunters into the modest size room. She knew the handsome young Army Officer's eyes would not remove themselves from the utter pleasure that awaits them both!

Nefertiti has dressed like this for hundreds of men in her years of pole dancing. Yes, part of the thrill was their attention! She knew how to capture all eyes as she commanded the stage. The other thrill was to make her rent in a day! At times she felt a pang of sorrow for the older gentleman who call strip club's their home. Still their pitiful loneliness was easy to cash in on and a girl needed to eat, pay her cell phone bills, get her nails done etc and ect..

Nevertheless, unlike some of the dancers, Cherish never felt the need to venture into the escort game. If she accepted you into her generally waxed vagina, it's because she found you sexy and interesting enough to freak with for a while!

She ran her fingers across the several paperback novels Lance has on his metal shelf before turning to Lance and saying.

"Lock the door please..."

Major Brown didn't need to be told twice, because he had already done it! As expected, Cherish had Lance's undivided attention when she said in a lustful baby doll type voice.

"I've been thinking about you soooo much. Oh, my goodness! I need you to lay back on that big of bed of money! Oh my god, all this cream, makes we want to...Cream."

As Lance moves forward, their lips meet in a full court press of pent of passion and species driven lust! Cherish's hands fumble with Lance's military metal buckle as his rugged hands clumsily fondle her twin mounds of firm booty meat. Squeezing them, pressing them and holding both warm ass cheeks as they spill out the palms of his hands like warm butter. Lance's smiling from ear to ear, knowing he had just found a cure for his loneliness in the Apocalypse!

Nefertiti slowly twirls around so Lance can take in her sex appeal, before jumping into his lap forcing him back on to his bed- *of nearly $12,350,780.00*. Cherish's hot pussy lips snuggly on to the front of Lance's Boxer shorts like they came made to order.

Her luscious deep mocha color breasts came equipped with clearly aroused chocolate chip nipples. Which appeared to be fighting their way through Major Brown's pressed tan Military T shirt!

Nefertiti left index and forefinger fumbled with the awaking of the Army Ranger's thick manhood. Her whispered ring illicit thoughts in his exposed ear.

"I know you don't have much time, but you have no idea how much I need this right now! I will admit a girl might enjoy eating a little VJ now and then. However, I am not ashamed to admit, boooyyyy I am A-DICK-TED. I need your consent, so, are we doing this?"

Before he could answer she licks Lance across his face like a cat in heat! Major Brown swallowed hard as he replied as cool as he can.

"No, I mean YEAH! Pardon the pun FUCK YEAH. Help yourself, huh, be my guest. I, I, I... shit I need this just as much as you do! Besides you are so fucking hot!"

Cherish places soft, sensuous kisses Lance on his neck, before sitting up and taking off her tiny blue backpack followed by her tight t-shirt. Exposing her perfect natural breasts for Major's Brown's inviting tongue! Being a modern woman Nefertiti reaches into her stylish blue backpack and brought forth a few condoms.

Without saying a word, she smiled as she puts the tip of the unbroken item between his lips and said.

"Open this for me baby.... "

Major Brown quickly bites into the container freeing the only thing stopping him from getting some!

Cherish leaned forward to kiss Lance's lips as she takes the condom and with the grace of an angel, unrolls the thin lambs' skin down his confused, yet waking shaft.

Cherish had to do an ole fashion- *thumb gently massaging the head of his penis as her fingers worked the shaft*- until Lance's Dong finally wakes up for their private party! Her vagina was already wet with thoughts of the moment she had been planning out in her head.

Nefertiti's moans were so soft, genuine and sweet they completely drove Major Brown fucking wild! Here's one of the reasons the nickname Cherish stuck with Nefertiti; she slowly inserted her moist vagina on top on the head of the pulsating shaft. When her palace accepted the tip of Major Brown's organ, Lance felt like he arrived in HEAVEN. Surprisingly even though the thin condom was supposed to dull Lance's sensation or deem the ability to truly appreciate the wonderful place his penis has ended up. It didn't work for Lance thought to himself this was the best Hump Day he has had in years! Bonus for Cherish held Lance's gaze, their eyes locked in synch much like their hormones.

Nevertheless, Cherish pelvis began riding Lance's rigged member like she invented black cowgirl style!-*By the way she was working it*! Cherish sat back fondling her own breasts for Lance's visual enjoyment for he was trapped in awe with childlike wide-eyed glare. Nefertiti was and still was in some ways a showgirl to her heart! She's adoring the attention and the delight of this abled bodied black man. The room quickly went from smelling of plastic and money to good pussy! Nefertiti removed her fingers from her right breast and placed them on to Lance's lips.

Allowing him to kiss and lick Cherish fingers like they were melting ice cream on a warm summer day! Slowly she smiles as she removed her fingers, then relocated them towards her awaiting clitoris. With the with the expertise of a Russian gymnast, Cherish's turned her body while managing to keep Lance's stiff weapon deep inside her so she may engage in a bit of reverse Cowgirl! Their rhythms mingled in synch, slowly grinding up, down, back and up, up, down, back and up, up down back and up. All awhile her right fingers rub quick tiny circles across the face of her womanly desire. Major Brown's fingers gratefully found that by squeezing Cherishes needy nipples, she would moan appreciatively.

"Oh that my shit... Oh that's how I like it baby!"

As if they were a combo made part by hormones and part by fate Cherish Lance's bodies synchronize, his up strokes gratefully catch her downward thrust. Lance wasn't a virgin, still he might have to confined in his mentor that he's never meet a woman with so much fucking pussy control!

To Cherishes credit, she had been a hardcore Yoga practioner for three years before the infection and danced Ballet and ran track until she college was no longer her calling!

Working in a strip club taught Cherish how to seduce men, women and somewhere in-betweens. Surviving this far in the apocalypse taught Nefertiti it's time to love! She knew with a condom on, that Major Brown probably would not orgasm, this time. Nonetheless that didn't stop her from having one mild one and another not so mild as Cherish fought the urge to scream or yelp for utter fucking joy!

Instead, she moved Lance's hands up to her mouth to muffle her sounds of pleasure as her body shook for an intense several moments. The air was thick with sweat, hormones and good vibes as Cherish rested her head on Lance's heaving chest and she said.

"I know you didn't get to you know finish. Sorry hon, I probably should get back to my little group and you to saying the world. PS, I think you're hot as well!"

Major Brown swallowed hard, nevertheless he's uber aroused and mildly confused. Still, he complies by saying.

"You, you are probably right. I have some wet wipes. Give me a minute to wipe your juices off my boxers."

A glowing Nefertiti's smile was as endearing as treasure chest of chocolate kisses and her dime size dimples made a person wish they could lick'em!

She knew her newfound beau was a bit unsure of what's going on between them, so just like middle school Nefertiti had to tell the boy she like what to do.

"I know this happen so fast. But I like you! Give me your boxers and I will wash them and wear them at night. Just to feel closer to you. Come on give'em up."

Lance kind of smiled as he grunted, "well, I like you too. How many other women you think I let in my twelve million dollar bachelor's pad?"

Cherish chuckled first, followed by a nervous Lance as she replied.

"Yeah right. I've heard about you military types..."

Major Brown replied, "Never judge a book by its cover."

Cherish slightly turned her head so she can kiss Lance on his cheek and whispered.

"The next time, I promise you, it'll all be about you. Boy, I'm gonna make your toes curl."

Lance smiled as he replies, "Remember blowjobs are like rose for men!"

Nefertiti laugh was a wonderfully upbeat sound of acceptance and joy as she counters with.

“Oh, I don’t mind giving my special guy a dozen roses. That’s on the menu much like me sitting on that handsome face of yours. Well, you know, I was thinking about anal! Ahh, you know there’s probably time enough for me to give you a sloppy bouquet.”

In a conventional workplace especially in the **#ME2** era that followed the election of a highly unpopular President. The thought of coworkers dating was generally frowned upon. Because a boss dating a suburbanite always ends in a firing and a lawsuit!

However, when faced with the end of humanity- *rules were taken down several notches as the decades proceed.* - people seem to gravitate towards the underlining motivation that drives our genetic code. Much like the COVID-MOMREL-6 virus, humanity needs to spread itself to be successful!

Colonel Lafayette, being a keen observer of military history, knew that armed people without something or someone to care about might lose their way. So, before they departed Camp McCormick, she did what any commander did best, endure. She asked for volunteers and made it a purpose to appeal to those that felt they didn’t believe anymore.

It wasn’t that the Naval Recruits or the Marines weren’t as loyal as the Regular Army and Air Force personnel that sided with Colonel Lafayette. Windu knew they suffered from horrible leadership. Notwithstanding, she was able to talk 19 Naval and or Marine Personnel to continue to press forward! Plus, it’s not amazing Windu convinced 23 out of the 48 females from Camp McCormick to follow her lead.

Dawn walks around Camp PAYDAY with an escort of several PFCs and SPEC 4 but no officers like Cherish! Yet, nature always had a plan, even so it’s up to you to be open to its possibilities. This time it’s in the form of a tall sort of goofy looking Marine dentist that helps lift Dawn Morehouse's spirits. Captain Belmont – *a 24-year-old hailing from White Chapel New Mexico*- strolled over towards the crowd of young men escorting the seemingly out of place ex stripper around Camp PAYDAY.

To the trained or even untrained eye their procession resembled a pack of wild canines following the only one of their pack that was in heat! Captain Belmont's Native American and Mexican features far outweighed his Caucasian and African American Ancestors! Eilliam's high cheek bones and sharp pointed nose, rested upon a bony 6'3-inch frame.

However, his hair was coarse, and his height can be contributed to his D-League Basketball player father. Even though the seven Military men that are escorting her around were various shades and body types. None was an officer and for whatever reason, Dawn's fragile ego would not let her settle for anything less! Eilliam's Belmont intentions was just to be a gentleman. Being raised by a single mom and his grandmother, Eilliam's accustomed to treating women will the utmost respect.

The enlist men begrudgingly scattered back to their post, leaving Dawn and Eilliam standing by the vending machines. He introduced himself with a deep voice, one that seems out of place for his thin frame.

"Hello, I hope me chasing away your fan club doesn't ruin your visit."

There's something about Eilliam that caught Dawn Morehouse's attention. He's not over handsome like Cherish catch, still he's cute and tall. Dawn so loves a tall man!

Nonetheless the tall- *6'3 – 190 pounds*- skinny man wearing OD green has an unmistaken confidence that Dawn Morehouse has seen once or twice before- *it's called big dick energy*! Tall skinny men, no matter their looks, generally oozes it. It was kind of a reflex action, for Dawn didn't even think about it before happened.

Nevertheless, Dawn's eyes glanced at Eilliam's feet and the index finger on his right hand. Before casting their way up to his groin. Interestingly the imprint sitting plain for the world to bear witness. Human nature or just a girl with a dream automatically persuaded Dawn to flirt.

"Thank you, I'm a woman that prefers quality over quantity. I prefer the quantity to be certified, pure beef, but not an prick about it.."

She knew her words would either shock or entice or both! She waited in silence of the moment, nevertheless the young Marine Dentist who grew up near a reservation in what was once New Mexico was a true cocks' smith. Eilliam's smile was warm and appealing and his long finger slight touches Dawn's shoulder when he leaned forward to whisper in her hear.

"I do understand miss, an on inch here and inch off there makes a big, big difference. I'm not able get rid of an inch or more for anyone, even someone as breath taking as you! So, you either hopefully take every inch of me or none at all."

Dawn let the image of a what Eilliam was promoting flashed through her mental bank. Now she can't but help stare at his package wondering if he's just being a typical guy! Bragging about his penis, before focusing in on his long middle finger on his left hand. Dawn can't help but she slightly licks the corner of her lip before saying.

"I bet you say that to all the pretty Navy girls...."

Marshal Aquila and Colonel Lafayette manage to spend a few moments alone in the quarters she shared with the twins. Robin's eyes pick up on the three cots, coloring books and Barbie dolls scattered around the room. Still when she turns back to look up into Wynolla's brown eye, it's hard to believe the woman she had a one-night stand so long ago was fostering two nine-year-old girls. Even though those same girls hold the cure to their salvation, it was still hard to believe.

Their first kiss must have sealed this consequence, few people that have survived the infection. Those did so with made it with blind luck and a bit of preparation. To manage to find someone that shared a night with seven states away, five years before the infection, can only be called a charitable act of fate!

She leaned forward to give Wynolla a soulful kiss that converges her hopes and dreams of a wonderful tomorrow or just a pleasant right fucking now.

Windu didn't fight it, she found Robin to be the same fireball of emotion, and courage and sex appeal that had her pulling out all the best moves when then met five years ago.

Now her capable hands roamed all over Marshal Aquila's well-toned body. Lips pressing, searching for answers they will never have answered. The heat of passion rising to a boiling point as Robin unbuckles Wynolla's fatigues, letting them fall to the ground, before allowing her to undone Robin's faded blue jeans.

Robin backs up to give Windu a full view of what this booty call has delivered on to her plate! Marshal Aquila is certainly out of uniform when sporting a tiny red thong! She lightly pokes Wynolla in the chest, smiles and lustfully whispers.

"We don't have much time. So, I will give you sixty-nine reasons to lay down on your cot?"

Windu wasn't shocked as much as she's got off guard by the timing for, she replies.

"Whoa my lady, as much as I would love to honor your request. I'm afraid, I need to shower away the sweat that's been pooling around my V J for the last three hours."

Robin smiling as she shimmies out of her faded blue jean skirt before saying.

"Well, I'm glad I'm freshly showered, so if you don't mind, I brought pie..."

She lays down on his cot with her hands firmly placed behind her head, she waited for one entire second before rolling her eyes and saying.

"Soldier! I didn't pilot a vintage Soviet made helicopter all this way just to leave without having at least one semi loud, long orgasm. You can either dive right on in face first or go take a shower so we can have a quickie...

Wynolla smiled giving Robin a half ass salute before saying.

"Well hell, god and country will just gonna to have to wait fifteen maybe twenty minutes."

Marshal Aquila rendered a lustful look towards Colonel Lafayette. When she moved the fabric from in front of her freshly manicured vagina lips, she heard Robin purred like a cute little kitten! Wynolla begins to slowly strip, stepping out of her BDU's, allowing the material to hit the carpet as she said.

"Allow me to reword that, my schedule just opened up for an entire wonderful hour.."

In the meantime, Colonel Lafayette had given John free roam of the work that's being done in the labs. However, it's his encounter with little Deanaa and Hanna sitting at a metal table the taller of the two –*Deana- is playing with a pair of blond Barbies. While her twin sister, Hana-* happens to coloring in a book.

None of the military of civilian personnel seem to be paying them no mind, not even attempting to humor the children by playing any sort of game. John strolls over with a huge non-threatening smile on his face and asks.

"Is this seat taken?"

The taller twin Deanaa cocks her head to look around and then sort of smiles before saying.

"I don't think so. I mean everything belongs to the greenies."

John smiles and inquires.

"The greenies?"

The short of the twin Hanna looks up from coloring to say.

"Colonel Lafayette's friends. They keep us safe."

John nods before asking.

"Does the Colonel take good care of you?"

The one coloring in her book looks up and asked.

"Are you a new Doctor? They only let Doctors in here."

John has the face and demeanor of a kindhearted grandfather, maybe that's the vibe at least one of the twins were picking up.

The other bashes one of her Barbie dolls down hard on the metal table, breaking its arm in the process. She said in a pouting voice.

"I hate doctors, they always poking me with GIANT needles."

John nodded his head in agreement, before he can chime in Hanna injects.

"I hate them too. But they said it will help fight the monsters. Plus, after we get ice cream!"

Her sister never loses the pouting face when she replies.

"I really like ice cream."

John can't help but chuckle has he said.

"Yes, ice cream is yummy for our tummy. What's your favorite flavors?"

One girl screamed, "CHOCOLATE" while the other twin screamed, "STRAWBERRY." Before returning to their separate tasks.

John couldn't help but say, "You two need to be outside playing..."

Both of the girls stopped what they were doing and blankly stared at John like he had said a naught word. Deanaa, the taller of the two was first to whisper.

"We can't play outside..."

Her sister chimes in, "that's where the monsters are silly!"

John nodded his head in agreement then suggests.

"Where I'm from the few children we have go outside at least once a day. Just so they can play under the sun."

The mention of other kids, nearly made both of the little girls lose their minds in sheer excitement. As their mouths drop open to show their shock and disbelieve, the twins said in unison.

"Whoa! You got kids?"

The older twin Deanaa makes a joke, "Where are you from, the moon?"

John laughed as he said, "you know sometimes it feel like I do."

A few hours later the Helicopter ride to Shangri-La has two more passengers. John asked Colonel Lafayette could Deanaa and Hanna do a sleep over and meet a few other children. For her credit, Wynolla didn't think twice before saying yes! The news that Robin's father brought to the table gave the survivors a bit of hope.

Plus, it didn't hurt that Marshal Aquila has recently helped release a great deal of pent-up tension with the Colonel. Besides with the twins' safe and out of the line of fire, Windu knew she could get on the hunt for that madman Lee! Even if that meant returning to Great Lakes Naval Base to raid their probably still intact armory.

Yes, when the task force originally left to establish Camp McCormick, they loaded up on small arms ammo, 50 Caliber belts, C4 and frag grenades. Still, they didn't grab any artillery shells, missiles or any stun grenades. If Lee somehow managed to not only survive infection and can now somehow communicate with RAGERS! The good Colonel Lafayette knew Lee must be captured or quickly killed! Either one was on the table.

No matter where Doctor Hammond's serum may lead. The question of Jefferson Bullraguard Lee's fate belongs to the US Army! Furthermore, Wynolla needed to prepare in order to put that son of a bitch in her cross hairs and finish his crazy ass off for good. So, this time Wynolla planned to rip out Jefferson's spinal tissue for good measure!

Later that night John sat alone in his lab staring at the batch of potential serum being spun in his centrifuge. He was so deep in thought he didn't hear Earl and Ernesto when they entered the lab. Truth to be told if they didn't want to be heard, both men have the capability to be quitter than a cat! However, that didn't last for long because the pair are exchanged in a deep conversation as Ernesto said.

"Mi amigo, chicks, even if they have a pena are very complicated! We both live with people that see the world through the eyes of their twats or bungholes. It's a very confusing time to say the least."

Earl's tone reflects he's in a sort of torment that has never felt before.

"I, I never suspected being in a threesome relationship could be so difficult! Semaj my chocolate queen is as easy going and huggable as they come."

Ernesto could not help but ask.

"How's the head?"

Earl cocked his head in a weird fashion before giving a quick two thumbs up then saying.

"It is like getting blown by cotton candy on Christmas."

Ernesto nodded cool, then enquired.

"So, I guess it's Paradise that's giving you fits?"

That's when Big John looked up with a faint smile on his face. When his two comrades see the look on his face. The two men shelf their conversation, pull up a couple of rolling stools so they can sit down in front of their friend.

Earl's slow Southern drawl breaks the stillness, "Hammond, what the heck's going on?"

John sighs, "Well I have to make a decision that might cost me, everything."

Ernesto asks, "Cost you want? Is it the Army doings?"

Before he could answer Earl asked, "Or does it concern Indigo?"

Big John Hammond chuckled as he said.

"Who would have thought we would have made it this far? From Death Row to Shangri-La, that's an amazing feat. Right?"

Earl's tone was not frightening, more likely a worried loved one.

"My dear John Hammond whatever has you in such a funk?"

When the pinging sound of the centrifuge signaled the process was complete John looked at the medical equipment, then to his friends before saying.

"I am 98% sure I just created a vaccine against the COVID-MOMREL-6 Virus."

It takes several moments before the speechlessness wears off as Ernesto states.

"Shouldn't we be celebrating or something? Vaccine is good news, Si?"

Earl on the other hand was a bit more cautious when he said.

"How does your vaccine work my friend?"

John let out a slight smile as he began.

"The COVID-MOMREL-6 virus was mashup of six separate diseases."

Ernesto was wise enough to say, "Which virus raises can raise the dead?"

John does his best to explain by replying.

"The measles virus combined with the Ophiocordyeeps or the Zombie Ant Virus and the Taiwanese Lecuco-Hloridium parasite will enable the continuing of electrical sparks being sent to the cortex and at the base of the brain stem. Which causes the repletion part of our brains to continue and provide basic motor functions."

Earl had to ask his friend.

"Are you telling us your vaccine will stop the dead from returning?"

John sadly shakes his head no, as he rises to gather the vials of serum out of his centrifuge.

"No sadly, no. In theory this serum will make the living seem like them. Like we are no different than the dead or the RAGERS. Hopefully it acts like camouflage, we just learn how to blend in from here on out."

Earl stood as he asks, "What do you mean like we would be invisible to their eyes, their noses and of course their ears?"

As Ernesto stood up asking, "Actually, what do you mean by in theory?"

John reached into the white centrifuge, pulling out six vials before saying.

"By in theory I mean I need to test this serum out before knowing if it works. And yes, if it works, we would be invisible to the infected as well as the dead. The virus will not see us as a host anymore, but kindred. Right now, that's about the best we can hope for."

Ernesto slowly asks, "So who do you plan to test this on? Here's a thought, let the Army test it out first!"

Earl's nearly three inches taller than John so he looked down in his friends' eyes and saw the unspeakable truth,

"You plan to test it on yourself? NO, no, no my friend you can't do that. We need you man! All of this wouldn't be here without you, John! Please, let the Army test it."

John felt the genuine concern for his life from one of the most notorious serial killer America has ever created, he places his hand on Earl's broad right shoulder then said.

"Thank you my friend and you are one of my dearest friends Earl. Who would have thought being on Death Row would have bought us together, but it did! Besides, you and Ernesto will lead if I fall.

Nevertheless, I will not ask anyone to do this! If I made even the slightest mistake... Well, it would certainly end up with a bullet to someone's head. I, I figure it might as well be mine."

John turned and prepared a syringe for himself as he said.

"I asked you down here to take care of me. You know just in case I turn."

John uses the needle to withdraw 20 CCs of the reddish liquid. He put down the syringe for a brief second to grab an alcohol swab. He turned back to find Ernesto with the serum in his hand and Paradise standing in the doorframe.

John and Ernesto don't have to wait for Paradise and Earl to work some things out. Because she pushed past the big man to speak directly with Dr Hammond. Before she could speak, John greets Paradise.

"Hello Paradise, I guess you heard some of what was said."

Paradise offers a fake sort of smile as she replies.

"I came in around the part of you saying this might mask us from the infected and you need a test dummy... Ok! I accept."

That stunned every-*fucking*-one, leaving Earl nearly speechless, Ernesto can only look on with a puzzled look on his face, as Big John does his best to deny her request.

"No, no, no Paradise you don't understand. This could kill you or anyone of us, I just don't know! I don't have any mice or rabbits to test this out on. This could be a one-way ticket to the grave."

Ernesto pointed out. "And maybe back out again!"

Earl's tone was soft yet firm when he said. "No, you will not."

Paradise stood back striking a pose with her hands on her slender hips, the young Transwoman said.

"You're not the boss of me and you don't owe me Earl. I might love, but you don't owe me. Nobody owns me! I choose to do this!"

Earl calmly replied but this time with a slight bit of anger, "I never said I did, because I thought you understood the difference! What I do, what we all have done is because we care for each other. This very well could be the end of humanity, so the bonds we form, have real meaning."

Paradise paused for only a quick moment before replying, "Then why do you plan to take this magic potion Earl? Or will it be you, Ernesto? I know you both will feel the need to volunteer to be with your friends at all costs to those around you!"

Earl held open his masses arms and waited, Paradise hesitated, she pouts for a bit before melting into his arms crying.

"Why Earl, why do you want to leave me too?"

John extended his hand towards Ernesto gesturing for his serum, slowly his friend hands it over. John nodded his head thanks then said.

"There's something I found out when I was at Camp PAYDAY."

Paradise looked up and out of Earl's massive pecks as John told the story of the one, they say can command the RAGERS. This Horde of death and insanity was like an unguided missile causing havoc wherever it lands! Giving alarm to the thought of what kind of madman could control the army of the purely insane?

"So, you see why I need to test the serum? If this type of man exists, he must be stopped. Or at least captured and studied."

Ernesto weighed the thought before saying, "It might be like how you say, getting rid of Hitler when he was still a baby, huh?"

John nodded his head yes, yet it was Earl that provided the path yet followed.

"It has to me or Ernesto, John you understand that. You can't sacrifice yourself..."

Before he could finish, John injected, "If any of us are going to survive this. Great sacrifice will be called upon us."

Paradise's voice was squeaky, still her words ring true as rain.

"The key word is US, right?"

Big John looked at the trio gathered in his lab, and he could feel that not only their intentions, but their hearts were in the right place. As much as he wanted to find fault in Earl's logic, he couldn't. So, he prepares another syringe, the first one for either Earl or Ernesto and the second one for whoever was willing to accept it.

Over one hundred miles away, the smell, sounds and fabric around what was once a military installation gives way to only one impression. DEATH! The numbers of Zombies lumbering around the area are beyond counting. The Army of Jefferson Bullraguard Lee, took the Air Force Reserve Station without much trouble. Women, men and children were not spare the chance to be reborn as either an evolved RAGERS or his army of the dead.

Shortly after Lee organized his RAGER force into cleaning the road of unmanned vehicles, pushing and pulling the obstructions from his path. Lee must have envisioned Caesar's march to Rome, where his legions return from battle to put the Senate on fucking notice!

When Jefferson found the helicopter, sadly, it didn't work. He contemplates his next move, while sitting in the pilot's seat of a decommissioned helio. His tone, at times bizarrely rational, even if he is clinically insane.

"I don't have the pieces to make this work. That means that the living may control the air, nonetheless I will control everything under the sky!"

Lee exited the aircraft, flanked by a dozen of the more evolved RAGERS. His variation of the virus hadn't affected all RAGERS the same. Fresh kills seem to absorb larger amounts of whatever Bullraguard was emulating, persevering a larger percentage of memories and basic motor skills. They followed behind him, along with some of the former Air Force Reservist and their infected families.

Clouds roll in overhead as Jefferson looked up towards the sky, while his personal RAGER escorts made sure the shambling Dead Heads don't wander too close with well-placed kicks to their decaying bodies. Or an energized blow to their rotten skulls! Lee's gaze fixed on his evolved RAGERS cleaning the path to Chicago. There he will find Colonel Lafayette and avenge his honor, Jefferson thought as he barked orders.

"That's it! Clear the path to Damascus! We will conqueror this land and all that possess it! No matter how long it takes you will clear me a path and using your strength, I will see my enemies cowering in fear before ME! In turn I shall provide you a buffet of pain and horror to feed your hunger!"

His audience gave Lee a series of grunts, groans and even a few cheers as they go about their task. Allowing early autumn rain to spew on the labor force without even a notice of awareness of its behalf.

Chapter III:

LOVE, LOVE WILL KEEP US TOGETHER, BABY FOREVER.

When Paradise grabbed the first syringe no one attempted to stop her. Her eyes locked with Earl's, and he must have read his woman's mind when he nodded his head yes. To a question that only they understood. Still, Ernesto did take a slight step back, while his keen eyes scanning the room for something sharp and pointy!

Earl on the other hand, reached down and grabbed one of the remaining syringes then said.

"If this goes horribly wrong, bury me near the outdoor weed garden. I think I would enjoy the smell of that."

Big John's face forced a smile as he said. "I don't think there will be any adverse side effects. Nevertheless, I just what to thank you for trusting my science."

Paradise has but one question, "how long will this, I mean your vaccine last?"

John shrugged his shoulders, signaling he had no idea.

Thirty minutes after their vaccination, Earl and Paradise equipped themselves to venture out among the locals. Semaj didn't take their volunteering in stride! When the young attractive ebony Transwoman broke down crying, her father's features were clearly defined. Nonetheless, the other parts of Semaj's love triangle embrace their crying member in a warm cocoon of genuine acceptance and most all love!

Both test subjects left Shangri-La armed with two semi-automatic handguns, one fully automatic assault rifle-both equipped with suppressors, 440 rounds= fifteen clips and a short sword. Ten days' worth of food, and water rations per person, 56 grams of weed per person, two CB radios, a red Subaru Forester-4x4 with a full tank of gas and two filled twenty-gallon gas cans.

Surviving the Apocalypse does have its advantages, in most cases real estate can be had for the low, low, low cost of nothing! Hence you don't get bitten by the dead, beaten to death or raped into a comma by RAGERs. Anything you couldn't afford is now just there for the taking!

Plus, you are free to be whoever you want to be, even if that's a motherfuckin Menace To Society! The happy couple found the red Subaru Forester was the perfect vehicle for traveling through and around the long parade of stalled cars.

The highway resembled a dead multi appendage orgasm running for miles upon miles upon miles! The four-wheel drive allowed Paradise to maneuver their transport off road and the couple couldn't be happier. Earl noticed that for the first time in over three weeks, he was witnessing Paradise, smile! He picked up a bag of CDs- *music storage devices*- thumbed through the bag until he finds the one that for him seals this moment. ***First Choice- Let No Man Put Asunder***.

The music was lively, upbeat and reflects its time- 1983, Paradise bob's her head as the music takes controls and she lip synchs the words

"It's not a perfect love, but I'll defend it, because I believe this is what fate intended. We got a love that, too, too good to throw away. Hey, it's not over between you and me, it's not over..."

Earl held out his hand and Paradise cheerfully wrapped her long thin fingers around his chubby digits as they both take took lip synching and having a great start to their day trip.

" *Baby , awww shucks honey let me tell you something.*"

Earl picked up the chorus, "Honey *let me tell you something..*"

Paradise chimed in a sassy, sexy tone, *"Now they call me an Aquarius. You know what that means?"*

Big Bad Earl Grimes was smiling like a kid, just like the time he caught his Grandfather dressed at Santa Claus going down on his grandmother.

Paradise sort of rolls her hips in his direction, laughing as she down shifts to avoid the shambling undead as they crawl out from of every abandon dwelling, stalled vehicle, gully or bloody stump positively tearing themselves from under huge rocks.

"See I got something you don't ever want to turn down. Understand what I'm talking about baby?"

Earl mouthed, " *aww shucks, aww shucks..*"

Paradise uses her right hand to stroke his face as she counters with, "I *got something for your mind, body and soul, every day of our lives..*"

Earl took Paradise's slender hand, brings her palm to his lips and providing a passionate kiss to one of his ladies. Most of all Earl was glad to see the shine back in Paradises brown eyes. As the song plays, she whispered the hook.

"I got something for your mind, your body and your soul. Come get you some boy, come get you some boy, come get you some boy, come on and get you some boy. Let no man asunder Let no man asunder."

Being they took the more scenic route; it took the happy couple nearly two hours to traverse the eighteen miles to downtown St. Charles Illinois. The smell of decay, festering garbage and raw sewage can't compare with the smell of nearly forty thousand walking corpses and their twelve thousand insane RAGER comrades!

Their little drive through pastures, gullies, roads and streams would have made a great pre-Apocalypse commercial. Instead, the red Subaru was like little Red Riding Hood attracting all the neighborhood riffraff in its wake!

Paradise parked their fiery steed in front of the public library as unwanted company was quickly closing in on their happy moment.

Paradise leans over, bringing her face inches from Earl's before loving said.

"Whatever happens, I, I just want to thank you for seeing this through with me."

Earl gave Paradise a soft long kiss on her thin lips before saying.

"I knew I couldn't stop you from embarking on this course. Instead, I wanted to support you."

She kissed him back, another slow, long full kiss on Earl's thick lips. Paradise moves her nose so she's able to rub it gently across Earl's before saying.

"You know this could be our last hurrah. Maybe we should..."

Paradise nodded her head to the back seat as her left hand tries to unzip Earl's size 46 inch jeans. Earl kissed Paradise harder this time and considers her offer. When the noises of several pair of hands banging of the roof of the vehicle alters the mood. Earl took Paradise's head in his meaty hands and whispers.

"Now it's time for you to listen! I could blame the way I used to be on my upbringing. You must understand I wasn't raised to express myself in a positive nature. I was raised by the lash. That was then, today I've never had more than I have now! So, when I exit this car and if Hammond's syringe fails to perform as promised. I need you to drive away."

He doesn't wait for Paradise to answer, Earl kisses her one more time and zips his pants. Before grabbing his weapon, his backpack and stepping out into the crowd of RAGERS and Dead Heads. Inside the red Subaru, Paradise fought the urge to leap out of the driver's side door right after him. Guns raging, let fucking fate be dammed! Fear, anger and then guilt finally all swoop down on Paradise like birds on wounded prey.

She saw the shadows and shapes crowding around Earl, their constant moaning and groaning makes Paradise cover her ears and bury her head into the steering wheel! It felt like forever, before she looked up and turned the car back on. Suddenly the door was snatched open, and Earl looked in with a huge smile on his face nodding for her to shut it off and follow him.

The next forty minutes Earl and Paradise causally strolled from the library to several of the remaining non burning or burnt structures. Which includes what's left of a Cracker Barrel Restaurant, sure all the contents were either spoiled or ransacked. Even so the package candy isle was mostly intact! A gaggle of Zombies and RAGERs stumble through the room as Paradise and Earl slowly entered the establishment. And the first of many smells to reach their nose happened to be the one of rotten vegetables. Followed by unattended moldy food, then the unmistakable smell of the Dead!

Nevertheless, that doesn't stop Paradise or Earl from enjoying themselves. Neither talked, instead they communicated using simple hand gestures and head motions. Not surprisingly just as John Hammond designed it, his vaccine rendered the dual partially for of the club. Dead Heads stumble towards them, before veering off at the last instant to give chase to whatever stoked the virus; need to spread. RAGERs provide them a hard look, but without the intent to take their action to that of murder, death, kill level.

Most if not all of St. Charles Illinois has been reduced to either rumble from numerous explosions of gas lines or unattended fires. Or that from the violence that only unsurely mobs or living can bestow upon an area. Nonetheless, the complete destruction only a Zombie Holocaust springing from the mouths of babies, wives and husbands alike could bring has still very much active.

One of the few remaining structures left standing was a four-star Hotel chain made famous for it started in out on the West Coast, in Hollywood! Earl had always wanted to eat in their café, however his long incarceration didn't allow for work release or delivery to death row. RAGERs roamed among the broken glasses and shattered dreams of those caught in the wave of infection that swept humanity into the arms of its own extinction.

By now the expensive carpet was ripe, wet with mold, dried blood and filled with tiny rode blocks of hardened rodent poo! Paradise wanted to wince as she did her best to step over the mounds of debris in her path. But any sound other than moans, grunts, snarls and shouts may not be received well.

Earl led the way and for a burly man was surprisingly light on his feet, avoiding and dodging anything bearing down on the couple. He headed to the registration desk, finding dried splats of blood and tiny pieces of desiccated organs spread across the counter! Earl's quick eyes scanned for the keys in their intended slots.

Out of the corner of her eye Paradise noticed a rather sad sight. A slender Transgender Zombie, shambling about in a ripped dress missing parts of its stomach and thighs. Remarkably, the penis was still intact! It was hanging in front of the dead corpse's bloody dress; the sight made Paradise turn her face in disgust and a bit of fear of fate!

Earl's big broad smile, signaled he had found what he's looking for. The swamp of walking corpses made it difficult to move through the isle. Nevertheless, Earl used the pointy end of his machete to gently usher the dead out of their path. While heading for the stairs Paradise fought the overwhelming urge to cry!

All this death forced her to ponder about people in her life she hadn't seen in years. Their faces flashed into her mind's eye and Paradise must focus on her footing as she made her way up the humid, dark stairwell. Using flashlights to light their way, it took more than twelve minutes to reach the tenth floor.

For whatever reason the tenth floor had a large amount of smeared human waste spread across walls. While mostly eaten corpses litter the hallway, some even reanimated waving their boney hands towards whatever moved their way. Stepping over piles of luggage, Earl and Paradise both wondered if their owners ever made it out of the building.

When they passed a maid's card with a ring or keys and plenty of towels and soap. Earl makes it his business to snatch the ring of keys and Paradise snagged the towels as three RAGERS exit the room directly across from the one Earl was using the master key- since the electric card readers were useless *it was back to old fashion keys.*

Luck had it that the massive suite had not been touched since the maid shift cleaned it before their world crumbled.

As Earl entered first followed quickly by Paradise and she swiftly locked the door behind them. The sliding glass door that led to the balcony was closed nevertheless the curtains are wide open and the mini bar was thankfully stocked! Earl's first to say in a low enough whisper that only Paradise should hear.

"Feels like this is our first date.."

He reached his massive hand into the mini bar and pulled out two bottles of water and a couple pack of gingerbread cookies. Paradise accepted, with a semi smile she replies.

“I generally tip twenty percent. Anyway, are you sure we should stay here for the night?”

Earl puts his pack down, before carrying a brown wooden chair to jam under the door’s handle. Sticking his head into semi dark bathroom, Earl noticed the rack of towels tidally placed for the next customer. Earl Grimes knew a thing about sound proofing rooms on the cheap. Quickly jamming the towels under the doorframe, followed by flipping over the mattress of one of two queen size beds.

Earl placed the mattress across the door frame and settled down to be with Paradise in the other room. As Paradise sat on the edge of the other bed; she took out a porcelain marijuana pipe. Like an expert her nibble fingers packed a bowl, as Earl took the time to remove a SAMSUNG phone and a pair of ear buds from his pack and whisperd to Paradise.

“I think II have the right song for this moment.”

The faint sunshine that was, gave the room a warm orange hue. Earl and Paradise sit on the unused hotel bed and placed the right ear bud into her slender ear canal. Paradise tilts her head to accept it as she fires up her bowl of 100% Sativa. When ***Michael Jackson’s THRILLER*** started up. “Darkness falls across the land..”

Paradise nearly coughs out all the pungent marijuana smoke she intended to hold in her lungs. Earl laughs as Paradise can’t help but chuckle as the song plays, she said.

“really?”

Before packing another bowl and handling it to Earl, who gratefully accepted as they both hum along with the classic Halloween themed song. Earl’s powerful lungs forced the embers of the pure

Sativa to burn brighter. Paradise stares as Earl held his breath until his eyes begin to water, then slowly lets the smoke exit his nose.

He hands the weed pipe back to his companion and scrolls to the next song. **Etta James- At Last**. When Earl a rose, his huge frame towered over the 26 year old transwoman, yet she felt no fear! He held out his hand signaling let's dance, as the slow music began. Paradise doesn't stand, as much as stood up in a posture that oozed so much goddam sex appeal! And the song played on...

"At last, my love has come along. My lonely days are over, and life is a song. Oh yeah, oh yeah at last my skies are sunny and no longer blue..."

Paradise nestled her head into one of the least celebrated serial killers of the old world and feels good about it! The couple moved in a nice slow n back and forth rhythmic motion as the music continued.

"My heart was wrapped in a clover, the moment I looked at you. At last, at last, at last, my love has come along, our lonely days are over and my life is a song..."

Back inside the control center at Shangri-La, Big John's on the SAT-phone having a conversation with former resident Indigo Roberson at her new home at one of the last Global Security and Logistics LLC outpost in North America.

His demeanor was certainly upbeat much like talking to a long-lost friend, as he listened to Indigo's reply.

"You mean, Earl Grimes is out in the wild with Paradise?"

John sort of chuckled as he replies, "yes for nearly two days now."

Indigo paused before asking. "How, how do you know that they are still alive?"

From anyone else John Hammond might have taken the question as an insult to his ability to run a controlled experiment! Nevertheless, he fielded the question from Indigo has genuine concern for either the dual or his vaccine.

"I know they are alive because I spoke to them both an hour ago. They check in every three hours. As of fifty minutes ago they were still staying in the Honeymoon Suite at Hard Rock Café & Casino in St. Charles!"

He could hear the marvel in her voice as John images her forehead wrinkling up as she fought to unravel a mystery, Indigo inquires.

"John you are telling me you made a vaccine, how?"

The scientist in Hammond's proud to discuss his finding! Even though the jury is still out on GS & L, John knew they are probably one of the few still standing labs with the potential to make quantity of his serum. Even so, he paused an uncomfortably long amount of time. Forcing Indigo to clear her throat as she tried to explain.

"I, I want to thank you for saving my life. I, I know I probably can never return to Shangri-La again...."

She paused leaving the door open for John to step in, which he sighed a deep sigh or regret before saying.

"Yeah, my daughter is still working though her grief, I hope she may be passed it by now. However, I have no idea where Paradise's head's at!"

This time it's Indigo's time to sigh as she said. "And she has the ear and heart of the big bad wolf, so that is that."

John smoothly changes the subject by saying. "None of that matters, my vaccine works at least so far. That's what you and your cohorts at GS&L should be focusing on the data drop your people can pick up from Colonel Lafayette."

Indigo huffed and scoffed at the words, "Co-Horts? That's a bit..."

She decided not to finish what she was thinking because in fact John's words were not harsh enough!

Changing the subject, Indigo stuck to the science behind the serum.

"What, I meant is how did you do it?"

"One of the key components of this virus is how the genetically modified Rabies virus hijacks our immune system forcing it to ramp up our adrenaline."

Indigo chimed in, "Yes I see on the data drop you just sent how it enlarges our brain around three hours after intimal infection."

John was so happy to be sharing his knowledge with at least someone who got it as well as someone he's at least familiar with. Well, that made him smile before saying.

"Yes, you are right! The fever attacks our hemoglobin forcing it to explode on a cellular level!"

Indigo chimes in, "Yes I see and it's the Ebola virus which assists in the rapid spread of infection! Yet, how does the Zombification start?"

John paused a second before saying, "I suspect it's how the Necrotizing effects of the Ophiocordyeeps and LeucoHLoridium combining with the other viruses on a micro cellular level. The modified Rabies enlarges the brain, so the brain is still working after death."

Indigo giggled before saying, "And as we can see that's not good. Still how does your vaccine work?"

John proudly states, "did you know that Octopod can repair their own DNA, rewriting it as they go?"

Indigo pauses before saying. "No, I mean yes, I've heard that before. Are you telling me, you used Octopus DNA in your serum?"

John's assured that he has at least a knowledgeable and personable ear to bend his theories on. Not that the former CDC and WHO doctors at Camp PAYDAY have been anything but professional and friendly. They just aren't someone he had considered a friend! John continues by proudly saying,

"Yes, I did! It allowed me to rewrite the virus just enough that I could extract properties that mask us as being infected..."

Indigo's voice showed the respect as she said, "But it removes the side effects of the infection? John that's brilliant! If I was there, I would give you the biggest hug..."

She hesitated, knowing that returning to Shangri-La was out of the question for now and maybe forever! John was sensing the hurt and pain in the tone of her voice as Indigo goes on to say.

"I've, I've never killed any, anything before. I cry just about every night, I, I see Sky's face as I turn to see her holding her throat. The dark red blood flowing freely from under her clenched fingers."

As a friend John can only listen, knowing anything he said would confuse the matter. Instead, he let a few movements pass, before clearing his throat and then said.

"Time heals most wounds and if that doesn't work. I strongly recommend a joint of Indica and a decent glass of red wine every day until it no longer hurts as much..."

Meanwhile a hundred miles away, the RAGERS infected by Lee's mutation have regained a certain amount of brain power, hence one of them figured that tying ropes around the dead would help them haul abandon cars from the highway. Those who decaying bodies will not be split into bloody halves by the force of heavy labor will have nonstop workload running all day and of course all night. Lee's horde has been clearing four miles a day! Now with this innovation pushing, pulling and prying tens of thousands of pounds of personal motor vehicles, commercial transport and military vehicles off the beaten track. The road to Chicago seemed less further than a week ago.

Overturned Semi Trucks positioned to clog congested highways are no match for tens of thousands of Dead heads put to good use! If the RAGERS had been interested in illicit black-market goods like kilos of cocaine, heroin, flat screen television, fireworks or cigarettes. They would have hit the fucking jack pot, one hundred times over!

For among the long-ago gallons of melted ice cream, broken eggs, dead cattle and smashed smart televisions. Laid shipments of firearms that were headed towards the border, which make a far better prize for Lee's Red Army than cocaine. For RAGERs on god's GO-GO powder is a sight no one really wants to experience!

Lee's mutation was spreading from RAGER to the next host and then to another RAGER. The army of the insane was growing in numbers that will be hard for any standing structure to withstand. There are probably thirty thousand Zombies in an area. Quietly mingling with eight thousand unevolved RAGERs in the area! However, there were at least sixteen hundred evolved RAGERS in that same area. Each one that comes in contact with a unevolved RAGER, gives off a dose of the Lee's mutation of COVID-MOMREL-6 virus. Somehow, it's able be passed to the next unaffected host. Completing the circle or life, sorry I mean death!

It's the ninth day of Earl and Paradise quest, their SUV was still in decent condition, so they started driving west on old country roads. Paradise had so much fun holding her head out the window. She was much like a French Poodle on a brisk autumn day, lapping up sunshine and insects to boot! Earl had no idea where he was going, he's just following the path of least resistance.

Much like a pack of mangy junk yard dogs chasing a loud delivery truck, the Dead Heads gave chase, tripping, and falling while doing their best to keep up with the mere 35 mph Earl was doing in the Red Subaru Forester.

When Paradise stuck her head back inside smiling, and Earl knew it was time to pop the question.

"Now we know Big Joh's serum works very well, why don't we take off and see what's left of America?"

Paradise fired up her bowl, she took a long drag, held it for a moment, before coughing cheerfully she chimed in.

"Cool, we could stay in every Governor's mansion across the land. Raiding weed dispensaries as we go..."

Earl added on with, "We could also head to Hollywood and find the Movie Stars we used to hate, now as Zombies, then kill them."

Paradise handed Earl a freshly packed bowl as she unzipped his cargo shorts.

Earl Grimes might have been the template when it comes to serial killers- *loner, obese, white and male*. Even so he's above average in one accord. His penis length is over seven inches with a waistline of 42 inches- *which was down from 46 1/2.*

Paradise took a wet wipe from her pack and apologies for it being cold. Earl never misses a beat by saying.

"If this is going where I think it's going, cleanliness is next to; oh my god it's in thy mouth said the altar boy to the Priest!"

Paradise's voice dripped with lust, " Baby, I was an altar boy."

Earl's tone responded in the same lustful nature, "My child, I wanted to be a priest. Did you know a14th century Pope was once heard saying that happiness was best served covered in baby oil and on thy knees?"

Paradise not to be outdone in their verbal wordplay responded in that spoiled hottie voice that turns men on by saying.

"I'm sorry, Father. Mary mother of God, may I reach heaven by taking part of the bread of, Earl..."

She never finished her rhyme as Paradise's warm mouth engulfed Earl's- *semi hard, cleanly wiped* -penis into her willingly orifice. He began humming, **Do You Know The Way To San Jose**.

Fun Fact; Paradise has had a male organ willingly sliding in and out of her mouth since she was fourteen and if Semaj's head game was like really like fucking warm, sticky cotton candy? Well Paradise was like a warm bath engulfing a hard organ in Hoover vacuum cleaner! It wasn't that Paradise couldn't give bomb head. No, it was like, now she had a reason to care, that the other person involved in said action was at least being entertained. She gave Earl a reason to not be Chicken Head and he gave Paradise a reason to finally believe in love!

Three months ago, Earl's then massive gut would not have allowed him to accept road head. Now at nearly eighty pounds lighter, his dick looked like a pale rapier impaling her face over and over and over fucking again! Ps, they were both, loving it.

Earl had to slow down to nearly 10 mph in order to stop from hitting a bump and having his cock ram the back of Paradise's throat. The long line of shambling dead fought hard among each other to see which caught their prey first! The feel of Earl in her mouth makes Paradise's own penis stiff, with thoughts of bending he massive man over once more to impact his small intestine with the love of her slender gay, Jesus!

However, it's what the road beheld in front of them gives caused for Earl to slow their vehicle to a slow and steady halt. The curious tone of Earl's voice adds with his patting her softly on the back of her head, forcing Paradise to retract the erect penis from her mouth resembling the smacking sound of a wet blow pop!

"Paradise my love, I, I think this is something you sound see with your own green eyes."

A Zombie train of sorts, in the form of three lines of Dead Heads hauling a flotilla of RAGERS atop an empty flatbed of a semi-trailer. More than that, the sound of other RAGERS screaming PULL. PULL from the police car they happen to be driving was, different. Paradise used the back of her hand to swipe the saliva from her red lips, before muttering.

"Well, now I have seen everything my dream board told me I would see!"

Paradise chuckled before giving Earl a passionate kiss, then asked.

"Shouldn't we report this to Hammond or the Army?"

As Earl contemplates his answer, Paradise uses the time to replace her ruby red lipstick.

Earl pointed to the parade flotilla approaching them. The sight of infected RAGERs standing on top of luxury RV's barking orders to their elk was a bit frightening. While Dead Heads were used to haul stalled Semi Tractor Trailers off to the side of the road was more than frightening. For the implications further pushes humanity of the face of the planet.

She licked her thin lips, kissed Earl on his cheek and seemingly purred like a spoiled sexy cat, "Well, I can see what could be considered more important than me giving you the best road head I have ever given!"

Back at Camp Pay Day Colonel Lafayette has been busy the last few weeks. Her small force has been able to liberate HEAT seeking missiles and high caliber enriched tracer ammo from Great Lakes Naval Base. Which now belonged to either RAGERS or the dead! Even with the knowledge the Sailor assigned to the armory provided. The sheer volume of walking hazards made the mission problematic!

The amount of fuel used up while luring large herds of the infected away for the building they needed to enter was indeed costly. Nevertheless, in the end, Windu' s birds loaded up twenty missiles to be divided among her five aircraft. Along with seven thousand rounds of ammo. However, the sight of some many undead children walking around in diapers combined with their constant moans of hunger. Nearly made even the proudest warrior break down in tears. Everyone understood in some way or fashion that Lee was the cause of all this suffering! Great Lakes Naval Station was his command.

These poor souls were his charge, naval families trusted in command and command failed them! Slinking away in the middle of the night like the coward they were. Damm them to hell, both Dunston and Lee she thought. Colonel Lafayette and Major Brown made good on their heist, even so the memory of the aftermath of that failure will linger with them for days to come.

Meanwhile back at Shangri-La, it's been over twelve days since John's first trial of his vaccine had been successful applied in the field. By all accounts Doctor Hammond's work has been a success! He has been busy developing the next generation of his wonder drug, when his daughter called him to the COMMS Center.

It didn't take long for John to ascend the five flights to their COMM center. Robin handed her father a cup of coffee and then said.

"Dad, Earl has something to tell you."

His voice was strong, and Earl was using his words like he's painting a landscape for all to witness in its horror.

“My friend on the road once traveled, Paradise and I happen upon a Wildman living among RAGERS. Half dressed in military fatigues, wearing sunglasses and what looks like the head of a still blinking woman for a hat! The eyes of the hat roll and move around taking in all the surroundings with nothing to say about the sights they behold. I have glared in many of mirrors on countless days zeroing in that I was among the poster children for what crazy looked like. Well John, today I must admit I was wrong!”

The sight of a flotilla of RVs, Semi flatbeds and school buses being ferried by the Dead was surreal. In practical terms, the Dead were being used like slaves of old. Thousands of stinking, decomposing’s, shuffling and moaning death merchants have been harnessed and put to general labor. Paradise was first to crack a joke.

“I guess that’s how Egyptians made the pyramids.”

Earl counters with, “I’m sure they’re not all Jews. Nonetheless I get your point. Watching this reminds me of an Aryan I met behind bars.”

Paradise frowns up her pretty pug nose and then said.

“Phew, I hate Nazis! Cheap meth using bastards.”

Earl nodded his melon size head in agreement and continued. “This guy was obsessed with Zombies. So much so while on a meth inspired beige, ole Zeb killed and ate the poor Hispanic post woman who delivered his mail. Then his Polish Neighbor and an Asian delivery boy! Well to make a long story short, he swore he was vegan before that day...”

That’s when Lee and Earl locked glares! Even though Earl could not see his eyes, Chicken Head knew the look of pure insanity when he laid eyes upon it.

From Lee’s POV he took notice of two noninfected people standing among the sea of death and nothing was going out of its way to beat, rape, murder or eat them! Which in this environment, was strange.

Earl whispered to Paradise to make sure John heard what was going on around them. Seconds later hundreds of armed RAGERS bum rush towards the couple, encircling Earl and Paradise! The foul Army was grunting and pointing their weapons in their general direction. However, the lot seemed a bit confused! John's vaccine worked, so they are not actually sure want they are pointing weapons at.

Paradise and Earl stood VERY STILL, as Paradise kept her thumb on the receiver of the ham radio. Earl talked even more slowly than usual, yet very loudly.

"Hello there ole boy! I'm Earl and this is Paradise. I see you rather enjoy traveling like Pharaoh! Good for you. Which way are you heading?"

Lee leapt off the top of the RV and landed like a cat hoping to sneak up on its prey. Slowly he rose, cracking his neck so loud it resembled a clap of thunder! Jefferson Bullraguard Lee pushed through his sea of insanity until he was standing mere inches from the massive Earl Grimes. Lee was at least three inches shorter, even so at that moment, he was four levels crazier than Earl!

The two quickly get into a pissing contest, neither saving a word. Charging the already tense atmosphere. It was Lee who broke the silence by saying.

"Strange you stand in front of me, alive and not infected. Yet my flock has not harmed yee."

Earl's slow Southern draw delivers the right line, however to the wrong man.

"My father was a Jehovah Witness, a real fire brand of Preacher. Yep, my father was fond of savings, small miracles are Gods way of saving he still cares."

Lee repliesd in a flat emotionless tone.

“The old Gods are dead as my flock! You and your companion shall join me, for I shall make camp here.”

By the time Shangri-La relayed the message to Camp Pay Day the connection with Earl and Paradise had been lost. As much as Enestro wanted to go searching for his friend. Everyone that knew Earl Grimes, understood Death was never coming directly for him. John started vaccinating everyone under his care, for he understood, DEATH was indeed on its way!

Later that morning when their Helicopters landed back at Camp Pay Day the duty Officer’s voice in Wynolla’s headset explained there was an urgent message sent by Shangri-La! It didn’t take long for Colonel Lafayette and Major Brown to walk down the two flight of stairs from the roof.

Making their way to the converted command center, Navy Chief Warrant Officer Henry Oakerson- *A bald thirty-Year-Old Jewish Male from Philly*- greeted his superiors by saying.

“Great Day to you both. We have an Urgent Message from Dr. Hammond.”

Colonel Lafayette replies, “Let it rock Chief.”

Chief Oakerson plays the audio file, he recorded a few hours earlier. The voice made Wynolla’s blood boil, but the Officer didn’t show it to her command.

“I am the new God! Nature has selected me to cleanse this world. Like a tidal wave, my flock shall bludgeon, and we shall burn the old world down! We shall strangle the young and eat our way from sea to shining fucking sea…”

It took Major Brown to break the silence by saying.

"FUCK! It's, him. It's..."

Windu replied with a bit of spite.

"That psycho shit heel LEE!"

Confused as the rest of them Chief Oakerson asked, "I thought you said you left him in an ocean of RAGERS?"

Major Brown replied, "We sure did Chief! I don't know how that crazy bastard did it. But he's alive and kickin!"

Colonel Lafayette took a few moments to access the information before saying.

"The chatter we have been hearing about RAGERS using tools and working as an army. It's Lee! Somehow, he's a mutation. One different from Deana and Hana."

Chief Oakerson asks, "How the fuck is that even possible?"

Wynolla sighed before saying. "We won't know, until we nab the insane son on a bitch! Chief, I need you to get Shangri-La and GLS on the horn. I need to speak to our allies ASAP!"

The town once name Lincoln, was a city in what was once Logan County, Illinois, in what was the United States of America.

It was the only town in the United States that was named for Abraham Lincoln before he became president. **Fact** he practiced law there from **1847** to **1859**. The town was first settled in the 1830s, and before the plague, Lincoln was home to two colleges and two prisons. The two colleges were Lincoln College and Lincoln Christian University!

On the grounds of Lincoln Christian University, Lee's flock made its camp. At the present time Lee's RAGERS Army numbered a bit under six thousand. If the RAGER flock should be compared to pod of Great White Sharks. Consider then the tens of thousands of Zombies wandering about represented a school of Piranha!

Moaning and groaning on the outskirts and underbelly of the infected force. Their numbers are five times the number of the RAGERS in the area. It's only because they don't see the RAGERs as a source of passing the virus, do the two co-exist. Even so, the herd of Dead Heads could probably obliterate the RAGERs army if they could pass the virus or just get tired of their constant fucking abuse!

By now Earl and Paradise have been relieved of all their weapons. As guests of Lee, they have been allowed to at least keep their clothes, for now. While RAGERS scavenge the University grounds looking for survivors, other RAGERS and of course water.

Standing in front of the statue of Abraham Lincoln, Jefferson Bullraguard Lee pondered for all to hear.

"This madman did more to destroy American than MOMREL-6 virus ever could do! White men were placed on this world to RULE! Wouldn't you agree with me Mr., what did you say your last name was?"

Earl wondered if he should just snap the lanky man's neck and be done it with, before saying.

"Grimes, Earl Grimes. Brother, it's written somewhere that those cloaked in the will of the lord do so in his name!"

Lee's laugh had a familiar sinister ring to it one that Earl knew all too well. It was the sound one made when they had the upper hand on your prey. Jefferson directed his attention to Paradise when he asked.

"How did you two survive?"

Paradise didn't like the red-faced man standing in front of Abraham Lincoln statue. She wanted to reach over and touch the back of

Earl's massive hand. Nonetheless instead, Paradise put on her best phony face and replied with a smile.

"The short version, we meet at a strip club! Earl saved my life, we wandered a bit, before encountering a group known as Global Logistics and Security."

Lee turned and stared at Paradise for an uncomfortable of time before asking Earl."

"Mr. Grimes is it?"

Earl's slow Southern draw had been perfected over the years to conceal any hint of emotion. Furthermore, he was five out of five in beating lie detectors in his day..

"That's what my departed mother named me and what's your friend?"

Lee turned to face Earl and his week old stank breath reached the big man before the words.

"I was once known as Jefferson Bullraguard Lee. Now I am known as the Reckoning! A worldwide tsunami, the Dao one must take to reach enlighten! Even so, that's before I met two more like me. Tell me, how did this Global Logistics and Security help you survive?"

Paradise replied before Earl by saying in a baby voice.

"They gave us a yucky shot in the bun-bun and it made us sick, until it didn't..."

Before the Transwoman could finish speaking, Lee turned to her and spoke without a hint of emotion.

"I asked him. Speak out of turn again and I will have your degenerate yellow behind skinned alive."

Earl looked around to see hundreds, upon hundreds of RAGERs milling around and he knew this was not the time to let Chicken Head out. Instead, he smiled and replied.

“Two Southern boys such as us have no quarrel friend. My companion will keep quiet until spoke to! White Power brother! White Power…”

Lee asked Earl once more.

“Are you telling me, you have not been comprised by a cowardly Nigger Army Officer? One who stole my command and left me for dead?”

Paradise body language stiffed up just enough is caught Lee’s attention.

He slowly turned to her and asked.

“You, do you know whom I speak?”

Paradise doesn’t smile this time around. Her tone was flat, however her eyes signal anger and hate towards the stank breath man standing in front of her.

“I have a few black military lovers before, if that’s what you are asking.”

Earl moved closer to Paradise, shielding her with his large frame. Coming nose to forehead with Lee and then said.

“Brother, we won’t bother you any longer. We will be on our way.”

That’s when Lee’s demeanor switched from murderous, to phony friendly!

“Where to, friend?”

Earl replied, "It's a great big land brother, GL&S gave us a gift! So we plan to see where it takes us. Friend, I suggested to my traveling companion we head to Hollywerid and look up movie stars we hated and if they are still alive, kill them!"

Lee laughed a deeply demented laugh and replied, "That does sound like fun! Oh yes, that sound like a bucket of fun and I would love to go with you! However, first you must tell, where can my flock find these mad fucking scientists at Global Logistic and Security? I can't allow them to make more such as yourself."

Earl's grin hid his deadly thoughts as he replied.

"Have no other Gods before thee! Yes, I do understand your motivation Brother Lee. All I can tell you; they fly midnight black Helicopters, and they placed black canvas bags over the heads of everyone they contact! Effectively kidnapping persons of interest."

When it comes to spinning the truth, like I stated Earl Grimes had beaten 5-5 lie detection machines in his lifetime. However, Paradise was past the point she felt uncomfortable! She's frightened and Lee picks up on it.

"What about you? Do you know the location of this mysterious entity known as Global Logistic and Security?"

Paradise swallowed hard, attempting to put up a strong presence. Nevertheless, the red faced man was making her skin crawl.

Lee asks once more, yet this time his tone was not phony friendly, just sinister.

"Did you not understand the question? Is English not your first language? Tell me about this GL&S."

That's when Earl had no choice but to place himself directly in the path of the storm when he said.

"Leave her be! I told you all we know. I have no reason to lie to you."

However, Lee's reply nearly floored them both.

"Come on now. Mr. Grimes. I read about you long ago, when the world still spun of gossip and social media nonsense. I even followed your exploits for years! Watching your case snake its way through the court system. Truly you were an American icon, isn't that right Chick Head? Honestly, I am a huge fan of your work!"

Earl Grimes knew it was now or never, as he prepared to pounce on the madman. Still a second squandered was a second lost as Lee's guards moved a step faster!

A large group viciously began clubbing and merciless stomping the wholesale shit out of Earl until the big man was bloody submitted! While others restrained the screaming Paradise as they ripped off every piece of clothing she was wearing. And yes, their love would last until their dying breath.

Chapter IV:

WHEN LOVE HAS TO DO WITH IT?

When Earl and Paradise missed their next two check-ins, even Ernesto began to worry! Down in the armory, the Ghost Face Killer examined the weapons he planned to take with him into the field. Several rows of automatic weapons stood silent sentries for any warriors who are willing to take up arms on a quest.

Ernesto pushed his shopping cart down the aisle, carefully selecting the proper weapons to fit his needs. First an American bolt action Sniper Rifle, followed by an Israeli made assault weapon. Ernesto was busy pondering his handgun choices when his beloved entered the room.

"Que? Are you planning a surprise picnic for us?"

Ernesto turned to face his wife and even he can tell Celeste has a glow about her.

"No, my love, I, I am thinking about going to search for Earl. Armed with John's miracle serum of course..."

Celeste face wrinkled up in a semi frown as she said.

"Honey, I know Earl's our friend. Even so, we have bigger things to worry about."

Celeste moved closer to her husband, allowing her left hand to gently stroke his face. He turned his face so his lips can kiss her palms. In a motherly voice, she said.

"We are with child. I don't know if you noticed how I stopped drinking, doing blow and even smoking motta."

Ernesto slowly puts down the .45 caliber handgun and happily hugged his wife. Happiness swells deep inside, bubbling up in the form of happy tears and he whispered.

"Yes, I noticed, I thought you were just drying out. But a BABY! Mi Corazon, that's the best news I've heard all Apocalypse!"

The couple embraced, their kiss was soft, slow and filled with joy. At that moment they shared in one of life's happier moments, then his wife said.

"My love, you can't leave me or our child. I know you Ernesto, you will go get yourself killed. Hoh, Earl, well... he was a serial killer! I am not throwing shade, for we were pieces of shit hired killers as well! Even so, Earl knows how to survive. Please stay here with ME, with US!"

She placed his hand on her belly and Ernesto succumbed to the fears of being a family man. He chuckled as he replied.

"A pappi, me? I never thought it was possible. Every moment I laid rotting away on Death Row. My thoughts were consumed by YOU. Now here you are in my arms, with promises of our family! Yet, all I can think of is what happen to Earl and Paradise?"

She placed her head on his heart and muttered.

"I know. It sucks, but we have a little one to raise. Us..."

Up three levels and Semaj was a nervous wreck as the young ebony Transwoman had no clue on what to do! She was all alone in her empty hatch, nevertheless every which way she turns, Semaj was reminded of her former bunk mates. Armed with the news the duo has now missed four straight check in, Semaj sat alone waiting for the knock on her hatch to say, Earl and Paradise were indeed dead!

Salty tears flow freely down her chocolate cheeks and there's no one around to help comfort her sorrow. Even under their present condition Semaj has been perfecting the **GFI**= genuine femmie illusion. Her skin's softer than warm butter, with no signs of razor stumble.

Robin happened to stop by to do a well-being check and the conversation turned towards love and how intimacy is important. If asked Robin would admit, Semaj was a head turner! Nonetheless, the poor child was overcome with worry and anxiety. Marshal Aquila remembers the feeling well. After Sky was killed, she nearly allowed her heart to be harden with hate! If it were not for the rekindling of flames with Colonel Lafayette, Robin might have gone over the edge.

She allowed her words to guide Semaj to a better place.

"Look I am not going to write those two off just yet! However, if the time comes honey, it won't be easy. Still, we are here for you! Don't you dare let despair rob you of your joy. I can see it inside you and so will others."

Semaj was at a loss for words for several moments before saying.

"Thanks, but there's not many Trans people among us, well not allow the living you know. I, I guess Paradise was probably the last of the fiercest Transwoman to ever walk the earth!"

Once again Semaj broke down crying and that took Robin back a few weeks when she was all anger and sorrow. She begins to cry as well, yet Robin does manage to say.

"No hon, you are the fiercest Transwoman walking the planet! I bet you if we can make it to Brazil, we would find an island filled with alive, fit and gorgeous Transwomen tanning nude in the afternoon sun. With booties bouncing and big ole dicks swinging in the warm South American wind!"

Semaj managed a chuckle before replying.

"Oh, that would be a wonderful sight to behold."

Inside John's lab he sat wondering if his vaccine somehow failed! Was it his efforts which exposed his friends to the harshness of the Apocalypse? Colonel Lafayette wanted forty dosages of the vaccine ASAP! Whatever was happening in the wastes what was America's currently working its way to their front door! The fight was on whether the wanted it or not.

Nonetheless, without the proper data, John couldn't be sure if his vaccine was the reason no one has heard from Earl or Paradise in now seven days. John only could be sure of one thing, he needed to save as many people as he can.

Lee's Horde had made what was once the city of Lincoln Illinois their base. However, even before the Apocalypse, Lincoln was the post card rendition of a small American town on its last legs!

It's only due to the efforts of a small Christian college that this hard-working farming community got itself on the map. Now, all its citizens have joined the parade of dead heads or the ranks of evolved RAGERS. The once proud town was washed in filth, grime, garbage, shit and smoke! Armed RAGERS patrol the area around Lincoln College's student union building. Making sure the tens of thousands of Zombies keep it moving with their endless shamble. With no reason to venture pass their makeshift defense Deah Heads encircle the student union with no direction to go.

Found inside among the mounds of burnt books, stinking trash and various body parts, happens to be where Lee had established some sort of makeshift throne room in the student café.

It was several days before Earl awoke with the feeling that his massive arms had somehow been restrained and his vision obscured by some sort of dark hood or maybe even a blood-stained pillowcase! He could hear the shuffling of feet and Jefferson Bullraguard Lee's voice in the background.

To Earl the aroma of the air was a familiar blend of sweat, blood, tears and overall despair. He knew them well, for so many times in Chicken Head's life, he has been the one playing the spider to a helpless victim's fly!

Well that stopped being a rule of law about several days ago. Strung up like a helpless Christmas goose, Earl could feel a jolting pain to his left eye socket and a warm wet liquid flowing from his throbbing bunghole!

That's when he heard Lee's hoarse voice in the background as Earl groaned ever so slightly.

"What, what have you done with Paradise?"

Jefferson Bullraguard Lee tone was upbeat as he directed his full attention to his captive.

"Ahhh, our honored guest is finally awake. Generally, when I slam my cock into a new slave, they react with something. You, you, magnificent bald sonofabitch, you stayed unconscious the entire nine minutes I was breeding you. Re-fucking-markable! "

Earl groaned once more.

"Tell me, where is Paradise?"

Lee's slow tune tone turn upbeat and sinister as he replied.

"You mean your stubborn and condescending Asian He-She- fucking It? Well, pick your own pronoun, whatever, it would not cooperate, at first! Nonetheless, by the time I finished instructing my RAGERS on how to run a proper fucking gang bang! Well, let's just say, He-She-fucking IT opened up to us rather nicely. Here take, a good goddam look for yourself bucko!"

On Lee's signal one of the nearby RAGERS snatched the dark blood-stained pillowcase off of Earl's head.

It takes a few moments for his remaining blue eye to focus on his surroundings. A few dozen armed RAGERS mill around, while Lee stood like a proud artist unveiling his work. The image was complete, a bruised, battered and barely breathing Paradise for Earl's one good eye to see. The anger building inside Grimes could only be measured in one phrase, nuclear explosion!

He screamed, "NOOOOOOOOOOOOOOO! Paradise, please get up. Please..."

Lee's tone was in his usual slow delivery yet wielded with total disgust.

"Mr. Grimes what the fuck happened to you? I saw your docudrama, you were portrayed as a Great White Shark! I even fashioned some of my efforts after your exploits. Riding around with your victims' head on a mannequin so you could access the carpool lane. That was classic fucking Earl Grimes!"

Lee clapped his hands, his mood once again is upbeat, he laughs before saying.

"That was delightfully priceless! Now look at you, falling in love with an IT. Someone that should have been your victim. Why? It's Armageddon, why choose to be on the side of light, over darkness? Why choose so-called good over the evil that freely flows through your goddam blood! I can smell it in you! Your action makes no fucking sense to me Mr. Grimes. Listen, we started off on the wrong foot. So, I will offer you a choice, join me brother. Let's you and I get back to what making America great..."

Earl's voice boom, so loud than nearby RAGERS take a step back as he said.

"FOOL, I never harmed anyone for who they were! I killed for loneliness and those with poor manners. You took my Paradise from me, today I kill only for RAGE."

Lee not to be out done. He sort of kicks the barely breathing body, so Paradise lets out a muffled moan, before Lee continues.

"Listen up Chicken Head, yeah, I figure we can be on first name bases since I've had my cock wedge up your surprisingly loose asshole! Your little plaything spilled the beans. Sadly, or not! It took twenty-nine RAGERS dry fucking every hole to get her to cooperate. Earl let me tell you, she-him-IT could really, really take some infected dick. And you slept through all her petrified screams, horrified pleas and of orgasms, big boy! She-He-They even got a message through on your SAT PHONE. So just you sit tight brother, would be help is coming! Then you can join your IT, together walking with the fucking DEAD."

Colonel Lafayette knew the stakes and she didn't allow Major Brown, Robin or John Hammond to talk her out of this course of action! Wynolla knew anyone traveling with her could be used as leverage! Lee wanted her and to make the plan work, Colonel Lafayette must deliver herself into the hands of their enemy.

Even with that, Windu enjoyed the drive in a drop top Volkswagen Beetle! The sun was shining, the air was crisp, and the roads were clear. Colonel Lafayette inserted herself twenty miles outside the town of Lincoln. After an intense short walk through a field of mingling Dead Heads. Wynolla found a working vehicle, she placed her government issued suppressed M-17 assault weapon, with grenade launcher on the passenger seat and drove toward the enemy's lair.

The scientist in Colonel Lafayette marveled at how Dr. Hammond's vaccine worked! The Zombies had no interest in Windu and RAGERS don't seem to take notice as well. The only thing that was more of an interest to Wynolla was witnessing how the RAGERS are working together like a colony of Army Ants!

As she zoomed by doing 45 mph Windu could see that Lee must be captured and studied! No matter how she felt about the asshole, Jefferson Bullraguard Lee was an anomaly and humanity needed to find out how's and why the psycho cocksucker mutated!

Earl Grime's friends wanted to mount a rescue mission the moment Paradise's muffled voice provided the painful recanting of events. Even Major Brown wanted to come up with another way of doing this. Nevertheless, the burden of command fell on Wynolla's shoulders. The former Admiral was a problem that Colonel Lafayette created when she failed to put a bullet in Lee's diseased brain!

Now as she drove down a lonely road to nowhere, Wynolla went over the plan in her mind repeatedly. Major Brown and four teams of Operators will join her once she lays eyes on Lee and can access the situation.

Robin will land her Russian made vintage attack Helicopter with a small team to extract their people, Wynolla and hopefully Lee! The recovered news helicopter had been fitted with a 50 Cal. mounted in its door, manned by 31 year old Gunny Sergeant Ken Marcus *of Cleveland Ohio*. It and GSL should provide backup by reigning fire!

Under Windu's rain poncho, the twenty pounds of C-4 strapped to her chest was more mentally uncomfortable than physically uncomfortable! She rather not suicide bomb herself, even so all cards must be on the table to get close enough to Lee for the plan to begin.

Before the drive Windu selected the only song that represented the moment.

David Bowie and Queen singing Under Pressure*, and she* can't help but sing along.

"Pressure, pushing down on me, pressing down on you, no woman ask for. Under pressure that brings a building down, splits a family in two, puts people on streets. Um ba ba be, Um b aba be, Eh day

da, Eh day da. It's the terror of knowing what this world is about, watching some good friends SCREAM. LET ME OUT! Pray tomorrow, gets me higher."

As she drove towards her destination, the sight of a moving car not alone a speeding one along with the sound of a woman singing at the top of her lungs, well that's priceless! Zombie and RAGER alike stop and turn to catch a glimpse of Colonel Lafayette as she belts out.

"These are the days it never rains, but it pours. People on the streets, Ee da de da de, People on the streets, Ee da de da de, It's the terror of knowing what this world is all about. Watching some good friends scream let me out...Turned away from it all like a blind man, keep coming up for love but it's so slashed and torn why.. WHY, why love, love, love. Why can't give LOVE just one more chance? Insanity laughs under pressure we're breaking can't we give ourselves one more chance? Why can't WE give love one more chance, give love, give life, give life one more chance...."

Earlier that morning Major Brown handpicked the Operators for this OP, Lance knew the fate of is mentor and even humanity itself was at stake! If this miracle vaccine failed to perform as billed. Lance knew there's an angry ocean of infection between them and their objective!

He needed Operators with nerves of steel and steady trigger fingers. It's ONE SHOT, ONE KILL time.

Every round they take in the field must equal certain death to their foes. **Fun Fact** for the last four years leading to the end of the world there was a contest between branches of our military. Not surprising to them, even so it was Army Snipers who took the grand prize as the best our Military had when a shot had to been made!

If they were ever to be considered the "Best of the Best", now is the time to prove their metal! Four teams of six will repel down to meet the terrain one half mile from location. Allowing the Helios to carry out the second part of their mission. Create a distraction by the tactical use of high explosives!

Each Helio was equipped with four heat seeking missiles and several thousand rounds of 50 caliber ammo. The infected may control the land, but their task force will dam well control the air and everything beneath their rotors!

Back at Shangri-La, Robin waited for her group to board their Russian made vintage attack Helicopter. After much back and forth it was decided that Ernesto would accompany Big John, Celeste, Semaj and Cherish on their bid to rescue their friends. Celeste wants to come, at first Ernesto will not hear of it, nonetheless for once he listened to Calamity when she said.

"My love, we ride together! We love together and we'll die together as a family if need be."

John didn't have to put the screws to GL& S, pretty much whoever was running that bastion of covert research wanted a look at the anomaly! They pledged two black helicopters filled with troops and scientists. Every one of them will be armed with John Hammond's miracle vaccine and a sense of that the fate of humanity hung in the balance.

The dead have no reason, no will, just drive and desire to feed and spread the infection! The living on the other hand must prepare for as the Chinese Martial Artist use to say, "ten thousand things to come." Flying nearly two thousand feet above the soon to be battlefield, the four Army Black Hawks were seemingly prehistoric beast ranging the earth for one last meal!

Major Brown for a moment allowed his mind to ponder want to do about Cherish. Lance found her amazing and very, very flexible! He wanted to be all up in her mix, however what will their future hold? Will they be able to defeat Lee and his Army of RAGERS? The last bit of wisdom Windu planted with him was simple. Kill the head, the ass will follow! Also, named their second child after her.

The road that led to Lincoln University was manned by RAGERs and Dead Heads alike. Which meant Wynolla must swerve several times not to plaster any Dead Head that lumbered into her path. Much like frightened deer, they tend to stand their ground even when a one-ton vehicle is bearing down on them!

When she approached the sentries posted at the front gate of the University, without warning Colonel Lafayette slowed her vehicle to a quick, tire burning halt! Nearly a dozen Armed RAGERS mingled at the entrance. Most firmly stood in the middle of her path , even so Windu thought to herself.

"Either they don't see me or don't seem to fucking care about being run over! If I ever see John Hammond again, I promise to buy that wonderful man a cold beer."

Nonetheless, Wynolla blew the car horn several times before a small path opened allowing the Colonel to gun the shiny red sports sedan on through. In her rearview mirror she watched the path slowly close behind her. Much like a Viking funeral, the path to Lee was lined with his warriors!

Red Faced former men, women and even child stand shoulder to shoulder pointing towards the direction of their commander and their demigod! It's a hot and humid day for early fall and if the RAGERs had been professional soldiers, they might have questioned why they follow Lee.

Or why Wynolla was wearing a rain poncho on a clear day, these questions would have caused a seasoned Solider some concern. One or two might have thought about searching her or better yet emptying their sidearm into Lee's face themselves! Nevertheless, RAGERs evolved or not are not soldiers. When Colonel Lafayette exited her red sports sedan smiling, she tossed the keys to the nearest RAGER then said.

"Hey bud, it's yours. Enjoy, I tell you the sound system is booming!"

The RAGER didn't catch the keys, instead they fell towards its grimy boots and Wynolla didn't stay around to see if anyone of them picked the keys out of the pool of dried blood. Without much fanfare she jogged up the white granite stairs towards the Great White Dope!

In her Army career Colonel Lafayette had parlayed with Somalin warlords, Afghans Black Marketeters and Islamic clerics. Even so, Lee will be her greatest challenge, for they hated each other with a passion reserved for scorned lovers and the falsely accused!

If John Hammond had not had a breakthrough on his vaccine, the capture of Lee would be critical! Now, it's a want, not necessarily a need. Yet, Wynolla knew she had to play this just right or she would never be able to buy Doctor Hammond that cold beer!

The smell of so much death filled Wynolla's nostrils with an aroma she will never be able to get out of her mind's eye. The illumination of dozens of torches also provide the air a stench of sulfur, plus it's muggy as hell! Nonetheless, only Windu seemed to be sweating.

The first image that flashes through Colonel Lafayette's mind was the last half of Francis Ford Coppola's film**, Apocalypse Now** and she muttered to herself.

"Colonel Crazy Pants- has really gone fucking native!"

RAGERS line the halls, standing shoulder to shoulder, each seemingly not aware or even awake! Nevertheless, their presence pointed towards the objective. Each step Wynolla too, she noticed the sound of footsteps keeping up behind her. The hallways have collapsed and now they follow Wynolla like the mighty Mississippi River flowing back towards its source!

When Colonel Lafayette reached the former student cafe, the room opened to reveal several hundred more RAGERS encircling a makeshift throne of milk crates and human skin. From across the room, Wynolla and Lee's locked eyes as she slowly approaches.

When Jefferson Bullraguard Lee stood up, it was he who spoke first.

"Oh my, oh my, oh my. It looks like the knife in my back has returned! Tell me what happens when two Jews and a Jigaboo enter a bar?"

Wynolla flung back her poncho to reveal a suicide fest made of C-4 and ammo clips as she replies.

"Hopefully get a clean glass and a chance to catch the CLAP like any paying customer!"

Lee was silent for a few moments, before letting out a chuckle then saying.

"Well, I can certainly arrange that. If you want to catch several strains of VD, get in line over there! I think MISS THANG still has a bit of life in IT."

That's when Colonel Lafayette noticed of the other side of the room, a huge man bound in-between to pillars much like the biblical Samson! His face was partially covered by a dirty, bloody bandage, even so Wynolla knew he was Hammond's friend. Directly in front of the poor soul -*much like the display has been put on solely for her benefit*- nearly a dozen naked RAGERs were apparently having sex with either a lifeless or soon to be lifeless person.

Wynolla forced a weak smile before calmly saying.

"No thanks, now let's get down to brass facts. Do you know what fifteen pounds of C-4 and a bandoleer of twenty clips of 5.56 NATO caliber tracer rounds; a alongside four FRAG grenades will do to ruin your fucking week, Lee? This is the detonator, take my thumb off this red button and this room, along with several acres of land, simply disappears! Nod, if you understand the words coming out of my mouth."

Lee spits before replying with his slow, yet sarcastic delivery.

"Oh, well I never knew Sand Niggers allowed goofy dykes to be goddam Muslims terrorist! Your God will not provide you 72 Virgins, you know that right?"

Still calm as the other side of your pillow, Wynolla replies.

"FYI dick face, I'm a Daoist. Yet, it's surprising to see you are still asshole Lee. Funny, but how come death didn't cure you of that? Nonetheless, I have no plans to end up like your other guest over there before you at least hear me out. So, either you talk NICE or we all go BOOM! Your choice."

"The RAGERS behind Colonel Lafayette begin to close in on her, she this time shouts at Lee.

"I swear I will blow us to whatever happens after this life is done! Tell the RAGERS to take twenty steps back, their stale hot breath on the back of my neck has me feeling a bit nervous Lee!"

The air was thick with unbridled tension as the RAGERs waited for Lee to make up his mind. His bond and utter control of their behavior marveled Wynolla! Even so, she kept this observation to herself.

It takes a few moments before the entire group takes several steps backwards and Lee to say.

"Fair enough, however if I'm to hear what you think, may sway thy righteous hand of thy jealous god. Then I might as well do it sitting down. Follow me.."

Lee performed a quick about face and walked back into the cafeteria, turned into his makeshift throne room.

His long stride has him well in front of the vigilant Colonel Lafayette and the armed escort of RAGERs. Jefferson Bullraguard Lee's path took him pass the wheezing, battered, bloodied and barely still breathing Paradise Hunter.

The once beautiful, bold and artsy profound transwoman had both her eyes swollen shut, at least four broken ribs, and from Colonel Lafayette's experience, it sounded like a punctured lung! She laid in a puddle of her on blood, RAGER semen and lots of foul-smelling piss.

Even though Wynolla knew these are the friends of John Hammond, she could not let that bit of information slip, just in case Lee wasn't aware. A blind Earl lets out a loud moan of pain, anger and frustration when Lee crosses is path.

"Let me go to her or I swear I will eat your heart and wear your skin as a coat!"

Lee stopped long enough to say to both Earl and Wynolla.

"Here rests a white man that could have had the world but chose to not live up to his full fucking potential! His eyes offended the new GOD, me. So, I ripped them out of his goddam head and ate them in front of big blind ass! However, I allowed him to keep his tongue, so Mr. Grimes could turn his face and praise the new God. ME! Sadly, this beast hasn't learned any manners."

Earl grunted and said with a bit of humanity, "Please, my lord, allow me to go to her side..."

Lee smiled before nodding his head allowing two RAGERs to step forth and unbind Earl from the concrete pillar. The big, blind man crawled towards the labored sound of Paradise's breathing. As he moved by Wynolla, she could hear him mutter.

"My love, I, I'm sorry. So sorry, just rest all will be over with soon..."

To her credit, Colonel Lafayette's left thumb never left the red button as she follows Lee towards his throne of milk crates covered in dried human skin! Before Jefferson Bullraguard Lee took his sit, he nodded to a series of RAGERS to place their loyal mindless selves in front of his throne. And they did so, two rows deep of infected human shields! This makeshift barricade aimed their assorted small arms, hunting rifles, shotguns and semi-automatic weapons at Colonel Lafayette. Lee sighed as he said.

"Well?"

If the situation wasn't as dire and deadly as possible, for whatever reason Wynolla let out a chuckle, be it nerves or not. Lee has never enjoyed being anyone center of ridicule.

"Do you find your situation funny? Go ahead blow yourself up, see if I give a fuck! I am far above your ridicule, your judgement, your ant like approach to life. I am supreme!"

Windu allowed a few moments to pass, before replying in a calm and steady voice.

"Ridicule you, no, no, no. I am in awe and I'm wondering if there is still a man of science upon that blood-stained skin you are sitting on? You hold the key to controlling if not defeating this virus! What's left of humanity needs you, don't you see that?"

It's Jefferson's time to take a few moments before replying. His answer was a portion of honesty, mixed with a huge amount of arrogance and a lot of I don't give a fat flying fuck!

"Ohhhhhhhhhhhhhh, now your black ass needs ole Jefferson Bullraguard Lee, do you? Frankly, didn't you leave me for dead? Yes you did, however I had no doubt in mind that I wasn't done! You left me and that nincompoop Dunston to our fate and what fate showed me was that I, Jefferson Bullraguard Lee was not to be written off so fucking lightly. And if humanity truly needs me as a savior, then humanity shall serve me and my Red Army!"

Wynolla's voice had a pleading tone to it, something she picked out at Pych-ops 101 while working out of Fort Bragg.

"Okay maybe you're right! What if just maybe you are wrong and now you get to be the hero you always dreamed of being Lee? You have been bitten; I can see the bite marks. The man of science in you must be screaming to you, why didn't I turn? Or how is it I can control other infected?"

Lee's reply was quick.

"You first! A quick pro quo if you will. Why did you abandon Camp McCormick?"

With that Colonel Lafayette knew her location has been compromised and Jefferson can see it on her face and his laugh was filled with evil glee.

"Ohhho, you thought I didn't know and your alliance with some ex Chair Force Entomologist and Death Row survivor? This mysterious John Hammond!"

Lee let his words hang in the air before saying.

"Well, let me tell you, when you are being brutally gang raped before having your pupils scooped out of your face! Ohhhhoh, you will tell me everything! So, stick around, or go BOOM! I don't give a fat flying fuck you, fucking monkey."

Wynolla sighed, for she had to buy some time for the plan to work, instead she continued talking.

"It's hard to believe you wore the rank of Rear Admiral, Lee. You could hold the key to saving humanity! Dammit, is this how you want the last light of humanity to be snuffed out? What the fuck?"

Lee yawned and replied, " Yes what the fuck! Now what part of I don't give a fuck anymore don't you get? Burn it the fuck down! Fate lite a match, and life belongs to the strong!

Lee's snarls as he continued." Before, before all of this, I hated you for the color of your skin! And yes, I hated women who thought they were superior to men. Now, I detest the scent of your precious humanity! Humanity has never done anything for me! Where was your humanity when you exiled me to the wildness? I didn't die as your sneaky black ass envisioned! So once again why did you abandon Camp McCormick?

Colonel Lafayette gritted her teeth as she took off the bandoleer of C-4 and rested it at her feet. Her thumb never released its stead, yet Wynolla does take a step back before saying.

"First, I didn't exile you Lee, you murdered a fellow officer! Second, I didn't abandon Camp McCormick, we chose to move our efforts to a secure backup location after your exploits poisoned our community with HATE! We had a chance to restart civilization without the all the bullshit, but you could let all the hate go."

Wynolla had to fight back tears of anger as she went on to say. "Sadly, the Camp fell when what looks like some sad sack of shit decided to make moon shine and blew a hole in the side of the North Building exposing it to the fucking dead."

Lee was silent for several seconds, before probably sharing his most lucid thought when he said.

"Moonshine? What backwoods, dumb fuck felt the need to make goddam moonshine?"

Inside the vintage Russian attack helicopter, the COMM was picking up Colonel Lafayette's mic loud and clear! The only thing clinched tighter than Marshal Aquila's teeth were her toned, tanned butt cheeks. She had logged so much time during the Apocalypse in the cockpit of their Russian beast that Robin was flying it like she was an honorable **K**-krazy-**G**-gripping -**B**- beautiful spy!

Inside the cabin even if the inhabitants wanted to speak, the roar of the engines would only drown their voices. So, everyone sat silently in thought. Celeste rests her head on Ernesto narrow chest, this was as close as they have ever been. For the first time in a long time, both were scared! No sense being armed with false bravo, no more rage against the machine. The thought of bringing a child into a world of certain horror made both their heads spin! Nonetheless, the couple would face the world together, holding hands as they truly share the of bound; **WE**, **Ride Until We Die**!

Semaj and Cherish grew up on the West Side of Chicago and senseless violence has always been a sad part of their existence. Cherish strongly felt with the world in shambles, violence, death and destruction was so much a part of their everyday life, that fighting for something had to make a difference in this world. Or we are no better than animals!

Semaj on the other hand was worried about her pod mates, Earl and Paradise! Because from the sound of Colonel Lafayette's open mic, their health was in jeopardy.

The young ebony Transwoman had only fired a weapon on the range of Shangri-La, and she didn't have to accompany this mission. Semaj wanted to! She knew Cherish had her back, which meant someone must have Paradise and Earls as well!

As Earl crawled forward his outstretched arms searched the floor for the sound of swallow wheezing somewhere in front of him. A few helpful kicks to his side or his exposed buttocks point the broken giant on his path. The wheezing gets louder letting Earl know he was getting closer! The mere sight of Paradise would have enraged Earl to unspeakable acts, if he could see.

Paradise Hunter had been through a lot in life, she has been beaten and raped before! Sadly, and very shortly she will go through even more as a Dead Head. Paradise could only lay still, among a pool of her own blood, human waste, alongside RAGER's piss and sperm. She was a crumbled pile of broken bones and only a callous piece of shit would not feel a bit of sympathy towards her plight!

As Earl's bruised hands pushed through pools of unknown liquid, he found an exposed femur and he heard Paradise's softly muffled moan of pain. Earl felt the need to hurry, still he gently touched his way up her body until he found her face and he softly begged for her forgiveness.

"My love, I'm here, I'm here. I'm so sorry, I, I never thought I couldn't protect you! I am so sorry. I love you Paradise do you hear me, I love you!"

Over Paradise's wheezing, and his own sobbing, Earl can hear her crying as well. Through a broken jaw, shattered teeth and at least one puncture lung, her raspy, hush voice manages.

"I lo,lov,love you too E, Ea, Earllll."

Like a mother holding her sick child, Earl Grimes gently cradled the battered head of the departed Paradise Hunter. He didn't want to, nonetheless did feel the life slowly fade from someone who he had actually allowed himself to deeply care about! Much like a dormant volcano, the murderous rage in Earl Grimes was boiling, slowly seeping its way to the surface and is ready to explode. And the song that popped into his head, told their tale. **Whitney Houston's I Will Always Love You.**

Outside, the sound of approaching helicopters was sort of masked by the approaching sound being broadcast through the heavens via Major Brown's musical taste. He went full head banger when choosing **Limp Bizkit's, Rollin ft. Redman, Method Man, & DMX**!

From two miles out RAGERs and Dead Heads alike cast their blood-stained eyes towards the sky. Searching in vain for the source of the sound that seems to have attracted all their attention! Flying nearly one thousand feet about sea level, the task force was no more than approaching tiny spots against a mostly blue morning sky.

The courtyard of what was once Lincoln College was filled with Lee's conscripts. He had armed them to the tee and taught them how to look like they were military. Nevertheless, when the first missile came veering down from the sky like a thunder bolt from

Thor's Hammer! The explosion *-which was equal to that of over 2,000 pounds of TNT-* sent a shockwave that causes a ripple effect of pure goddam consequence!

The next explosion happened a moment after Colonel Lafayette's red sport car turned in a Baghdad IED. Two tons of Detroit's finest goes up in a fiery blast that would have made many a Jihadist proud! For her effort the pristine walls of what was the entrance to Lincoln University's student union was promptly vaporized in the baptism of white-hot flames. Future generations will debate if the smell of rotting skin of hundreds of Dead Heads was harder to mask than the sound of approaching aircraft!

GS&L's commitment of three Black Helicopters approached from the West just a promised, swooping in like the prehistoric beast of prey they now are!. Not much was known about the "Operators" from **Global Security & Logistics**. Nevertheless, their sleek Black Bell Company Helicopters swoop, dip and drive like a Hawk catching mice across the battlefield. They caught the attention of Lee's RAGERS and Dead Heads alike, their aircraft took an assortment of small arm fire. Still, they give better than they got.

Jefferson Bullraguard Lee's mutation has brought back enough motor skins to his RAGER force that they are able to lock n load. Point, then somewhat aim and most of the time shoot their weapons. That's doesn't mean they always hit their marks! Nevertheless, the rouse of black flying aircraft caught their attention. Drowning out the sound of Major Brown's four Helios dropping out of the East firing missiles like invading ET's making War of what's left of the dominant species!

Brilliant explosions of red, orange and yellow cascade across yellow faded lawns, catching fire to anything in its path. The 50 MM cannons of Major Brown's birds of prey chew up concrete, Detroit steel and rotten fest with the same bravado! RAGERs who have not been infected never bothered looking for cover as the barrage of hot lead ended their suffering! All while directly behind Major Brown's task force, Marshal Aquila's Soviet Beast roared upon scene with the fury of a woman intent out not losing another soul she cared about.

Earl could hear the commotion going on around him, even so he felt the moment Paradise turned in his arms! John Hammond's miracle vaccine was still working on Earl, because his former love didn't want to bite him as much escape Earl's embrace. Her trashing around signaled for Earl it was time to let go, so Earl let loose his emotion in a song. Even after the savage beating Earl had take, his voice, his voice was still American Idol worthy!

"I will stay and I promise to never get in your waayy, I won't go, because I know I will be thinking of you every step of my day-ayyy. And I, I will always, love you, ooh always love you. You, Paradise my darling, you! MM..."

The sound of Zombie Paradise attempting to raise its frame on a broken leg. Wasn't half as sickening as the sound of Lee screaming at the top of his lungs.

"Kill her! I want that black bitch dead! And you better fuck her corpse to be sure!"

When the first missile hit, Colonel Lafayette had already unslung her AR 15 with grenade launcher off her shoulder, while sliding into cover behind a marble Statue of Jesus Christ! Wynolla may have been an infectious disease specialist, nevertheless she has been deployed in hot spots such as, Iraqi, Somalia, Colombia and Afghanistan. Plus, a rather wild weekend in Juarez Mexico! She was the United States Army and was accustomed to gunfire; the Colonel had been in her share of spontaneous firefights. Even so, no one can say the same about Lee's RAGERs!

They might have regained a bit of nerve control, but still for the most part their hand to eye coordination seems a bit, off! RAGERS take makeshift defensive postures aiming their assorted weapons at the area occupied by Colonel Lafayette. Twitching, grey muscle tissue of trigger fingers repeatable squeezed off rounds in many directions.

In some cases, it was Lee literally handing a toddler a weapon and hoping for the best! An assortment of rounds exploded near and all around Wynolla. Nonetheless, it must had been divine intervention for Jesus had the steering wheel and not one round ventured in Windu's direction.

On the other hand, her three round bursts put members of Lee's RAGER militia D.O.A, and flat on their backs! A lot of strange happening were going on, still the one that held Wynolla's eye had to be Earl. The blind giant slowly walked towards Lee whose barking orders and no one seemed notice or bother to stop him. If sad opera music had been playing in the background compiled with a sudden release of white doves, the entire scene could have been a broadcast of a violet action or indie horror movie!

Bullets seemed to not be interested in Earl as they whizzed past his face, his massive body and unique frame! As he continued to sing softly to himself, *"The memories of us are what's driving me, so goodbye and yes, I will cry, because we both know what we need-eed! And I will always love you, love you. I hope death treats us kind, for you are all I ever need-eed, and I will always love, you, you, Paradise my darling you..."*

All Earl wanted was to continue to draw closer to the sound of Lee's voice.

"Goddamit! Will one of you rush over there and drag her cowardly ass from behind that image of a false god and beat that lazy bitch to death already! What the fuck is wrong with you people!"

Their answer was yes; however, the busy end of Colonel Lafayette's silenced AR 15 made it hard for any RAGER to comply with Lee's request.

On the West side of the Campus, GS&L three black corporate Helicopters landed to expel three sets of six commandos. Much to their credit, the GS&L Mercs entered the fray without hesitation!

Their highly trained hand to eye coordination was clearly displayed by their tight three round shot selection. They came prepared to party, using suppressors on their automatic weapons made their attack sound like angry hornets on the move!

Three rounds to the heart stop most RAGERS, even so for the truly stubborn a double tap to their soiled forehead sealed the deal. Even through what will come to be known as Hammond's cure, concealed their presence. The sound of all that gunfire whipped the Dead Heads up into a large-scale Piranha sort of feeding frenzy!

Their loud constant moan echoed off vacant dorms and athletic buildings alike. It was the dinner bell for nearly forty thousand of Zombie were aching for warm human flesh. Frankly from their experience where there was gunfire, so was breakfast, lunch and probably dinner! The shuffling of skinless feet in no particular direction caused even the most hardened combat veteran a sudden case of bubble guts!

The rush of Zombies into the courtyard even startled Lee's RAGER force. Like a wave of filthy water, the Dead Heads slam into evolved RAGERs with teeth chomping at the air. RAGERs did as trained raising their weapons shoulder high and began firing into the Zombie horde! However, on that day, maybe it was the humidity, maybe it was they grew tired of the RAGERs bullshit. Nevertheless, something changed in their relationship.

The Zombie Horde responded like any APEX predator should, they attack! Drawn towards the sound of gunfire, Dead Heads rushed past GS&L Mercs straight into Lee's bowl-shaped lair.

Out of seemingly nowhere, the sound of the great vintage Russian attack helicopter competed with zombie moaning, rapid gunfire and the screaming of RAGERS being eaten alive!

Robin had Wynolla's tracker signal loud and clear and luckily the roof of the student union was mostly clear. However, she had no way to know if the stress level of the roof would hold this seven-ton beast. She guided her transport past Major Brown's Helio's which were scraping the battlefield with 50mm gunfire and a few well-placed missiles for good luck! "God, the Army Rules!" Robin shouted out loud.

Windu stopped firing her weapon when the mass of Zombies crashed into Lee's makeshift command/throne room. She must hold her breath and try not to fart for Colonel Lafayette was a rock caught in a torrid of blood! A hard place to be for sure. Endless streams of Dead Heads shuffled past Wynolla as if she wasn't there. Their sole focus was on the RAGERs firing their useless weapons into a moving mass of certain fucking death!

For the first time in a very long time, Jefferson Bullraguard Lee's fucking speechless. If he had hair, Lee would be ripping it out by its strands. He muttered more to himself.

"Noooooo, no, no, no, no. What are they doing? NO!"

Fun Fact; looking back across the pages of history those were probably the same last words of late and not so great, **7th Cavalry commander** Colonel George Armstrong Custer!

Lee doesn't seem to be bothered that his one-time prey, Earl Chicken Head Gaines was nearly within arm's length. Nonetheless, the serial killer that is Earl Grimes was on a mission to find the only person that has brought him a great deal of pain in a very, very long time!

Days into his captivity Earl's ears had learned to signal out Lee's breathing in a room. Now Chicken Head's massive frame lumbered forward, much like the Dead Heads that moan and march right next to him. Earl picked up his pace for he wanted nothing to reach his prey before he did!

Wynolla very much wants Lee alive, or at least a large amount of his spinal fluid. Valiantly she rose from behind her cover, braving the horde, Windu called upon her internal force to move as quickly as she can among the flesh eaters in an attempt to reach her former commander first! Lee backed up as the crowd was heading directly towards the last few hundred evolved RAGERs under his command.

Any RAGER firing a weapon was immediately pounced upon by an overwhelming amount of gashing teeth, clawing nails and over all painful fucking death! Their line broke easily under the pressure of the Zombie horde. Lee could have ordered his army to put down their weapons. That might have at least turned the fire down on the Zombie bomb going off all over the face of his master race! However, under pressure Lee once again, froze, he never rose to meet the challenge.

Much like the Great Lakes Naval Base that he allowed to be overrun, his current base has also been overrun! Not by an outside enemy. No, by what should have been his greatest ally, DEATH!

Jefferson Bullraguard Lee somehow had weaponized the remnants of the virus and in turn, they turned on him. Once again blinded by RAGE, Lee looked past what he should have paid attention to, shouting.

"YOU DID THIS!"

Lee snarled when he noticed Colonel Lafayette weaving in and out of traffic. Nevertheless, he should have noticed Earl Chicken Head Gaines launching his bloody right fist towards Jefferson's exposed puss filled face! Furthermore, the loud SNAP of Lee's jaw breaking was clearly heard by Wynolla as she made her way towards the front of the class.

Lee dropped quicker than a hot load on a willing partners backside and Earl hastily places his bloody bare foot on his one-time tormentor's neck. Chicken Head's wounded whisper carried as loud as a high school marching band!

"You took everything from me, everything! Allow me to return the favor ten thousand-fold, brother!"

Thirty seconds prior, Robin decided to chance it as she allowed the heavy Russian aircraft to gently touch down on the two-story roof. At first, the sounds of the load bearing being stressed out made her want to throw the throttle in reverse and fly towards the heavens!

Yet, Marshal Aquila knew that every second counted. So, she silently counts to five before allowing the rest of her burden to rest securely on the rooftop of what was Lincoln College.

Meanwhile, Wynolla was doing all she could not to break out in a full sprint to reach the front of the Zombie horde. For now, their efforts were centered on what's left of Lee's evolved RAGERs. Their constant gunfire grew less and less by the passing second and Colonel Lafayette can see Lee's diseased head high above the crowd. It's not until she gets closer did Windu see why.

Earl Grimes, even in his severely weaken state had enough strength to lift Jefferson Bullraguard Lee two feet off the ground! Lee's feet were violently thrashing as Earl slowly strangled the life out of him. There are a few of Lee's RAGERs attempting aid by kicking and punching Earl in the back of his head.

Still ancient **Chinese proverb states**, *nothing deters a person on the road to revenge, except themselves!*

Wynolla uses her suppressed 9mm Smith & Wesson to place six well placed rounds in the back of RAGERS heads before moving within ear shot of Earl and she offered in a soft tone.

"Sir, please, it's me Colonel Lafayette. We need him alive."

Earl replied, "I don't."

Colonel Lafayette can see the light passing from Lee's eyes. Slowly she raises her weapon to aim at Earl's head. That's when suddenly, John Hammond came up beside her. John placed his hand over Wynolla's weapon, gently lowering it to the floor. He stepped past the Colonel, followed by Ernesto, and together they approached their friend. As Hammond was first to say.

"My friend, it's time to go home. If you would please, please put him down. This, man offers humanity our best chance of survival."

It took Earl a few seconds before he complied by at least lowering Lee's feet back to Earth, nevertheless he doesn't release his grip off his throat. The emotion in his voice was real.

"John, John is that truly you?"

John Hamond was nearly in tears, no matter what Earl Grimes had been in the past, in the present he has been a good friend! Even the Ghost Faced Killer was hard pressed to contain his tears of compassion. From their own eyes they can see the torment and abuse their friend had taken from an even bigger sociopath than himself!

Ernesto said, "We are here to take you home, mi amigo."

Earl would cry if he could, but he has had his eye lids burned shut, so instead he chuckled before saying.

"Oh, my lord, I truly must look a mess!"

John replies, "Nothing Semaj wouldn't mind helping you clean up, I am sure. She's in the helio waiting for..."

Earl loosens his grip a bit as he said with such sorrow in his voice, that he sounded like a wounded lion!

"He killed Paradise, he, he had her gang raped. This foul cockroach allowed my love to turn into one of the dead. HE'S MINE! Tell Semaj, I, I will always hold her dear, as I wish she will do for us."

Hammond once again attempted to offer a way for those he holds dear.

"Earl please, I need spinal fluid from this man. That will be a painful process for him, very painfully. He will pay for what he did to Paradise. I promise..."

Earl cut him off by saying, "Like Indigo John? No, no, no I think not! John, I love you brother. I mean that! I love you an Ernesto more than anyone except, my Paradise."

Earl allowed his words to sink in before continuing, "Besides, your serum got us this far. Trust me when I say, this man is the DEVIL! You need a true Monster to kill a Devil. We may have been kindred souls this one! Even so now is time we both, usher into the long night."

Nine members of GS&L assault team finally made their way through the fray, but keep their weapons firmly trained on Earl, Wynolla, John Hammond and Ernesto. One of the black masked intruders' barks orders.

"Unhand that, that thing. He's coming with us! Anyone makes a fucking move, and you will catch one to the face, I shit you not!"

As the chaos of RAGERs being eaten by Dead heads swirls around them, the group of Earl's friends were for the moment speechless. It took Wynolla speaking into her headset to break their silence.

"Major Brown, we have just been threatened by any ally turned hostile force! If you have not heard back from me in twenty seconds, use the remainder of your missiles to blow those expensive black corporate taxis out of our sky!"

Colonel Lafayette was fed up and she let her words linger. Her next action might be considered as an act of war.

"Then quickly proceed to hunt down any of their personnel on the ground, using whatever means at hand to convince these MERCs to reveal their base location! Travel to said base find any survivors and be sure terminate with extreme prejudice!"

Windu lets her words sink in before turning her attention to GS&Ls Merc and whispered.

"Time's ticking fuckers! Either lower your weapons and leave. Or you and your entire shadow organization joins, them."

Wynolla pointed to the ramble around them. Lee was squirming for his life in Earl's capable hands, even so he manages to say.

"I am GOD! I shall eat your..."

Earl squeezed harder as the GS&L goons slowly back out of the area, before running walking towards their aircraft. Colonel Lafayette talked once more to his second in command.

"Delay that order Major, the threat is on longer critical."

John Hammond once again attempted to reason with his friend.

"Please Earl, let him go, allow me to see how his mutation..."

Earl's voice was overflowing with a pain neither of his cell mates had ever heard from the huge man before. That's even when Prison hacks beat Chicken Head for nearly an hour over him saying how much he wanted to eat one of the guards he just knew was a closet queer!

"John, NO. The power to have those things under control will only lead to more like HIM. If not now, one day in the future some charismatic psychopath will come along and weaponize your research, you know that! No,no,NO!, He belongs to Chicken Head. Now good Colonel, if you would please place those fancy explosives at our feet and when you are airborne... Well, send us all on our way."

Ernesto tried once last time.

"Earl, I am going to be father and my child needs you as it's godfather. Please amigo, I am begging you, let us take you home.."

Earl Grimes replied with warmth.

"Oh my, oh, my that's great news, for you and Calamity! Nonetheless I must go, and this bastard goes with me! The world is filled with Monsters now, we, we no longer needed."

With that Wynolla laid the bandoleer of explosives at Earl's feet, turned and headed towards the roof. And was promptly followed slowly by Big John and Ernesto.

The force of nearly forty thousand Dead Heads were agitated and in need of release. Their former relationship transformed with their RAGER cousins, as their battle or slaughter continues to unfold.

The joint task force from Campy PAYDAY and Shangri-La sling off heading towards the Southwest. As the Black Helicopters from GS&L head towards the Northeast. Maybe the last vestiges of humanity in North America take off towards much different fates.

What was undeniable for all parties the red, yellow and white fireballs that erupted from 15 pounds of pounds of C4, hundred rounds of 5.56 NATO tracer rounds and several FRAG grenades exploding in the early morning dew, was pretty fucking awesome!

The shock wave collapsed the entire student union and whatever vehicles that are parked outside, detonated with the fury of Naval Battleships lobbing ordnance across a continent! And with that, the legend of Chicken Head and sad song that was the Life of Earl Grimes, Killer, Convict, Companion and Friend. Met his long overdue tragic end.

Even so, Ernesto nor Big John would have never consideration their friend would have died of a broken heart!

Chapter V:

THERE ARE BIRDS AND BEE, FLOWERS AND TREES

It took a while for life to find a way, nonetheless the world was still spinning fall was still in full effect and the Dead still rule the planet. Yet, due to the efforts of Colonel Lafayette and her OPERATORS and the residents of Shangri-La the mutation of the former Jefferson Bullraguard Lee did not become the rule of thumb!

RAGERS are still violent, but they do not behave like an organized machine. In the days, months and years that follow. Shangri-La and Camp PAYDAY's personnel become intertwined.

Ernesto and Celeste have a baby girl who they named after Robin, since she saved their lives. And a year later a bouncing baby boy they Named John Earl, because those were Ernesto best friends to the end!

Cherish and Lance have the second marriage in Shangri-La- *Ghost Face and Calamity were first*. Not soon-eight months- after the new Mrs. Brown gave birth to twin boys. And eighteen months later one of the cuttiest baby girls in the apocalypse!

Dawn and the tall Marine Dentist from Oklahoma decided marriage was an outdated concept of the forgotten past. He was her man, and she was his woman, yet they did stay together for twenty years, having a baby girl in the process. Dawn even found a calling as a dental assistant.- *Which had nothing to do with her voted most like to suck someone other than her boyfriend's cock, while in High School*! Yeah, we are all good at what we do.

Big John who so much was owed, finally loved once more. He and Nabila Hussein hit it off while talking about ways the vaccine could be administered world-wide! They were the official grandparents of all children born to CAMP PAYDAY and Shangri-La. They lived and loved each other for seventeen years until John Hammond died of a heart attack.

After Ernesto and Celeste had their child, Destiny knew her time had come. She refused to play the third wheel any longer. Would she die alone, the ex-stripper thought? Luckily Staff Sergeant Belladonna had an eye for tiny dancers and she and her new girlfriend Destiny took for to see the rest of America, both armed to the teeth. And carrying vials of Hammond's vaccine for survivors they encounter along the way.

It took Semaj a while to get over the death of the only two people she felt understood her. However, once she opened herself up to the possibilities of living with some many Navy people, it didn't take her very long to find the Shipman that was looking for an emotional investment with a Bootylicious brown bottom homebody and her semen.

Robin joined Wynolla at Camp PAYDAY, their love helped the Deana and Hanna grow into the women that will help drag this world back from the RAGERS and the dead. She talked with her dad every day and was there when he died many years later.

The plight on Indigo and GS&L was murky at best, they went totally dark six months after dealing with Lee. No one knew their location so there was no way to check for survivors. Maybe they moved to a backup base or maybe their actions and the way they did business came back to haunt them!

Wynolla allowed anyone who wanted to return to their places of origin and look for their family members all the ammo they could carry and a hundred vials of the cure. Their mission was a success.

All that mattered was that life had gone one. Earth without the plague of humans creating, consuming and destroying without as much as a thought for the balance of nature. Had become to heal and healing is what the planet needs now more than ever.

Pods of whales swim happily in the Hudson Day. On the other side of the world baby elephants no longer worry about Ivory hunters in their native lands! It's a wonderful sight to see Bees have returned to making honey!

Yes, the dead still make up the dominant population. Yet now they are less of a threat than a generation ago. Even their decay has led to miles upon miles of fields of fresh flowers!

The information left by Colonel Lafayette in what was Camp McCormick was left for future generations on how to rebuild civilization. The twins only went on this mission to retrieve several jump drives, because of chatter on the CB about another transmutation running through the RAGERS.

It's been nineteen years since the Lee alteration and this current mutation may be the key in turning RAGERS off for good!

The only good things that happen in this Apocalypse was the death of RACISM, SEXISM and the pursuit of being rich! Now every living human must cooperate and respect that all life is indeed precious.

We are each other's keepers, religion didn't help during the RED DEATH. No Gods came down from heaven to heal the sick and destroy death! No magical Gods appeared to turn off nuclear plants when they melted down across the globe.

Yet humans are still around! What happens for the next generation must be paid by those in the here and now. Remember we are the sum of our parts, not the sum in a greedy person's ledger.

Burt Bacharach- *what the world needs now is love, sweet love it's the only thing there's so little of. What the world needs now is love sweet love. It's the only thing there's so little of...*

Etta James- - *I want a Sunday Kind of love. A love to last past Saturday night and I would like to know it's more than love at first sight and I want a Sunday kind of love. Oh yeah, oh yeah. We all need a love that's on the square, my oh my, got to find someone who cares.. For I want a Sunday kind of love....*

CAPTAIN & TENNILLE *Love, love will keep us together. Think of me baby whenever some dead fucker comes along, singing their song. Don't mess around, you got to stay strong. Just stop, cause I really love you! Stop cause, I really love you. Look in our hearts and see, love, love will keep us together. You and me forever, thinking of you...*

EPILOGUE.

We should all give thanks to those to choose to defend the principles of Truth, justice and liberty for all with no thought of loss of life or limbs.

We should honor the sacrifice of those that came before us. Let's be clear all branches of our nation's military have added to our continuing purist of freedom. None of us own the word Patriotism! Understandably our United States of America is more than a collection of land masses. It's a collection of people, most came looking for wealth and freedom.

Others had their freedom, wealth and land taken. And no matter how far we have come, 14th through 20 century thinking and terms still plague our society today.

We should all ponder that our entire civilization was based on a single thought process. White Men Could Do Anything To Non-White People! Women where property and gays were looked at with taboo- even though it seems the lifestyle was practice by Royals and Poor alike..

In the end what divides us can no longer be how we interact with each other. America was patterned after Ancient Rome and in Rome you were either a Roman or a slave! You weren't Nubian, Gual, hailed from the British Isle, or a Wildman from Ire, a Syrian, an Egyptian, or a Greek. You were either free Roman or slave!

Which are you?

For there's only one culture we should be celebrating if you live in our land, American! Are you a proud free Roman or are you a slave to greed, lust, murder, lies and corruption? Over the last twenty years, "We the People in order to create a more perfect union" has lost its luster, yet it should never lose its intent.

When we surrender our ability to think, to be presented the truth, as well as not having access to justice for all. Then, America goes the way of all crumbling empires! The only question's will the people behind the mask cash their chips in and destroy us all so they can rebuild in their image? Or will they join us in actually making America the great nation we hope she can be?

Fun Fact: *This novel was not well received in* ***Texas, Alabama or Florida****. However, the state of Texas ranks 47 out of 50 States in* ***Literacy****. Alabama ranks 39 and poor, ass-backwards Florida ranks, 48.*

Enclosing, the actual likelihood they understood the meaning of this material is as unlikely as the person they call ***Jesus Christ- Hebrew name's Yehoshua (Yeh-HO-shoo-ah)*** *was born in* ***Indiana-*** *which ranks 17 in literacy.*

<u>The END, Roll Credits.</u>

Milton Keynes UK
Ingram Content Group UK Ltd.
UKHW052053300624
444882UK00001B/84

9 781977 273932